The
FORSAKEN
THRONE

THE KINGFOUNTAIN SERIES

BOOKS BY JEFF WHEELER

The Kingfountain Series

The Legends of Muirwood Trilogy

The Covenant of Muirwood Trilogy

Whispers from Mirrowen Trilogy

Landmoor Series

The FORSAKEN THRONE

THE KINGFOUNTAIN SERIES

JEFF WHEELER

47NORTH

Text copyright © 2017 by Jeff Wheeler

Published by 47North, Seattle

www.apub.com

Amazon, the Amazon logo, and 47North are trademarks of Amazon.com, Inc., or its affiliates.

ISBN-13: 9781477807736
ISBN-10: 147780773X

Cover design by Shasti O'Leary Soudant

Printed in the United States of America

To my other parents, Pete and Suqi

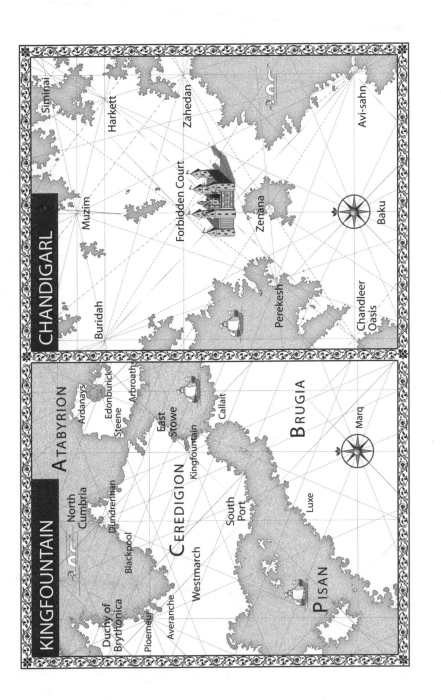

KINGFOUNTAIN

ATABYRION

North
Cumbria
Ardanays
Edonburick
Steene
Arbroath

Blackpool
Dundrennan

Duchy of
Brythonica
Ploemeur
Averanche
Westmarch

CEREDIGION
Kingfountain
East
Stowe
Callait

South
Port

BRUGIA

Marq

Luxe

PISAN

CHANDIGARL

Siminai
Harkett
Zahedan
Muzim
Buridah

Forbidden Court
Zenana
Perekesh

Avi-sahn
Baku

Chandleer
Oasis

CHARACTERS

MONARCHIES

Ceredigion: Andrew and Genevieve (House of Argentine): The army of Kingfountain was nearly defeated at the Battle of the Kings, but a tenuous peace has been established. Gahalatine, the Overking of Chandigarl, swore fealty to Drew as his sovereign lord and pledged to help rebuild the devastation inflicted by his people. This peace was forged through a marriage alliance between Gahalatine and Trynne Kiskaddon sealed at the sanctuary of Our Lady following the battle. The vast treasure ships were unloaded of their precious cargo, and Gahalatine's men began rebuilding and educating the people in Chandigarli customs.

Chandigarl: Gahalatine (House of Dainik): Gahalatine is still the Emperor of the East Kingdoms, the vast territory he conquered through his ambition and Fountain-blessed ability to lead. He has succeeded in maintaining control of the empire's formidable military, but the Wizrs of his realm lead the bureaucratic government of the empire through the Mandaryn. Gahalatine's long-term power struggle with the Wizrs has shifted since the death of their leader, Rucrius, whom Trynne slayed in the fountain of the poisoner school in Pisan. His land's traditions prohibit him and Trynne from consummating their marriage until Trynne turns eighteen or until one of her two parents can be found to grant permission for the match.

Averanche, Brythonica, and Westmarch: Tryneowy (House of Kiskaddon): Trynne is now the most powerful ruler in Kingfountain next to the king and queen. As her parents are both missing and her younger brother was killed in a carriage accident, she controls the sizable domains of both her parents as well as the city she holds in her own right. It is now publicly known that she is the Painted Knight, King Drew's champion and protector. Trynne is also responsible for the training of the Oath Maidens, an army of female soldiers that played a pivotal role in defending the king during the Battle of the Kings. Although her marriage to Gahalatine is political in nature, she is grateful their alliance has brought an end to the bloody conflict between the empires. She is now preparing to visit him in his domain and be hailed as the Empress of the East Kingdoms.

North Cumbria: Fallon (House of Llewellyn): Fallon would have lost his life in the Battle of the Kings if Trynne had not interrupted the battle between him and Gahalatine's sister. He willingly relinquished his position as the king's champion to Trynne herself, the woman he lost and still loves.

◆ ◆ ◆

My father is dead. My half brother is still the king. All that I had carefully built has crumbled around me. Sometimes I wish I had never found that secret tome in the poisoner school in Pisan. I can still hear it whispering to me. Can a book be alive? It tells me that all the great ones have suffered defeats. That glory comes to those who struggle on past disappointment and failure. I was born to be a queen, not that Kiskaddon girl. She has robbed me of what was truly mine. How easily I could do away with her. But that would not be enough.

She must suffer as I have done. She must lose all that she has gained. I can be anyone I want to be. A poisoner. A Wizr. A duchess. A queen.

Morwenna Argentine

◆ ◆ ◆

PART I

Wizr

CHAPTER ONE

The Assizes

A month had passed since the Battle of the Kings. The feeling in the audience hall was somber as the members of King Drew's council sat around the Ring Table in the palace of Kingfountain. They had gathered today to decide the fate of a criminal and a traitor.

Trynne Kiskaddon sat next to the king in the seat called the Siege Perilous, reserved for his champion. It had once belonged to Trynne's father. She still remembered where she had been standing, years before, when the Fountain had whispered to her that she would one day sit in that seat. A shudder passed over her at the thought. She had never wanted it. And now she would have to help the king pass judgment on two people whose trespasses had shaped her life: Dragan and Morwenna.

Dragan was her father's enemy. A Fountain-blessed thief who'd not only attacked her, but had also played a role in her father's abduction. And Morwenna . . . the king's blood-sister had admitted to trying to sabotage Trynne's family. She'd also committed treason against her own brother.

King Drew had given the task of judging the Assizes to Lord Amrein, the master of the Espion and the king's chancellor. Lord Amrein had spent countless hours interviewing witnesses, seeking to reconstruct the events of the last few months, and now he was presenting evidence to the council while they ate from trays brought stealthily in by servants, and sipped from gilded cups. Together, they would decide the fate of the prisoners, and then the king would render his judgment.

Though Trynne had seen it countless times, the majestic Ring Table, hewn from a tree so massive it took up the majority of the audience hall, never failed to impress her. And yet the others' stern expressions, revealed by the flickering flames of the torches mounted in sconces on the walls, were a reminder that none of them wished to be there.

Most of the chairs were full. The King and Queen of Atabyrion were both present. Trynne had rescued Lady Evie from Chandigarl herself, and Trynne's husband, Gahalatine, had dispatched one of his Wizrs to retrieve Iago from a ship that still had yet to make it to the Forbidden Court. It almost made Trynne smile to think about how upset Iago had been to miss all the action at Dundrennan. He had complained vocally about it until his wife, rather patiently, had suggested he count his blessings instead. Atabyrion had been attacked and defeated, and now engineers and builders from Chandigarl were reconstructing the defenses and beginning improvements on the harbor.

Iago and Lady Evie held hands as they listened to the evidence of the case. That simple evidence of their love for each other made the chair next to Trynne, the one meant for her own husband, feel more conspicuously empty.

She glanced at the others at the table, at the Dukes of East Stowe and Southport. Finally, her gaze found Fallon, brooding as he stared at Lord Amrein, his face a mixture of pain and anger. His eyes shifted to meet hers, betraying deep suffering. They had not spoken since the battle. He had remained in Dundrennan to guard Morwenna and Dragan and had then escorted the prisoners to Kingfountain under heavy guard.

To prevent Morwenna from escaping, Gahalatine had revealed the use of the astrolabe—a device that he and many of his people wore around their necks. It was a metal ring of sorts surrounded with spokes, almost like a sunburst in appearance. But its purpose was to enable the wearer to see the invisible ley lines. Armed with them, Morwenna's guards had been able to ensure she was kept away from the ley lines, thus preventing her from using her Fountain magic to escape. She had promised to submit to the judgment of the council, declaring that she had been a pawn of the Wizr Rucrius, whose control over her was now gone.

Trynne looked away from Fallon, wondering if she should try to speak to him following the meeting. She was preparing to go to Chandigarl to participate in the coronation ceremony that would officially make her Gahalatine's queen. She was nervous and excited, and part of her wanted to share those emotions with Fallon—as a friend. She hoped that her marriage would help him finally overcome his feelings for her. Now that she was wed to another, she had forced her own feelings for him into a cage deep inside her.

"I think the facts of the case," Lord Amrein said as he paced around the Ring Table, drawing near to where she was sitting and capturing her attention, "are confusing and muddled at best. I have no fewer than twelve witnesses who swear the man in custody is the thief Dragan. We have the sworn word of Duke Fallon, who lured and trapped him." His tone showed his respect. "I must give you credit, lad. For all my resources with the Espion, I couldn't do it."

Trynne shot a look at Fallon, who shrugged as if the compliment meant little to him. He made no reply.

"The problem, as I explained," Lord Amrein continued, "is that the man has suffered a strange form of amnesia. He does not know his own name. He has no idea where he is from. Curiously, he still has the ability to steal, and every time the Espion searches him, they find small things he has stolen from his jailors here in the palace. He's being held in Holistern Tower at the moment, awaiting the judgment of this council."

Duke Ramey leaned forward in his seat with a disbelieving scowl. "Is there really any point debating this? The man is a thief and a liar. He tried to *kill* Lord Owen. Throw him in the river and let's be done with it. Next case."

"We can't throw him in the river," Lady Evie said, shaking her head. "He's Fountain-blessed."

Duke Ramey reddened. "Maybe we could try *several* times," he said with a hint of malice. "Or fill the boat with chains."

Iago smirked at the statement. "I can't say I disagree with the sentiment," he said with his amiable brogue. "The only good serpent is a dead one, but why risk executing a Fountain-blessed in the river? Should we not take the man to the mountaintop and let him freeze? Is there anyone at the table who objects? Based on all the things Lord Kevan has told us, some of which I didn't even know, the man is a villain. Let's get to the king's sister. That's the more perplexing case we must decide."

Duke Ramey gently thumped his fist on the Ring Table and then pointed to King Iago, nodding in agreement.

Silence hung in the room for a while as Lord Amrein looked from person to person. "Does anyone intend to speak up in favor of the condemned . . . ?" he said, his voice full of assurance that no one would.

Trynne felt as off-balance as if she were aboard a ship in a storm. She had been invited to witness the interrogation, and to her soul, she did not believe that Dragan was lying. When he looked at her, there was no recognition in his eyes. He'd asked a guard who she was and how he'd wronged her.

Trynne cleared her voice. "My lords," she said, wondering if she were being foolish. "I know we went through the evidence already. I am one of the witnesses who identified the man." She sighed, rubbing her palms across the table. "When I captured Rucrius, he told me something that has haunted me ever since. My father is alive, he said, but he has forgotten his family completely. He doesn't even know his own name. Rucrius claimed that we have no comprehension of the power that the Wizrs of Chandigarl possess." She interlaced her fingers. "My husband has been searching for an answer to this riddle. Lord Fallon and I both believe Dragan was complicit in my father's abduction. He admitted as much. Before we condemn him to death, can we not defer the decision until we find some means of restoring his memory? It feels . . . unjust to condemn a man who has no knowledge of his crimes. And if we do discover a way to restore his memory, there may still be some use left in him."

They were all looking at her. They could see the evidence of Dragan's mistreatment of her on her face. Her smiles were all crooked, her left cheek still slack because of how he had injured her as a child. That she, of all people, was speaking out for him had affected them. A hush fell in the room.

"That is very noble of you, Trynne," Lady Evie said with a tone of respect. "I think we all *want* to see him punished because of what he did to your father. What he did to *you*."

Trynne nodded in agreement. "I'm expecting Gahalatine to arrive any day now. Can we not wait until he arrives to see if he has brought us any new information from the Wizrs?"

Lord Amrein walked to his seat, returning to the leather folder containing the notes he'd compiled. "I don't think we have any disagreement as to the man's guilt or a suitable punishment. We will leave the matter to the king's discretion." He looked at Drew and nodded deferentially.

Drew glanced at his wife, who leaned in close to whisper something in his ear. He nodded and then reached for Trynne's hand, giving it a reassuring squeeze before he released it. "I trust your judgment, Trynne. More than you know. Lord Amrein, keep him confined to the tower. For the time being."

Lord Amrein bowed stiffly. "Very well. Now we must discuss the case of your blood-sister, Morwenna." He let out a deep sigh and shook his head. "This one will not be as easy. But it is our duty to decide guilt and to recommend punishment." He clasped his hands behind his back and began to pace again. "Morwenna Argentine, daughter of Severn Argentine, conspired with the Mandaryn and the Wizrs of the East Kingdoms to overthrow her brother and place herself on the throne of Kingfountain. There is ample evidence of her collusion with them, as I have discussed in great detail with many of you during our interviews. This is treason. There can be no other charge suitable for such crimes."

Lord Amrein interrupted his pacing and wagged his finger. "There are, however, many factors to be considered. She testifies that she was under the sway of the Wizrs, controlled by a powerful ring given to her by Rucrius. Without Lady Sinia or Myrddin to confirm or reject her claim, we are flummoxed. Lord Gahalatine took the ring with him to Chandigarl and is seeking answers. But we will likely never have conclusive proof that she was willingly complicit." He paused and looked at those assembled. Trynne noticed that Fallon was pale, his fists clenched, his eyes serious. He was emotionally invested in the outcome. While he had testified against Morwenna, openly revealing his knowledge of her actions against king and realm, Trynne had found some of his clothes in a chest under Morwenna's bed in the poisoner's tower. How compromised was he?

She told herself it was none of her business. As a married woman, she had no reason to care about Fallon's romantic life. And yet . . . she did.

Lord Amrein held up his hands. "It's undeniable that her aid during the battle saved many lives, but it is my opinion as chief justice that we should view her collusion with the enemy, regardless of coercion, in the harshest light. Is it possible that she was a complete pawn of Rucrius? Yes. But the evidence suggests that she was a willing participant."

An awful feeling of dread came into the room. Trynne squirmed in her seat. She herself felt conflicted about Morwenna. Lord Amrein's position was not an enviable one.

The chancellor paused and riffled through his papers. "It is my suggestion, based on the evidence, that Morwenna Argentine fell in league with Rucrius at the poisoner school in Pisan. My interviews with Lady Trynne and others suggest that this happened shortly after she began attending the school, when she was very young and malleable. By all accounts, she excelled at her studies—one of the brightest to have passed through that school in a generation. There is no doubt she was ambitious and determined. It is my belief that Rucrius began grooming her to be a double agent for the East Kingdoms. The Mandaryn were charged with finding a suitable bride for Gahalatine, and based on the evidence, it seems they settled on Morwenna. The king entrusted her to visit Chandigarl on multiple occasions. She could have easily used this as an opportunity to provide information to both sides. I do not believe it was her intent to destroy her brother." He held up his finger as he made that point. "No, based on Gahalatine's reputation for supplanting rulers and reassigning them, she may have justified her treason in her own heart and mind with the knowledge that King Andrew would not be killed but sent elsewhere." He tapped his finger on the solid table. "But it is *still* the crime of treason."

"Are you suggesting that we execute the king's sister?" Iago said in apparent disbelief.

Lord Amrein pursed his lips. "I am not. There is another suitable punishment that does not require her death."

"What then?" Iago asked. "Speak up, man!"

"Attainder," Lady Evie said, sitting forward, her eyes twinkling. "That's what he is going to suggest."

Trynne blinked in surprise, but the answer fit—it seemed an ideal solution.

"My lady, yes," Lord Amrein said with a chuckle. "I think your knowledge of history exceeds even that of Master Urbino. Do not tell him that I said so, if you please. Yes, she is correct. A bill of attainder against Morwenna Argentine would strip her of all rights, lands, and privileges of her noble blood. It would not preclude her from inheriting, say, lands in Atabyrion, or anything else from her *mother's* line. But it would strip her of all rights to the throne of Ceredigion. It would, in essence, remove the opportunity in the future of her *ever* becoming queen."

Some murmuring began around the table as the peers of the realm began considering the solution.

Lady Evie spoke up. "Normally attainder follows a crime of treason or felony. For example, if a member of the nobility arranged a murder against another peer—not the king, but a peer—a bill of attainder could be passed to strip away the rights of the criminal's spouse and heirs before he or she is sent into the river. What you are suggesting is the same legal precedence, only there would be no execution."

"Precisely," Lord Amrein said with a bow. "It protects the king's interests while showing compassion for his sister."

"Brilliant," Duke Ramey muttered, nodding vigorously.

"But she'll not continue serving as his poisoner," Iago said, tapping his fingers on the wooden round, shaking his head vehemently.

Lord Amrein nodded in agreement. "Clearly not," he answered. "She would be confined to an estate, a castle, for example, that could not . . . be reached easily." His underlying meaning was clear—she would not be allowed near the ley lines. Banished, in essence. "She seems . . . contrite. She's cooperated fully with my investigation. Then again, she may be trying to avoid execution."

"Attainder," Duke Ramey said, knocking his knuckles on the table.

There was unity in the decision. Trynne felt a twinge of relief, but it was accompanied by a feeling of foreboding. Where could they keep someone like Morwenna? Someone both powerful and dangerous? It seemed like no genteel prison could hold her.

A loud knock sounded at the door and the king's herald entered. "Lord Gahalatine of the East Kingdoms," he announced before sweeping the door open to introduce Trynne's husband.

Trynne's heart thrilled when she saw him march into the audience hall, but the feeling was instantly extinguished when she saw the look on his face. There were soot stains on his cheek and his eyes were wells of grief and raw anger. Trynne pushed away from her chair and rose. Something awful had happened.

Seeing her seemed only to aggravate his wounds. There was no look of love in his eyes now. His nostrils flared, his lips curled with contempt. She sensed his Fountain magic was nearly spent.

"My lord, what is wrong?" Drew asked, rising also from his chair.

Trynne approached Gahalatine, reaching out to touch him, but he glared at her, as if warning her not to draw too near. Flakes of ash covered his cloak and his hair. His hands were red and blistered.

Gahalatine's emotions were so roiling he could hardly speak. "My city is burning," he said hoarsely. "The palace is destroyed. My sister . . . is dead." He tried to speak, but a shudder of emotion stayed his words for a moment. Finally, the words came out in a rush. "*Rucrius* came. He said the Fountain would punish us for surrendering to you. And then lightning struck. Everything is burning. Burning to ashes."

CHAPTER TWO

Forbidden Court

Gahalatine's words, his apparent grief, stunned everyone into silence. Though ambitious, he was a man of honor, not prone to exaggeration or misrepresentation. Trynne and Morwenna had visited the Forbidden Court together to rescue Lady Evie—before Morwenna's treachery had come to light. Trynne had marveled at the wealth on such ostentatious display. From a stone barge crossing the great lake at the center of the city, she had seen the golden rooftops glittering in the sunlight. Now her mind imagined roaring flames licking at those rooftops, destroying everything in their path. All that beauty and opulence gone. She reached out her hand to touch her husband's arm, but he stiffened and backed away from her, his look one of repugnance.

"This is indeed tragic news," Trynne said with concern, cringing at his rebuff. She wanted to comfort him, to try to soothe his grief. She had lost her own brother in a tragedy. She understood the kind of pain he was feeling.

His cold stare sent a shaft of fear into her heart. "Can you even pretend you did not know?" he said in an accusing tone. He looked next at Drew, pinning him with a glare. "Was this not your ruse all along, my lord? Your trickery and deceit? Well, I have sworn myself, and even though it would seem my oaths were made under false pretenses, I am still bound by them."

Trynne's fear gave way to terrified panic. "What are you saying? We had nothing to do with this."

"Indeed not," Gahalatine countered angrily. "*I* bear the blame and I accept it, for I *trusted* you. As I trusted your king." He glared at Drew. "The Fountain has punished me for my blindness. For abandoning the charge it had tasked me to complete. It was my decision, and I made it willingly. That is why I am so wretched. I was tricked and deceived. By you"—he looked pointedly at Trynne—"and by the sovereign you would do anything to protect. Your loyalty bound you, no doubt. Just as my honor now binds me."

Trynne felt her cheeks flush with indignation and dread. Her stomach roiled with confusion. "I have done nothing to deceive you, my lord husband! How can you be so changed? You wrong me to accuse me like this."

Gahalatine's cheek muscles twitched as he silently shook with emotion. Trynne reached out to him again with her magic, trying to divine if he were an imposter. No illusion had ever worked on her before. Her senses might be fooled, but not her heart. No, this was Gahalatine—injured, furious, and betrayed.

"Did you not tell me that you killed the Wizr Rucrius?" he challenged.

"I did it with my own sword," Trynne answered firmly.

"I saw him myself!" Gahalatine snapped. "Very much alive and boasting that the two of you have been in league all this while. That he *gave* you the Fault Staff to enable you to destroy his fleet at Ploemeur. He says that you have it still." He held up his hands. "What am I to think, Tryneowy? All along, I suspected he was trying to induce me to marry the Argentine girl, but he fooled me into falling in love with *you.*" His lack of love, the violence in his eyes and voice shook her to her core. She was speechless, dumbfounded, horrified. "He arranged for you to be fed information about my kingdom's financial straits. I've been such a fool. Such a trusting fool. And now the Fountain is punishing me for my arrogance. For my pride. I wed myself to someone far below my station in the hopes of overthrowing the very chains that are now locked about me in every possible way. I rushed into it, heedless of the cliff."

He turned his brooding gaze to the king and the council seated around the Ring Table. He looked at them each in turn, his gaze full of disgust and loathing. "I only came here to concede my defeat, Your *Majesty.*" He nearly spat out the words. "My city is still burning. I cannot tell you how many have burned to death in their homes. The devastation is unspeakable." He quivered again, trembling. "I forfeit my seat at this table. Now I must attend to my suffering people. It was my decision that brought this calamity on them. Farewell."

"No," Trynne gasped, reaching out and taking hold of his arm. "This is not true. None of it."

"Do not touch me!" he roared at her, jerking his arm away. "I loathe the sight of you. Albion, take me back to the *zenana* at once."

Trynne's attention had been so fixed on Gahalatine, she had not noticed the Wizr's presence. "Yes, my lord," Albion said, but he wasn't looking at his emperor. He was looking at *her*, unable to conceal a victorious grin. It brought her no comfort to learn Gahalatine's destination. On her short visit to his land, she had sensed a subtle but persistent evil rooted in that place.

Gahalatine glared hotly at Trynne. "I will come for you in Ploemeur when I am ready for you. You are my wife still. Await my coming."

Trynne watched in horror as the Wizr Albion hooked his finger on Gahalatine's sleeve and the two vanished through the power of a *Tay al-Ard.*

The room was spinning as she blindly clutched at her chair. Trynne felt her pulse in her temples, herself at the verge of fainting. This could not be happening. It had to be a nightmare. Surely she'd awaken from it gasping and terrified in her bed.

And yet she did not.

Someone was there, holding her as she trembled. It was the queen, and Genny had a look of grief and fierce concern.

"How dare he?" Genny whispered with almost a growl. She held Trynne, squeezing her tightly, stroking her hair. Trynne couldn't think. Her mind was whirling as fast as the room.

"I would not have imagined such words coming from such a man as he," Drew said in disbelief. "He is a man of honor, but he speaks as one convinced that he's been betrayed. This tragedy has addled his senses."

"What he did to Trynne was inexcusable," Genny said, still clinging to her. "I have no doubt that the devastation he depicted is true. Based on what we've learned, the buildings in the Forbidden Court are arranged close together. A fire could easily devastate such a place."

"But what of Rucrius?" Lord Amrein wondered. "I've been fixed on that point since he repeated his name. Trynne, you killed him in Pisan—isn't that true?"

"I did," she answered, her voice sounding strained in her own ears. She avoided glancing at Fallon. It would be unbearable to see his face at such a moment. "I left his body in the fountain that we appeared in. I can go back there . . ."

"No!" Genny and Drew said in unison.

Lord Amrein shook his head. "That may be exactly what the Wizrs are expecting you to do. You are their greatest threat. I know that some Fountain-blessed can disguise themselves. Isn't it obvious that someone was impersonating Rucrius? You took off his head, did you not? Forgive me for being sordid, but one cannot be revived from that, correct?"

Trynne swallowed, trying to contain her emotions. "I do not know for certain," she said, trembling violently. There was a story in *The*

Vulgate, the ancient book of magic, of a man who was enchanted and could be revived after being decapitated. She wanted to be sick. She was afraid it would happen in front of all of them.

"Come sit down," Genny coaxed, helping her to a nearby bench.

"What purpose could this serve?" Lord Amrein said, tapping his fingers on the table. "Clearly we're still at war."

"Or the game is still being played," Lady Evie said, speaking up. "Another game. One whose rules we don't know."

Trynne could still imagine the roar of flames. The cries of Gahalatine's people. They were *her* people too. She was their uncrowned queen.

"I must go there," she murmured, shaking her head.

"To Chandigarl?" Genny asked with concern.

Trynne nodded forcefully. "Don't you see, Genny? If someone is pretending to be Rucrius, I'm the only one who can unmask him. Gahalatine will not be deceived if I am near him. You saw him. They've poisoned his mind, and he abhors me now. He thinks that I tricked him into surrendering. Could it not appear that way to others as well? I must go. Whenever there has been a disaster, the people of Brythonica lend help. We always have. I will send every ship if I must."

"Not just yours," Drew said, walking toward her. "I am still his liege lord. We are innocent of these accusations—something we must attest with our actions. We will send relief to Chandigarl. It will take time to get there, but we'd best begin now." He straightened and pointed to Lord Amrein. "Send word to our captains. We will send food and workers to help rebuild the city."

The king hadn't allowed offense to cloud his judgment—and Trynne admired him all the more for it. It was exactly what her father would have done, she thought with a pang.

"I will go there," Trynne said, squaring her shoulders. "He is not himself, surely. I can help."

"Not alone," Genny said, shaking her head. She noticed Fallon rising from his chair, his look intense and incredulous. His clenched fists on the table said much about his worry.

"I must go alone," Trynne insisted. "He's my husband. I *must* resolve this."

The queen's eyes still glittered with emotion. Trynne could see the resentment festering there. Genevieve was incensed at Gahalatine's accusations.

"Go then," the king said. "Go with the Fountain's blessings."

Lord Amrein closed his leather folder. "We will postpone the decision on Morwenna, then, until the next time."

"No," the king said grimly. "Write up the bill of attainder now. Morwenna will forfeit all rights and privileges of her rank and station. She will be a ward of the crown. See it done, Kevan."

"Aye, my lord," he replied with a sigh. "In the attainder do you grant her the right to marry? As we discussed, it would bar her heirs from assuming the throne."

Drew looked at him and then nodded brusquely. "But who will want her now?"

◆　◆　◆

Genevieve walked with Trynne to the chapel, arm in arm. Trynne's abrupt marital discord had left her feeling hollow. She could see in her mind the pitying looks on the faces of the king's council. She wanted nothing more than to be alone, but she was determined to face down the imposters and soothe Gahalatine's misery. It was a trick, a deception. Nearly any Wizr had the ability to disguise themselves. Trynne had seen Rucrius take on the guise of King Drew, and she herself possessed a ring that could change her appearance at will. Morwenna had a similar artifact, although Fallon had confiscated it.

At the thought, the darker part of her feelings bloomed. Had Fallon known something about this through his Espion connections and not told her?

"Where will you go first?" Genny asked softly as they reached the chapel entryway, guarded by the king's knights.

"The ley line going east can be reached from the south. I was planning to go to Marq first and then join the east–west line. I wish I had evidence of Rucrius's death, but I don't dare go to Pisan. I'm sure the poisoner school must have found his body."

"They may have hidden it," Genny said thoughtfully, "not wanting to be implicated in his death."

"True," Trynne said with a sigh. She stepped over the rail and into the waters, which radiated away from her without soaking her. Soon, she stood on a circle of dry tiles.

"Be careful," Genny said. She clutched a hand to her own bosom and looked forlornly at Trynne.

"I will," she answered. Then, closing her eyes, she thought the word that would transport her away. *Kennesayrim.*

The rush of the Fountain magic surrounded her and she was falling, embraced by the power and transporting herself through the ley lines across the world, bouncing from city to city in a blur. In her mind, she remembered the fountain that she and Morwenna had visited together on their journey to the Forbidden Court. It would be dark in Chandigarl. She could imagine smelling the cinders.

The magic ebbed much more quickly than she had anticipated. She blinked, finding herself standing in the fountain at the Chandleer Oasis. The fountain was calm, and glowing stones lit the floor, making the water shimmer blue. The ley lines had only taken her part of the way.

She summoned the word of power again, willing herself to go east, only to be thwarted by the magic. There was nothing there. It was as if a wall had been put in front of her.

The fountains had been destroyed. The ley lines were blocked.

The whisper from the magic brought the dreadful realization. The fountains had *all* been destroyed. The Wizrs were cutting off access to the Forbidden Court from the rest of the world. There was no way she could quickly intercede. In fact, she could not go to Chandigarl at all. A voyage there took months, and she had sworn to her mother that she would maintain the protections of Brythonica. If she left to see her husband, her people would drown.

His angry words throbbed in her heart.

Await my coming.

He'd left her with no choice.

CHAPTER THREE

Forsaken

Trynne walked a corridor of the palace of Kingfountain, feeling ill and dejected. She was cut off from her husband, and the memory of his look of betrayal still stung her. He was an honorable man at his core, but he had accused her of duplicity in front of the entire council. She wanted to prove herself by her actions, to lay bare her very soul to him and convince him that she had not tricked him in any way.

The corridor was abandoned until she reached Genevieve's room, where she found two Oath Maidens on duty protecting it. Mariette looked at her in concern. The tall Oath Maiden had become somewhat of a trusted intermediary between Lord Amrein and the queen. Trynne had often spied Mariette, who was a widow, deep in conversation with the Espion master. She suspected the two fancied each other.

"My lady," the woman said worriedly. "Rumors are rife throughout the palace. Some swear they saw Gahalatine return to the palace and then leave again abruptly. Is all well?"

Trynne was not up to any deception. She felt the frown tugging at her mouth, but she would confide herself to Genny. No one else.

"There is grievous news," Trynne said. "Is the queen in her chamber?"

"Yes, she is." Mariette nodded to the other maiden, who quickly knocked on the door and then opened it for her. Giving Trynne a knowing look, Mariette warned her, "She's with her brother."

If Trynne had known, she would not have come. Part of her wanted to flee. She couldn't face Fallon, not now, not with her cheeks still flaming. If she could have vanished, she would have.

The other maiden opened the door wider and gestured for Trynne to enter.

Squeezing her hands into fists, Trynne took a deep breath and stepped into Genny's private chambers. A hint of lilac was in the air. Sunlight slanted in from the curtained windows, exposing Fallon's slouched form on the window seat, his injured leg propped up on a stool. He was watching for her, his eyes seeking hers, but he looked away as soon as they made eye contact.

He grunted as he brought his leg off the stool and then stood. For some reason, the badge of the Pierced Lion on his trim leather tunic made him achingly handsome to her. His hair was unruly, as if he'd raked his fingers through it in frustration. His mouth attempted to be neutral, even welcoming, but she saw the anguish he was struggling, and failing, to subdue.

"I'll be on my way," Fallon said courteously. He walked over to his sister with a pronounced limp and kissed her on the top of her head. "Are you going to come see Father and Mother off when the tide comes in? I'm not sure I fancy a walk down the steps to the docks."

Genevieve squeezed her brother around the waist, pressing her cheek against his chest. She looked up at him, a serious look on her face. "I was planning on it. You should come too, Fallon."

He shrugged and then gripped her shoulders. "Best if I leave the two of you alone for your conference." He looked at Trynne furtively. "The ley lines are closed. Aren't they?"

"Did you already know about the fire in Chandigarl?" she asked him, trying to keep the tone of accusation from her voice.

He shook his head no. "No, I did not know about the Forbidden Court. I haven't heard any intelligence about the ley lines either. It was just a guess based on today's . . . display. I had no idea Gahalatine would arrive today." His eyes began to smolder with fury. "If I had, I wouldn't have come." He gently pinched Genny's cheek. "I'll see you at the docks."

"Would you like me to have some of the maidens carry you down?" she joked.

Fallon pursed his lips, trying not to smile. "I'm half-tempted. I'll be punctual. Punctilious even. Sadly, I cannot think of a third to make it a set. I must be tired." He rubbed his eyes, gave his sister an affectionate smile, and started limping toward the door. Trynne stood stock-still, though her heart ached with pain.

Fallon stopped in front of her. "By your leave, *Cousin*."

She bit her bottom lip. "I'm *not* your cousin, Fallon."

"You are now, Trynne," he said. His look was full of poignant meaning, unspoken grief, and firmness of purpose. With those final words, he left the room.

Trynne felt her own emotions bubbling up from the place she'd hidden them, coming to a boil and threatening to spill out. She bit her lip again, willing herself not to think about all she had lost. Not to cry.

Genny's hand touched her shoulder, the comforting gesture pulling her back from the storm raging inside her.

"You never made it to Chandigarl." Genny turned her away from the newly closed door.

Trynne shook her head. "Fallon was right. All the ley lines have been severed. Every one. They are cut off from the rest of the world." She cupped her hands over her mouth. "It takes months by ship to reach that part of the world. I cannot go there."

Genny looked sympathetic. "No, you cannot. We will send as many ships as we can to help."

Trynne nodded, but it didn't make her feel any better.

"Where will you go?" Genny asked. "Ploemeur?"

"Yes. My duty to Brythonica is the most urgent. Besides, there is more good I can do for my husband from there." Even using the words hurt. *My husband.*

"He will come around, Trynne," the queen said. "When one loses something they treasure, they do not always think clearly. He's been deceived. He will see our goodwill from the ships and assistance we send. He will judge us by our actions and not the hollow words of traitors. Even he realized that the Wizrs were manipulating him." She squeezed Trynne's shoulder. "Truth will win out."

"But meanwhile I must endure the torture of suspense," Trynne said. "I must wait for him to come to me. How long will it take? A fortnight? A month?" The agitation made her break away and start pacing. "Longer? I cannot bear this, Genny. I cannot bear that he thinks so ill of me. That he *believes* I am capable of such treachery. That I would willingly marry him in order to deceive him." She touched her heart with her fingertips and then dug them into her skin. "What's strange is that I had fallen half in love with him this last month. Even though he attacked us without a cause, I'd come to forgive him. There is much I admire about him. And I thought . . . I believed that he truly admired me."

"He did," Genny said emphatically. "Which is what makes his pain all the greater. He was in love with you, Trynne. He manifested it in a thousand different ways. Perhaps he was in love with the *idea* of you at first. You have your father's gifts from the Fountain. You're uncommonly pretty."

Trynne glared at her.

"You *are*! Despite what happened to you. You radiate courage and goodness. You're reliable and faithful. You are exactly what he needed. What he *needs*. Which makes you the biggest threat his Wizrs have ever experienced. Coldly and deliberately, they removed your father from court to make Drew vulnerable. What they didn't expect was that the Fountain would call you to defend us."

Genny paused and clasped her hands in front of her. "People are ruled by superstitions," she finally said. "Even ours! Take a coin from the fountain and you'll be thrown into the river. The Fountain didn't punish the Forbidden Court, but Gahalatine upended his Wizrs' plans by swearing an oath of fealty to Drew. He made a decision that could not be easily undone. What horrifies me is how many people the Wizrs were willing to kill to try and counter it. How many of their *own* people." She gave Trynne an impassioned look. "Such power cannot be trusted without firm control. I see that now. I have a feeling these Wizrs will want revenge against us for their defeat. And you, Trynne, are the last Wizr that we can trust."

Trynne knew it was true, and it grieved her, for she had never wanted to be a Wizr. Myrddin had vanished over a year before, telling them that the Fountain had called him to help settle a desperate situation in another world. Then it had called her mother, Sinia, to the Deep Fathoms. Morwenna had been allied with the enemy all along, so she could not be trusted to save Kingfountain.

"I don't want this," Trynne whispered helplessly.

Genny walked up to her and took her hands. "I know. I know your heart, Trynne. But still I must ask you to help us. We don't have your mother's visions to guide us. We don't have your father's strategies. You must be both of them right now. Even while you endure heartache. Even though you'd rather be in the training yard with Captain Staeli. I hear he's on the mend."

Trynne nodded forlornly. "I will do my duty," she said. It was not what she wanted. But when did life ever work out the way one wanted?

"I know you will," Genny said. "Go back to Ploemeur. Send your husband whatever aid you can. Over time, his heart will soften to you. He will begin to see the truth."

"I must hope that he does," she replied.

The two embraced, holding each other for a long moment. When they finally drew apart, Trynne gave the queen a serious look. "What did Fallon talk to you about?"

The question had obviously surprised Genny. Her cheeks flushed slightly and her eyes narrowed.

"Oh no," Trynne groaned.

Genny patted her cheek. "I don't know if I *should* tell you. I was hoping to bear this burden for you. At least for a while. Nothing may come of it."

"Please tell me," Trynne pleaded.

Genny turned, pacing slowly away from her. "It was a private conversation. One between brother and sister, not between a duke and his queen. He didn't tell me to keep it in confidence. He was merely asking for my advice."

A feeling of panic and doom was building up inside Trynne. She hadn't thought it possible to hurt more than she did, but . . . it always was . . .

"I'll be miserable if I don't know. Please, Genny."

The queen nodded but still paused, choosing her words carefully. "You know that Fallon has always looked up to your father as a role model, as an example. The years he spent under Owen's tutelage are some of his fondest memories. It's where he fell in love with you." She turned and looked at Trynne. "Much, I'm afraid, like our mother did with your father. The water wheel keeps turning, doesn't it?" Genny was silent for another moment, pondering her choice of words carefully. "I still have memories of when Severn ruled. I was but a child." She smiled self-consciously. "I even remember asking Owen if he still loved my mother. How brash I was back then! He was truthful. I've always admired that about him. It was the truth that helped him defeat Severn in the end."

Trynne was still on tenterhooks. She gazed mutely at Genny, waiting for the awful truth to spill out.

"Fallon wanted to know if I thought Owen had wasted too many years mourning the loss of our mother."

A shudder rippled through Trynne. Her mouth went dry. She understood the implications immediately. "Fallon wants to marry . . . ?"

She couldn't bring herself to say the other woman's name.

Genny looked at her. "He didn't ask specifically if he could marry Severn's daughter. His feelings for her are rather conflicted. He's sorry for her. Afraid of what may happen to her. They have been friends for many years."

Trynne bit her lip. "You didn't mention that I found his clothes in her tower, did you?"

Genny dimpled and winced. "No. I *am* still his sister. There are some things I might not wish to know about him." She breathed out heavily. "As I said, I was hoping to bear this burden for you by not telling you. Will he ask the king's permission to marry her? I don't know. He can be rather rash, although you must admit he has gotten better."

Trynne shook her head, still amazed at what Genny had told her. Part of her wanted Fallon to find happiness with someone else. Someone who would inspire him to be someone. To make himself the best he could be.

Anyone *other* than Morwenna Argentine.

"I will say this in my brother's favor," Genny said, coming up and hugging her once more. "He does not resent that Gahalatine chose you. He respected him for it. That respect has been tarnished because of the way he treated you earlier today. Fallon told me that if he hadn't been so weak, and if he hadn't known you would disapprove, he would have punched Gahalatine just as he did Elwis all those years ago. You remember that affair?

"But even though he was furious, he knows firsthand that someone stops thinking clearly after they've lost something dear to them. He said that about himself mostly. About how it felt to lose you. But he also realizes that he would have *died* in Dundrennan if you hadn't intervened in the battle. He would have lost everything, including his own life."

Genny smiled and pressed a kiss to Trynne's cheek.

"We must be prepared for what is coming," the queen said. "Something is approaching. Right now, we are blind to it, so we must step cautiously. Standing still isn't a good choice. We must all move forward, even though it hurts."

Trynne knew Genevieve had spoken the truth. But it still hurt.

♦ ♦ ♦

Emotions rule people. The stronger the emotion, the more vivid and influential it becomes. The Dochte Mandar discovered a magic in another world that controls emotions. It's contained in a little medallion, a series of twisting vines, which they wear around their necks. It can produce fear. It can feign love. It can imbue one with courage. It can make one a coward. The Mandaryn believed they could control me through my emotions. They believed they were chaining me. That I would submit and yield to their whims if they threatened to kill my father. Well, my father is dead now and I can't even feel it. Love is a manipulation. An illusion. They believed that Rucrius controlled me. Now they are beginning to know that he was only my tool. I've broken the power of the East Kingdoms. And I will break down Kingfountain as well.

Morwenna Argentine

♦ ♦ ♦

CHAPTER FOUR

The House of Pillars

Trynne caught herself nodding off during the loquacious speech given by the ambassador of Genevar. She bit the inside of her lip in the hope that a little pain would revive her, but the endless meetings, petitions, and reports weighed her down and sapped her strength. In the six months since lightning had struck the Forbidden Court, she had grown ever more weary of her new responsibilities.

She had never wanted to bear the burden of the two most powerful duchies of Kingfountain. Her grandfather had been a capable and wise counselor in Ploemeur, and now that he was gone, killed in the same carriage crash that had taken her younger brother and her grandmother, the duties of the bureaucracy rested on her shoulders. The things he had handled were brought to her and she was beset day and night. Emissaries from Tatton Hall were getting more and more demanding for a piece of her time, and Thierry was in a constant state of agitation as he tried to prioritize the endless tasks for her.

Trynne's only solace was rising before the sun and taking the ley lines to Averanche to train with Captain Staeli and the Oath Maidens. As soon as the sun crested the wall of the training yard, she hurried back and was assaulted immediately and relentlessly with her duties until well after midnight each night. She was young, but the toll felt heavy enough to break her.

So did six months without word from Gahalatine. Six months with the torture of not knowing.

"My lady, I think my words are boring you," the ambassador said with a tone of reproof. "I will not take any more of your time."

Trynne realized her eyes had drifted shut and she snapped them open. "I'm sorry, Ambassador," she said, shaking her head. "Please go on."

"How much from my report should I repeat?" he said, his bald head dripping with perspiration. He mopped it with a sweaty kerchief and then put his hand on his hip in a belligerent posture.

"I think we've heard enough for the day," Thierry said. "Return tomorrow morning, please."

He grunted. "I had hoped to be on my way to Genevar with the tide."

"By all means, leave if you must," Thierry said in an offhanded way. "You are dismissed."

Trynne felt her cheeks flush with embarrassment as the ambassador gathered up his papers.

"Clear the hall," Thierry ordered.

People began shouting for their turn for an audience with Lady Trynne, but her pikemen herded them out of the audience chamber. It took several minutes before the noise abated and the doors shut with an ominous thud.

Trynne pressed her fingers into her temples and rubbed circles. Her mind felt lost in a fog of misery and regret. "I'm sorry, Thierry," she apologized. "I think we've offended the ambassador."

Thierry sniffed and approached her. "Come, my lady. Let's take a walk on the beach. Even your mother, with her prodigious patience and the assistance of your father and his father, was taxed by the demands on her time. *And* her emotions. The sea air will do you good."

His tenderness brought tears to her eyes. After rising, she followed him out of the rear doors of the audience hall. Accompanied by a detachment of guards to protect her and keep the crowds away, they strolled to the beach and climbed down the stone steps leading to the sand. The noise of the surf crashing against the rocks and hissing on the shore, the smell of the breeze, and the feeling of sunlight on her face as the huge orange orb dipped down the horizon—all helped soothe her. All reminded her of her mother.

"Your mother always came here for solace," Thierry said gravely. "I miss our walks together. She sought my counsel, even though she is much wiser than I could ever hope to be. Would you hear my counsel, Lady Trynne?"

"I would welcome it," she answered, clasping her hands behind her back, feeling the tickle of her hair as the wind blew it against her neck. The feeling of the sand changed as they approached the shore, the fine grains now mixed with beautiful colored beads of glass that had been pummeled and trampled by the waves for centuries. The colors were vibrant and dazzling. A family of curlews chased along the beach looking for little crabs.

"You are carrying too much on your shoulders," Thierry said. "The ambassador from Genevar should be making his report at Kingfountain, not Ploemeur. The land disputes in Westmarch should be postponed for a year. Refuse to hear them."

Trynne gave him a serious look. "I am being kept in suspense, but that does not require that everyone else should suffer the same way."

He raised his eyebrows. "Then you must empower someone else to make the lesser decisions for you."

"I am waiting until my mother returns," Trynne said, gazing at the sea. There had been no word for months. Each time Trynne invoked the magic of the protections, she silently prayed to the Fountain that Sinia would return. Until then, Trynne was trapped in Ploemeur, a hostage to her own promise and the fears and concerns of her people. Every time she returned from Kingfountain after consulting with Drew and Genevieve, the people looked relieved. No, that word wasn't strong enough. They were absolutely terrified whenever she left. If something happened to her, they knew Brythonica was doomed. It would be drowned by the Deep Fathoms just as the kingdom of Leoneyis had been before it. The evidence of that fate lay beneath their very feet. The beautiful beads of polished glass had been stained-glass windows once, in the kingdom that had long since been destroyed.

"She may not return for some time still," Thierry said. "Might I make a suggestion?"

"Please, Thierry. I am so busy of late that I do not have time to think of solutions to my problems. As you clearly saw this afternoon, I'm drowning."

"We all see it," he answered sadly. "Running a duchy was always a burden meant for two. For one person to run two? Unthinkable. And since your . . . your *husband*"—she could hear the disapproval in his voice—"has been too preoccupied with his problems to visit you, you must call upon capable, trustworthy people. Take your aunt Jessica, your mother's lady-in-waiting. Her husband is a sensible man and a proud Brythonican. Lady Jessica has served your mother well, but she is also a Kiskaddon. Send her to Westmarch and let her and her husband stay at Tatton Hall for the time being. Let her hear the cases brought to her and she can give her recommendations for solutions that serve both duchies.

"Your mother put great power and trust in Marshal Brendon Roux in ruling the realm. His family was most experienced in the arts of war. Most do not know this, but his father was the squire of the Maid of Donremy during the wars between Occitania and Ceredigion. You need someone like him, my lady. But we cannot simply wait for such a person to appear." He paused and met her gaze. "I would humbly ask that you let me share this burden with you. I know how your mother thought and the way she would decide. The only reason I have not mentioned this before was because I feared it would be presumptuous on my part to recommend myself."

She hugged herself, feeling a shiver run through her. After her family's combined duties and responsibilities had fallen on her shoulders, she'd felt the need to perform them on her own. But to what end? The work was wearing her down to the point of exhaustion. She would much rather be searching for her father than listening to boring speeches and reports of the latest conflicts between the relief ships sent to Chandigarl and the Mandaryn. The Mandaryn had seized all the cargo and wouldn't dispense the goods to the suffering people unless the goods were brought in on treasure ships bearing their own flags. Their machinations infuriated her.

"I will heed your counsel, Thierry," Trynne answered. "Will you send word for my aunt to come and see me this evening? Then draft the delegation of my authority and I will sign it. Thank you for helping me make it through these difficult months."

He put his hand on her shoulder. "My lady, you have experienced grief that is unsurpassed in recent memory. Some of the people . . . some of the citizens have begun calling you the Lady of Sorrows." He cast a wary look at her. "Perhaps I shouldn't say so, but others are saying that your family has been cursed by the Fountain."

They had been strolling slowly along the shore, staying just beyond the grasping reach of the foaming surf. Her guards had kept the area clear for them, but they must have allowed someone to pass. A man was walking across the beach toward them, someone she did not recognize.

Thierry noticed her gaze and turned to follow it. "That is Aumbale of the Espion if I'm not mistaken."

Trynne did not recognize him, but they met him partway. Aumbale had a strong stride and wore a tunic splattered in mud and riding gloves that he tugged off and stuffed into his belt as he approached. He'd not shaved for several days and looked saddle-weary.

"My lady," he said, bowing stiffly and producing a letter. "I come from the Star Chamber at the behest of my master, Lord Amrein. I left three days ago. I watched him pen this note with my own eyes before he fixed the seal. I'm certain the news will be coming at my heels. Your husband, Lord Gahalatine, arrived in Kingfountain by treasure ship. He awaits you there."

♦ ♦ ♦

Trynne's hands were shaking so badly that she had to ask her maid to help arrange her hair. Now that the time had finally come, she felt unprepared to see Gahalatine. She'd expected him in Ploemeur, but he'd come to Kingfountain instead. Why?

There was no time to consider it. They were waiting for her.

Once she was dressed to befit the occasion, she made her way to the chapel and stepped into the waters. Taking a deep breath and closing her eyes, she invoked the word of power, and in the next moment she was standing in the palace. Two of King Drew's knights awaited her.

"Welcome, Lady Trynne," one of them offered. "The king has been expecting you. He asked us to direct you to the solar when you arrived."

She thanked him and started down the corridor, wringing her hands as she walked, unable to quell the feelings of doubt and worry. She had not seen Gahalatine in six months. She had turned seventeen in that time, bringing her ever closer to her eighteenth birthday. According to the laws and customs of the East Kingdoms, Gahalatine could not consummate their marriage, without her parents' permission, until she turned eighteen. The thought of continuing their marriage this way—with him hating her, avoiding her—filled her with dread. She had to dispel the lies the Wizrs had told him about her. This was her moment to speak the truth.

As she approached the double doors leading to the solar, she reached out with her magic, not wanting to be caught off guard. She immediately sensed the presence of several Fountain-blessed in the room opposite her. One of them was Gahalatine himself. Magic was being used in the chamber and its essence hung in the air.

Trynne could sense Gahalatine's power had been restored, though it was not as vast as it had once been. His power had been connected to that of his sister. Her death had diminished him, but his reserves were full. He was not the one invoking his power. It was coming from someone else.

The guard at the door announced her and she strode into the solar, a place she had often visited to see her father. A room full of maps and globes and a comfortable table always supplied with trays of food and wafers. A crackling fire was in the hearth, for the sun had gone down, and the candles and torches were the main sources of light. The feeling of magic began to ebb immediately.

Her husband sat at the window seat, arms folded, his eyes leveled on the door as she entered the room. He looked guarded and impassive, in total control of himself . . . until their gazes met. There was a twitch at his cheek as she walked in and a mixture of emotions welled in his eyes. The Wizr Albion stood in front of Gahalatine, the same one who'd accompanied him on his ill-fated visit to the council six months ago. She sensed a piece of magic around his neck in the form of a medallion. It was still cooling from recent use. *This* was the source of the magic she'd sensed.

The other Fountain-blessed was not a Wizr but King Sunilik. She was startled to see him in the solar, even more so to find his daughter Sureya at his side. There were several warriors wearing the leaf armor, all of whom gave Trynne angry looks as she entered. They were there to protect Gahalatine from harm. From her.

"Trynne," Drew said, his voice sounding strained. "I'm glad you came so quickly."

"Of course I came," she answered, approaching Gahalatine at the window seat. He stared at her as if she were a threat to him, as if she were a distrusted enemy. Part of him responded viscerally by backing away, leaning against the window behind him. She cast a defiant look at the Wizr and then knelt before Gahalatine.

"My lord, I am so grateful to see you," she said, looking at him with pain and entreaty. She still felt the lingering effects of the Fountain magic in the room. She could almost see it twisting Gahalatine's heart into hate.

Her husband looked wary, his brow furrowing at the sight of her kneeling before him. He looked conflicted, as if part of him were at war within himself.

"I'd almost forgotten," he said in a low, husky voice, "how beautiful . . ." Then he shook his head and abruptly stood. "Rise, my lady. You are my equal, not my inferior. Even though the coronation has not happened, you are still my wife. You need never kneel before me."

She clung to the bit of hope dangling in front of her. He was conflicted. The Wizrs had discovered a way to manipulate him with their powers. Well, that would not work with her nearby. Rising to her feet, she wondered how to greet him. They had shared a kiss at their marriage. Several, in fact, but they had all been tame kisses of brotherly affection. Nothing like the kiss Fallon had given her atop the tower at Dundrennan. If they overcame this obstacle, she was convinced their relationship would change with time, that passion would grow.

"So you arrived three days ago?" she said, at a loss for words. "By ship?"

"Indeed," he answered coldly.

She glanced around the room. Lord Amrein stood at the table with the king. Genevieve was there, but not the young princess. The queen looked stern and serious. She was studying Gahalatine with a slight frown of disapproval.

"I thought you would come to Ploemeur," she said, still feeling the awkwardness of the moment. She wished to be alone with him, not in a crowded room full of witnesses.

He looked at her incredulously. "How could I risk that?" he said with a curt laugh. "After what you did to my fleet?" His anger was still evident but under control. "None of my crews dare enter your waters, my lady."

The scene was becoming more befouled by the moment. "Why did you come, then?" she challenged.

"King Sunilik convinced me," Gahalatine answered. "And by my troth, we must work out some arrangement. Some *truce*, if you will. The Mandaryn insist I cannot trust you, but Sunilik has advised me to hear your side. To listen patiently to your explanations." He swallowed, looking down for a moment before meeting her eyes again. "I knew this would be painful. For us both. But I am determined to endure it. I believe that I wed myself to you in a cunning ploy. I do not see how the evidence can be interpreted differently, but I will listen to you. The Mandaryn have agreed to these conditions. Apparently I did not require *enough* stipulations or conditions last time." His barbed words stung her.

"I will gladly justify myself. I look forward to the opportunity," Trynne said. She wanted to throttle the Wizrs who had corrupted his mind and his feelings.

"Very well. My conditions are as follows. We will have our conversation in your domain. In Ploemeur, in fact. I have wanted to see Brythonica's people and customs with my own eyes. Lord Amrein has agreed to escort me. We will be accompanied by my faithful warriors, and the king has pledged to send knights for my protection. Sunilik will remain in Kingfountain on board the treasure ship. If I do not return safely in seven days with the Fault Staff in my possession, he has orders to set sail and return to Chandigarl. There will be perpetual enmity between our empires ever after. So I ask you again. Do you accept my terms?"

There was a pit of coldness in her stomach. "I must bring you the Fault Staff?"

He nodded firmly. "I require that it no longer be in your sole possession. You are too dangerous to be entrusted with such magic."

Trynne's anger was quickly turning to fury. "If my king commands it, then I will give it to you."

CHAPTER FIVE

The Chapel Fountain

The mood in the solar was dangerously hostile. Trynne clenched her fists and looked at King Drew for guidance. She felt humiliated and dishonored, but she could discern that there was magic at work, that her husband's feelings and attitudes had been consciously manipulated by his Wizrs.

Drew pursed his lips, looking warily at Gahalatine. "So you are saying, Lord Gahalatine, that none of our efforts to aid Chandigarl during these many months have convinced you of our honest intentions?"

Gahalatine frowned. "Your tactics amount to a bribe," he answered stiffly. "Which is a fitting punishment considering our own use of that ploy. The Fountain has punished me most harshly for not seeing through the illusion."

"What illusion?" Drew answered. "You came here as the aggressor originally. We did what we could to defend ourselves."

"And you did so most admirably," Gahalatine shot back. "As I said, I believe I was caught in a snare." He gave Trynne a reproachful look. "You entered my kingdom. You learned what you could to your advantage. But the power of the Fault Staff is too much of a temptation."

"And you would trust your Wizrs with it?" Trynne demanded.

Gahalatine shook his head. "No, I would trust no one with it. If it were in my hands this very moment, I would break it over my knee and see its power destroyed. That is my intention."

Drew rose from his seat and started pacing. "I would agree to that," he said. "Better if neither of us had it. There is an imbalance of magics between our peoples."

"That is not my doing," Gahalatine said dismissively. "We have ever been the more powerful empire. My humiliation pains me, but as I said, we must form a truce of some kind. Tryneowy is my wife, even though I have seen Rucrius with my own eyes and she claimed to have—" He stopped short, sighing. "No, we will not have this conversation here. I do not believe my terms are onerous. I will go to Brythonica, but not by sea. Not by the ley lines. Let me see it with my own eyes, without trickery. Let me walk the shores where my doomed fleet perished. Let me say a prayer to the Fountain for their souls. Sunilik promised to send his daughter, Sureya, to accompany my wife back to Ploemeur to ensure no double dealing. I trust him and his daughter."

The barb was not well buried, and Trynne felt it keenly. Reya gave her a sad smile from across the room.

"My lord king," Gahalatine continued, "if we can agree that the Fault Staff should be destroyed, then let us do so here in Kingfountain with your council as witnesses. I promised Lady Tryneowy that she would not be forced to move to Chandigarl. We will, if we can, agree to a prescribed frequency for her visits." His cheek quivered with suppressed emotion. "And then I will return to my people and continue to repair the damage done there. Even after six months, the city is horribly scarred. My Wizrs advised me not to even come here. But I hearkened to Sunilik." He gazed at Trynne with a hint of longing. "Maybe we can, in time, build anew what was destroyed between us."

Her throat was thick as she saw the war raging inside him. The Wizrs had attempted to turn his heart to ashes, but there remained glints of heat, hissing cinders. A strong part of him that still cared for her.

"We are in agreement on the terms. You have my permission to leave," Drew said. "Lord Amrein will escort you and your guard. You will see for yourself that we are still recovering from the devastation you wrought on us. But peace has always been our goal. We never provoked this confrontation, Gahalatine."

"That is true enough," Gahalatine said, then pressed his lips together in a firm line. Even though she had been hurt by him, even though it would take time to heal, she admired his strength, his determination to do what was right despite the wily counsel—and strange magic—of his advisors.

"I will see you in Ploemeur in three days' time," Gahalatine said. He took her hand, and his touch made her feelings rouse like a shaken beehive. For a moment, he seemed on the verge of pressing her hand to his lips. His eyes seared into hers. "Why is it that I feel so differently when I am near you?" he whispered, pitching his voice so softly she barely heard it.

"It is the truth freeing itself," she answered him. "I am not what you have been led to believe. Allow me to justify myself."

He nodded. "I've heard the sweetest berries come from Brythonica. We cannot enjoy them in the Forbidden Court because the distance is too far and they perish before they can arrive, except the ones preserved in jellies. I know there is a beach made of broken glass from drowned Leoneyis. My ancestors once traded with that kingdom and learned much wisdom from it." His thumb grazed her knuckle. "I will come in three days." She saw the look of hurt in his eyes, the pain he was experiencing from being so near her.

Then he let go of her hand and turned to Lord Amrein. "Shall we not start at once, my lord? I have no urge to sleep."

♦ ♦ ♦

Genevieve and Trynne walked to the chapel fountain together after watching Gahalatine's group ride off from the castle bailey. Though Reya was to join her at the chapel, Trynne had urged her not to hurry. She knew her friend wanted more time with her father, and Trynne herself wanted to speak with the queen alone.

"That did not go as I expected it would," Trynne said, squeezing Genny tightly just beyond the doorway to the chapel.

"It went worse than I had feared," the queen replied. She motioned for the knights guarding the chapel to leave and they promptly obeyed. "The coldness and anger of his greeting." She shook her head. "I'm sorry, Trynne, but I grieve for you. I could not bear it if Drew looked at me like that. With such antipathy."

Trynne nodded. "There is magic at work, Genny. That Wizr has something with him. Something he was wearing around his neck, a medallion perhaps. I sensed it before I even entered the room. He has been using it to control Gahalatine's feelings, but it cannot work while I am with him. You don't know how tempted I was to attack Albion then and there."

Genny smiled. "I wouldn't have blamed you. Well, perhaps you'll have your chance. The Wizr is riding with Gahalatine for protection. Sunilik will be our welcomed guest here at the palace while he awaits their return. He expressed his gratitude to me for sending you to the oasis to rescue Reya. Their reunion was touching."

Trynne smiled. "I should have liked to see it. Well, I must go back to Ploemeur and prepare for my husband's arrival. I suppose this is a little how Mother felt when she was waiting for Papa to come to Ploemeur for the first time. He was so rude to her."

The queen smiled and rubbed her arm. "Well, hopefully his visit will help resolve the situation. There will be fewer people around to distract you. I wish the Wizr wasn't with him, but I have to say I'm grateful he left. We all felt horrible until you arrived. There was so much tension in the air despite our efforts to be civil."

Trynne nodded. "I'm glad I missed that part. It was good seeing you, Genny." She pressed a kiss to the queen's cheek.

"Trynne," Genny said hesitantly. She glanced to make sure no one else was around. "I wanted you to know that I did speak to Fallon. About the clothes you found in Morwenna's chest. Actually, I had someone go up there and look for them. His things were there, just as you said, and it gave me the pretext of asking him about it."

Trynne's stomach began to churn with worry, and a queer, bitter ache throbbed inside her. "And?" She could tell the news wasn't good because of the subdued look on Genny's face.

"Fallon was surprised by it, actually. He said he had never been to her tower before. It was a place she never brought anyone."

Wariness and suspicion mixed with relief, which was quickly squashed when the queen continued.

"He rode to Marshaw to ask her about it." Seeing Trynne's confused look, she explained, "Forgive me. Not many know of it. It's a small manor in the Forest of Bowland, close to Blackpool. There are no ley lines in or around that wood, so Morwenna has been sent there. He confronted her with the tunic." Genny sighed. "Well, she confessed that she'd stolen it from him during one of her stays in Dundrennan. She'd kept it in secret to comfort herself." Genny's gaze was piercing. "Trynne, when he returned from Marshaw, he was changed. I think Morwenna has been in love with him for some time. I don't know much about their conversation, but he was noticeably altered. He asked Drew for permission to marry her. He promised to watch over her in Dundrennan. It's his belief that she was fully under Rucrius's sway, and he thinks she deserves better than to spend her life in isolation." Her hands reached and clasped Trynne's between them.

"When was this?" Trynne asked, nearly choking on the words, the ache inside her growing unbearable.

"It's been two months already," Genny answered. "Drew hasn't given his permission yet. He wanted to be sure that Fallon's feelings were constant. His requests have become more and more agitated and ardent. I've never seen him . . . well, I thought you should know. Drew is planning to grant his consent, but he may make them wait until the Feast of St. Benedick."

"What were you going to say?" Trynne asked, feeling miserable. At least this settled one of her concerns. Fallon had not been wooing both of them at the same time, but she was still disappointed in how quickly his feelings had altered.

"That's all I wanted to say," Genny said, squeezing her hand.

"I know you're only trying to save my feelings, but I would prefer to know everything. You said you'd never seen him so . . . ? What? You stopped yourself just now."

Genny was always honest, even when it hurt. "I've not seen him so lovesick. Not since he told me how much he loved you. I was frankly startled by the violence of his feelings. But she is a handsome woman and he has ever been vain. Her very vulnerability was probably alluring. And her secret feelings, when they finally came out, gave him succor. Something to hope for. That he's smitten with her, I have no doubt. It pains me, but I want to see *both* of you happy."

Trynne let out a strangled sigh. "Thank you for telling me the truth, Genny. And for dismissing the guards first. I'm glad it was just the two of us."

The queen hugged her again. "Go back to Ploemeur and remind Gahalatine that he's desperately in love with you. I wish we could prove that Rucrius was dead, but the Pisan school still won't admit to having found his body. Even so, I know you can help him see reason. Gahalatine is still grieving from losing his sister and seeing his city destroyed. He's misguided, but there is no reason why we cannot mend this rift. Ah, there is Reya."

Trynne turned and saw her friend approaching. It was small comfort, but it was some. "I will do my best, Genny, but it wouldn't hurt if Gahalatine showed more trust and humility. He should have come to me straightaway. We've been married for more than half a year, and look at us. We're still strangers."

When Sureya arrived, Trynne reached out and they clasped hands as friends. They all smiled at one another, enjoying this small moment of peace.

"My father has done all he can to persuade Gahalatine to trust you," Reya said. "He can be very stubborn when making a point."

"I know," Trynne answered. "And I'm grateful he advocated for me."

"Then you two must fix this together," the queen said brightly. "When you and Gahalatine return, I hope to see some evidence that things have improved."

"I hope so too," Trynne sighed. "I desperately hope so."

CHAPTER SIX

Transgression

Gahalatine's approaching visit to Brythonica was heralded with shock and nervous anticipation. The short time to prepare had driven the staff at the palace, normally staid and composed, into a fit of hurry. The arrangements started immediately upon Trynne's return—the capital city eager to properly welcome her husband to the ancient duchy so richly blessed by the Fountain. Trynne hoped that Gahalatine would feel the presence of the Fountain magic as he entered the peaceful domain. The berry farmers were hard at work with the spring planting. The climate was mild and the sky could not have been a purer shade of blue.

Trynne paced in the audience hall, feeling her stomach tingle with both worry and hopefulness. She had sent Sureya and an escort to greet her husband at the borders of the wood. Word had reached her from Lord Amrein that Gahalatine's mood had softened as they crossed Westmarch. He'd become more prone to laughter and intensely curious about the history of the land. But his laughter always seemed to wane, his mood to sour and darken, after he consulted with his Wizr each evening.

The company of travelers had made fast progress through the realm, exchanging their horses for fresh mounts to ensure they were not delayed.

Because the road to Ploemeur led directly to the sacred wood, Trynne had left explicit orders with her mother's aging battle captain, Marshal Soeur, that none of the entourage was to visit the grove. Only a command from her personally could revoke the order. Any of the Fountain-blessed who passed through that wood would sense the magic there—and be intrigued by it—but Marshal Soeur had promised that her order would be obeyed.

Thierry entered the audience hall with news from the baking guild that all the food would be prepared and in order. "They seek to honor and welcome your husband with the finest fare that Brythonica can offer," he said with a hint of smugness. "I think, my lady, that he will be duly impressed."

"Thank you," Trynne answered, feeling herself start to fidget again. "Any word on their progress?"

Thierry pursed his lips and rocked back on his heels. "Word just arrived from Sir Louden that the travelers are on pace to reach Ploemeur in time for dinner, if not earlier. The meeting with Marshal Soeur at the border was amicable. No demands were made."

Trynne bit her lip and nodded. "Excellent, thank you."

"I have duties to attend to with the goldsmith guild," he said, bowing to her before departing.

She walked to the nearest window seat and stared out at the beautiful cove, the rippling waters of the bay, and the city hunkered down amidst green hills decked with manor houses and gardens. Ploemeur was truly an idyllic setting, but her fears would not be settled until she had reconciled with her husband. She would do anything in her power to soothe his concerns and regain the lost trust between them. Deliberately, she had not reclaimed the Fault Staff from where she had hidden it, for its power could be sensed by anyone Fountain-blessed.

While she believed Gahalatine genuinely wished to destroy it, something told her Albion did not share his emperor's intentions. She had concealed it at the sanctuary of Our Lady at Penryn. No one knew where it was except for her.

Biting her lip, she gazed at the ships at harbor, all the Genevese trading vessels that came in and out. Part of her own fleet was anchored in the tranquil bay. The sight of all those ships made her think of her mother. Sinia had been sent to the Deep Fathoms—the great unknown—and yet she'd accepted the Fountain's summons with calm fortitude. Trynne felt none of her mother's serenity.

She tugged the window open by its handle, letting in the fresh ocean breeze to caress her face. She closed her eyes, listening to the trills of birds and the distant noise from far below. Easing herself onto the bench, she sat for a moment, enjoying the stillness, her mood contemplative.

She'd not been sitting there long when she heard the distant rumble of thunder from a cloudless sky. A pit opened in her stomach. Rising from the window seat, she walked briskly to the other side of the room. The view on that side looked down on the sacred woods. A layer of clouds had suddenly appeared on the horizon, overshadowing the trees. The pit in her stomach began to suck everything inside it. Her temples throbbed and her pulse quickened with fear. The magic of the silver bowl had just been summoned.

Without pausing to consider the implications, she stalked from the audience hall and hurried to the fountain she used to travel the ley lines. As she briskly strode, it felt as if some inner voice was howling for her to run, not walk.

"My lady?" one of the serving girls asked.

"Find Thierry," she ordered. "Tell him I'm going to the grove. Something's wrong."

The maid bobbed quickly and rushed away. Worries began to cascade through her. When the bowl was invoked, the guardian of the grove was summoned. Captain Staeli had been gravely wounded in the Battle of the Kings, but he had healed with help from her magic. He was the one who wore the ring of the grove and would be summoned to defend the place. If he was defeated, the ring could be claimed by another person. This thought, this fear, was what made her stop her determined walk and break into a run. Servants stared at her in concern as she rushed past them. The knights stationed at the fountain looked at her worriedly as she stepped inside.

"My lady?" one of the knights demanded.

"Send knights to the grove," she ordered. "At once. I fear something awful has happened."

With the message still on her lips, she thought the word of power to cross the ley lines and felt the magic engulf her, as if she'd plummeted off a waterfall.

She arrived in the grove instantly. Chunks of ice as big as fists crashed down all around her, the hailstorm creating a cacophony. There were soldiers all about, some huddled under shields, arms raised to deflect the bombardment. Most were sprawled on the muddy ground that was thick with frozen shards of ice, bleeding from the impact of the jagged chunks.

Her father had brought her to the grove long before he was attacked there. He had shown her how to summon its magic and what it did. The storms summoned by the silver bowl had always terrified her, but the magical assault never lasted long.

"Aspis!" she cried, creating a shield around herself and those nearby. She gazed through the pelting storm, trying to find someone she recognized. The aura of Fountain magic was everywhere. The air tingled with it.

The hailstorm ended abruptly, and in the wake of its commotion, she heard the groans of the survivors. People had collapsed everywhere. There were no horses. They must have all bolted away.

The sounds of pain were dissonant with the angelic song of the birds that suddenly appeared on the limbs of the denuded oak tree. The hauntingly beautiful chorus had always wrung tears from her eyes in the past. But today she was desperate to find her husband and her friend, to help them and the wounded men.

Lord Amrein was lying on the ground, a jagged wound on his skull and blood covering most of his face. He looked like a dead man. Trynne gasped with shock, but she could not absorb what her eyes saw.

The presence of another Fountain-blessed drew her gaze to the cleft of the riven boulder, and she caught the swish of a pale-colored silk skirt. It looked familiar and she squinted, trying to make out the shape as the person disappeared into the cave beyond the great rock.

She took a few steps and then saw Gahalatine struggling to sit up. His big shoulders were trembling with weakness and he pitched forward again. She felt the throb of his Fountain magic, but it felt wrong—like a bubble that popped each time it attempted to coalesce. Hurrying to his side, she knelt in the melting ice, soaking her skirts.

She looked at his face, his brow twisted into a rictus of pain. There were chunks of ice in his hair, along with a matting of fresh blood. She wrapped her arms around him and invoked a healing word, pouring some of her magic into him.

Some of the soldiers were upright now, gazing at the tree and listening to the anthem from the beautiful birds. But only a few had managed to stand. Most lay still. Many, she realized, were unbreathing. Marshal Soeur was among the dead. Her breath hitched, but she would not let herself cry. Where was Reya?

"Where am I?" Gahalatine muttered, wincing, staring around the grove in shock and confusion. Her magic was working through him, repairing the injuries he'd sustained during the hailstorm.

"You'll be all right," she said soothingly, choking on the words. She stroked his shoulder and then wrapped her arms around him, wanting to both give comfort and take it. "You weren't meant to come to this place. Why did you come here?"

He turned his head, gazing up at the skies as if afraid of them. He looked shaken and fearful. Then he looked at her, his eyes tracing her features. There was no anger or hatred in them now. Just fear and worry and confusion. He struggled to sit up and was successful this time. She couldn't stop holding him.

"What is this place?" Gahalatine murmured, gazing at the silver bowl chained to the stone plinth. At the riven boulder, at the oak tree that was now full of leaves and glistening mistletoe. The magic of the grove always revived it following the storm.

"It is a sacred place," she answered, gazing around for a sign of Captain Staeli. Where was the grove's defender? The magic was supposed to summon him in the case of intruders. "Why did you come here, my lord? Why didn't you go straight to the palace with Reya?"

She saw Lord Amrein's chest rise and fall and nearly sobbed with relief. She noticed that another body lay crumpled beside Lord Amrein. It was her friend's small form.

"I don't know," Gahalatine said, shaking his head. "I don't remember coming here." His eyes searched her face, as if he wanted to say something to her but was ashamed.

The song of the birds vanished and the birds with them. She rose and hastily went back to Lord Amrein, sinking back down to her soaked knees. Judging by the scene laid out before her, the Espion master had protected Reya with his own body and borne the brunt of the storm. His life seemed to be ebbing before her eyes. Trynne touched him, invoking the same words of healing. His wound was more grievous than Gahalatine's had been, so she had to pour more of herself into him, draining her stores of magic. Then she saw the Wizr Albion, sprawled out on the ground. She hadn't sensed his magic, and the reason was instantly clear. His face was pale, his eyes frozen open.

He was dead.

Keeping her hand on Lord Amrein's back, she continued to feed magic into him, fusing his crushed skull. His wounds were mortal. She poured as much power as she dared into him. It had weakened her. She touched Reya's neck, sighing with relief when she felt the throb of her friend's heart. Then she rose and stalked toward the cave. She'd seen the shadowy figure disappear into its depths, but she didn't feel the presence of someone Fountain-blessed coming from it. Reaching out with her defensive magic, she probed the darkness of the interior. It was empty.

This was where her father had disappeared. Clenching her fists, she stared at the gap in the rock. The empty rock. Somehow it had stolen from her again. What was the key to this place's strange magic?

Trynne approached the cave, but she felt a strange throbbing of warning not to enter it. Something would happen to her if she gave in to temptation. It was a warning from the Fountain. Her curiosity and pride almost made her ignore it, but she had taken an oath to obey the Fountain. Trynne backed away from the stone and went back to Gahalatine, who was standing now, gazing at the bodies of the fallen in shocked abhorrence.

"I'm sorry this happened," she said, shaking her head. "I'd left orders for your party to be kept away from this place. I was going to explain it to you, my lord, when we spoke."

He was looking at her oddly. All his anger and negativity were gone. He looked confused more than accusing. "Where am I?" he asked her.

"You're in Brythonica, my lord," she said, fresh worry blooming in her chest.

The name seemed to mean nothing to him. Nothing at all. "Brythonica," he sighed, gazing around the grove in wonderment. Then he shifted his focus back to her. "And you are the mistress of this grove?" he asked.

The awful truth crashed down on her like an avalanche. Gahalatine's memories had been stolen from him—like her father. Like Dragan.

"I am," she answered. "What is your name?"

He looked at her helplessly. "I . . . I cannot remember." He walked in a slow circle, gazing at the towering trees. "I remember nothing. I don't know . . . who I am." He finished the circle and looked at her pleadingly. "Can you help me? I need to remember. You know me? You recognized me, yes? Who . . . who are you?"

Trynne's heart shrank with pain. "I am your wife, my lord," she said forlornly.

CHAPTER SEVEN

Ignominious

Wounded and dead alike were brought to the palace at Ploemeur. The scale of the disaster was almost incomprehensible. Trynne was devastated by all the injuries and death. There was no doubt at all that it had been a deliberate attack, orchestrated by her enemies, and yet the Wizr Albion had been killed as well. Surely a simple shield spell could have saved him from the ravages of the ice storm. It felt as if a game of Wizr were in progress, only she was blind to all the moves.

Healers tended to the injured. Reya had revived but had swooned soon afterward from dizziness. The soldiers who had survived were frightened and in a state of shock from the calamity that had befallen them. Gahalatine was befuddled with confusion. His wounds were treated, although her magic had already started to heal him. Of the survivors, Lord Amrein was in the most perilous condition. He was still unconscious and struggling with each breath. She checked on him constantly, afraid he too might die under her care.

She remembered the threat Gahalatine had made before leaving Kingfountain. If he did not return in seven days, Sunilik was to return to Chandigarl and declare a state of enmity between the kingdoms. There was already plenty of ill will between them.

She sat on a stool beside Kevan's sickbed, her hand touching his arm, feeding part of her magic into him. Her reserves were draining steadily, and she had no time to restore them. As she lent him her strength, one of the healers wiped away some of the grime from his face with a warm towel, revealing pale cheeks.

A strong hand gripped her shoulder from behind. She turned and found Gahalatine standing over her, his face pinched with concern.

"My lady," he said hesitantly. "Can you spare a moment? I'm growing anxious." He cast a look around the room. "None of this is familiar."

His touch was like a stranger's. There was no recognition in his eyes, no fondness or hatred. Just bewilderment.

She looked down at Lord Amrein and released his arm. Shifting her gaze to the healer, she met his eyes and said, "Let me know if the chancellor revives. Let me know at once."

"Yes, my lady," he said with concern. "He may not wake for some time . . ."

The words he left unspoken were the loudest: *or ever.*

She rose from the stool and guided Gahalatine toward the balcony, entwining her fingers and tapping them against her mouth as she walked. The stress of the situation was taking its toll on her.

Before they made it very far, he turned to her with a look of fear. "I still cannot remember anything. Not a flicker from my childhood. No memories of my mother or my father. None of *you.* You say we are husband and wife. Yet should I not at least recall something about you? About this place?" He stared at her with hopelessness. "It feels like . . . a trick. A deception."

The sight of his confusion filled her with even more pain. Her father had been like this. According to Rucrius, he was masked and incarcerated in a dungeon under the threat of death. There had been no one to guide him or remind him of who he was.

She looked at Gahalatine firmly and gripped his arm. "I tried to explain this at the grove. I know it will be difficult for you to understand. But your memories have been washed away."

"But how?" he demanded.

"I do not know," she confessed. "It has happened before and we do not know the cause of it. I also do not know if it is temporary or not. You may get your memories back." She shrugged, forcibly reminded of the fact that so far Dragan had shown no signs of recollection whatsoever. For seven months. "You may not. For now, you are safe. I am, as I told you, your wife. We were married seven months ago at Kingfountain."

He stared at her blankly. "And you say that I am the Overking of Chandigarl, a kingdom across the sea," he stated without any conviction.

"You are. You attacked our realm, but we arranged a truce between our kingdoms. You needed a wife and I'm of one of the noble families. Your counselors, the Wizrs, have tricked and deceived you at every turn. They may be the ones who blocked your memories."

"And I chose . . . you," he said with concern throbbing in his voice. "What happened to your . . . to your face? As you've been speaking, I've noticed that . . . I see that part of your face doesn't move like the other." He raised a finger to point at her, though he was still clearly struggling with a way to make his query polite.

The words were like an arrow through her heart. Gahalatine had fallen in love with her because of how she had overcome adversity. This handsome man was seeing her flaws without the context. He did not love her. He didn't even know her. Her head started to spin with despair. She needed to sit down.

She wasn't sure she could trust herself to speak, but she tried. "Yes, I was . . . injured as a child," she said, feeling enormously self-conscious. "That is not important right now. We did make an alliance between our people. The customs of Chandigarl demand that a husband and wife wait to consummate the marriage if the wife is too young and her parents are unable to give permission. My parents are both missing. So we have not"—her cheeks flamed scarlet—"*been* as man and wife yet. When you returned to Chandigarl after our wedding, a lightning storm struck your palace and burned down a large part of the city. You blamed me . . . blamed the Fountain for it. You were coming here, to Ploemeur, to reconcile with me."

His lips parted in surprise. He stared at her, listening to her words as if she'd spoken in a foreign language, wrestling to make sense out of them. The apathetic look on his face revealed that he was less than entranced with her. Did he think he had taken her to wife out of pity? She could not bear to consider it.

"My lady!"

Trynne spun around at the sound of the healer's voice.

"He's waking!"

She saw Lord Amrein leaning up on one arm. He'd just vomited into a bowl. Several other healers had gathered around his bed. She felt a thrill of relief, a spark of hope amidst a blackness of soul.

The healer knelt by the chancellor, gripping his wrist and pressing the back of his free hand against the man's forehead. "He's very weak still. My lord, do you know your name? Do you know where you are?"

Lord Amrein glanced around the room in confusion. Those who'd been injured in the grove lay all around him, receiving treatment from other healers. "I recognize the symbol of the triple face on the pillar over there. This is Ploemeur, is it not?"

"Thank the Fountain," Trynne gushed, spanning the remaining distance between them.

He looked at her, his brow furrowing. "My lady," he said broodingly.

"I tried reviving him with salts and it did the work," the healer said. "My lord, you sustained a head injury along the journey."

"It was a hailstorm," Lord Amrein said.

"Indeed," Trynne said, nodding. "When you are feeling more rested, we will need to leave for Kingfountain immediately. There is news I must share with the king and queen at once."

Lord Amrein frowned, his brow knitting. "If I could sit on a horse, I'd go now," he said.

"No, there is no need. We could take the fountain and be there straightaway. But you look so ill."

He nodded and leaned forward on the bed. "If I could be helped there? We should go at once."

Trynne directed two of her knights to help carry him there. Then she waved over Thierry, who was still baffled by the abrupt turn the day had taken. He could hardly be blamed. One moment they'd been preparing for Gahalatine's visit—the next, the hall had become a sickroom. And where was Captain Staeli? Why had he not appeared in the grove to defend it? Not knowing only made her anxiety worse.

"I need to know Captain Staeli is well and to seek his counsel. Please send a rider out and have him come to Ploemeur at once. I'm taking Lord Amrein to the palace to warn the king about what has happened. I leave Gahalatine in your charge. Answer his questions. Help explain who he is and why he is here. I will return as soon as possible. Talk to Reya when she awakens again. See if she can explain why they went to the grove against my express command."

"I will do so, my lady," Thierry answered. "Can you explain to me what has happened? Was it a freak storm? The weather was so clear. It doesn't make sense."

She couldn't share the grove's secrets, but her steward had expressed her own thoughts so precisely. "I know, Thierry. None of it makes sense."

◆ ◆ ◆

When they arrived at the chapel fountain in Kingfountain, Lord Amrein dropped to his knees from the rush of magic, planted his hands on the rim of the font, and then proceeded to retch once again in a series of spasmodic jerks that produced nothing but a little bile. The Espion assigned to the chapel rushed in to help him out.

"What happened? I've never known him to travel this way," one of the Espion asked Trynne. The chancellor was clearly in no shape to answer the question himself.

"It was urgent we both arrive." Invoking the word of power for healing, she reached out and touched Lord Amrein's shoulder. Her own stores of magic were continuing to dwindle, but her effort had improved his color noticeably. "We need to see the king and queen at once."

Both Espion exchanged a look before glancing back at her.

"What is it?" Lord Amrein demanded. "I saw the look you gave each other."

One of the Espion leaned in and whispered something in his ear. The chancellor's head jerked back. "Take me to the king."

"What has happened?" Trynne asked in concern.

Lord Amrein stared at her. "The baby, Kate, is critically ill. The whole palace is concerned she will die."

Trynne blinked. "Where is she?"

"The queen has been nursing her. The doctors are all baffled as to the cause. She was healthy three days ago when I left, and now she's . . . failing?" He looked again at the Espion who had conveyed the message.

The Espion nodded, his lips pursed.

"I must go to her," Trynne said, knowing how desperately worried Genny would be. Trynne's powers had been depleted, but she felt—no, she *knew*—that things here were not as they were supposed to be.

"The king is in the council room," the other Espion said. "The queen is in her chambers."

"Help me get to His Majesty," Lord Amrein said to one of them. Then, pointing to the other, he made a quick gesture with his wrist. "You accompany Lady Trynne."

"Aye, my lord."

Trynne didn't need the escort, nor did she understand the subtle Espion sign that Lord Amrein had just given his man. Fallon probably knew what it meant. Without a word, she walked at a forceful pace through the corridors she knew so well. The expressions of the servants and the subdued atmosphere only added to the impression that something was badly wrong.

She turned to her escort, who was barely keeping up with her. "The babe fell ill immediately after we left?"

"Aye, my lady," he said circumspectly. "No cause or reason for it."

"Have there been any visitors to the palace?"

"Just the delegation from the East. Sunilik has met frequently with the king and queen. Do you suspect him?"

"I don't," she said, shaking her head. "No, I believe he is trustworthy. But no other visitors have come? Is Duke Fallon still in the North?"

"Aye," the man said, arching his eyebrow at her question. What she really wanted to know was if Morwenna was still under guard at Marshaw, but she would only ask that question of someone she trusted. Besides Captain Staeli, she didn't know many of the Espion personally.

She gritted her teeth and hurried to the chamber. As she approached, she felt and sensed the dim aura of magic coming from beyond the door, which immediately put her on her guard. She had never sensed magic coming from Genny's room before. The Espion waited at the door, and Trynne was announced, her concerns growing with each breath.

"Yes, send her in at once," she heard Genny's voice say in a worried tone. Something about her voice sounded strange to Trynne's ears, though she couldn't say what. Worry wriggled inside her more violently.

The room looked the same, but the smell had changed. An odor of sickness hung in the room. Genny stood by the cradle, wearing a dark-green gown that was almost black. Her hair was elegantly coifed, which surprised Trynne. Would a concerned mother have taken the time to groom herself so elegantly? The look of grief on her face was belied by the satisfied glint in her eyes. As Trynne approached, she sensed multiple sources of magic, like a series of musical instruments playing softly in the background, unobserved by any but the most practiced listener. The effect was very subtle, but any Fountain-blessed would probably sense it if paying attention.

First, there was a ring that was hiding the true appearance of the queen. The woman looked and sounded like Genny. But it was a lie. Trynne could sense it clearly. Such tricks had never worked on her. Another magic was worn beneath the lacings of the woman's bodice. A medallion of some kind. It felt similar—no, it felt *exactly*—like the one Albion had been using when Trynne had arrived in the solar a few days before. There was almost a sickly-sweet odor that came from the magic, one that tried to put Trynne at ease and make her feel safe in the presence of a trusted friend. A woman whom she had shared a bond with for so long, one she trusted implicitly with all her secrets.

But this woman was not Genevieve.

It was Morwenna.

It is time for the blacksmith's hammer to fall. I will forge this kingdom into my own making. What gives the smith's arm the strength to continue the strokes? Anger. Revenge. Tryneowy ruined my last plan. She will suffer for it. Dearly. She will lose everything she treasures. Her reputation. Her husband. Her lover. She will understand what it means to be a pariah, an outcast, an enemy. She will understand for herself the trials I have borne my whole life. And when she is done suffering, she will beg me for a poison to end it. I may or may not give her what she asks. She has no idea what I am capable of. She has no idea what curses I will bring on this land. If I cannot rule Kingfountain, no one will.

Morwenna Argentine

CHAPTER EIGHT

Threat

Trynne only had a moment to decide.

One of her gifts from the Fountain was that of discernment, both of people and of complicated situations. Even as her gut wrenched with disbelief and shock, her mind assembled the pieces. It was obvious to her now. Morwenna had a Tay al-Ard. She also had a ring that could disguise her into anyone she chose. And she had poisoned Genny's baby.

All of Morwenna's contrition and helplessness had been feigned. In that brief moment of sun-bright clarity, Trynne recognized the face of her enemy, the enemy of the realm. She'd had suspicions before. She'd seen the shadows on the wall. Now she knew exactly who was blocking the light.

At the same time, Trynne's own magic was sufficiently drained that she would not prevail in a contest with Severn's daughter. No doubt the poisoner was anticipating her arrival. She had set these events into motion in preparation for it. She knew how the memory spell worked. No doubt she was the one who'd lured the men into the grove and stolen Gahalatine's memories. That flash of a pale skirt had been *hers*. What reaction was Morwenna expecting from Trynne?

All she knew was that she needed to survive getting out of that room.

And so she chose to feign ignorance.

"Genny, I came as soon as I could," Trynne said as she hurried into the room. It was not difficult pretending; her emotions were already wringing with concern for the child. "Poor Kate! Can I see her? You must be frantic."

Trynne did not reach out with her magic. She was sorely tempted, but such an action would give away her distrust immediately. Her actions needed to imply she wholeheartedly believed Genny was standing there. Trynne approached, keeping her eyes fixed on the cradle. The babe's labored breathing could be heard from across the room and Trynne reflexively pressed her fist against her own mouth, the shock of it piercing to her core. How could someone harm such a defenseless thing? The thought made her shudder with revulsion.

She arrived at the crib. "Oh," she gasped, staring miserably at the child. The babe's complexion was green, and she struggled fitfully in her sleep. She reached out and touched Morwenna's shoulder, just as if the girl were truly her best friend and not a monster.

"It came on suddenly," came the reply. Morwenna was trying to act the part of a suffering mother. "The doctors cannot say what is causing it. She vomits over and over and grows weaker by the hour. The *king* is frantic, as you can imagine." There was a slight inflection in her words, as if she could not totally disguise her utter animosity for her brother. "The Fountain is cursing us. I fear the child may die." Was there an implied threat in her words? Trynne swallowed, wanting to snatch the baby and run.

"Can I . . . can I try to heal her?" Trynne pleaded, glancing imploringly at the queen's beautiful face. "My magic is nearly wrung out, Genny. I have little left. But if I can save her, if there is *any* way I can save her, I will."

Morwenna positioned herself closer to the crib and put her hand on the railing of it. She slowly shook her head. "No, I don't think so. It's because of you that she's so sick."

Trynne's heart was hammering wildly. She struggled to maintain her composure. "What do you mean?"

Morwenna gave her a warning look. "Your powers have been rather . . . erratic of late, Trynne. Drew and I are worried the burden you've carried is beyond your capabilities. Even a stone will crack under stress. We've seen the signs in you."

Trynne needed to get out of the room, but she sensed that Morwenna had no intention of letting her walk free.

"Well, I have been preoccupied of late," Trynne said, taking a single step backward, watching to see how Morwenna would react. Her adversary took a step forward to compensate.

"Of course you have," Morwenna said soothingly. "When the mind is burdened with guilt, a person can sleepwalk at night and not remember what they did in the morning. Do you have any lapses in your memories, Trynne? Things you've done but have since forgotten?"

Coldness seeped into Trynne's bones. She took another step backward, knowing if she turned to run, a dagger would be plunged into her back. Still, she resisted the urge to summon her magic to defend herself.

"What are you saying?" Trynne stammered. "Genny, this isn't like you."

The look in the queen's eyes was unforgiving. "You gave your heart to one man and married another for wealth and power. It's been tormenting you, hasn't it? And now Fallon wishes to marry Morwenna Argentine. He loves her, you know. He always has. I didn't want to tell you, but I think you always knew the truth deep down. Their secrets. Their friendship was deeper than you know. He used you to get information for her. He used your feelings for him to deceive you. He does not love you now. Not after you betrayed him."

Trynne's mind was whirling, but she knew the words were intended to provoke her, to make her defensive. She felt the power of the medallion and blinked with surprise, experiencing the user's intent to give her the emotion of jealous rage.

But the magic could not force her to feel it. She understood the cause.

"You've always known this about him and you didn't tell me?" Trynne said in challenge. "I thought you were my friend."

Morwenna smirked. "Yes. I know you did."

The door opened without a knock. Morwenna's eyes flashed daggers at the interruption. "What is it, Mariette?" she asked, barely bridling her fury.

"I'm sorry for the intrusion, my lady," Mariette said. She had been assigned to protect the queen after the battle in Dundrennan and was still serving her. "King Drew wishes for Lady Trynne to join him at the Ring Table at once."

Morwenna glared at the Oath Maiden with barely concealed frustration. "By all means take her there."

Trynne backed into the hallway, her eyes fastened to Morwenna's body, especially her hands. When she was out of reach, she turned and hastened to Mariette, who had joined her. There were six Espion in the corridor. They hadn't been there before.

"Mariette, what is going on?" Trynne asked in a low, frantic voice.

"I think the baby has been poisoned," Mariette said in an undertone. "Everyone is praying to the Fountain for her, but something is wrong."

"Indeed, it is," Trynne said. She noticed that while the Espion had allowed them to pass, they'd begun to shadow them immediately. She saw them exchange the subtle hand signals that allowed them to communicate without words. "Have you noticed a change in the queen's behavior?"

"A pronounced one," Mariette said with concern. "She's slow to respond to any questions, and her personality seems to have transformed overnight. It happened two days ago."

"It's *not* the queen," Trynne whispered.

Mariette's breath hissed. "Who?" she mouthed, giving Trynne an alarmed look.

"Morwenna," Trynne replied quietly. "She's in disguise. I imagine Genny is being held captive . . ." And she knew instantly where. Marshaw. A place that could not be reached by use of ley lines. Morwenna wasn't imprisoned in her manor. With a Tay al-Ard, she could come and go as she chose. Obviously she'd managed to hide it from her captors. And she had clearly used the medallion to seduce Fallon into his fiery impatience to marry her. Trynne boiled with fury.

Morwenna was using the people Trynne loved like puppets.

They were approaching the doors of the audience hall, but Trynne felt like she was walking in an enemy fortress. Even the guards were watching her with suspicion.

"That baby will die if we don't save her," Trynne whispered to Mariette. "Do you know where the Espion tunnels are?"

"I do," Mariette answered.

"I'm going to cause a bit of a disturbance in there, Mariette. I think Morwenna will come after me. I'm hoping she does. You need to get Kate to the sanctuary of Our Lady. I will try to meet you there and bring you both to safety. If we don't act now, it will be too late."

"Would she really kill a baby?" Mariette wondered with horror.

Trynne turned to look at her as servants opened the doors to the audience hall. "Yes," Trynne answered emphatically, her gaze burning into Mariette's with a silent plea to trust and obey.

Mariette bowed to her and then turned and walked back the way they had come. Her heart afire with emotions, Trynne strode into the audience hall. She immediately noticed there were additional guards in the room. Many more than was usual. There were already several people seated around the Ring Table. Kevan Amrein was slouched in a chair, drinking from a cup and waving off a servant who offered him bread and cheese. The deconeus of Our Lady and Duke Ramey were also present.

Upon seeing her, Drew immediately rose from his chair. The seat next to him was conspicuously empty. The king looked haggard and soul-sick. His eyes were bloodshot and he had smudges beneath his lids. He looked like a man tormented. The warmth and kindness in his eyes were gone, replaced by distrust and apprehension. He looked at Trynne as if she were a danger to everyone in the room.

This was an even sharper turnaround than the one she'd experienced with Gahalatine. Drew was not himself. She could almost smell the effects of magic on him.

"My lord, I came straightaway," she said, taking a deliberate path through the middle of the room. She couldn't help but notice that all the doors were guarded. The king glanced at his captain, an Atabyrion swordsman named Thasos, and gave him a subtle gesture with his hand, as if to stop him from pouncing on Trynne.

The king looked like he was struggling to stand upright. He rubbed the back of his hand across the stubble on his normally clean-shaven chin.

"Yes, you did. I thank you." His voice sounded hollow. "I wanted to see you immediately. To ask you to defend your actions."

"My actions?" Trynne said with confusion. "What are they? My lord, something is wrong—"

The king held up his hand in a jerking motion, cutting her off. "Let me speak plainly, Trynne. You are here to answer some serious allegations." His eyes were smoldering with enmity. "I am normally a very patient man. But at this moment, I feel troubled. Greatly troubled. Lord Amrein tells me that he escorted Gahalatine to Brythonica without incident *until*"—here he paused, holding up his finger—"they reached the wood. That grove in the woods is meant to be a carefully guarded secret. That is the way your father wished it to remain, but as the company came up the road, Lord Amrein said you were waiting for them. You directed them to tether the horses and follow you into the grove. *You.*"

Trynne heard the words with disbelief. But she understood the ruse. Here was further evidence Morwenna had been at the grove. She'd deceived everyone, including Gahalatine. And then she'd worked her spell to steal his memory.

"I was not there," Trynne said forcefully. "I was at the palace in Ploemeur . . ."

"Surely those loyal to you would say and *do* anything you bid them to," Drew countered. "I trust Lord Amrein. I thought I could trust you. Where is Sunilik's daughter? Why did you not bring her with you?" His countenance darkened with anger. "I see that you have not brought Gahalatine either. Do you wish for us to send Sunilik home empty-handed? To start another war?"

Lord Amrein leaned forward, his face full of confusion and doubt. "There may still be an explanation. Let her speak, my lord. I saw Lady Trynne with my own eyes, but my senses have been deceived before. It is unlike her to be so duplicitous."

Trynne sensed the power and presence of a Fountain-blessed person approaching down the corridor. It had to be Morwenna. She would not allow Trynne to defend herself.

She stared at those assembled at the table, calculating her next move. Genny had been abducted, and Drew was a shadow of himself. Their baby was going to be murdered unless Trynne and Mariette managed to steal her away, and Morwenna had used magic to impair the judgment of many of the people in the palace. The guards stood there fidgeting, waiting for the command to arrest her.

Just as Morwenna had been arrested. She had gone willingly, shoulders slumped in defeat. An act. She had never truly been caged at all.

Trynne was running out of time. This was not the moment to confront Morwenna. Not when her own powers were so weak. And if she allowed them to put her in a cell, she'd be helpless to rectify the situation.

Trynne stared the king in the face, beseeching him with her eyes. "Loyalty binds me," she said deliberately. Then she lifted her hand, twisted the ring on her finger in full view of everyone, and invoked a word of power. The twist of the ring was just a deception. She did not try to use the ley lines.

She borrowed Dragan's trick and turned herself invisible.

CHAPTER NINE

Treason

The invisibility spell she had learned studying *The Vulgate* was especially draining, and she knew she would not be able to sustain it for very long. Her objective was simple—force Morwenna to respond to her as a threat, giving Mariette time to sneak the babe from the castle.

The audience hall erupted with confusion and chaos as the king surged to his feet. There were gasps and murmurs and commotion, which enabled Trynne to walk around the table and head toward the nearest exit—a door on the opposite side of the room from the one Morwenna was likely to use.

"She's gone!" Drew shouted. "I wanted her captured. Now that she's back in Brythonica, it will be more difficult to snare her."

Duke Ramey made it to his feet. "I cannot believe she's capable of treason, my lord," he said with grave concern.

"Do you think I'm comforted by the thought?" Drew replied. "Even the queen was taken in by her deceptions. Summon our forces, my lord duke. We will flush her out like a thrush if we must."

Trynne saw a look flash between Duke Ramey and Lord Amrein. There was suspicion there. Drew's normal calm and patience were gone. He was uncharacteristically agitated.

"My lord," said Kevan Amrein. "There might be another explanation."

Trynne could sense the approach of Morwenna, and she hurried out the door as a servant opened it carrying a tray of uneaten cheese. Her pulse throbbed in her neck as she hastily walked down the corridor, dodging past the servants who'd clustered in the hall.

A powerful jolt of Fountain magic rumbled through the palace. Trynne instantly became visible again in the corridor, appearing out of nowhere and startling someone who nearly ran into her. Morwenna had invoked the spell to rip away Trynne's invisibility, just as Trynne herself had done to Dragan in Marq. But Trynne had been expecting it.

"Beg your pardon, my lady," the servant girl said, veering away from Trynne with a look of worry. She was well known at the palace and, until now, had been implicitly trusted. Most of the servants wouldn't be aware of the change.

Good.

Trynne quickly ducked down another corridor, trying to sense the presence of her pursuer. Yes, Morwenna was moving after her, probably disguised as someone other than the queen. Both she and the poisoner were walking briskly. Trynne knew that the chapel fountain was guarded by the Espion. That was where she would be expected to go, but there were other fountains within the inner grounds, ones that her father and Lady Evie had played in as children.

Morwenna had studied the Wizr magic much more ardently, which only added to Trynne's disadvantage. She experienced a sudden pang of regret for not having learned more. Had she memorized the precise location of the ley lines, her path would not be limited to the fountains.

Trynne suddenly darted to the left, changing her direction almost at random. Both she and Morwenna knew the layout of the palace. The upper part was really one continuous circle. If the poisoner had a Tay al-Ard, then she would be able to use it to catch Trynne by getting ahead of her. If she suspected her final destination. Trynne knew from experience that the magic of those devices was not infinite. Morwenna would only be able use it a limited number of times before it needed a recharge. How many? Three or four?

Trynne suddenly sensed Morwenna's presence in the hallway she had just left. She'd closed the gap almost immediately. A flush of panic rushed through her and she started to run. There was no cry of warning or shout to stop, but she could feel Morwenna behind her. Tracking her. Running like she was.

Trynne veered toward the door of an anteroom, jerked at the handle, and stepped inside. It was a decorative space, filled with chairs arranged in conversation areas. The far wall was embedded with tall windows. Trynne summoned her magic as she rushed across the room. She stepped up onto a chair, yanked aside a set of curtains, and then pushed at the latch of one of the windows.

There was a pulse of magic, and the door of the sitting room rocked open so forcefully it smashed into the wainscoting. Not even pausing to look back, Trynne hoisted herself up onto the window ledge and jumped down. She heard the splashing of the fountain at the garden, a sound that filled her with desperation to reach it.

Sprinting across the lawn, her skirts nearly tripping her, she raced to the edge of the fountain. Magic swelled behind her again, a freezing spell that should have stopped her in her tracks. The spell diverted away, and Trynne leaped into the waters, turning briefly.

She saw a woman standing at the window—it wasn't Morwenna's face, but Trynne could sense the illusion. There was a scarab-like ring on the middle finger of her raised hand. Even from this distance, she thought she could see the malevolence in the girl's eyes.

Trynne stared at her a moment, feeling the huge wave of magic building up inside of Morwenna. The fountain she stood in began to hiss and gurgle, and Trynne felt immense pressure thudding in her skull.

She invoked the word to transport herself away. *Kennesayrim.*

♦ ♦ ♦

With great agitation, Trynne walked the grounds of the sanctuary of Our Lady. Her ring disguised her as a commoner, but it didn't make her feel safe. She paced for several hours, hoping Mariette would come and terrified she would not. Always, she stayed in the portion of the grounds where she had a view of the royal docks across the river.

Trynne had always been good at playing Wizr, but there were moments in some games when an opponent's move irrevocably changed the whole game.

Morwenna had abducted the queen. She had poisoned the royal child. Her failure to become Gahalatine's queen—and by extension to rule all of Kingfountain—had clearly pushed her across a moral line. Her father was dead, his ties to loyalty and honor severed. She had changed the rules, and Trynne would have to outthink her and out-maneuver her.

At least all the pacing and plotting was helping Trynne fill her magical reserves. This was a challenge she relished, and she was determined not to let Morwenna win. She was the king's champion still, even if he was too addled by magic to recognize it.

Her eyes caught sight of a small canoe as it plunged down the ramp and hit the river at an angle. Trynne's breath quickened, and she hastened to the docks at the rear of the sanctuary. When she arrived, she dropped her disguise so that Mariette would recognize her.

Mariette was easily distinguishable in the small canoe, but Trynne could not see if she had the child. Anticipation stole her breath. When the boat came closer, she finally glimpsed a squirming bundle and heard the mewling of discomfort and hiccupping sobs.

Relief flooded her.

Mariette handed the child up to Trynne, who caught Kate in her arms and held her fiercely.

"The ride here reminded me of the cost," Mariette said, her voice a little tremulous. There were beads of sweat on her upper lip. "This is treason and I'd be thrown into the river. I want to run as far from Kingfountain as I can."

Cradling the child in one arm, Trynne reached out and helped Mariette up onto the dock. Then Mariette fastened the boat with a mooring line. "What next?"

"This baby's life is in great danger," Trynne said, shaking her head. "We must do all we can to save her, Mariette."

"She's very sick," Mariette said, looking pained. "Will she . . . will she die if we take her away? What if Morwenna is the only one who can cure her?"

That was a thought that made Trynne cringe.

♦ ♦ ♦

When Trynne returned to Ploemeur, she used every healing spell she knew from *The Vulgate* on Kate. But the baby's illness only grew worse. Perhaps there was another spell that could cure the princess, but finding words of power in the long, dry-as-dust book had always taken time, and that was something she did not have.

Reya had recovered her strength, and although she was still dizzy from her injuries, she was determined to help. Gahalatine, whose sense of honor had not been stolen with his memories, had also offered his assistance—especially after learning the babe was the princess of this kingdom. While she appreciated the offer, there was little he could do in his current state.

"How did this happen?" Trynne asked Reya, staring at her friend in confusion while she held Kate and tried to soothe her unsuccessfully. They had taken to a small sitting room, somewhere they were unlikely to be seen and overheard. Gahalatine stood by the window, listening to them with a slightly baffled look on his face.

"My lady," Reya said. "When you appeared before us, I was convinced it was you. The gown you were wearing was different than the one you had on earlier in the day, but I didn't think anything of it at the time. You brought us to the grove yourself and then poured water from the bowl onto the stone slab. You said you had something to show us."

"It was not me," Trynne said, shaking her head.

"But it looked like you. It sounded like you. Even your manners were the same. It deceived us all. My eyes could not tell what was true." She paused, then added, "But in my heart, I know it wasn't you. You wouldn't have led us to such an ambush. And now you say Morwenna has stolen the identity of the queen herself?" She looked fiercely angry. "This is the blackest of treason. And I fear that she does intend for my father to bring Gahalatine's message of enmity home."

He looked on in confusion. Trynne forced a smile and said, "It's a long tale, but suffice it to say that Morwenna has none of our best interests in mind." Turning back to Reya, she added, "I fear you are correct about your father. But neither of us can risk returning to Kingfountain at present.

"As for her ability with disguise . . . Morwenna is a poisoner. She was trained in the art of disguise, and she has a magic relic that allows her to assume the shape of anyone else. Her plan hinges on killing the princess. I must find a cure, but I do not know where to look. Maybe I should go to the poisoner school." The words felt toxic on her lips, but she was desperate.

"No!" Reya said, shaking her head. "You could not trust anything they told you. And they may not even know the answer. I must ask—does Grand Duke Elwis have a poisoner? Perhaps we could ask him?"

Trynne liked the idea. The thought of doing nothing but waiting for Drew to invade Brythonica made her desperate. "I could find out. He wasn't at the palace. Neither were Lady Evie or King Iago. We need supporters and quickly. I'm certain they would help us."

"Bring me with you," Reya pleaded. "Grand Duke Elwis and I have become . . . friendly"—her cheeks pinkened slightly as she said it—"and

I can speak to him on your behalf. By helping you, I help the queen as well. She is in great danger too."

Trynne nodded through her exhaustion. There was no denying it. Gahalatine knelt and gazed at Kate. "So weak and ill," he said, looking distraught. "Who would do this to a babe?" He looked at Trynne, still not recognizing her, but compassionate. "I wish I could help," he said again. "Might not the poison have come from Chandigarl?"

Trynne didn't even want to consider that. If he was right, Morwenna herself might be the only one who knew the cure.

◆　◆　◆

There were only two days of silence from Kingfountain. And then the word went out. Tryneowy Kiskaddon was a traitor to the crown. The king was gathering his army to march on Westmarch and Brythonica and subdue the two duchies. They would be made crown lands, and the rulers would be chosen by the king himself.

The grim news was brought by none other than Captain Staeli, who was not only unharmed, but was totally unaware of the attack on the grove, which only added to the mystery.

He arrived at dusk the day after Trynne had returned from Brugia with Elwis's poisoner. Reya had fainted after crossing the ley lines, and Elwis, very attentively, had insisted that she remain behind with his physicians until she fully recovered. He had listened to their tale and promised Trynne to do everything in his power to assist her as an intermediary with the king, even if it meant resisting the crown.

The poisoner Elwis had sent with Trynne, Michal, had served the grand duke's father. He was tall and gaunt, with shorn gray hair and a serious and unexpressive face. Every part of him was exact, from the length of his fingernails to the creases in his doublet. In his thick Brugian accent, he had told Trynne after examining Kate that, although he could not discern the specific poison by the symptoms, he knew his business well. In his estimation, he had announced in a colorless tone, the babe would die within the next two days. With that, he'd borrowed a steed and left. Trynne had been too loath to leave Kate to bring him back through the ley lines.

Though she knew Evie and Iago would give her their support, unquestioningly, should she ask for it, Trynne could not stomach the thought of making a visit in person. Not when she'd have to report that she'd saved Kate from Morwenna—but the princess was likely to die anyway. She'd sent a courier, telling them the whole sordid tale, and then she'd spent every waking moment poring over *The Vulgate*, hoping she'd find an answer.

She'd found none.

And now Captain Staeli had come to Ploemeur and told her that her parents' lands were about to be invaded. Trynne pressed her face into her hands in stunned acceptance that her worst fears had come to pass. "This is unbearable," she moaned. They had retired to her private chamber, where they could speak privately.

Captain Staeli had always been a taciturn man. He scratched his gray-flecked brown beard. His balding pate was moist with sweat from his ride from Averanche.

"It's as bad as that if not worse, lass," he told her, his lips pressed firmly into a frown. "Lord Fallon was named head of the Espion."

Trynne gaped in shock. "What of Kevan Amrein?"

"He was struck down by a mysterious illness," Staeli said. "He's not moved from his sickbed since you left. Folk are saying he met with foul play here in Ploemeur. What happened here, my lady?"

"Morwenna," Trynne said angrily, squeezing her fists. "She is behind all this anger and deceit."

"I know, lass," he said. "But that doesn't change the fact that the king's army is on its way. Severn's brat won't put you on trial, my lady. She'll kill you with her own hands, and then she'll destroy this kingdom. We cannot allow it."

Trynne rose from the window seat and began pacing, drumming her fingers together as she walked. "I've sent word to Atabyrion, but it will be too late. What can they do to help Kate? To help us?"

"You've little time left," Staeli said, shaking his head. "Your fleet, my lady, is supporting the East Kingdoms at the moment. Most of your soldiers are away."

Trynne stared at him, her stomach bunching into knots. "I can't defeat the king."

"Yes, you can," Staeli said, walking toward her. "You are the best knight in all the lands. You've proved it over and over. If he comes at you, then you fight him."

"But he is the king!" Trynne said in anguish.

"Aye, and he's been misled. And controlled by magic. You'll gain nothing by pouting and pretending. You need to fight, my lady. Defend your lands. You control the most powerful duchies and the king knows it. Conquering these lands won't be easy, nor should it be. Your father wouldn't lie down and die."

Trynne rubbed her eyebrow. "I wish he were here," she said. "I do not know how to take this news. I have a duty to my people. A sacred duty I cannot abandon. My mother charged me with defending our borders." She paused and looked at him. "You need to know what happened here. How this all began. Oh, where to start?" She quickly explained to him how Gahalatine had arrived suddenly at Kingfountain, demanding to see her in her domain. How the Mandaryn had filled him with distrust and wariness of her. She then related how the party had suffered the brunt of the magic of the silver bowl, and finally shared her theory—that Morwenna had tricked the men and led them to their fate. That the poisoner had used a spell to steal Gahalatine's memory, just as she'd done with Dragan.

"My question to you," she continued after finishing the disturbing tale, "is why weren't you summoned to the grove? That should have happened following the ice storm. Let me see my father's ring."

Captain Staeli wrenched free his glove and offered her his callused hand. The ring was invisible while being worn, so the first time she'd seen it was after removing it from the severed hand found in the grove.

The ring was made of white gold on top of yellow gold, with concentric circles around the band. Her father had won it after mortally wounding Marshal Roux, who had died after charging Owen to protect Sinia. The ring had forced him to defend the grove from any uninvited intruders.

"I sensed nothing when you said the magic should have summoned me," Captain Staeli answered sternly, gazing at his hand. "To be honest, I've never felt anything particularly special about this ring. Occasionally the magic has felt . . . active, but nothing ever happened. I only had the feeling of being watched. I thought it might be the grove's magic checking in."

A ring was only a ring. A master craftsman could have made another one that looked identical to it. A Wizr could enchant it and give it properties of invisibility. Perhaps the true wearer of the ring had been summoned to the grove by the hailstorm after all.

"Could this be another one of Morwenna's tricks?" Trynne said, shaking her head. "My mind is reeling from the implications."

A breeze came from the window, followed by a smell that infiltrated her chamber. The smell of flowers . . . *magnolia* flowers.

There was movement at the balcony window. Staeli reached for his sword when a man stepped away from the curtains, tall and lanky and dressed in black leather with the symbol of the white boar as a badge.

Fallon. Her eyes fell on a cylinder—a Tay al-Ard—as he stuffed it into his belt. His expression was dark and brooding and there was a wry look about him, as if he knew full well he'd startled them both.

"No, Staeli, you don't have Owen's ring," he said, tapping his lips gently with two fingers and then running his hand through his dark hair. "I have it."

CHAPTER TEN

Hetaera

Morwenna must have sent him to stop Trynne, to arrest her for treason and bring her back to Kingfountain. Panic shot through her, for she knew she'd be forced to flee, perhaps even harm him to do so.

"Well, lad," Captain Staeli said in a warning tone, positioning himself in front of Trynne. "I suppose we'll see if you're as good with a blade as everyone boasts."

"I'm not here to fight you," Fallon said, shaking his head as he stepped closer. Trynne summoned her magic, preparing herself for conflict. "In fact," he continued, "I'm relieved you're already here, Captain. It saves me from having to seek both of you out, and time is something we have in scant supply." He looked into Trynne's eyes. "Don't run. Hear me out."

"I think it's a trick," Staeli said. "Go, my lady. I'll stop him."

Fallon shook his head. "No tricks. Put your sword down, man. I'm not fighting either of you. Trynne, I know I must earn your trust quickly. Take the Tay al-Ard." He pulled it from his belt and held it out. "Both of us know what it can do. I took it from Morwenna. It's hers."

"Take it, Captain," Trynne said guardedly, still looking into Fallon's eyes, trying to understand what was happening. Her instincts said she shouldn't trust him. But part of her was desperate to. She needed help—and that could be exactly what Morwenna was counting on. She stared at him with suspicion.

"I'm on your side," Fallon said, handing the device to Captain Staeli. "I've *always* been on your side. I need to explain quickly what is going on. We don't have much time to save your father and stop Morwenna. I know where he is and how to get there. If we don't go immediately, he is going to die in a war that is consuming another world. It's the world Myrddin is from. Trynne, all the stories we heard growing up are true and frighteningly real."

"How can I trust you?" Trynne demanded. He'd given the captain the Tay al-Ard, but she was still unconvinced. Was he trying to play on her emotions? Was he being driven by Morwenna's magic even now?

He held up his hand. "I know you don't trust me. Will you at least listen to me? I wanted Captain Staeli to be here because he won't let you do anything he feels is foolish."

"You're right on that, lad." The captain nearly growled the words.

"Then we understand each other," Fallon said. "I drugged Morwenna and then took your father's ring and the Tay al-Ard from her. I tried to take off that black beetle-like ring she wears, but it won't come off. It might need to be cut off her finger. When she revives and realizes I'm gone, she'll come looking for me. She will try to kill me, I'm pretty sure of that. We don't have a moment to waste, so I need you to trust me. Can we sit? I promise I'm not trying to waylay you."

Trynne motioned for the couch and the chairs and they all took seats near one another. She watched Fallon closely for any sign of deception, but while he looked haggard and weary, he did not look guilty. There was a determination in his countenance she'd never seen before. A settled aura, one that spoke of his strong will.

He rested his elbows on his knees. "I've known for some time now that Morwenna deliberately betrayed the king. I've kept that knowledge secret from everyone except my sister. Morwenna has abducted her and hidden her in Marshaw, disguised as herself so that she won't be believed. I've put in motion orders to set her free and bring her to Dundrennan. They say you took Kate, Trynne. Is that true?"

She nodded. "She's here, but she's very sick."

Fallon's look darkened. "I hope I'm not too late to save her. Let this part of the story be quick. I've been training with the Espion for several years. You knew this. But I've also trained in secret to be a poisoner. Morwenna has been teaching me." He tapped his fingers together. "I think I can help Kate. I *hope* I can help her."

As if seeing the question in her eyes, he explained, "The main reason I wanted to study those dark arts was because of my interest in the properties of nightshade. Under a certain dosage, it can make the victim reveal what they know without leaving them the memory of unburdening themselves. Too much, and it's fatal. I've used it on Morwenna to learn about the scale of her plot to take over Kingfountain. Actually, her ambition doesn't end with this land." He pressed his palms together. "Morwenna is a *hetaera*."

Trynne looked at him in confusion. "What is that?"

"They are like poisoners, but they are from another world. They have powerful magic. You have no idea how powerful, Trynne. They have these medallions that can be used to manipulate a person's emotions. They can cause fear. Jealousy. Just about any emotion you can imagine, but more strongly, more powerfully than what is normal. They can even make a man fall in love."

He tilted his head to one side. "Or hate. The king doesn't realize that his sister is pretending to be his wife. Until now, she was maneuvering in the background, but she has begun to execute her plan. She poisoned Kevan Amrein so she could offer me the position she knows I've always wanted. But in order to claim the full powers of the hetaera, she needed to betray the one she loves." His eyes were dark. "Me. She didn't think I was aware of what she was doing. She won't remember telling me because of the nightshade. She gave me this—her medallion. It's called a *kystrel*."

He reached into his pocket and withdrew the medallion. It was round with a whorl-shaped pattern on the tarnished silver face. The chain attached to it dangled from his hand.

"I haven't worn it. I will *never* wear it. If I did, she would be able to control my actions. All part of the great betrayal, you see. She got it from that other world. She's gone there many times with your father's ring. I would not have been able to take the kystrel off on my own. Someone else would have had to break the chain and tug it off me. I'm telling you all of this because the place where we're going is overrun by the hetaera. Civilization is collapsing, and they are about to annihilate themselves in war and plague."

As Fallon spoke, Trynne had felt a few buds of hope bloom inside her, but his last comment caught her completely off guard. "What do you mean, where *we* are going?"

He stuffed the medallion back into his pocket. "The passage to this other world is here in Brythonica. In the grove. For some reason, Trynne, you are immune to the hetaera's magic. You and those who are near you. Your father was also immune, which is why I think he's still alive. I can't do this alone, Trynne. I need your help."

Fallon's gaze was intense and serious. "I've been trying to solve this puzzle for a long time. I had all the clues, and the nightshade finally enticed Morwenna to put the final pieces in place. Morwenna stole your father's ring. She learned about it from a story in an ancient book called *The Hidden Vulgate*. It is a book of magic she found in the poisoner school in Pisan. It tells the story of Owain, the man who married the Lady of the Fountain. That story spoke of a pathway to another world—the world the original King Andrew was taken to when he was mortally wounded by his bastard son." He rubbed his chin. "If we don't stop Morwenna, that story will repeat itself, Trynne. The king will die. But we can stop her together. Please."

Her heart welled with gratitude for him. But she also realized that if she left Brythonica, there would be no one to maintain the wards that protected the duchy from drowning. She had been trusted to safeguard her people. But she had also sworn an oath to herself to save her father. What was the right choice?

Fallon straightened and shrugged his shoulders, looking at Staeli. "Well, Captain? What do you think? Have I made this all up? You know," he said with raw emotion in his voice, "that I would give my life for hers. That I would never let anyone hurt her or harm her family. Not knowingly. I've kept silent to preserve the secret. Only my sister knew. If she were here, she would vouch for what I've done."

Staeli's brow was furrowed with suspicion. "And you know what I'd do to you if you ever did harm her."

"I do, Captain. And I would deserve it." He turned his attention to her. "I told you before, Trynne, that I might do things that seem suspicious. At least you know why now." He let out a long sigh and leaned back in his chair.

"What about Gahalatine?" Trynne asked, looking at his face.

Fallon nodded. "There is something about the oak tree in the grove that causes memories to be lost. Both your father and Gahalatine were brought there. I don't understand that part, but we may need to chop it down in order to restore their memories." He paused. "Sunilik has already left for Chandigarl."

The news was not unexpected, but it gave her another pang of unease.

"When he arrives," Fallon continued, "there will likely be war between our realms again. Not now, but in the future. Only Gahalatine can stop the war. If we go and rescue your father, we can return and heal them both. The Tay al-Ard is much faster than a ship. We could arrive in Chandigarl before Sunilik does."

"My mind is still reeling, Fallon," Trynne said, shaking her head. "But what you said makes sense. I feel like I've been walking blindfolded in a room and have kept stumbling over chairs."

"We all have," Fallon replied with a sardonic chuckle. "All except Morwenna. She was not always evil, Trynne. Her plan was not to destroy us, but to put her father back on the throne. She was ambitious for it. And her magic provided her a way to accomplish it. But Severn's death changed her. She was not accustomed to defeat, to setbacks, to being thwarted. She embraced the hetaera magic to get more power—and it ruined her." He stared at Trynne fiercely. "She must be stopped."

Trynne let out a sigh. "How are we going to find my father once we pass over to this other world? Fallon, the Tay al-Ard only works if you've been somewhere before."

"I know," he said. "It can help us get back to the portal after we've found him. But it won't help us find him. *This* will."

He was wearing a pack beneath his cloak and slung it off one of his shoulders. It was full and heavy, ready for a long journey. She saw a dagger strapped to it, along with a bedroll. He undid the ties and pulled out the bedroll. Then, fishing through the contents, he withdrew a metal chest with a rounded lid and a handle.

It was the Wizr set.

Trynne's eyes widened. "But Rucrius destroyed it!"

Fallon gave her a smirk. "So we all thought," he said. "But one thing I've learned about Morwenna is that she has a gift for forgery. She was in league with Rucrius all along, Trynne. She made an identical set. When the Wizr arrived and used his staff to crack the set, it was nothing but a show. She had already switched her copy for Drew's. She's been using the board all along. She can't move the pieces, but she can see where all of them are. When we travel to the other world, the game will shift to represent the politics over there. The board is based on geography. Your father is the white knight. The set will lead us to him."

"Open it," Trynne said emphatically.

Fallon removed a key from around his neck and unlocked the case. Then he opened the lid, and there . . . She'd not seen the board in several years. The pieces were arranged in an almost haphazard fashion. She knew that the rows and columns represented the various kingdoms. Blinking quickly, she rose from her seat and knelt by Fallon, looking at the board. Staeli came as well, his brows knitting together in confusion.

Trynne saw two white knights next to each other on adjacent squares on the western side of the board. Her throat caught when she looked up at Fallon's face and saw him gazing at her in compassion and determination. The two pieces were guarding a white king. Across the board, they saw the black Wizr piece. Morwenna.

"There is Genny, at Marshaw," Fallon said, pointing to the white queen up in the northmost corner of the board.

Trynne's eyes scanned the board. Where was Drew? She was looking for another white king. But there wasn't one.

Instead, she saw the black king near Morwenna's piece.

Her countenance fell and a cold feeling filled her stomach. Drew . . .

Should she go with Fallon? Should she visit a world on the verge of destroying itself? Or was her duty to stay, to try to block Morwenna's progress another way? She wasn't sure she could trust her own judgment, for she was filled with conflict. In the heart of her anguish, she heard the quiet murmur of the Fountain.

Save the king from himself. Go, or all is lost.

Fallon looked at her as he slowly closed the lid and twisted the key. "We don't have much time, Trynne. Will you come with me?"

She gazed into his eyes imploringly. "Can you save Genny's baby?"

CHAPTER ELEVEN

Into the Grove

Night had fallen over Ploemeur, and the sky glittered with stars and a waxing moon shone through the gauzy curtains of the nursery. Trynne, Fallon, Gahalatine, and Captain Staeli had gathered into the palace nursery, where Mariette was helplessly trying to ease the discomfort of the suffering infant.

"Light a candle," Fallon whispered.

Mariette balked at the suggestion. "It pains her eyes." She held Kate even closer, rocking her slightly.

"I know, but I must see her clearly," Fallon said.

Staeli went and lit a taper and brought the candle near. Fallon gazed down at the child, his face scrunching into a look of sorrow and controlled fury. He examined the babe's face, tilting up her chin and looking at her neck. The princess's skin had a greenish cast and she began to wail as soon as the light was brought near. Tears trickled down Mariette's cheeks as she watched.

"Shhh, lass," Fallon cooed. He pressed his fingers to her throat and cocked his head. Then he nodded and turned toward Trynne. The light of the candle flickered across his serious expression. "These are the symptoms of monkshood mixed with ellesbore. Both are deadly enough to kill a child within a few days. Morwenna taught me that ellesbore is more common in the East Kingdoms. I think she intends to implicate Gahalatine in this as well. The cure is white horehound." He reached down and took Kate's little hand, stroking her fingers with his thumb. "She might not have lasted another day." He looked at Mariette. "A little tea. Make her drink some every hour for two days. That should be enough. Her body will do the rest." Fallon leaned down and brushed his lips over the babe's brow.

Mariette's smile was beaming. They sent for an apothecary to get the herbs immediately.

Fallon smiled in response and patted Mariette's back. "Kevan Amrein needs some as well or he's a dead man. You'll have to find a way to get him the cure—a grown man will last a few days longer. Might be best to stage his death, though." He twisted a ring off his littlest finger. "This is Kevan's Espion ring." He handed it to Staeli. "You can do a lot of mischief with this. We won't need it where we're going."

"I'm coming with you," Staeli said, his expression fierce.

Gahalatine straightened. "I will come as well."

Fallon looked at them and then at Trynne. "Brythonica must be protected," he said, "and by soldiers who are brave enough to defy the king's army and buy us time to return with Lord Owen. My lord Gahalatine, you cannot come without jeopardizing your own people. There is a magic game of Wizr that has been under way for centuries. It ends when one of the kings is defeated—you or King Drew—and there is no heir. When it ends . . . it ends abruptly. I believe we can get your memories back, but if you leave this world, disaster will befall your people."

Trynne felt shaken by his words, and she saw Mariette's eyes widen with distress. So, the game was finally on the precipice of ending. The stakes were as high as they possibly could be. And yet . . . the thought of being alone with Fallon filled her with unease. Not because she mistrusted his intentions but because . . .

"Captain, can we talk over there?" Trynne asked, motioning for him to come with her. She nodded to Gahalatine, indicating that he should join them. Fallon offered to hold Kate while Mariette snuffed out the candle and went to fetch a teapot and warm water.

Both men followed Trynne to the window seat, but as they all got settled, Trynne found her eyes drifting to Fallon for a moment. Her heart wrung with emotion at the sight of him nuzzling Kate with his nose, whispering soothing words to her as he rocked her in the darkness. Comforting. Loving. Her throat caught with emotions and part of her melted at the scene. But then she saw her husband watching her watching him, and her heart clouded with trouble.

"I'm sorry, my lord, but this may not make much sense to you," she said quietly. "To Captain Staeli, it will. My father always told me the greatest lesson Ankarette taught him was the importance of discernment. He said it was the most important of the Fountain's gifts. Should I go with him, Captain Staeli? My heart tells me that I should. That it's the Fountain's will."

His bearded face turned down into a frown. "You want to know if I think he's being honest."

She nodded. "I'm not sure I can see things clearly right now. Everything was in confusion, but his words make sense. I also *want* to believe him. I *want* to believe that he's true to his sister, to his niece." She looked down at her lap and didn't articulate her final thought. *To me.*

Gahalatine leaned forward, his face showing concern. "Who is this man who has come?"

"The brother of the queen," Trynne said. "We were raised together since childhood."

"And you are a married woman now," Staeli said warningly. "I know your husband has recently treated you ill." He gave Gahalatine an accusing look. "Don't think that I'm not tempted to thrash him because of it, whether he remembers it or not." For a moment, Trynne wanted to smile because she knew he meant it. "But duty is duty, lass. If you go with the Llewellyn boy, you will be tempted to break your vow. Let me come with you." His eyes said more than his words. He knew how she felt about Fallon, although he respected her more than to say so out loud, especially in front of her husband.

Holding the captain's gaze, she answered, "I would never betray my oath, Captain. I am an Oath Maiden. Who else can I trust to carry out my will while I am gone? Thierry is a capable steward, but he's no battle commander. We need *time*. And I need you and Gahalatine to defend Brythonica while I'm gone."

"I don't understand why I cannot come with you," Gahalatine said seriously. "Your friend, he said something about a game, but it made little sense to me."

"I know," she answered, meeting his gaze. "You will have to trust what I say. To trust my promises. If you cannot trust me, then we have nothing together."

Staeli pursed his lips and fidgeted. "What you are asking tests my loyalty to the utmost. If you don't return quickly, I'll be condemned for treason for certain. Your husband may face the same fate." He let out a pained sigh. But then he lifted his gaze to hers again. "I will do it, lass," he said huskily. "If your father were back, he could fix this mess. I know he could. Who better to fetch him than you?" He reached up and stroked her slack cheek with the edge of his coarse finger. "I am and always will be loyal to your house. Your father had to rebel against the king once. It was the right thing to do then, and now that the king is under his sister's power, it's the right thing to do again."

Her heart gushed with appreciation for this man, her faithful mentor and friend. She hugged him, feeling tears sting her eyes. "I don't know what I would have done without you," she said, trying to contain her emotions. Part of her was afraid she would never see him again, and that thought made her squeeze him even tighter.

91

"Gack, lass," he said, patting her shoulder. "I'm naught but a soldier." He gently pushed her away and she saw him brush something from his eye. Then he put his meaty hand on hers. "You bring your papa back and this will all be worth it."

Trynne rose and then kissed his balding head. "Thank you," she whispered thickly.

Then she turned to her husband. "Do you have faith in me, Husband?"

He gave her an intense look. "I can only judge what I've seen. I have much to learn and I will have to ask this fine captain about why he resents me so. But it seems to me you are serving others above yourself. That is what a leader must do. If I can help in any way, I will. Trust must be earned. Be faithful to me and I will be faithful to you."

His words impressed her. He had always been good with words. She leaned up and kissed his cheek. "I will," she said firmly.

Mariette returned with a teapot and Thierry, who gave Fallon a wary look as he entered the nursery.

"What is the meaning of all this?" the steward asked with concern. "I only just learned of Duke Fallon's arrival. Why was I not told?"

Trynne took a deep breath. It was going to be a long night.

♦ ♦ ♦

Standing before the mirror, Trynne looked at her reflection as she tightened the strap of her arm bracer. She'd considered wearing the full armor she'd inherited from the Maid of Donremy, but such an outfit would have invited attention and conflict. Instead, she was garbed as a simple knight, equipped with a sturdy chain hauberk, a nondescript tunic, and a leather belt. She had both her swords in their scabbards at her waist. Captain Staeli was finishing going through her pack, which contained a bedroll, some food and water, and even some coins from various realms. Gahalatine stood nearby, his big arms folded, watching her with quiet interest. He and the captain had spent a long time talking in solitude, though she did not know what they'd said to each other.

As she stared at herself in the mirror, her hair tied back in a queue, she realized she could pass for a man to the unobservant. Worry consumed her. Glancing out at the night sky, she realized it would be dawn shortly. They needed to leave.

There was a soft knock at the door and Mariette entered with Fallon. The palace was asleep, but Trynne's night was just beginning. She tugged on her gloves as Staeli hefted the pack and helped her put it on.

"How is Kate?" Trynne asked the two as they approached.

"She's looking better," Mariette said with relief. "She just took some more tea and some broth. I'll depart to Edonburick with her for safekeeping. I have the sealed letter you gave me for your parents," she added with a nod to Fallon. Trynne quirked her brow at him.

"I've said my good-bye," Fallon offered. He gave her an urgent look. "Kate will be safest in Atabyrion. Genny is not yet free, and my parents can secure the babe in places that Morwenna can't find. Now can we go? It will not take long for Morwenna to figure out I've betrayed her. Once she does, her wrath will be unleashed to its fullest extent."

Trynne glanced at Staeli, who looked as somber as ever. He nodded brusquely as he crossed the room to Fallon. Even though the captain was shorter, he had an intimidating air. His hand closed on Fallon's elbow. "If anything happens to *her*," he said, jerking his head toward Trynne, "you'll have more to fear than Severn's daughter."

Gahalatine gave Fallon a distrusting look that mirrored the captain's.

Fallon swallowed and then nodded, trying to stifle a smile. But he sobered quickly and returned the serious looks sent his way. "My only intention is to get Trynne and her father back to Ploemeur safely. I give you my word of honor."

Staeli nodded to him, accepting his oath as fact. "I'll hold you to it, lad," he said. Then he withdrew the Tay al-Ard from his belt and handed it to Trynne. "I'll still feel better if she holds this from now on."

Fallon nodded. "Shall we?"

Trynne walked to the window and parted the curtain, gazing down at the rippling waves. The tide was coming in. From her vantage point, she could see the sea-glass beach. The wardings would hold for another fortnight before they needed to be reset. Watching the foamy waves filled her with dread. If she didn't return . . .

Trynne banished the worry, shoving it from her mind. She *would* return in time. She had to.

Fallon joined her at the window, his face partially covered in shadow. "I'll make sure you get back," he told her with determination. "Time passes the same while we are gone. Morwenna said as much."

She took a steadying breath and then gripped the Tay al-Ard in her hand. "I'm ready."

He put his hand on her arm.

Trynne turned back and stared at her mentor one last time. He gave her a curt nod. Gahalatine did the same.

An instant later, she and Fallon were standing in the dappled shade of the magic grove. The air was chilly and a morning mist crept through the undergrowth. The sun still slept but some birds had awoken and were trilling loudly in the trees. The cracked boulder loomed nearby, its dark maw open as if to swallow them. Myrddin had been trapped behind that boulder for centuries. Was there a way that Morwenna could do the same to them? Was this nothing but an elaborate trick to get Trynne out of the way? She remembered seeing the figure slipping into the cave when she had found Gahalatine. It made her confidence shrivel.

Fallon let go of her arm and marched deliberately over to the silver bowl chained to the plinth. The air smelled of earth and juniper and mushrooms and a thousand tiny smells that blended into a unique perfume. She could feel the immensity of the Fountain magic surrounding them. The grove had always been a spiritual place for her. It was a nexus of some kind, a well of power. Her heart beat wildly as Fallon carried the bowl to the small trickling waterfall and began to fill it.

The hulking oak tree spread its gnarled branches above them, a reminder of what it had done to her father. To Gahalatine. A strange sensation crept over Trynne as she gazed at the oak. Almost a warning feeling. It never used to feel that way before. It was as if this place had been turned against her too.

"Don't look at the tree," Fallon said, glancing at her. "There is some compulsion that makes you want to look at it. I don't understand the tree's magic, but it's real." Holding the bowl, he carefully stepped back down to the plinth. "I've never done this before, but from what I've read, pouring the water on the plinth causes a storm."

Trynne walked up to him, nodding as she went. There was an itch in her mind, a nagging to look at the tree. It grew more intense.

"How do we get to the other world?" Trynne asked him, trying to shake off the feeling.

"Through the cave," Fallon said, pointing. "The storm summons the power to open the gate. There are certain laws that bind this place. Whoever bears the ring can pass back and forth to the other world. They can bring others with them."

"Can an army cross through?" Trynne asked.

Fallon frowned. "I don't think so. I believe the magic is limited. According to *The Hidden Vulgate*, only a few people are able to pass in and out before the gate closes." He stood over the plinth, gazing at the grove. "Shall we?"

Trynne nodded and stood back as Fallon tipped the bowl and splashed water onto the plinth. A surge of Fountain magic filled her reservoir of power to the brim, making her nearly gasp. Her fingers tingled with it.

The immediate clap of thunder was so sharp and loud it almost deafened her. Fallon cringed, nearly dropping the bowl, but he quickly set it down instead. Then the rain started, huge plops of water that began to deluge the grove, followed immediately by shards and chunks of ice. The commotion was loud and angry and sent chills through her. They both ran into the cave, hands covering their heads, as the violent hail pummeled the forest. A gust of knife-sharp wind cut into the entryway of the cave, the violence of it shoving Trynne and Fallon into the cave entrance. There was another force in front of them, pulling at them like a river current. Their boots began to slip.

"This is it!" Fallon said, his eyes gleaming with triumph. The wind howled and raged and the very rocks and boulders around them began to groan. The interior of the cave was bathed in shadows, and Trynne could see nothing in its depths as it continued to suck at them, the roar of the wind growing louder and louder, keening.

Trynne found his fingers gripping hers. She wasn't sure if she'd reached for his hand or he hers, it had happened so suddenly. The world began to pitch and tilt and she felt like she was going to fall. Her stomach thrilled with giddy panic.

"Into the cistern!" she gasped, gazing in fear at the black void summoning them. She needed her father's words of bravery now more than ever.

She gripped Fallon's hand tightly, fearing they'd be tugged apart by the vortex. A crackle of thunder filled the air and the flat slope of the cave entrance pitched so that their boots were scrabbling to find footing. There was none.

They fell into the depths of the cave. She braced herself, half expecting to smash into the cave wall at the end.

Instead of crashing into stone, she struck something else.

Fallon has betrayed me. There can be no other interpretation of the facts. He is gone, and he took my Tay al-Ard and the ring. My kystrel is also gone. If he were wearing it, if he were doing my bidding, I would know. I would sense where he is in the world and I would be able to use him. My memory is muddled from last night, but there's one thing I do know. One thing I can see clearly. Fallon took Tryneowy to the Dryad tree. They have crossed worlds.

Without the ring, I cannot follow them. But I can destroy Brythonica before they return. And I will. Another lost kingdom, drowned by the Deep Fathoms. They will all learn the consequences of defying me.

Morwenna Argentine

♦ ♦ ♦

PART II

Knights

CHAPTER TWELVE

Ruins

It was dawn in the new world. Trynne had landed in the detritus of an oak, the sharp edges of many brittle leaves pricking against her palms and cheek as she opened her eyes. There was birdsong in the air, a sweet sound that greeted her merrily as she lifted her head and found Fallon sprawled next to her. He winced with discomfort and lifted his head, a few decayed leaves clinging to his dark hair.

"Ugh," he groaned, then turned his head and saw her lying next to him. His pained look softened into a relieved smile. He propped up on his elbows and gazed around the grove. "This is not Brythonica," he said in wonder. "Look at the size of this tree. It must be a thousand years old."

Trynne sat up, brushing the dirt and crushed leaves from her arms, and tipped her head to look at the oak tree looming over them. It was the shaggiest, most enormous oak she'd ever seen. The limbs were so thick and laden with boughs they dragged along the ground in some places. A morning breeze flitted through, caressing her cheek, as she gazed up at the canopy—endless tentacles of branches and thick clumps of mistletoe—in awe. Other oak trees were also nearby, but this one was the largest. Huge seeds the size of fruit were scattered amidst the debris. Her ears picked up on the sound of trickling water.

"It's morning here," Trynne said. Fallon rose quickly and then reached down to help her up. "I'm not sure if it's a coincidence."

Fallon shrugged, stretching his muscles. "It's quiet. I don't hear anyone."

Fountain magic pulled at Trynne, drawing her in the direction of the trickling stream. "There is something that way," she said, pointing.

He turned and gazed in that direction. "How can you tell?"

"I can sense it. It feels like the grove with the silver bowl. There's Fountain magic that way."

"Then we should go there first," he said. They started crunching through the dead leaves and twigs. Fallon lowered his hand onto his sword hilt as he walked, leading the way with his long strides. They both stopped at the same time, having seen the fletching and shaft of an arrow sticking out of the debris. Fallon slowed down and cleared away the detritus with his boot, revealing a mangled skeleton. The bones had been scattered haphazardly, as if by wild animals. A few scraps of cloth and chain mail—pierced by the arrow—were all that was left. Fallon looked at her somberly.

"That way," Trynne said, nodding.

A short while later, they reached a trickling stream at the bottom of a gulley. It was an easy jump, and as soon as they made it across, Trynne felt the tug of the magic leading her alongside the creek. The woods became thinner, exposing a huge mound of moss-covered boulders. No, they were too symmetrical to be boulders.

"What are those?" Fallon asked, pointing to them. They hiked the short distance and discovered a mound of stone boxes in a huge heap. They were rectangular, each one about the span of Trynne's arms. They were gathered at the foot of an enormous hill that rose high above them.

"What a strange place," Fallon said, walking around the perimeter of the mound of stone boxes. "Is this where the magic is coming from?"

"No, farther up the hill," Trynne answered. She walked in the opposite direction, running her hand along the stone. Many were broken to pieces. She could make no sense out of it, but it seemed that they had been pushed down the slope of the hill and had tumbled to the bottom in a heap. She glanced up the trail and saw more oak trees on top of the hill.

"Trynne!"

The urgency of Fallon's voice made her hasten around the stone debris to join him.

"Look," he said in wonderment. He was gaping up at the hillside, so she turned to follow his gaze. A series of stone steps was carved into the rock face. It solved the question of how they were going to reach the crest, but she was startled to find several huge boulders suspended in midair partway up the slope. The boulders were not attached to the hill at all, but hung as if by invisible ropes of magic.

"By the Fountain," Trynne murmured.

They smiled at each other in amazement and then started up the steps. As they climbed, she looked back down at the woods wreathed in fog. The air was chilly but not too cold, and the climb made their breaths quicken.

"At least we won't have trouble finding that oak tree again," Fallon said, pointing to the hulking tree. "It towers over its neighbors."

As they neared the floating boulders, Trynne's legs were starting to burn from the effort. The steps grew steeper, and they needed to climb up one of the floating boulders to get to the next spot. Fallon hoisted her up by the waist, allowing her to clamber onto it, and then she leaned over the side and helped pull him up.

"There's a cave," Fallon said, nodding in the direction of the hilltop. It was clearly visible from the floating boulder. They exchanged a look full of wonderment and descended from their perch. As they warily approached the cave, it occurred to Trynne that this was much like the cave at the beach in Brythonica. She sensed Fountain magic coming from inside. The floor of the cave was made of dirt and was dusty, with broken boulders holding up a giant mass of stones. A broken face was carved into the boulder at the end of the space.

"*Le-ah-eer,*" Trynne whispered, invoking the word of power for light. The stone obeyed and began to diffuse the room with a glow.

Fallon gave her a surprised look. Hands on hips, he gazed around at the small cave. "Is this the source of the magic—?" He cut himself off when the engraved boulder suddenly began to slide open.

There was a rustling noise, an impatient huff, and light flooded from behind the boulder, blinding them both. Trynne held up her hand to block the light and reached for one of her swords.

"No need for that, no need for that," a familiar voice said with a snort. "The Medium told me you were coming. Aye, you didn't startle me. Tsk, tsk, we are friends."

"Myrddin?" Trynne asked in astonishment. Her eyes were still adjusting. The last time she'd seen him, he'd left their world for another one more needful of his help—*this* world.

"Yes, it is I. So the *pethet* brought you with him, little sister? Of course he did. Come in, come in. If you are hungry, have some food. Just a little bit, the apples above are all mush now, but I have a few firm ones left. Come along. Come into my cave. You are welcome, even if one of you is a *pethet.*"

Trynne rejoiced to hear his voice and stepped forward, even though the light was blinding her. The brilliance finally ebbed and she could see Myrddin, dressed in the same cloak and robes he'd worn on the long-ago day he'd guided her through the oaths that had made her an Oath Maiden. He had a sour smell about him, as if he'd eaten too much onion, but she hastily controlled her thoughts, knowing that one of his Fountain gifts was the ability to read the thoughts of others.

"It *is* Myrddin," Fallon said with a short chuckle. "And what is a *pethet* anyway?"

"Bah, leave it to a *pethet* to ask the wrong question," the Wizr said with a huff and another snort, waving for them both to enter.

Trynne could tell he had been seated at a stone desk. It was full of strange metal books, the pages made of rectangular sheets of gold with rings set into them. There were heaps of them, some stacked on the floor, some set into stone boxes in the wall. She watched as Fallon gazed at them, his eyes brightening at the sight of so much treasure.

There were strange engraving tools on top of the stone table, along with a curious instrument. There were small metallic shavings all around them. It looked as if Myrddin had been in the midst of engraving when they'd disturbed him.

"Aye, there is much work left to do," Myrddin said, putting his meaty hand on her shoulder. "Much left to write still. But come, you are guests. I should be gracious even though you have interrupted my work. The apples are over there. They are very sweet. Famous in these parts. Here, take some. They will help sustain you on your journey."

"Where are we?" Trynne asked, seeing the pottery that held the apples. She was going to hand one to Fallon, but he hadn't followed her. He was standing over the stone desk, about to lower his head and read from the metal pages.

"I wouldn't do that, *pethet*," Myrddin warned, clucking his tongue.

Fallon straightened. "I've never seen its like. What is this?"

"So many questions. So many. Always questions. Bah. How do I know so much that everyone keeps asking me? I ask, seek, and knock. It's simple. You could do the same, *pethet*. But I must get back to my work. So I will not answer you now. Eat it, little sister. Taste it."

Trynne realized she'd stopped with an apple midway to her mouth. She'd realized, at the last moment, that she recognized these particular apples. Many, many years ago, Myrddin had given an apple like that to her brother in the audience hall of Kingfountain. The memory of how much little Gannon had enjoyed the fruit knifed into her, but she obeyed the Wizr and bit into the apple. The sweetness was muted by the memory.

Myrddin gave her a sympathetic look that revealed he was aware of her suffering. "You eat one too, *pethet*. It will give you strength for your journey."

Trynne handed an apple to Fallon and he took it from her. He paused, smelling it first, and then bit into it. His face practically beamed with enjoyment. "Sweet and tart," he said with approval.

"There. Now you are both eating and cannot pester me with questions. This is good. I will say what I can say. No more. No less. I am a Wayfarer. A traveler between worlds. I have advised kings and shepherdesses and many other folk for long and sundry years. There are rules that separate the worlds from one another. And you are here now because your *father* was brought hostage here." He gave Trynne an arch look.

"Do you know where he is?" she asked desperately.

"Eat! Let me speak! I will say what I *can*." He sighed, shaking his head. "Always so many questions. Your father is in this world, but he is not nearby. He was taken far away and locked in a dungeon. You will go there, little sister. You will see it. It was the Fountain's will that he should come. He cannot remember your world, but he serves the Fountain's purposes. There are rules, as I said. Rules that separate the worlds. You must acknowledge this or turn back at once."

His gaze turned to Fallon.

"Ach. I see now. I see."

Fallon's eyes blazed with sudden anger.

"I will say nothing more on that. I see it clearly. I did not create the rules, mind. Even I must abide by them. I was trapped in this world for many centuries, little sister. I was trapped here because of a woman. The portal was shut until your father and the king returned to open it. It is not the only portal. There are others like it. The Black Wizr knew all about it. Yes, the Black. My enemy."

"Rucrius?" Trynne asked.

Myrddin puckered his lips. "No. The Black Wizr has another name. An ancient one. Shirikant." He said the name like a curse, his cheek muscles twitching with revulsion. "His power was bound to a book. You call it *The Hidden Vulgate*. It is an unholy and evil creation. This is the book that the king's sister found. Always it hides in shadow. It cannot be destroyed. It is more ancient than this world. It is the fullness of evil."

Trynne shuddered. "Morwenna found it while studying in Pisan."

"Yes, little sister. It is what has corrupted her. What has corrupted so many others from the beginning. If allowed, it will destroy Kingfountain just as it has destroyed this realm. It is the evil of pride. Of greed. Those emotions are what drive us to revenge, and revenge is never satisfied. There is no sating it."

His words sparked a memory in her mind, something Rucrius had told her when she'd bound him in a cell in Ploemeur. *You've shied away from the truth, but you'll find that revenge endures forever.*

Myrddin nodded to her. "The lips may be a man's. The words may be a woman's. But the *thoughts* belong to the one who sat on the forsaken throne. The one who gave up all wisdom and power because of ambition and revenge." He shook his head. "Morwenna is but a tool. Her grief, her loss has driven her to hatred. The book was here in this world. I have watched it destroy other kingdoms. I am watching it destroy these last two. It was moved to your world, which will suffer the same fate unless you stop it."

"What must we do?" Trynne asked in desperation.

"Save your father, lass," Myrddin said. "This world is too far gone to survive, and he will perish with the others unless he leaves now. Take out the Wizr board and I will show you what it means. Hurry, *pethet*! There are two kings clashing. Every inhabitant of their kingdoms will be destroyed in one great battle. All save one. One of the two kings will live. Your father is serving one of those kings. I must write the ending. It is my task. Yours is to take him away and return home before the end comes. Lo, it comes quickly!"

CHAPTER THIRTEEN

Bearden Muir

Fallon twisted the key in the lock, making a little snick sound, and then opened the lid of the Wizr board. The setup had indeed changed, the pieces much sparser and in a new configuration. The black and white kings were on opposite sides of the board.

"Your father," Myrddin said, pointing to the white knight on the board next to the white king. The board was nearly devoid of pieces, mostly little pawns. But there were two queen pieces on the board, both positioned near the kings. "Count the pieces, lass. There are but few left on each side. The final conflict comes. The king of this land, Comoros, prepares his fleet to attack the land of Dahomey. They come by sea. He summons all of his strength here"—Myrddin's finger pointed to the black king's square—"to the east. Only partway across the board, see? A terrible plague ravages his kingdom. The people are dying faster than they can be buried. Every warrior is conscripted for the fight. You will not cross this kingdom without being caught. Men betray one another for coins or favors. Take the main road east and it will bring you to the king's city, to Comoros. It's along the way of your journey, before you meet the sea separating you from Dahomey and the cursed shores. Gack, you will *smell* it before you see it." His cheek twitched with revulsion. "Your father is across the waters in the next kingdom, there. The board will draw you both toward the last battle. The current is strong. There is no stopping it now. If you stay too long, you will perish with the rest."

Trynne looked into Myrddin's eyes. "Can it not be stopped? Could these kings be persuaded to stop fighting?"

Myrddin arched his brow. "You will see for yourself, lass, ere this is through. Now come, let me show you something else. Be quick." He snatched his crooked staff from near the stone desk and hastened toward a tunnel leading deeper into the cave. Fallon gazed back at the golden record, his eyes hungry. "Come, *pethet*," Myrddin growled. "We must hurry!"

Trynne gave Fallon an arch look, reproving him with her eyes, and he smiled sheepishly and followed them into the tunnel. The ceiling was so low that both men had to stoop slightly to walk, but it was a comfortable height for Trynne. Myrddin moved at a brisk pace for such an old man, and they both had to struggle to keep up.

His voice boomed back down the hall. "Tunnels that wind and twist," he cackled. "Tunnels beneath the ruins of an old sanctuary. Naught but rubble now, but she still bears secrets. Aye, she does."

"Myrddin," Trynne called as he took them through dizzying passages. She would never be able to remember the way. "We saw a pile of stones at the bottom of the hill. What were they?"

"Eh? What were what?"

"The pile of stone boxes," Trynne repeated, increasing her pace.

"Ossuaries," he answered sharply. "It is the way the dead are buried in this world. The traditions differ from Kingfountain. Almost there. A little farther still."

The corridor was illuminated by glowing stones, which lit up upon their approach and then winked out into darkness after they passed them. There was a strange feeling in the air, the ripple of Fountain magic. She felt the sense growing stronger as they drew deeper into the catacombs.

Myrddin paused at a stone boulder blocking the way. He muttered a word that Trynne couldn't hear and the boulder moved aside just as the one protecting his chamber had done. The opening revealed a set of steps, and Myrddin instantly mounted them, gesturing for them to follow. The stairs ahead were dark. No lights greeted them as they cautiously followed the Wizr, and the boulder ground shut behind them, leaving them in the dark. Fear clung to her like cobwebs.

"Almost . . . just a bit . . ." Myrddin panted. "Let me shove this slab and . . ."

Light pierced their eyes, causing Trynne and Fallon to both reflexively shield their faces. Myrddin had pushed a square stone slab, connected to metal hinges like a trapdoor. The steepness of the steps made her legs burn as she and Fallon followed the Wizr up into the daylight.

The sight took her breath away. They had emerged into a large rectangular pit the size of the audience hall in Kingfountain. Broken stone and rubble were everywhere, and broken walls and lone buttresses lined the top ridge of the pit. The flagstones beneath their feet had grass and weeds growing in the seams. Overhead, the sky was blue with a few lacy clouds, and birds swooped across the upper chasm. She craned her neck, and so did Fallon, gazing at the strange and otherworldly sight. Light shone down from a broken arch, and she could almost imagine, in her mind's eye, what this great sanctuary had once looked like whole.

"This is all that is left," Myrddin said forlornly, scraping the bottom of his staff on the stone floor. "What took years to build and endured through centuries of upkeep is now crumbling to dust. Thus is the way of the world." He spread his arms wide, encompassing the breadth of the ravaged space with his gesture. "This is the heart of the sanctuary. This is where men and women were taught and trained in the ways of the Fountain. They call the magic by a different name here, but it is one and the same." Myrddin walked a short distance to a heap of rubble.

"This is where the altar was," he said, poking one of the crumbled stones with the staff. "But one of its secrets still lies buried here. This is where King Andrew was interred."

Fallon shot him a quizzical look, his brow furrowing.

"Aye, *pethet*," Myrddin said, his voice full of grief and longing. "This is where they buried my *friend*. It was long ago. Very long ago." His staff drooped as he hung his head low in respect. "He was wounded in a great battle. Stabbed by his bastard son." His voice was soft, but his eyes were stern, fierce. "He killed his son defending his throne. His sword, the blade Firebos, was lost to him by then. Stolen by his blood-sister. Lost for centuries. Now the story happens again. Over and over it repeats, teaching the same lesson. But will we learn from it? Hmmm? Will we ever learn?"

Trynne felt an odd swelling feeling in her heart as she gazed at the ancient Wizr, a man who had lived through the ages, bearing witness to the patterns and repetitions of history. How had he become this way? What had imbued him with such an unnaturally long life? They were questions she knew he would never answer. She felt humbled being in his presence and being on such hallowed ground, which had been so terribly desecrated.

Myrddin clenched his crooked staff with both hands, his knuckles turning white. "King Andrew was mortally wounded. His body was committed to the Fountain in a boat in an effort to find a way to heal him. He was taken to the island sanctuary of Toussan. No medicine or spell in your world could restore him. But there was healing to be found here. King Andrew did not die, but spent the remainder of his days in this place, a fell swamp called the Bearden Muir. He tended the apple orchard over yonder," he said, nodding with his brow. "He was not Fountain-blessed. He never had been, although he had always desired it. Taming the orchard was part of his training. Come, I will show you."

The staff clacked against the stone as Myrddin led them to a small alcove with a broken stairwell leading up. When they emerged, they were up at the main level and could see the spoiled grounds of the sanctuary. The stone was blackened as if a great fire had laid waste to it. It filled Trynne with wrenching sadness, and tears stung her eyes and burned her cheeks as they fell. The rubble was overgrown with moss and lichen. Slowly, nature was reclaiming the debris with wildness. As she gazed around, she saw Fallon pointing to a structure that was unharmed. Just a short distance away, the stone hut was still standing, unbesmirched by the fire.

"What is that?" Fallon asked, walking toward it. Beyond, Trynne could see the apple orchard Myrddin had spoken of.

"It was the Aldermaston's kitchen," Myrddin said solemnly. "The walls surrounding the grounds have all fallen. The village was put to the torch. But the kitchen stands." A small smile pursed his lips. He was lost in a tender memory.

"I wish I could have seen it as it used to be," Trynne said, rubbing her hand along one of the remaining stone buttresses. "I can still feel something here. This place is ripe with memories."

"Aye, little sister. It is." He gently swung the butt of his staff through the long grass. "This way."

As they crossed the grounds, Trynne gazed at the beautiful scene. A lopsided hill in the distance caught her eye. There was a haze in the lowlands, tendrils of fog that were quickly burning away with the sun's warmth. Her boots whisked through the tall damp grass, and she let the feathered tips tickle her palms as she crossed. The ruins were over-grown and unruly, but she could almost imagine seeing this place in its full glory.

They passed the kitchen and crossed into the derelict orchard. Myrddin tapped one of the stubby trunks with his staff and looked up at the crowded limbs. Withered apples still clung to some of the stems that had gone yellow and parched. Spoiled fruit was everywhere, and a sickly-sweet smell hung in the air. Trynne wrinkled her nose.

"Andrew tamed this orchard," Myrddin said, gazing tenderly at the limbs of grayish bark. "And it was here that he learned to *hear* the whispers of the Fountain. By taming these trees, he began to tame *himself.* All his life, he had been so busy. Going from one conquest to another. From one trouble to another. Bah! Most troubles we bring to roost ourselves. There are some words spoken too softly for ears. But they are spoken still. There are some truths we can experience with our eyes and still not see. Andrew learned the patterns of the seasons. He finally learned one of life's great truths."

He slipped his hand into the pouch he wore at his waist and withdrew a single apple. "What is the potential of one tiny black seed in one small piece of fruit?" He grinned at them both. "This!" he whispered, spreading his arms wide, indicating the horde of trees around them. "This orchard was once famous throughout the kingdoms for its sweet fruit and cider. But what if these trees were neglected for long enough that they no longer produced sweet fruit? What would be the purpose of the orchard?" His lip twisted into a sneer. "It would cumber the ground. It would waste its potential. How many seasons, how many years would a gardener give it before deciding there was no hope left. Eh? How many seasons of ill fruit before the gardener shook his head and cut down the trees? The gardener is patient. But when none of the fruit is sweet . . ." He shook his head sadly. "Firewood. That is all the grove would be good for. And so culling must happen to save the orchard. This is the way of things. As Andrew eventually came to accept."

Myrddin bowed his head reverently. His voice was soft. "Andrew married again," he said. "After his first wife was dead, he married the ruler of this sanctuary, who was a widow herself, the daughter of a king. They had children, even in their old age. They were mighty children. All Fountain-blessed. They produced generations of stalwart rulers who founded their own kingdoms. They were stronger than the inhabitants of this land and began to rule them. The Dochte Mandar—whom you know as the Mandaryn—hunted this family. Be wary. They will sense that you are not of this world too. Now go and reclaim your father, little sister. Ere he is destroyed along with the others when the flames come."

"What about the book?" Trynne asked. "Where is the book that caused this evil? Does Morwenna have it?"

He shook his head. "You cannot touch that book, little sister, without falling under its thrall. It destroys whoever touches it."

"But surely it must be destroyed!" Trynne said.

Myrddin shook his head. "One cannot destroy evil, little sister. It can only be bound for a season. It plants its seeds the moment we stop fighting against it. I have told you enough. Now you must go. But I will give you both a Gifting from the Fountain ere you depart."

♦ ♦ ♦

As they left the ruins of the village and sanctuary, Trynne could sense the Fountain magic behind them. The feeling faded with distance, and the serenity and peacefulness she had experienced in that place faded, replaced by ominous thoughts and feelings of dread. She was grateful for the lingering comfort of Myrddin's Gifting. Before parting ways with them, he'd bestowed to each a spell that would linger with them throughout their journey. To Fallon, he had given the Gift of Xenoglossia, which bestowed the ability to speak and understand languages. To Trynne, who could bestow that ability on herself, he had given a blessing of strength and fortitude and increased insight to be able to hear the Fountain's whispers, even when she was in desolate places.

One such place was the main road, which was choked, overgrown, and abandoned. It was obvious that years had passed since any wagons or horses had come this way. There was no sign of inhabitants anywhere. No telltale plumes of smoke from distant chimneys. The forest was full of black, mossy oak trees, and it crowded in on both sides, leaving them with but a tunnel to pass through. Within a few years, Trynne could tell, even the tunnel would revert to fenlands. She and Fallon trampled along the path, skirting budding trees that were beginning to fill the void.

"What do you think about what Myrddin said?" Trynne asked him. Their pace was strong. They'd packed food for several days, thankfully, so they wouldn't need to stop and forage.

"About what part? He said a lot." Fallon swatted a mosquito that was hovering over Trynne's ear. She flinched and scowled at the insect.

"Well, what parts stood out to you?" she persisted.

Fallon rubbed his mouth. "I didn't know that King Andrew had offspring in this world. Think of that, Trynne. The Argentine dynasty is only five hundred years old. King Andrew lived a thousand years ago. That's a lot of history. How much did Andrew influence this world? It's humbling to even think on it."

Trynne gave him a probing look. "Did you know Myrddin would be here when we arrived?"

"How could I know that, Trynne?"

"Well, he kept talking about the rules and things that governed the portals, looking at you as he talked. It almost felt like the two of you had spoken before. Is that true?"

He shook his head and held up his hands. "I didn't know he would be here, and no, I did not arrange that little discussion. I feared he would try to talk us *out* of attempting to rescue your father, and I wasn't going to sit still for that. We came all this way for a reason." Staring into her eyes, his gaze intent, he said, "Your father is coming back. I promise you he will."

"Don't make promises, Fallon," she said. "We will both try. But there is a lot of ground to cover and we have no horses. It won't be easy."

"No, I don't imagine it will be. One of the things I learned from Morwenna is that she promised Dragan he would be allowed to come to this world. He was eager for it. The laws are crumbling in this place.

There is no trust. The kings look after their own self-interest, and the nobles squabble among—"

There were loud cracking sounds in the woods on either side of them. Fallon stopped talking, but they did not slow their stride. Dark shapes began to emerge from behind the trees on both sides of the road. Fallon halted, sizing up the situation. Trynne followed suit.

"What do I see?" said one of the rabble. The man was wearing mismatched leather armor and holding a crossbow. His tunic was muddy and ripped, the once-white fabric a dingy gray, and the brown-and-red cross-shaped design in tatters.

"I think we caught us another pair of *mastons*," said another man in a dangerous tone. The word was said with such contempt and hate, it filled Trynne with unease.

"They're not the first we've caught," the first said, leering at her. "And they'll meet the same fate as the others."

CHAPTER FOURTEEN

Hunted

Trynne heard the subtle noise of grating metal as Fallon drew his sword. She quickly followed suit, crossing her arms and drawing both of her blades.

"Oh, ho ho!" one of the brigands crooned. "They have some fight in them! Most start babbling and sniveling before they die."

Fallon pitched his voice low for her. "Do you want to take the ones on the right?"

"Yes," she answered. "But let them attack first." Her magic was strongest when she was acting in defense. There were at least a dozen men coming at them, and a few more were ghosting through the trees. If they remained still for too long, they'd be boxed in.

Fallon flourished his blade, cutting two sharp circles through the air. "I anticipate some blood, lads. Ours or yours is the question."

The grimy-faced attackers continued to converge. "He's got a mouth on him. Bold as a rooster. Pluck him, then. Now!"

The man with the crossbow hefted it to his shoulder, aiming at Fallon first. Trynne stepped forward, putting herself in the line of fire. The crossbow twanged and time seemed to turn sluggish. She saw the shaft streaking toward her, then arced her blade to intercept it, deflecting it off its course. It struck an oak tree with a loud thunk. The marauders raised their battered weapons in stunned surprise. The swords all had nicks and dents and clearly hadn't touched a whetstone in ages. The men shuffled forward and roared in challenge, attacking as a mass.

Trynne lunged forward, ducked the first swipe at her neck, and scissored her blades in front of her, slashing her assailant's armor open and following up with a swipe of her boot to send him crashing down. Her training with Captain Staeli rushed into her mind, along with the memories and experiences of Oath Maidens from the past. She'd defeated greater odds than this. She and Fallon fought back-to-back, protecting each other from the onslaught.

Fallon smashed the pommel of his sword into a man's skull, dropping him like a stone. Every now and then, there was enough of a lull in her own battle for her to glance back at him. He'd proven himself more than a match for his foes. There was a graceful elegance in his attack, the sign of a man who had trained in his craft for years. But he was also not afraid to use brute force when the need arose. She watched as he stomped on a man's boot and then cocked the brigand's head back with an elbow strike that literally sent him spinning into the grass.

Trynne used both her weapons equally, cutting at wrists and hands to disarm rather than slay her opponents. They were bumbling fools, accustomed to winning through sheer force of numbers.

"Flee!"

The shout was quickly taken up, and the ill-trained men scattered like roaches caught feasting at the dregs on a table. Trynne and Fallon stood side by side, watching their assailants flee. "Get the sheriff, get the hounds!" one of the men shouted as the group melted away into the woods.

♦ ♦ ♦

Several hours passed as Trynne and Fallon groped their way through the tangle of the woods, tracking the sun through the snarled branches overhead and trying to bear eastward. Clouds of gnats and mosquitoes swarmed, drawn to their warmth, to their blood. It was a miserable slog that brought them up and down little hills, thick with mossy trees that clawed at them.

Then they heard the baying of hounds in the distance.

A sour expression twisted Fallon's mouth. "They found the dogs," he muttered. He sniffed the air. "They'll be able to track us at night now."

Trynne looked back, the direction the sound had come from. "How far away do you think they are?"

He cocked his head. "Still a ways. Ah, there's the hounds' call again. Now that they've found our trail, they'll converge."

"Do you think they'll catch up by darkfall?"

Fallon scratched the back of his neck. "The trees will slow them down, as they did us. But I don't want to roam these woods for weeks. We don't have time to get lost."

"I thought all the soldiers were being gathered for the war," Trynne said. They kept walking, hiking through the dense thickets, not bothering to hide their tracks.

"They are likely deserters," Fallon said. "They don't want to fight for the king. I don't blame them. They were pathetic." He flashed her a knowing smile.

"They could hunt us for days," Trynne said with growing frustration. "All the way to the city where Myrddin said the ships are. How many will we have to fight off next time?"

Fallon shook his head. "Nary a one."

"How can we avoid them if they have hounds?" she asked.

"I might not play Wizr as often as you do, Trynne, but these men rely on the dogs. What do dogs rely on?"

"Our smell," she answered.

"Exactly. If they can't smell us, they can't find us. We've been skirting around ponds all day. The next large one we find, we're going to cross through it. Stagnant water is smelly stuff. It'll confuse them."

"Not to mention soak us through," Trynne answered archly. "I'm not sure I like your plan."

"Ah, but you're forgetting." His eyes gleamed mischievously. "I wear your father's ring. You remember the story of how he jumped into the river by the sanctuary of Our Lady to save my sister's life when she was a child?"

The memory surfaced in an instant. The river had parted down to the rocky floor, allowing Owen and Genny to climb back up, unharmed by the current. "The ring repels water," she said, dipping her head to him. "Well done, Fallon." She was used to being the one giving orders, coming up with strategies. It was a relief to have a partner in the adventure.

It didn't take long to find a bog to cross.

The path ahead was soon interrupted by a huge expanse of filthy, muck-strewn water. The noise of bullfrogs became deafening as they approached it. Fallon tapped his nose and winked at her, motioning for her to join him where the chorus was the loudest. Some gray reeds drooped ahead, providing almost a screen. The bog stretched out as far as they could see, interrupted occasionally by small hills that rose above the waters and were crowded with stunted oaks.

Fallon stood at the edge of the pond and cocked his head. The sounds from the hunters and dogs were still miles off, though drawing closer. The afternoon light was beginning to wane. He nodded and then motioned for her to wait at the edge while he stepped into the brackish water.

She felt the magic rush around them as his foot pushed into the water, repelling it away from him as if the waters were shivering in terror. Instead of becoming mired in the mud and muck, his boots stepped easily onto the surface of the ground beneath the water—as if it had suddenly hardened. He looked down at his boots as he was standing there, the magic splaying the water away from him. Then he motioned for her and reached up to help her join him. She thought he'd take her by the hand, but he surprised her by fixing his grip on her elbow instead. She joined him in the small dry patch and together they started making their way through the pond, the path opening ahead as they walked, and the waters closing in behind them. She smiled at the thought of the hounds and men reaching the shore, only to be baffled by the abrupt end to the trail.

They walked swiftly, getting accustomed to the influence of the magic as it cleared the way for them to pass. She glanced up at Fallon's face, feeling grateful to him . . . but also confused. They were alone together in another world, traveling companions. She was married to a man who didn't remember her—one who'd shunned her shortly after their marriage. But she was here with Fallon, whom she had loved and cared for since childhood. It was a dangerous thought and she found herself wanting to look away from his face. Except she noticed the tightness around his eyes, and his slight pained frown. Something was wrong.

"Fallon?" she asked worriedly.

"Yes?"

"Are you all right?"

"The ring is . . . painful," he said, his voice neutral, barely hinting at his discomfort. "It's like a toothache, except on my finger. I can bear it."

"Did it start when you invoked the magic?" she asked him.

He nodded firmly, saying little else. "I'll be all right."

Knowing that the ring was doing him harm, she hurried her pace, trying to force him to lengthen his stride. The pond was vast, and when they reached the other side, she was grateful to return to normal ground. Again, he was wincing, rubbing his hand surreptitiously.

"Let me see it," she insisted.

"It's all right, Trynne. I'll be fine."

"Please, Fallon."

He showed her his hand and her eyes widened with surprise. His ring finger was gray, the nail fringed with black. She took his hand in hers, gazing at it with concern.

"It feels better already," he said dismissively and tried to tug it away.

She held on tightly and began whispering the words of healing magic. She felt her stores diminish, but only by a little. He sighed and nodded.

"Much better. Thank you."

She patted his hand and they continued their walk. Shortly afterward, they heard a frantic series of barks and shouts of surprise coming from the direction of the brackish pond behind them. Several dogs were howling and baying in confusion, and loud shouts of anger from men, the words indistinguishable, joined the mix.

"Well done, sir." Trynne complimented him, and again he shrugged as if it were of no importance. She eyed him furtively, struck again by how much he had altered. He had once been dependent on praise and kind words. Now he shunned them.

◆　◆　◆

When nightfall caught them, they chose to hunker down on a hill in the middle of another secluded pond. They made a little camp beneath an oak. Neither thought it wise to risk a fire, so they hurriedly ate from their provisions before the sun was completely gone.

There was a fluttering sound above their heads and Trynne saw little gray shapes streaking in and out of sight, just barely visible in the deepening gloom.

"Bats," Fallon said, wagging his eyebrows at her. "I hope they gorge themselves on these malevolent insects. You have six lumps on your face. They probably itch. How many do I have? I think a dozen."

She had to smile at that, but she hadn't bothered to notice—or count—so she just shrugged and ate a portion of her bread in silence.

When their scanty meal was finished, they packed up their gear and brought out the sleeping blankets.

"I'll keep first watch, if that's okay," Fallon whispered. "I'll wake you at midnight. Or whenever I guess it to be midnight. I don't know the stars in this place. Or the moon. Do you think they will look different from ours?"

"I imagine they must," she said, drawing the blanket around her. She cleared away some of the debris and nestled down onto the earth. She was exhausted, but her mind was alive with thoughts and worries. Where was her father on such a night? She felt closer to him than she had since the night he'd disappeared, but still so very far away . . . She shivered beneath the blanket.

Fallon stepped away a pace or two and settled against the trunk of the oak tree, his sword in his lap. He was silent, but she heard his breathing and found herself listening intently to the little noises he made while trying to get comfortable. Her heart ached to talk to him. More bats continued to flutter overhead, and the drone of mosquitoes and water bugs was soon conquered by other night sounds—the distant hoot of an owl, the croaking of frogs, and the ticking noise of some unfamiliar insects. The waters of the pond lapped against the hillock. But Fallon was silent. She was grateful that he showed her respect. Not once had he taken a liberty with her.

"Can I ask you a question?" She said it in a whisper, hoping they were still close enough to speak in low voices.

"Aren't you weary?"

"I am, but my head is too full to sleep. You don't have to answer."

"There's more time now than we had last night. You can ask me anything. But if I fall asleep during your interrogation, revive me, since I'm supposed to be keeping watch."

"But will you be honest with me, Fallon?"

"Yes, Trynne. What troubles you?"

She was still not quite warm enough beneath her blanket, so after a shiver and adjusting her blanket more tightly around her, she broached her question. "How do you feel . . . about Morwenna?"

He let out a long breath through his nose. "You're not going to throw anything at me if I tell you the truth?"

"I promise I won't."

"Good. At least there are no magnolia trees nearby." He chuckled to himself, but when he spoke again, his tone was serious. "Morwenna Argentine. She is . . . she is like fire. I think it is normal for a person to be attracted to something even though you know deep down it will burn you if you touch it. The essence of your question, I suppose, is whether I'm smitten by her. I suppose yes. To some degree. It plays to any man's vanity to have a beautiful woman show interest in him. But I've never forgotten who she was. Or what she was." He fell silent a moment, brooding. "I think it's time you knew her story."

CHAPTER FIFTEEN

Unseen

"The thing you must first understand about Morwenna, Trynne," Fallon said in a quiet, thoughtful way, "is she was just as fiercely loyal to her father as you are to yours. She sought his approval beyond all others. She pitied his fall, and I think the notion of avenging him was what drove her from the start."

"She told you this?" Trynne interrupted. She was grateful she couldn't see him in the dark. His words had already sliced through her.

He hesitated. "In a way. I've learned a great deal from the Espion. It is no secret to you that I admire that organization and have the ambition to lead it someday. Over the years, I have coaxed Morwenna into confiding in me. I didn't share everything I learned with my sister. But I shared most of it. Morwenna has been secretly manipulating events to overthrow her brother. Not to kill him, but to depose and exile him, just as happened to her father. To do that, she needed to first banish your father. As much as she resented him for removing Severn from power, she thought she may need him if the Mandaryn ever united against her."

He paused and they listened to the sounds of croaking for a while.

Trynne thought it a good opportunity to ask a question. "During the Battle of the Kings, she joined our side in fighting Rucrius. Without her, Rucrius may have destroyed our army with the storm he summoned. Was that planned? It didn't feel so at the time. He murdered her father in front of her."

"Ah, yes. That was *not* planned." His voice grew more somber. "You know how one move in Wizr can trigger subsequent moves that shift the power of the game? Sometimes there are too many unknowns to account for every possible outcome. *You* were the unknown in this situation, Trynne. You kept interfering with their plans. Morwenna didn't know about the Oath Maidens you were training in secret early on. She certainly didn't know you were the Painted Knight. I kept your secret and never told her. During that battle, I think Rucrius and the Wizrs realized Morwenna wouldn't be Gahalatine's chosen bride. He was so clearly fascinated by you.

"Morwenna was the mastermind behind the plot, and they saw her weakened condition as an opportunity to throw off her control. She was completely spent after that battle. All her Fountain magic was drained away. They would have won, but you chased down Rucrius and killed him, toppling the board. You thwarted their plans. Again. You cannot understand how much she resents you. Because of you, her father is dead."

"So it's my fault her treason failed, is it?" Trynne asked cynically.

He shrugged—a small gesture barely seen in the dark. "You stole her husband. You ruined her plans. When a person has little or nothing left to lose, it alters their thinking. Risks they naturally would avoid become acceptable . . . no matter how far-fetched. As you no doubt guessed, Morwenna caused the lightning storm in the Forbidden Court. She impersonated Rucrius and set the city ablaze. She killed Gahalatine's sister. Imagine, if you would, what would have happened after King Eredur's death if Ankarette had run amok and began executing the nobility of Ceredigion rather than staying loyal to the queen. Morwenna has become . . . reckless. She wants revenge on *you*—and at any cost."

Trynne shuddered. She had never told Fallon about the caves on the beach of Brythonica, the magical protections that held the waters at bay. She had only a fortnight to return and make sure that the proper words of power were said to maintain them. If Morwenna wandered onto that beach, she might be able to sense the magic. *Please no,* she thought in her mind. Worry radiated through her whole body.

"One of the ways Morwenna sought revenge," Fallon continued, unaware of her silent struggles, "was with me."

Trynne rolled over, turning her back to Fallon, clinging to the blanket in anticipation of the words that were coming.

"She used magic on me," Fallon said softly. "The power of the medallion that I showed you, the kystrel. The feelings she tempted me with were very real. Very powerful. It was like finding myself in a strange waking dream. I fell madly in love with her. Even though I *knew* nothing had changed between us. Even though I *knew* I was being manipulated. But the feelings were so powerful, so real." He sighed. "I also knew she had the ability to watch me from afar. I played the role of besotted lover in front of my sister and even Drew. Only after she gave the medallion to me and I refused to put it on did the magicked feelings truly begin to abate. But I'll be honest, as I promised I would be. She has compromised me emotionally. When I drugged her with the nightshade and she revealed her full plans to me, part of me was deeply tempted to give her more of the poison . . . enough to kill her." His voice was very low, very soft, and she could hear the turmoil in his words. "But I . . . I couldn't. It would have been like stabbing myself in the heart. She has power over me. I had to escape, to run away. I cannot face her again, Trynne. I'm afraid of what I might do." He fisted his hands on his lap. "I knew that she was intending to betray me. She revealed her plans, almost laughing at her mischief as she did so. She's impersonating my *sister.* She was willing to murder my little niece to clear the way to the throne. She's become the very monster we all feared she would be. The same kind of monster her father became. There is no longer any loyalty that binds her to anyone. Not even to me. I had hoped . . . whatever happened . . . that I could keep her from doing her worst, but she's beyond help. Knowing all of this, I still could not hurt her."

He sniffed and sighed again. There was hurt in the sound, the sound of a man betrayed by a friend. Trynne felt anguish for him and wished she could comfort him. She imagined herself holding him, stroking his hair, and whispering soothing words. Then she imagined him kissing her cheek in thanks, and her blood began to quicken with heat, hoping he would kiss her jaw, then her neck, then . . .

As heat radiated through her, she became aware that they were not alone on the hillock anymore. There had been no noise, not the cracking of twigs or the rustle of bushes, but she still sensed a presence—some force she could not see. There was almost a mewling sound, so high-pitched it was nearly lost in the sound of the wind. A feeling of dread and fear mounted inside her.

"Do you feel them?" Fallon whispered darkly.

Her skin crawled. It felt as if something catlike was nuzzling her back. She quickly sat up, and more thoughts crowded into her mind. She loved Fallon. She always had. Her husband didn't love her. He would never know. She would never tell.

"What are they?" Trynne asked, her voice quavering.

"I don't know," he said. "They started coming soon after we began talking. Maybe they were drawn by the kystrel in my pocket." She heard the scratching sound of his nails against the stubble on his throat. "They must feed on our emotions somehow. We should stop talking, or at least stop until daylight. Why don't you go to sleep?"

"I'll try," Trynne whispered, shaking with horror at the feelings roiling inside her. The feelings were unnatural. They were forbidden. After she lay back down, she reached out with her mind. With her magic, she could sense the presence of the unseen beings. She could sense the malevolence, the frustration that she and Fallon had become aware of them.

She had another thought, a memory of Fallon kissing her on the pinnacle of the tower in Dundrennan. The feelings intensified and she slammed her mind down, focusing on memories of her father. Of playing Wizr with him and trying to outsmart him. Of her favorite berry pies from Ploemeur.

A hissing, angry feeling came from the presence around her.

Be gone, she thought, snapping the command with her mind.

The hissing sound grew worse. She continued to focus her thoughts, bringing back memories of the training yard and Captain Staeli. This was a different kind of battle. But it was a fight nonetheless.

She fell asleep, still hearing the angry purrs from the unseen monsters as they slowly withdrew and abandoned the hillock.

◆　◆　◆

Fallon's hand touched her back and then her shoulder and jostled her awake.

"It's your turn," he whispered through chattering teeth.

The night was black and cold and too dark to see anything. She could not make out Fallon at all.

"Thank you for waking me," she said, rising quickly. Her feet were frozen and the temptation to linger under the blanket was intense, but he deserved a chance to rest.

"I'll be honest, I did fall asleep a little," he said with a chuckle. "Those creatures have been prowling around us all night. They feed on feelings and influence thoughts. I've kept myself awake by debating with them. I tend to fall back on sarcasm, you know."

"I hadn't realized that," Trynne said dryly. She rose and walked tentatively, moving higher up the hill.

"The ground is warmer where you were sleeping. Don't mind if I borrow it, do you? Wake me at dawn. Pay attention to the direction the sun rises. According to the Wizr board, east is still our goal."

"I haven't forgotten."

"I know you probably hadn't, but it doesn't hurt to be clear. Good night."

"Sleep the best you can."

Trynne walked around the oak at the top of the hillock a few times before settling down to wait out the night. There was so much to think about that she didn't have trouble keeping herself awake until morning. The pale light of dawn revealed the thick fog layered over the moors. It was especially thick over the murky water, and it felt like they were on an island oasis amidst the deep gloom. When it was bright enough to see their surroundings, she decided to wake Fallon.

He was wrapped so tightly in the blanket and had burrowed so deeply in the dense debris of fallen leaves and twigs that she almost couldn't find him. His mop of dark hair, tangled with fragments of undergrowth, was the only thing that stood out. She gripped his shoulder and rocked him slightly until his eyes fluttered open.

Trynne had always loved the gray-green color of his eyes, so similar to the foliage of trees. His brow wrinkled and he lifted his head. "You look as bad as I feel."

"Thank you, gallant sir," she said with a snort.

"But I feel astonishingly well." He recovered quickly, grinning at her. They ate a quiet meal from their stores and then prepared for the journey, anxious to be away from the dreadful place. As they continued to march through the muck and rugged terrain, the sound of dogs howling grew more and more distant—and it had completely disappeared by midday. The insects were constantly nagging at them, which only gave Trynne and Fallon more determination to escape the confinement of the woods. They stopped several times during the day to check the Wizr board and make sure they were still headed in the right general direction.

They encountered an abandoned cottage in late afternoon. The door was broken open and the insides had obviously been derelict for many months. While there was nothing to eat in the larder, there was a well from which they drew some fresh water to refill their flasks, and Trynne was lucky enough to find a small herb garden that had been left untended. They harvested some greens, which were sour tasting but fresh, and they took some onions to eat later in case there was a shortage of food.

"Look over there. Those are berry vines," Fallon said eagerly. The sight of the overgrown trellises gave her a pang of homesickness—no place had berries quite so fine as Brythonica. After searching through the leaves, they spied some unclaimed fruit.

"What kind are these?" Fallon asked, carefully plucking one and plopping it into his mouth. He thought for a moment. "A bit tart, but edible. Here, try one." He pulled another and handed it to her.

She examined the small pink fruit made of little sacs of juice. "Thimbleberries," she said and then ate it. He was right about the flavor, but they harvested more to eat and some were sweet and delicious. Trynne noticed that for every berry Fallon picked for himself, he offered one to her as well.

After a league or so, there was evidence they were approaching a town. Smoke scented the air, rutted roads began to branch away, and ramshackle huts could be seen through the trees. Not wanting to risk trouble by venturing too close, they observed the town from a distance, hiding in a copse of trees. From their vantage point they spied a small wagon train heading down the road. It did not stop at the town, but instead bypassed it completely. It was heading east. The direction they needed to go to find Trynne's father.

So they began to follow it as the sun went down.

◆　◆　◆

I have persuaded my brother-king to wage war on Brythonica. The army of Kingfountain has been summoned. The ships are being gathered and arrayed and will blockade Ploemeur and deprive her of her allies. I've told the king that Trynne is a threat not only to us but to herself. She murdered the baby. He is mad with grief and despair. He cannot understand why Trynne would have forsaken him. I told him that he does not understand a woman's capacity for revenge. When this war is over, I will seek my revenge against him next. Shame is a powerful emotion. I will fill him with it.

Morwenna Argentine

◆　◆　◆

CHAPTER SIXTEEN

The Queen's Revenge

The city of Comoros could be seen from a great distance. It had taken two more days of hard walking for them to finally reach it. All the roads leading to the city were choked with armed caravans bringing food and war supplies to the capital. Trynne and Fallon had managed to join the one they'd found earlier. The merchant, Nellic, had promised to pay them well for protection because they already wore swords and armor. Some of the nobles in the realm had defied the royal summons to fight Dahomey. But most, Trynne and Fallon discovered, were hot for revenge against the former nobleman who was now ruling the enemy.

Trynne had new appreciation for the splendor of Kingfountain as they approached Comoros, walking alongside the trudging oxen and gazing at the massive city before them. It was black with soot, and the defenses were crumbling where siege engines had battered them away. The city was split by a huge befouled river, but the other side had been put to the torch and never rebuilt. Nellic pointed to the mass of blackened stones and called it the Stews. His face twitched with antipathy.

"It burned down years ago," the merchant said, shaking his head. "Nothing is ever repaired around here. I wouldn't trust crossing a bridge unless I saw another cart, equally laden, go over safely first. Some have collapsed without warning. Buildings fall all the time. It's a wreck."

Fallon flinched as if physically repulsed. "Are there no craftsmen who can do the work?"

Nellic shrugged and scraped his dirty fingernails on his hairy throat. "The king has done nothing but tax us since the war with Dahomey started. All trade has halted. Everything is for the war. We're going to hit Dahomey hard. So hard she'll never rise again. I've heard rumors that there is a massive blight in that land already."

Trynne could see the anger burning in the man's beady eyes. "You think we will win?" she asked softly.

"Of course we will!" he spluttered. "We're a stronger kingdom by far. After we've littered Dahomey with their corpses, we'll rebuild our lands with the spoils we take. In the meantime"—he waggled his brows—"this cargo of wool will fetch five times its value in Comoros. Every man must do his work to meet his own ends."

A haze hung over the city, and the road leading into it was full of ruts and holes big enough to rattle the wagons. The stink of the air made Trynne want to cover her face. Carrion birds flew in lazy circles in the sky. The land had a sick look to it. All the vegetation was stunted and the weeds were vast and filled with thorns and bristles.

The royal castle, perched on higher ground, could be seen from a great distance looming over the river, which was choked with vessels of all sizes preparing for a voyage across the sea. White gulls zipped above the harbor in huge flocks and dived for spoiled food that had been left to rot. The smell in the air was sickly sweet, the odor of all manner of things rotting.

"I had expected more grandeur," Fallon murmured to Trynne.

"It's quite a contrast to Gahalatine's Forbidden Court," she observed.

Fallon's mouth turned down in a sour frown when she said her husband's name. But he said nothing.

"We'll part company after we pass through Ludgate," Nellic said. He paused, looking back and forth between the two of them, and then gave them a wary look. "I had an eye on you day and night. I thought you'd try to rob me, but you never did. I'll pay you when we reach the city gates."

When they reached the huge stone buttress called the Ludgate, the entryway was clogged with people waiting to get in. Stern soldiers wearing blotted tunics stood on either side of the massive double doors, directing the traffic.

"There's no one leaving the city from the gate," Fallon observed to Nellic. Trynne hadn't noticed it until then. Comoros sucked in everything but released nothing.

Nellic shook his head. He had a shifty look in his eye that Trynne distrusted. "Everyone is leaving on the ships. It's easier to get work and higher wages in the city. Many have left their families to work here for coin. I brought all the wool I could with this shipment. They'll take my cart and buy my oxen too. No sense going back to my Hundred with pockets full of coins, only to be robbed. No, I'll stay here until the war ends and the king's peace is reestablished. I'd offer to join the soldiers, but I've got a game leg." He patted his and began to limp, although he'd been walking just fine for the whole journey.

The soldier who met them at the gatehouse scowled as he approached the wagon and began inspecting the bound bundles of wool. He climbed up onto the cart and prodded and poked the different bags. Then, looking down at Nellic, he said, "The quality is decent. Bring this load to Hawden Street. There are crowds of spinners there turning wool into tunics day and night." He jumped down with a huff and waved them on. His eyes narrowed when he noticed Fallon and Trynne.

"What are these two?" he asked.

Nellic bobbed his head agreeably. "I brought them for the reward. Ten apiece, eh? They can serve in the king's army." He sneered at them, obviously pleased with his ploy. He would not only be freed from the burden of paying them, he'd also get reward money.

"We came to fight for the king's army on our own," Fallon answered, his voice tight with anger. Not strictly true, but they'd decided it might be their easiest way to Dahomey. To her father.

The soldier snorted. "You mean the *queen's* army," he said with a chuckle. He nodded to Fallon's sword. "Can you use it? Can you prove it?"

Fallon shrugged, his cheek muscles hardening. "I'm all right with a sword."

The soldier dumped some coins into Nellic's greedy palm, and the tradesman left with a final mocking wave that reminded Trynne of Dragan. Then the soldier brought his fingers to his mouth and let out a sharp whistle. "Cap'n!" he shouted.

A graying middle-aged man approached with a frown. "Two more? What Hundred are they from?"

"Dunno. They *volunteered*." He bared his rotting teeth in a grin.

The captain hocked and spat. He sized them both up, giving Trynne special attention. She was tempted to use the Tay al-Ard to escape. She reached behind her back, but Fallon gave her a subtle gesture and a warning look.

"We take lads as young as twelve. Your brother?" he asked Fallon, nodding at Trynne. She bristled inside but kept her expression carefully controlled.

"Cousin," Fallon answered, a hint of humor in his voice. Trynne nearly elbowed him in the ribs for that.

The captain's brow furrowed. "Get them some tunics, a pass to bear arms, and bring them to the castle for training. The queen's ship departs soon, but they'll have to train for two months before going to the cursed shores."

"Thought so," the soldier responded. "Thank you, Cap'n." *Two months?* They certainly couldn't wait that long. They'd have to figure out a way to get on the queen's ship.

"Be back sharp, or I'll flog you."

"Aye, Cap'n."

The soldier escorted them inside the gate to the barracks. It was crowded and noisy, and everywhere Trynne looked, older men—and very young ones—were being arrayed in armor and given weapons from barrels full of swords and pikes. There were a few who looked to be their own age, but it was conspicuous that the older youths and young men had already been taken.

The soldier brought them past the weapons to a series of trunks stuffed with tunics. The tunics all looked the same, dingy gray with the cross symbol she'd seen on the tunics of the men who'd attacked them on the road. The soldier handed a larger one to Fallon and a small one to Trynne. As she took the rough wool from him, she noticed the scrubbed-out bloodstains and the stitching that had closed the gashes made by weapons. How many other soldiers had worn this tunic? How many had died in it? There were so many trunks, such an excess of swords, pikes, shields, and helmets. This was a land perpetually at war. Such a desolate place . . .

Her insides gnawed at her as she drew the tunic over her head. She had to find her father and get him away.

♦   ♦   ♦

It was midafternoon and the city was warm, the air heavy with smoke. There were fountains at the major crossroads. Trynne noticed that each had a sculpture with a stone face carved into it, like the ones she had seen elsewhere in this place—and in Gahalatine's pavilion. She could barely sense the faint whisper of Fountain magic emanating from them. The fountains were not spewing water, and she watched as men carried buckets of water to refill the fonts. There were long, winding lines of women approaching the fountains with pots and smaller buckets waiting to receive. She sensed, intuitively, that the sculptures could summon water—but no one was left who could summon it.

As they reached a gatehouse to the castle, not the main drawbridge but a porter door, the soldier spoke a few words to the sentries, one of whom motioned for Fallon and Trynne to follow him. As they crossed beneath the arch of the hulking wall, it felt as if they'd entered a prison. She gave Fallon a worried look.

The impression quickly changed as they entered the inner grounds and found that the yard was better maintained than the city beyond it. The pathway crossed a splendid garden with smaller fountains, trimmed hedges, and brushed pathways. The soldier took them to a greenyard that was full of men going through a series of drills. The clang and battering of weapons could be heard, as well as the barked orders of the commanders assigning the drills. There were archery butts and lines of peasants standing with bows trying to hit the marks. Trynne observed the crowds. It appeared a culling was taking place—those inept with bows were sent to train next with staves.

"You've got blades, that says something, but we'll see if you can use them," the sentry said gruffly, leading them past the bowmen to where the swordsmen were practicing. "The pay is better if you can." He sized up Fallon and ignored Trynne. "How did you escape the summons so long?"

"I wasn't trying hard enough, it seems," Fallon quipped.

They were thrust to the end of a line of would-be swordsmen, all waiting to face the sword master at the front of the line. He was a knight by the look of him, one trained with a weapon from a young age. The people in line were sent against him, one by one, and he disarmed them each in quick fashion. Then he'd bark a command and they'd be taken away, replaced with the next person. No one lasted longer than a few seconds and the line quickly shortened. Those who were sent away joined another group where instructors were holding drills on stance and technique. Captain Staeli would have felt right at home.

Trynne gave Fallon an arch look. "He's decent," she murmured, nodding to the knight.

Fallon shrugged. "He's bored." His eyes were focused on the knight. "The question, though, is how good *should* we be?"

Trynne was itching to swing her swords. She was still angry at Nellic's deception. "No use pretending."

"I was hoping you'd say that," Fallon said with a wink. "The better we are, the faster they'll send us to Dahomey. Either way, we need to get on the queen's ship before it leaves."

"Agreed," she said.

"Do you want to go first?" he asked her.

"You can. I'd like to watch you humiliate him."

"I don't plan on losing," he said.

When they reached the front of the line, Trynne watched as Fallon drew his sword, which was a much finer make than the blades the others had carried. He marched into the open space and the knight sized him up.

"You are tall," the man said, flourishing his weapon.

"And you've a gift for stating the obvious," Fallon quipped in return. "Shall we?"

Trynne felt a pulse of excitement and restrained a smile. The knight approached, holding his blade in an upper guard, crossing his legs in a battle stance as he moved. Fallon replied in kind, showing a similar technique and a complementary pose.

"You know your footwork," the knight said as they slowly circled each other.

"I know the sharp end too."

Then the knight came forward, dipping the sword down while swinging his armored elbow around at Fallon's face in a surprise move that would have knocked another man to the ground. Fallon didn't fall for the feint and stepped back as the knight's elbow went wide. He could have taken advantage of the opening to strike at the knight's back, but he deliberately paused, letting the man regain his defenses. Trynne suspected Fallon was purposefully prolonging the fight a little so as not to utterly humiliate the man.

"You're quick," the knight said approvingly. "Who trained you?"

Fallon answered with a flurry of blows that the knight struggled to answer. The group of men assembled began to whoop and cheer, and Trynne felt like joining them. After multiple attempts, Fallon eased back again, letting the knight recover his composure. His eyes were wide with surprise, his mouth quivering with delight and fear. He'd not been tested like that in some time, and Trynne could see that he was enjoying it, even though he was losing.

"You're playing with me," the knight said, shaking his head and gritting his teeth.

"Noticed that, did you?" Fallon answered smugly. He lunged in, the knight countered, and the two locked hilts. Then Fallon used his size to wrench the blades, and the knight's weapon clattered onto the yard. A chorus of cheers began to rise from the mass of men and a big smile lit the knight's face as he stared down at his fallen weapon.

"At last! You can have my job!" he said with a barking laugh.

Fallon bent down, fetched the knight's sword, and handed it back to him. "I'd be wasted here. My cousin and I want to spill blood in Dahomey. Their king is quite a swordsman, I've heard. I've been practicing."

The knight laughed. "To face him? Well, that remains to be seen. Well done. You go over there through that arch and see the captain of the guard."

"My cousin comes with me," Fallon said, motioning for Trynne to step forward.

"Every *man* must earn his place," the knight said, shaking his head as he leveled a disrespectful look at Trynne. She stepped away from the crowd and drew both of her swords. The knight's eyes bulged when he saw her do that.

"That's fine," Fallon said nonchalantly. "My cousin is even better than me."

"Captain!" the knight shouted as those around them started to guffaw.

Trynne shifted her gaze to the gatehouse, where she saw a man already watching them. He had dark brooding eyes and a graying beard, and wore a chain hood pulled down around his tunic front. The look he gave them was fierce and intense as he stepped out of the shadows. "By Cheshu, what is the matter, Sir Peter?" He had a strange accent, one that was reminiscent of Fallon's family in Atabyrion.

"You'll want to see these two, Captain," the knight said.

"I saw the tall one put you to shame already," the gruff captain said. "You can't handle the little one either?"

"He has two swords!" Sir Peter complained.

"Aye, and so do I."

Trynne noticed that he had two short swords belted to his waist. He drew them, revealing two curved blades, reminiscent of tapered leaves. Sir Peter backed away quickly, as if grateful to leave this fight to the other man.

"Well, lad," the captain said gruffly, facing Trynne with a catlike posture. He wasn't tall, but she could sense the prowess in him. He reminded her of Captain Staeli, except this man had more hair. "My name is Martin Evnissyen, and I am captain of the queen's guard."

"Hello, Captain," Trynne said. She crossed her blades in front of her.

Martin's eyebrows knit together. "Where did you train to handle two blades, I wonder?"

Trynne summoned her magic, letting it prod the captain's defenses. He was hale and strong for an older man. He had fought and trained for most of his life, and there were no glaring gaps or weaknesses in his defenses, except for his hands. She could tell his hands were scarred and pained him.

He gave her a curious look, as if he sensed the magic coming from her. As if he were aware of it . . . But there was no time to think about it. He immediately attacked, lunging at her neck with both blades and trying to stomp on her foot at the last moment. She tucked her foot back so he stomped on the stones instead and then levered her foot behind his ankle as their blades clashed.

It happened in just a moment. She saw his intention, and suddenly he was flailing backward and landing on his back, his blades clattering from his hands.

She had done nothing to disarm him.

Sir Peter gasped in shock and surprise and Trynne found herself staring at the crowd, who gaped at her in awe. The captain, this Martin Evnissyen, shook his head at her, chortling. He had lost to her on purpose and ended the fight just as it had begun.

"Well, I'll be a goose in a pot," he said. He tugged off his gloves and then reached up a hand for her to help him up.

Trynne sheathed her swords and looked at him more closely, not able to understand what had happened or why. She glanced at Fallon and saw a look of concern on his face. He was trained enough to know that the fight had ended too abruptly. She stepped forward to take Martin's hand, keeping her magic ready in case he tried to sweep her off her feet.

His grip was like iron as she pulled him up. He brushed off his legs with one hand, still gripping her hand with the other, shaking his head ruefully.

"By Cheshu, I've not been bested in a while," he confessed with hearty approbation. "You both will come to the castle. Sir Peter, finish off this crowd and then lock the gate for the night." He was still holding Trynne's hand, and he tapped each of her fingers individually with his littlest finger. She tried to jerk her hand away but he tightened his hold on her. What was happening? Was he an enemy? A friend?

"Come, lad," Martin said to Fallon, taking them both by the arm and leading them to the archway he had come from. As soon as they were inside the small guardroom beyond the arch, he stopped and whirled Trynne around, pushing her back against the wall. His demeanor changed in an instant and his voice dropped to a low growl as he turned his face to Fallon.

"Are you utterly mad bringing *her* here?" Martin said, very low and covert, his eyes raking Fallon accusingly.

CHAPTER SEVENTEEN

Corruption

Martin turned his sharp gaze to Trynne, his eyes full of suspicion. "You both have some explaining to do. For all I know, the queen was watching from the windows over the yard. Speak quickly, or I can't help you. Where were you caught? Muirwood?"

Fallon looked anxious and determined. Martin had put himself between them. There was no one else in the small guardroom, which had polished marble floors, giving the feeling that it was once used for another purpose.

"Who do you suppose we are?" Fallon asked, edging closer. Trynne had the suspicion he was preparing himself to fight the captain.

"It's obvious you are both mastons," Martin said in his thick brogue. "At least *she* is. Your disguise may fool most, lass, but I saw through it, and your fingers reveal the truth to anyone who cares to see it. You can always tell a girl by the length of her different fingers."

Trynne squeezed her hand into a fist, feeling vulnerable. "I'm not a maston," she said.

Martin snorted. "I know what I *felt*, lass." He shook his head curtly. Then his eyes shifted back to Fallon. His voice became less agitated. "I've helped smuggle many mastons out of the city, out of danger. The man I served in my younger days, he was a wise and able prince." His voice throbbed with emotion. "I'll help ye if I can. But you are in the king's city, Comoros, and they *kill* mastons here. Are you indeed from Muirwood?"

Trynne shot Fallon a warning look, but she could see Fallon was not disposed to trust the surly captain. "We're going to Dahomey. Can you get us on the queen's ship?"

Martin chuffed as if Fallon were completely mad. "The queen's ship? The queen's ship? Aye, she's set to depart for Dochte Abbey. 'Tis the only abbey *left*." He gave them a grim look. "But you won't be find-ing shelter there, I promise you that. The Aldermaston leads the Dochte Mandar now, not the—ah, so you *know* that name?"

Trynne hadn't been able to conceal her startled surprise when he'd mentioned the Dochte Mandar. This man was keenly observant.

"Yes, we know of them," Fallon said. "We still need to go. Can you get us there?"

"That abbey is blighted," Martin said with an angry scowl. "What seek ye in Dahomey?" His eyes seared into Trynne's. "Do you wish to join them, lass? As a hetaera?" She saw his free hand tighten around the hilt of one of his short swords. He still held her to the wall with the other.

Trynne was very reluctant to say anything, but he was judging whether they were a threat. Besides, his gruff and taciturn way put her even more in mind of Captain Staeli.

"Never," Trynne said vehemently, shaking her head no.

He eased his grip on the short sword. "That's a relief. I'm asking about your Hundred because you both look like you have been dragged through the Bearden Muir." He plucked a twig from Trynne's cloak and then smelled it. "Och, yes. I recognize that stench. I used to be the hunter at Muirwood Abbey in that Hundred. Now I'm captain of the queen's guard." His voice had a cynical edge to it. "Queen Ellowyn Demont. I don't want to draw any more eyes to us. I'll find you some fresh tunics. These rags you're wearing are for common soldiers. If you are truly bound for Dahomey, mayhap I can help. But if you try to escape, you'll only cause trouble for yourselves." He turned and fixed Fallon with a pointed finger. "I take it you're her protector? Hmmm? As if she *needed* one, by Cheshu."

"You're right. She doesn't need one," Fallon answered with a wry smile.

♦ ♦ ♦

They'd been left in a small barracks room to bathe and change. There was a washing bowl, a pitcher of water, and a smoking brazier that warmed the space. The hearth was empty, but a soot-stained, dead-eyed carving at the back had a lingering air of Fountain magic. She could sense its ability to summon fire. Fallon stepped out from behind the changing screen, dressed in a new clean tunic that bore a richly embroidered symbol of Comoros on the front. Martin had also given them shoulder armor and capes before leaving them to change.

Trynne had washed the dirt and grime from her face and was worried now that she looked too much like a girl. As she cupped water in her hands, she remembered the ring that could disguise her. But if there were any Dochte Mandar in the castle, they might be drawn to its power.

She stared at herself, wiping her mouth, and the delay festered inside her. Even a few days seemed too long to wait.

"Can we trust Martin?" Fallon asked, adjusting his sword belt on his hips. He looked gallant and darkly handsome in his new uniform. The tips of her ears began to burn and she looked away.

"Trust is a stronger word than I'd use," Trynne answered. "The delay weighs on me too. But if Martin can help us get to Dahomey faster, it's worth being patient." Feeling bashful, she paused and then added, "Let me change next."

He nodded and she took her tunic and armor and slipped behind the changing screen. She had not felt this self-conscious while they were traveling in the woods, but the room was so cramped and sparse in comparison.

"My first instinct is that he *is* trustworthy," Fallon said, his voice ghosting over the partition. "If they had an Espion in Comoros, he would be part of it. He's highly trained, probably even better than Staeli. His accent reminds me of home. You?"

"I noticed that too," Trynne said, tugging off the chain hauberk and wincing as it rattled. She hurriedly put on the tunic and was amazed at the quality of the velvet. The design was much more flamboyant than the ragged tunics they'd been given in the barracks. "That probably puts you at ease."

"I was always more at home away from Edonburick," he admitted. "Someone is coming."

She had noticed the sound of rapid footfalls as well. Working fast, she lashed her sword belt around her waist.

Martin barged right into the room, huffing and muttering. "You *were* seen," he grumbled.

"By the queen?" Fallon asked with concern.

"No, by one of her handmaids. By the time the queen went to the window, we were gone. She has just asked me to bring you both to her." He did not sound pleased. "Och, this doesn't bode well for either of you."

Trynne stepped around the side of the changing screen, working on the shoulder-guard strap. "Why not bring us to the ship bound for Dahomey now?"

Martin rubbed his eyes. "No, that would be unwise. The hunter is patient. The prey is careless. The handmaid nearly swooned," he said, eyes flashing daggers at Fallon. "You've roused my lady's curiosity, and she . . . the queen is a hetaera. Have you ever been in the presence of one before, lad?"

Fallon looked chagrined by the compliment the lady-in-waiting had inadvertently given him, but he managed to look humble instead of proud. "Yes. Does she wear a kystrel?"

Martin shook his head. "No. The king wears hers. He'll do or say anything she bids him to. He's a jealous sort, but he's impotent against her power." He gave Fallon a respectful nod. "You're not as wet behind the ears as you look."

"Thank you, grandfather," Fallon said provokingly.

Martin chuffed, folding his arms across his chest as he started to pace. "Well, delaying your meeting will only heighten her anticipation. Best to get it over with quickly. Like setting a broken bone."

Fallon approached Trynne and patted her back softly, his hand thumping against the Tay al-Ard she had secured to her belt beneath the cape. The reminder that they had a ready escape route only made her feel marginally better. He gave her a knowing smile and gestured for her to go first.

The corridors were lit by torches to dispel the evening gloom. The palace looked tranquil, something that was belied by the tension in the air. Their boots clicked against the smooth marble tiles—a noise that was drowned out as they approached the sound of music and laughter. The guards stationed there opened the doors for them, and a raucous peal of laughter escaped—the sound setting Trynne's teeth on edge.

The air was thick and hazy with smoke. The room was full of nobles and ladies wearing fancy doublets and ceremonial swords that were so thin they would likely shatter if struck against metal. Titters and giggles from painted faces flooded Trynne's senses. But a sickening feeling permeated the room, one that was instantly recognizable.

She had felt it before in the zenana in Chandigarl. There it had been covert and subtle; here it practically flooded the hall. She sensed the magic of kystrels coming from multiple sources. Her hand lowered to the hilt of one of her swords, and her eyes scanned the room, searching for the danger she felt but could not see. Then she noticed that all the women in the room had strange tattoo-like markings on their throats and faces, even the servants. *From the kystrels,* she realized in a spark of intuition. It was a sign of the magic's taint. It had to be.

"This way!" Martin bellowed over the din, directing them through the crowd. "The king is the one carving the stag on a spit with the knife," he said back to them in a lower voice. "He's rarely sober. He won't even notice you."

Trynne glanced back at the man with the knife. His reddish-brown beard contained flecks of meat and glistened with sweat. For a moment, she saw Drew Argentine in her mind and blinked rapidly to banish the image. This king was nothing like hers. He was guffawing over something someone near him had said, and his exaggerated laughter made him seem silly and obtuse.

They were approaching the queen, and Trynne could smell not only the woman's perfume, but also the power of her magic rippling beneath the surface as if she were Fountain-blessed. She was strong in the magic, Trynne could tell.

Her unease only increased when she got a clear view of her. The first thing she noticed was the woman's mass of golden curls and the filigree coronet nestled amidst them. She wore a black gown with a red bodice, and rich gold cloth formed elegant stripes down her arms, around her waist, and at her shoulders. One of her ladies-in-waiting, a plain-looking brown-haired girl, said something to the queen and pointed at them as they approached. The lady-in-waiting was heavily tattooed, the markings extending from her bodice up to her cheeks and reaching the corners of her eyes.

Trynne was trying to absorb the different culture and style of this world, but she felt she was a foreigner, a stranger, that she didn't belong there at all. Every instinct screamed at her to flee with Fallon and find another way to Dahomey.

The queen turned to face them. Her lips were painted ruby red, and she too had the tattoo markings on her bosom, neck, and cheeks.

The cut of her bodice would have been deemed scandalously low in Kingfountain. The whorl pattern of her tattoo had clawed its way up her breastbone and across her collarbone and neck. She wore an amulet around her neck—an eight-sided star fashioned out of gold, not a kystrel. Trynne sensed it was a mocking gesture. The queen looked past Martin and Trynne and her eyes lit up when she saw Fallon. It was a look of interest, almost fascination. The queen was older than they were, probably as old as Genny. Trynne felt a surge of possessiveness, but she tamped it down. Still, she took a step closer to him to be within arm's reach.

"One of my ladies has taken a fancy to you," the queen said with an alluring voice. "I think I can see why." She gazed at Fallon in open admiration, arching her eyebrows. The coronet on her smooth, unwrinkled brow fanned out like a large maple leaf. She had an imperious, haughty look, and her pose was one of confidence and command. "You think she is pretty, do you not?"

As the words were spoken, the queen's eyes began to glow silver.

CHAPTER EIGHTEEN

Frozen Heart

Trynne shuddered with dread as she felt the queen's control reach out to smother Fallon's heart. An oily sensation filled the air as the power rolled off the queen like dirty smoke. It did not come from a specific source, certainly not from the medallion twinkling in the torchlight, but exuded from the woman like Fountain magic, and it was just as powerful.

Fallon would have been struck by the full brunt of it had Trynne not been standing nearby. Instead, the magic parted and sliced to either side of them.

"Passably pretty," Fallon answered with a hint of boredom in his voice, "but she pales in comparison to *you*, my lady." He gave her a formal bow.

The queen's eyes narrowed slightly; her nostrils flared a little. Was she surprised by his reaction? Her eyes were eerie and otherworldly, burning with an inner darkness that made Trynne sick inside. There was another pulse of power, another rush of magic that sought to entangle Fallon. But again it sloughed off, unable to touch him.

"Was there a reason you wished to see me, my lady?" Fallon pressed, very formal and composed.

"My lady-in-waiting saw you in the courtyard today," the queen answered, her voice a little waspish now. "So, you have joined the ranks of my guardsmen?"

"Aye, my lady," Martin answered for him. "He beat Sir Peter with hardly any effort."

"Sir Peter is not my best knight," the queen said condescendingly.

"No, he is not," Martin said. "These two new recruits are both talented swordsmen. They are going to sail with us to Dochte Abbey. If it be your wish."

She gave Fallon another long look, taking in his physique and presence. Her tongue darted down to her bottom lip and another jolt of magic slammed at them. It felt like the brunt of a hurricane. Trynne kept her awareness of the magic to a minimum, seeking to hide her ability from the queen and growing more anxious by the moment.

"What is your name, Sir Knight?" the queen asked in a sultry tone.

"Fionan," he answered with a slightly mocking tone, bowing slightly. "It is my pleasure for my cousin and I to serve you."

The queen seemed to sense some hidden banter in the words and her brows furrowed because she did not understand it. She gave him a sidelong look as she raised a cup of cider to her mouth and took a swallow. Her lips pursed. "Oh, I see now. You've already been claimed. I thought I sensed a kystrel about. You have one, don't you?"

Fallon began to look uncomfortable, the corners of his eyes creasing. "Yes, my lady," he said, his voice more subdued. Trynne's worries increased in pitch and concern.

The queen wrinkled her nose. "I should have guessed sooner. You are far too delicious not to have been claimed by another. I sensed the . . . *resistance*. Well, I won't fight her for you. Yet. Captain, they may join us. That would please me." Then, with a dismissive toss of her head, they were excused.

Trynne felt a trickle of sweat down her back as Martin led them away from the queen's company. He was scowling, but when they reached the tables laden with food, he motioned for them to take some.

"This is your supper," he said gruffly. "Don't drink the cider. Not if you want to keep your senses." His eyes cut daggers at Fallon. "You enjoy teasing the flames, lad. But your gambit worked, so I won't fault you."

Fallon shrugged with unconcern, though Trynne noticed a bead of sweat trickling down his cheekbone. "How long before we leave for Dahomey? We must get there soon."

"Soon, lad? By Cheshu, you're a fine one to be giving orders. No ship leaves for Dahomey without the queen's consent. Their ports are all blockaded. Dieyre and his queen have moved their forces inland to lure us into his lair for the fight. We're set to sail in three days, depending on the weather. If that *suits* you." He chuffed again.

Fallon frowned with impatience and then nodded. "The sooner, the better, Martin. That is all."

The impertinence of Fallon's comment made Trynne stare at him in surprise.

Martin's look of anger shriveled into mirth. "So I'm dismissed now too?" He started to chuckle to himself. "You both have guard duty tonight. I'll send Deven to fetch you and teach you the ropes. That *is* all." He chuckled again to himself and sauntered away, shaking his head.

As soon as he was gone, Trynne nearly punched Fallon. "What were you thinking?" she asked in a low, controlled voice.

"I was thinking very quickly," Fallon answered. He was leaning back against the table, his face to the room, his eyes darting swiftly from person to person. He reached absently for a chalice. She nearly warned him not to drink it, but he said, not looking at her, "I'm only pretending to drink it. Keep talking to me. I'm watching the room. The queen has lost interest in us for now. Good. She has a fragile sense of self. Did you notice? She's surrounded herself with girls who are less pretty so that she dominates by appearance." He tapped his finger on the cup. "I poked the very bruise she conceals . . . Did you feel how she turned her magic on me the moment I commented on her looks? I guessed it right."

Trynne studied his face as he continued to peruse the crowd with a mocking look.

"Her magic didn't affect you because I was nearby," Trynne said.

He gave her a sidelong look. "I know that. Your father has that gift as well. But that is not the only thing that saved me." His eyes burned into hers. "I've been resisting a hetaera's magic for quite a while. I've learned to harden my heart. To focus my devotion to one person above all else. To shield my thoughts from entertaining affection for any other person." He shook his head slowly and looked away. "I don't underestimate their power. But surrendering to it is a choice. So is *not* surrendering to it."

A flush of admiration rose inside her. She could not help but realize what he meant. That he still loved her, that he safeguarded those feelings against all others. The conflict within her began to rage again.

"Fallon," she said softly, struggling with her feelings.

"I've gotten better at judging people. I try to read their minds by observing how they present themselves. At seeing through the disguises they use to shroud themselves. Take Martin, for another example. He used to serve a prince. A wise and able prince, he said. He longs for that. To feel important. To serve someone he admires." His gaze narrowed. "Something has drawn him into serving this queen. You can see plainly he's unhappy doing it, but there's a connection between them. I haven't figured it out yet." He pretended to sip the goblet again and then took a piece of meat from the platter and tried it. "What do you think?" He chewed for a few moments, his gaze distant and brooding. "He serves her but betrays her at every opportunity."

"But why would he do that?" Trynne asked in confusion. "Why take the risk?"

"I don't know. We need to figure it out."

"But how?" she pressed.

"The same way I figured out Morwenna had betrayed us all." He took another piece of meat.

Trynne helped herself to the food and found that she was ravenous with hunger. The noise and commotion and threats were stifling, but they could not abolish her appetite completely. There was a surfeit of food, more to eat than could possibly be gorged by those attending the feast.

After a little while, another man clad in the queen's uniform approached them. He was older than they, with long dark hair and a chin that had gone at least a day without shaving. He was handsome as well, another clue that helped Trynne see the kind of person the queen preferred to take into her service.

"My name is Deven," he said. "Martin suggests getting some rest before the night watch begins. Follow me." Then his voice lowered conspiratorially. "I too am one of the Evnissyen. I'm at your service."

♦   ♦   ♦

The final watch was from midnight to dawn. Deven woke them up in time, and they exchanged places with the previous watch guarding the corridor outside the queen's rooms. She had not returned from the feast yet, so the three of them guarded an empty chamber. Deven explained the procedures of inspection, checking each door and window, examining all the places large enough for a man to hide.

The queen and her ladies-in-waiting returned well past midnight and paid no mind to the guards in the passage. They were all sleepy and drunk except for the queen. Her senses were sharp enough to notice them, and Trynne breathed a sigh of relief when they locked themselves in the room.

"I'm the watch captain, so the others will check in with me soon, now that the feast is over," Deven said, arms behind his back. "There is a procedure for everything. Martin is very thorough."

"Indeed," Fallon said, rocking back on his heels. "How long have you served Martin?" he asked.

Deven gave him a wary look. "Quite a long time, actually. He saw that I needed . . . protection when I was rounded up by the sheriff of Walin." Silence descended between them for a moment. "Martin said I could trust you," Deven added, having apparently come to some sort of decision. He tugged at his collar, revealing the glint of silver mesh rings beneath the tunic. Trynne didn't understand what that meant, but Fallon nodded knowingly.

"I see. So you did not leave with the other mastons," he whispered.

Deven shook his head. "I heard the warnings to flee," he said guiltily. "I felt duty-bound to remain at my post. By the time I went to Muirwood, it was nothing but ruins. Everyone was gone." He sighed. "The sheriff in that Hundred has many hounds and constantly tries to capture any who come there. It is still a beacon, even though the abbey is no more. I deeply regret that I didn't leave when I could. Now I'm too late."

There was a noise down the hall. The soft scuff of a boot that was out of place. Trynne had been listening for the thud of sentries marching to report. Something didn't feel right.

Gazing down the corridor, she saw someone approaching, trying to make little noise. The person carried no light. Trynne instinctively reached out with her magic, sending tendrils into the corridor for a warning of danger. The person approaching was a man, very healthy and fit despite his feigned clumsiness. She sensed the danger about him, sensed poison and daggers and even a cord for choking.

Fallon saw her look and walked up to her. "Who goes there?" he asked guardedly.

"A poisoner," Trynne whispered back, keeping her eyes fixed on the strange man.

"What?" Deven asked, turning around.

The light from the torches suspended on the wall near the queen's chamber revealed a courtier approaching, wearing a fancy doublet and comical-looking pointed shoes. As he appeared in the light, his gait began to stagger slightly—the mark of a man who'd been drinking, though Trynne sensed no intoxication. The man was dissembling.

"Who are you?" Deven challenged.

"Mwa?" replied the man with a slur in his voice.

Deven put his hand on his blade. "Go back, you drunken fool. This is the queen's chamber."

Trynne felt her pulse quicken with worry. Fallon's attention was riveted on the newcomer. She too dropped her hands to her swords.

"This is wha . . . ?" the man said with a slur. He careened into the wall and then staggered, dropping to one knee.

And that's when Trynne sensed the second man in the shadows.

"You fool," Deven said, shaking his head. "Get out of here." He started to walk toward the man, to lift him to his feet and shove him back the way he'd come.

He'd be stabbed in the heart if he did that.

"Deven," Trynne said in warning. The night-watch captain paused, turning to her in confusion.

The sound of Fallon's sword scraping clear of the scabbard filled the air. Trynne drew hers only a moment afterward.

The man kneeling beneath the torch suddenly lunged to his feet, grabbing the torch and yanking it from the iron ring fastened to the wall. Trynne and Fallon both charged down the corridor toward him. The man with the torch swung it at Fallon's face. Trynne raced past him, intent on catching the other man, who had turned to run. She pumped her legs and arms, gaining ground. The man ducked around the corridor, and as she followed, she saw a small group of guards approaching from the far end with torches, talking in low voices amongst themselves. They also wore the queen's tunic. The stranger was trapped between them.

"Stop him!" Trynne shouted ahead to them.

The guards had just enough time to draw their weapons before he reached them. The intruder attacked viciously, knifing one of the guards in the stomach and dropping him. The others tried to attack him, but he was far more skilled than they. His boot landed a kick to one of the soldier's faces, propelling the soldier into the wall.

Trynne reached the scene moments later, summoning her magic to defend herself. The assailant turned and threw a dagger at her. It whistled past her ear as she dodged, and a moment later she was upon him, her sword arcing toward his side. The attacker stepped in so that her forearm struck him instead. He trapped her arm and his free hand shot up to her throat to crush it.

Trynne reacted instantly, kneeing him in the groin while she brought her other arm up to defend her neck. Shouts from the other guards filled the corridor, although most were sprawled helplessly.

She released her sword and tried to knee him again, but he pivoted his body and swung her around. They were both about to fall, him on top of her. That would be the end. Reflexively, she seized his belt, tugging on it just so, and she ended up on top of him instead of the other way around. Trynne jabbed his throat with the heel of her palm and he started choking. One of the soldiers managed to stab him in the chest with his longsword.

Trynne hit his face next, crushing his nose, and then jumped away from him as he twitched and convulsed on the floor. She was breathing fast and hard, terrified, yet in control. Another soldier stabbed him again, delivering the deathblow.

Soon Fallon appeared around the corner, his eyes wide with worry. When he saw her standing, he sighed with relief. The other sentries had backed away from the dead attacker, gazing at him in surprise.

"He . . . he was a kishion," the man said, gibbering in fear.

When Fallon and Trynne returned to the corridor leading to the queen's room, they found the queen herself standing next to Deven, her lips curled with anger.

"*Two* of them?" the queen said in outrage.

"Yes, Your Highness," Deven said, still in shock from the sudden attack. "They came to kill you. I have no doubt of it. These new guards saved your life."

The queen turned her gaze on Fallon and Trynne. Then her eyes locked on Trynne's. "I felt something in the corridor. Sensed it. It was *you*, wasn't it? Come closer. Who are you?"

CHAPTER NINETEEN

Hillel Lavender

The queen's eyes narrowed. "Drag the carcass away, you two. *You*, remain here." Her gaze was fixed on Trynne.

Deven promptly obeyed and hefted the dead man beneath the arms. Fallon shot Trynne a concerned look, his jaw clenching, but after a brief pause, he grabbed the dead man's ankles and hoisted him up. The Tay al-Ard pressed against Trynne's back—a tantalizing reminder that she could escape. But she wouldn't leave without Fallon.

"Your Majesty?" Trynne asked in a submissive voice.

The queen stepped closer, studying her face. "What is your name?"

"My name is Fidelis."

"The Pry-rian word for 'faithful,'" the queen answered, raising her eyebrows. "Curious. Are you Pry-rian, then? That is my heritage. My father was a mighty prince who was slain by the King of Comoros. As a baby, I was sent to Sempringfall Abbey to be raised a wretched. A nameless one. Unwanted." Her voice betrayed deeper emotion. She paced slowly in front of Trynne, eyeing her guardedly. "Even my name was stolen from me. I worked in the laundry as a lavender. I was called Hillel, but that was not my true name. Let me see your hand."

Trynne frowned, feeling more and more uncomfortable. "My lady?"

"Your hand. Now."

Trynne hesitated, but though she was fearful the queen would see what Martin had seen in her, she had no recourse other than to open her hand.

The queen gripped Trynne's wrist and examined her palm, looking for something. The urge to pull away, and the knowledge that she could not, was maddening. The queen stroked her finger along Trynne's palm.

"You have calluses like a knight," the queen said. "But you are no maston. I thought you were." She released her grip and Trynne pulled her arm back, feeling vulnerable and worried.

"I am not," Trynne said, shaking her head.

"A pity, then. All the mastons have fled. They fear me, and rightly so. But where are they? Where did they flee to? It is a great mystery."

The noise of bootsteps hurrying down the hall announced the arrival of another person. Trynne risked a glanced back and saw Martin approaching, his eyes livid, his face twisted into a frown.

"You were attacked?" he said, his voice throbbing with concern.

"I was not," she said disdainfully. "My new knights were there to protect me. You chose them well. They defeated both kishion."

"Two?" Martin shouted in outrage.

"Yes, there were two. This one detected them." She gave Trynne a pleased nod.

Martin gave Trynne a grateful look. "Well done, lad. One of them was carrying *this*," he said, holding up a folded note. The seal was broken off. He handed it to the queen. "I cannot read this, my lady. You must."

The queen frowned and snatched the note from his hand. Her eyebrows furrowed as she perused the contents. Martin gazed at her, a look of relief evident and naked on his face. It was not feigned; he looked as if he had truly been frightened for her safety. She realized that Fallon's instincts were right—something bound these two together.

The queen's nostrils flared. "They were sent by the Aldermaston of Dochte Abbey," she hissed, crumpling the letter in her fist. Her hand shook with rage. "The Aldermaston sought to kill *me*?" She started to pace, her expression that of someone who had been betrayed by a friend. "Condemned by his own hand. So he has betrayed me as well. So be it."

Pure hatred flooded her eyes. "Ready my ship, Martin. I want to depart with the morning tide. We sail for Dahomey at once. Tomorrow. Have someone rouse the king and get him ready. Carry him aboard if he's too drunk to walk." Her words were full of derision and venom. "If the Aldermaston has sided with Dieyre over me, then he will suffer the consequences. He will suffer as he made so many others suffer." Trynne saw the tendons in the queen's hand straining as she crushed the letter. "Rouse the castle, Martin. If I do not sleep, no one will. We must be under way at once."

"Aye, my lady," Martin breathed, bowing his head in submission.

The queen whirled and stormed back into her room, slamming the door behind her.

When Martin finally lifted his head, he gave a cunning grin. "Soon enough for you?"

◆　◆　◆

It surprised Trynne how quickly the queen's orders were obeyed. The entire castle was roused from slumber to prepare for the journey. By the time the sun was rising, Trynne and Fallon were on the deck of the flagship of the fleet, a hulking four-masted galleon that could have been a Genevese man-of-war. But it was nothing compared to Gahalatine's massive treasure ships, nor was the fleet anywhere near as large.

The queen was finally bedded down in the royal suite. Her husband had literally been carried aboard and was too addled with cider to do more than moan in discomfort. Martin barked commands like a seasoned sailor, and the squeal of pulleys and the stretching noise of ropes mixed with the cries of the myriad gulls swooping overhead. The vessel lurched from the harbor and entered the wide river heading downstream toward the sea.

The crew was efficient and there was no work left for Trynne or Fallon after coming off their night-watch duty. Too agitated from the night's events to rest, Trynne leaned against the railing and stared at the burned and charred remains of the quarter of the city on the other side of the river. The ruin of that part of the city had been complete. Only a few brick chimneys stood like sparse sentries over a vast wasteland. She wondered how the fire had started and why that portion of the city had never been repaired.

Fallon joined her at the rails, leaning down on his elbows and hunching his back. His tallness was a major part of his insufferableness.

"This place is devoid of good feelings, Fallon," she murmured softly, gazing at the ruins. "The queen is terrible. Mighty, but terrible."

"Quite a contrast to Genny," Fallon said with a chuckle. Then he sighed, his gaze faraway.

"How I miss your sister," Trynne said sadly. "I miss Reya. I miss home. Every time the sun rises, I grow more anxious to return there. It's only been a few days, but it feels much longer. What is happening at Kingfountain?

"I'm grateful for Martin's cleverness. One of the sailors told me that we'll reach Dochte Abbey by tonight if the weather holds. If there's a storm, it can take days to cross the waters. I hope there's not another delay."

"We could try using the ring," Fallon said, giving her a wink. Both of them knew such an effort would kill him. "It will take Drew several days to muster his army. There's no way he can compete with your fleet, Trynne. Even if many of your ships are still in the East. Ploemeur is safe by sea. At least for a while. He'll have to bring his troops by land."

She sighed, feeling her insides squirm. "Captain Staeli must detain them for as long as he can. How fast can Drew reach Brythonica once he marches?"

Fallon rubbed his chin. "If it were Severn leading, he'd be at your borders in five days. Your father? Maybe three."

The mere mention of her father made her heart ache with longing. *Soon,* she told herself, *soon.*

"Look at the two of you, idle as princelings," Martin scoffed, coming up from behind them so quietly they hadn't heard him approach.

Trynne flinched, but Fallon merely looked over his shoulder. "You came to chide us for laziness or just to eavesdrop, Captain?"

"To eavesdrop, lad, of course," Martin said with a snort. "You've given me precious little to go on so far. But I make do."

Trynne turned around, leaning back against the railing, and folded her arms.

"So now we have mention of a *father,*" Martin said, his eyes twinkling as he looked at her. "And certain names I've heard naught of. Bryth-won-wick. Didn't quite catch it, but I know of no city by that name. And naught in Pry-Ree, for I know every hamlet there. Is it the place where the mastons have all gone, I wonder?"

He was pressing for information, trying to get them to reveal more about themselves. They needed to turn the tables.

"The queen said she was from Pry-Ree," Trynne offered.

"Aye," Martin said with a shrug. "The blessed shores. My homeland as well, by Cheshu."

"She seemed particularly upset about that note you brought her," Trynne continued. "That note you *forged.*"

A crooked smile flickered on the captain's mouth, but not without a flash of ire. "You could say that there is no love lost between the Aldermaston of Dochte and myself."

She wanted to ask what an Aldermaston was, but doing so would certainly be a mark of her ignorance of the world.

"Why did the queen feel loyalty to the Aldermaston?" she asked instead. "Why was his betrayal especially bitter?"

Martin rubbed his thumb into his other palm, as if trying to soothe the memory of an old pain. "I want to help ye. But I cannot if I don't know who I'm trying to help or why," he said in a low, sincere voice. "We are going to Dahomey, as you asked. But once we get there, what next? Whom do ye seek?"

"Give us a reason to trust you," Fallon said in a quiet, deliberate tone. "There is something binding you to this queen. You say you once served a noble prince. She is not very noble."

His mood turned black in an instant. "I know, lad. There is very little to trust anymore in this world. The most worthy of it are done and gone. Disappeared. I could have gone with them. But I chose to stay behind because of her. Because of the queen." His dark eyebrows cinched together. "She is my granddaughter."

The pieces fit together in Trynne's mind snugly.

"So it's blood loyalty that drives you," she said, nodding.

"Aye," Martin replied. His shoulders bunched up and he folded his arms, as if he were suddenly very cold. "My master . . . the prince that I served . . . had a certain Gift from the Medium. He could see the future ere it happened."

Trynne's interest was piqued at his choice of words, and she and Fallon exchanged a look.

"I see my words struck a chord with you," Martin said with a laugh. "Though, in all blazes, I know not why. He was the Prince of Pry-Ree. His wife was with child, his wife being the cousin of the King of Comoros, mind you. She was murdered by a hetaera—a midwife skilled in treachery—but the babe survived. A wee lass." His voice thickened with emotion. "The Medium's will was for the child to be raised at Muirwood Abbey in secret. The King of Comoros knew that the prince's child might inherit his powers. A decoy was needed." He stopped, gritting his teeth. "My own daughter . . ." He locked his lips, struggling with his emotions. "My own daughter was dying too. She also had a wee girl . . ." His voice choked off.

Fallon leaned forward. "You had the infants swapped. Everyone thinks the queen is Ellowyn Demont, the prince's daughter, but she is not."

Martin nodded in agreement. He sighed out through his nose. "She was brought to Dochte Abbey. Against my will, I may add. But fighting the Medium is like trying to shove a river backward with your hands, or so I've learned. I tried to rescue her from Dochte before it was too late. You see, Dochte is where the hetaera make their foul oaths. There is a special Leering there, one with a serpent on it. It is the symbol of those who swear allegiance to Ereshkigal, the Queen of Storms. The ruler of the Unborn. There are many marks of a hetaera—her eyes glow with the magic, and sigils form on her chest and throat—but you can *always* know a hetaera from the serpent mark on her shoulder."

Martin stepped closer to them, gritting his teeth. "I've told you what I've not shared for many years. I have my own reason for bringing my granddaughter to Dochte Abbey. I seek to destroy that Leering. To stop more of the hetaera from being made and to unmake my granddaughter's curse. But I cannot go inside the lair. Only a woman can."

His eyes, reddened with emotion and wet with unshed tears, seared into Trynne's face. "So you see, lass, before I assist you further, I will be needing *your* help to *save* my granddaughter," he said in a dark, determined voice. "Then I'll help you save your father or whoever ye seek in the cursed shores."

CHAPTER TWENTY

The Aldermaston's Fate

What struck Trynne vividly when the ship rounded the jagged coast of Dahomey and she first saw Dochte Abbey was its remarkable similarity to the sanctuary of Our Lady of Toussan in Brythonica. Both had been constructed atop islands along the coast of their respective lands. The sight sent pangs of homesickness through her, filling her with the feverish desire to finish this mission so she could return to her own world, where things made much more sense and where her own enemy was plotting her duchy's demise.

Fallon approached her from behind. For a moment, she thought he was about to put his hand on her shoulder, but he ended up bracing himself against the rail of the ship instead.

"Martin explained to me that the island is landlocked when the tide goes out," he said, gazing out across the waters. "Doesn't it look like Our Lady of Toussan?"

"I was thinking the same thing," Trynne mused. "It feels so ancient. Was this place the model for ours or the other way around?"

"Only Myrddin knows," Fallon said with a curt laugh.

"How long do you think they will hold out?" she asked, nodding at the formidable island surrounded by thick defensive walls.

Fallon smirked. "Martin just now told me that Dieyre withdrew all his forces from the towns on the coast. There are no soldiers defending the island."

Trynne's brow wrinkled. "None?"

"They've all been summoned to the interior of Dahomey. It's as if he . . . wants us here. Are you sure you're willing to enter the lair of the hetaera, Trynne? I have a bad feeling about it."

"I should try," she answered. "Martin promises to keep helping us if I do this. Besides, if there's something I can do to destroy the magic of that Leering, won't it also break its grip on Morwenna?"

He gazed at the sea, his mouth tugged down with concern. He brooded a while before answering. "I would hope so. But I'd rather not risk you to save her."

His words touched a chord in her heart.

◆ ◆ ◆

Before the sun set that evening, the queen's fleet had captured the island sanctuary and manned the walls with knights from Comoros. The rest of the fleet began unloading troops and supplies with rowboats to form a beachhead. The ships would linger in the bay when the tide went out to avoid being trapped in the sand.

Fallon and Trynne were part of the guard that brought the queen onto the island after it had been taken. The queen's narrowed eyes gazed up at the torchlit fortress, her lips curling into a strange grimace. It was clear to Trynne that her memories of the place were not benevolent.

Martin arranged for the rest of the queen's escort to bring her up to the pinnacle of the hill. He told her that he'd go on ahead to make sure his men had secured the castle. Instead of taking the main road to the abbey, Martin brought Trynne and Fallon on a series of byways, which he demonstrated previous knowledge of, and led them through a secret gate into the gardens cloistered within the abbey grounds.

The smells of the garden struck Trynne instantly. The fragrant aroma of star jasmine and other night flowers filled the air, but her heart was full of foreboding at the secret errand that lay ahead. There were trellises and comfortable benches, and the gardens were sheltered by enormous trees. As they passed under a magnolia, Fallon bent down and picked up a seed pod.

"Don't," she said, giving him a warning look, remembering how they had flung such seed pods at each other at the gardens of Kingfountain.

The impish smile on his mouth promised nothing, but he did stuff the seed pod into his pocket instead of hurling it at her.

"It's over yonder," Martin said, encouraging them to follow. "We don't have much time before the queen reaches the abbey." They trod across the greenery and Martin brought them to a small secluded area, heavily overgrown.

"This is the entrance," he said, stopping and pulling his pack off his shoulders and setting it down. He hastily undid the straps and pulled it open. He withdrew several torches and handed them to Fallon with a flint and iron. Then he pulled out a piece of wrapped canvas and quickly untied the bindings.

Fallon had a practiced hand, and it took him but a moment to light two of the torches. Martin took one from him and brought it to the bundle he had brought out. His demeanor was grave and determined, his mouth twisted into a frown. "Every Leering is carved out of stone by an Aldermaston. Time can weather the face away year by year, but the *power* remains so long as even a part of it is left."

He flipped open the canvas, revealing a series of heavy mallets and chisels. "Your work, lass," he said, shooting her a fierce look. "The lair is beneath that stone cover. Go down there and smash the serpent off the stone Leering. Unmake it." He grabbed one of the mallets, hefting it in his palm. "You do this for me, lass, and I'll do everything I can to help you find the one you seek. The boy can stand guard. If the queen comes before you finish, I will delay her as long as I can and warn you before she comes. She may try to return to this very place."

Trynne took a deep breath. "I will try my best, Martin."

When he nodded his acceptance, she wrapped up the bundle again. After securing it inside her pack, she put the pack back on. She felt unsure of herself, but she'd trained long enough that she trusted her arm muscles to be up to the work.

"I'll hold the light, lad. You drag away the stone," Martin said to Fallon, gesturing with the flaming torch.

Fallon handed his torch to Martin before kneeling by the stone. Trynne watched him strain against the heavy lid. It took a few moments, but it finally moved under his effort. Only a little at first and then it slid off with a grinding noise. Fallon rocked back on his heels and stepped away.

The depths of the hole were blacker than the night.

Trynne crouched by the entrance, looking down into the darkness. She did not sense any magic coming from it, but a bleak feeling emanated from within. Suddenly, she felt the nuzzling, agitated presence of unseen beings all around them—just like she had on her first night in this desolate world. It put her on her guard, and she swallowed thickly.

"Be careful," Fallon said seriously, looking her in the eye.

"Help me down," she said.

He gripped both of her hands as she stood poised over the hole. She leaned backward, pulling against Fallon's arms as she scrabbled against the edge of the wall with her boots, finding toeholds. Fallon looked stern and worried as he helped lower her down. She felt grateful his reach was so long. By the time her feet reached the ground at the bottom, the darkness had engulfed her like smoke.

"Take a torch, lass," Martin said. "There be snakes down there."

"You waited to tell me until now?" she asked with a tremor in her voice. She stood aside and Martin dropped one of the torches down to her. It landed with a hiss on the sandy ground, thankfully still lit. Reaching down, she picked it up and peered into the gloom while she drew one of her swords.

There *were* snakes.

Dead ones.

Her skin crawled with revulsion as she gingerly stepped forward. The withered serpents were everywhere, black scales turned a musty gray. She felt her courage failing but edged forward anyway.

There was a hissing noise. A serpent slid from underneath the husks of its comrades, drawn to the light, to the heat. Trynne slashed down quickly and severed the creature in half. It convulsed in agony and quickly died. Her heart hammered as she saw more heads poking out through holes in the walls.

"I don't like this place, Martin!" she called over her shoulder.

As she walked, she struck down the hissing reptiles one by one. They were lethargic and weak. Her boot crunched against the desiccated spine of one, and she groaned at the sensation before shoving it away with the edge of her foot.

The tunnel was not very tall. Someone like Fallon would have needed to stoop in such a place, but she was unburdened by the need to crouch. Something darted out at her face from a hidden warren in the walls—a hissing tongue, fangs, a gaping maw—but instinct served her well. She instantly reached up and sliced the snake in two. The air had a sick smell to it, the musty odor overridden by the stench of decay. Her anxiety grew as she walked cautiously down the corridor, holding up the torch to see.

There was a small chamber at the end of the tunnel. Six pillars held up the stone ceiling. Each had a face carved into it, but the faces had all been broken off. Something had been wedged into the stone floor at the center of the room. A drain of some kind, or a brick removed. She'd wondered why she had not sensed any Leerings as she made her way down the hall.

They'd already been destroyed.

On the far side of the room, a stone door stood between two of the pillars, slightly ajar.

The door was so heavy, Trynne had to sheathe her sword to heave on it. It slowly ground open, and cool air gushed out of the interior. Many snakes lay dead in the chamber beyond.

With the torch held firmly aloft, she gazed into the room. All was empty and quiet. Void. And she realized before her eyes adjusted to the dark that the hetaera Leering was already gone.

♦ ♦ ♦

The Aldermaston of Dochte Abbey was in chains, cowering in a cell, trying to shield his face from the glare of their torches. He looked terrified, his clothes incongruously wealthy and mostly unspoiled for such a fetid location, save for a few blotches on his elbows and tunic front. The iron cuffs binding his wrists together made him look almost like a supplicant as he tried to see against the painful light. He was middle-aged with streaks of gray in his pale brown hair.

Martin stood in the entryway with Trynne and Fallon next to him. The captain looked like he was about to explode from built-up fury and resentment.

"Well, how the mighty have fallen!" Martin said with a scoffing tone.

"I know that voice," the Aldermaston whimpered. "The Pry-rian accent. You have been here before."

"Aye, and you were a miserable host. I've come for my vengeance and the queen has come for hers."

"She will not hurt me," the Aldermaston said, his eyes flashing with enmity. "I *made* her."

"But the question is, can you *unmake* her?" Martin challenged. He stooped by the cowering man. "We've been to the garden. The Leerings on the pillars were all broken. But the serpent Leering, the one that brands the hetaera, it is no more. I don't know how you managed to move such a stone, but it was done. Where is it?"

"I don't know," the Aldermaston said, and Martin struck him hard across the face. Trynne jolted from the sudden violence. Her stomach twisted into knots.

"It wasn't moved without your knowledge or assistance, Aldermaston," Martin said with feigned patience. "That Leering outside won't summon fire for me, but there is a brazier full of coals, and I will pour them into your hands if you don't answer me."

The Aldermaston's eyes blazed with sudden fear. "I didn't say they took it without my knowledge. I said I don't know where it *is*. It was too vulnerable here. The mastons may return someday—"

"Aye, and they will!" Martin growled.

"Naturally they would seek to destroy it! It's been moved to another abbey. I was not told which one. It is to be lost from memory." He licked his lips. "I was to pretend it was still here. The works were done at night, in secret. You saw it yourself! The Leering is gone."

"If you are lying to me . . ." Martin said, shaking his head in wrath.

"To what purpose!" the Aldermaston wailed. His shoulders slumped and he leaned back against the wall, a broken man. "Everything is taken from me now."

"Why?" Martin demanded. "You served the hetaera. You condoned the Dochte Mandar despite all the mastons they've murdered. Why would they forsake you now?"

The Aldermaston's lip twitched. "Because I failed to keep . . . because of who I let escape."

Trynne's insides began to burn with heat. She gazed at the cell, gazed at the chains the Aldermaston wore. Then she stepped forward and knelt before the Aldermaston.

"There was a prisoner here," she said, her voice trembling.

The Aldermaston looked at her face. He nodded. "I never knew who it was. It may have been the Earl of Forshee, the man Hillel has been looking for so persistently. If I still had him here, she surely would have spared my life."

This was the cell where her father had been kept. She'd never been more certain of anything. She rose, swaying slightly, and pressed the back of her wrist to her mouth. It was horrible to imagine her father in this dank confinement.

Martin nudged the man with his boot. "You know what Forshee looks like. How did you not know whether it was him?"

"He wore a mask," the Aldermaston said with a sigh. "We kept him drunk on cider at first. But after a few months, he suddenly became more lucid. He played with the bits of stone over there. He'd stack them up and then knock them down." Trynne and Fallon exchanged a look of recognition. Stacking tiles was one of the ways her father replenished his Fountain magic.

"He even carved a Leering into the wall, we discovered," the Aldermaston continued. "It's still there. It would have taken months of persistence. We had orders to kill him immediately if someone tried to rescue him. I thought it might be Forshee. A hostage to sway the queen. I wasn't sure . . . I didn't know what was the truth. Dieyre was born to speak falsely. But the man in the mask escaped. He got off the island. None of us could find him. Dieyre and the queen were so angry. So angry." He shook his head.

"Where is Dieyre now?" Trynne asked coldly.

"Drawing all his forces into the mountains east of here. Surely the three kingdoms combined will not fail to defeat him." He shook his head. "But he is relentless. He will fight them all. Surrender? Not

Dieyre. I think he'd rather everyone died than admit failure. This will be a war unlike any other."

The Aldermaston stared fixedly at the wall, his cheeks twitching as if in contemplation of the looming destruction.

The noise of marching boots heralded new visitors.

"The queen has come," announced a guard who had hurried ahead.

The Aldermaston's face blanched. "I am a dead man."

CHAPTER TWENTY-ONE

The Cursed Shores

There was a sniveling tone to the Aldermaston's voice as he pleaded for his life. Trynne watched the scene unfold before her eyes in the dark dungeon beneath the abbey.

"I beg you, spare me," the Aldermaston whined as Martin held him up by the collar of his fancy arrayments.

"It is interesting that you speak now of mercy, Aldermaston," Queen Ellowyn said with loathing in her voice. "Where was *your* mercy when you sent innocents to die in the flames? Where was your mercy when you sent two kishion to murder me? How can you beg for mercy now yourself?"

The Aldermaston made a strangled sound. "I did not send—"

His voice choked off as Martin throttled him.

"We have the orders you sent," the captain growled. "You've betrayed the name of Aldermaston in every possible way. Face your fate like a man!"

"I beg you," the Aldermaston pleaded, the chains on his wrists rattling. "Spare my life! I may still be of use to you. Remember," he said, staring up at the queen, "it was I who first trained you in your powers. I who lifted you up to become Comoros's queen!"

She looked at him with revulsion. "Yes, I remember you very well. The fetes and parties. The Dochte Mandar whom you sent to teach me. To *bind* me to your allegiance. But as you can see, we are stronger than you. We are many now. I think it is fitting that you should die like those you condemned. The abbeys must burn, Aldermaston. *All* of them. Including this one."

His eyes widened with horror. "But Dochte was to be spared! It was promised to me!"

She took obvious glee in his pathetic pleading. "All of them, Aldermaston. The reign of the mastons has ended. Even Muirwood was burned to the ground."

"No," the Aldermaston pleaded, sprawling out in front of her, his shoulder convulsing. "I beg you, spare this final one! I was promised, by Ereshkigal *herself*, that it would be spared!"

"You thought a promise made to a *man* would be honored by Ereshkigal? Was it not your own teaching that women are mutable? Changeable by nature? Are we not water that molds to the shape of the dish? Poor Aldermaston." She crouched down by his prostrate form and gently stroked his head. "Where is the Medium to aid you now? Where is the power you once took for granted? You have nothing left that I need or want."

The Aldermaston sobbed like a broken man, his shoulders heaving.

"Poor Aldermaston," she crooned. Her voice pitched lower. "Gideon wept as Muirwood burned too. He heard the screams from inside as the fire consumed it. As will you."

The feeling in the room grew so bleak the torches seemed to dim. A sick, strangling feeling seized Trynne's chest as she listened to the queen's voice. It had stopped sounding like her, the voice slowly changing to another's, as if multiple voices were speaking at the same time. Trynne's thoughts went blank with fear, and cold sweat seeped from her pores.

"Look at me," the queen said, her eyes glowing silver and swallowing what little light there was in the fetid prison.

The Aldermaston lifted his head, his mouth wet with drool. He shivered uncontrollably as the queen lifted his chin to face her. Her power swept over him, compounding his grief and remorse, his fear and desolation. The room seemed to echo with hissing noises, but Trynne *felt* rather than heard them—the delighted purring and growling of those unseen monsters feeding on the man's desolation.

"A rich bounty indeed," the queen said with relish. "You served me well, Aldermaston. But now I release you."

The queen bent her neck and kissed the Aldermaston's forehead. As soon as her lips touched his flesh, Trynne felt a little prick of magic, a spell of some kind imparted by the kiss. She felt the invocation of something, like a whisper of death, and the Aldermaston's shoulders slumped as if he knew what would happen because of it.

"I . . . I . . . speak your true n-n-name, Eresh—" the Aldermaston tried to utter, but his voice thickened and he could say nothing.

She stroked his cheek, relishing his impotence. "You will never speak again," she whispered. Then she rose and turned her shining eyes on Martin. "Assemble the servants and every living thing in the area to the abbey and then bar the doors. Bring this man to the gardens to watch it burn. Then tie a Leering to his neck and cast him into the sea when the tide comes in at dawn."

Martin looked at her incredulously. "My lady, you can't mean—"

She rose imperiously, looming over Martin as if she were a giant. "You will obey me, or you will join him."

Those terrible whining and hissing sounds—no, sensations—intensified. Martin stared at his granddaughter in horror for the command she'd given. But *she* had not given the order—it was the *thing* inside her. Trynne felt Fallon's hand close around her wrist. She glanced at him, saw the fear in his eyes. The warning to flee. There was nothing they could do here. No further help they could give.

Trynne reached behind her back to where the Tay al-Ard was fastened to her belt.

Martin stood transfixed, his brow furrowed with conflict, his teeth bared like a dog about to snarl.

Trynne felt Fallon squeeze harder, as if saying, *Now!*

She closed her fingers around the Tay al-Ard, feeling her heart cringe from the blackness of the deeds about to be committed. The queen turned toward her. Those uncanny silver eyes locked on hers.

And then she and Fallon vanished.

◆ ◆ ◆

Trynne brought them to the harbor where they had disembarked from the queen's ship. There were no vessels there now, for the tide had gone out, but there were plenty of soldiers and rowboats.

"I've never felt so awful in my life," Fallon whispered to her, shaking his head. He turned and looked up at the black face of the abbey. The stars swirled in a vast configuration in the sky, but the island itself looked dead and dark.

"It was pure evil," Trynne said, shuddering. "I've never been so afraid."

"Nor I," he agreed. "This place is cursed."

They approached a group of soldiers wearing the queen's tunic, and Fallon said they had orders to leave the abbey and row to the mainland. A few minutes later, they were on a boat. With each stroke and grunt of the soldiers' oars, Trynne felt a little better, but she still ached for Martin and his granddaughter. He had wanted to save her by destroying the Leering that made hetaera.

But his plan had failed. And the failure also meant they would not be able to break the hetaera's curse from Morwenna either.

The night was cold and Trynne gathered her cloak more tightly around her. They had brought their packs with them and would seek out her father after reaching the shore. She brooded on the scene they had witnessed, on the way a fell creature had possessed the queen. She had never experienced such a thing before, and never wished to again. Despite some similarities to her home, this land felt so foreign and bizarre to her, like an oozing wound that wouldn't heal.

She didn't know how long she was lost in her thoughts when she heard one of the soldiers murmur, "Look! It's burning!"

She had been facing forward on the bench, hip to hip with Fallon, and they both turned at the same time and saw that the abbey atop the spike of the island was ablaze. Her heart panged with dread and sadness as she watched the flames roaring. How could a structure made of stone burn like that? But it did burn, and unwanted tears blurred her eyes as she watched it. How many centuries had that abbey stood there, a beacon in the water? She could almost hear in her mind the distant echoes of hammers and chisels and creaking ropes. And yet it would be destroyed in a single night.

"By the Rood," one of the soldiers muttered. "She was the last abbey."

"Aye, man. They're all gone now. Good riddance," said another.

Trynne's heart was heavy as she watched Dochte burn.

♦   ♦   ♦

The shore was full of soldiers and tents when they arrived, but Trynne and Fallon were both wearing the tunic of the queen's guard. They were neither challenged nor questioned. Even if the queen had sent word right away for them, the Tay al-Ard had helped them outrun the speed of any messenger. While they had no intention to linger, they found a small tent for some privacy. Fallon removed the Wizr chest from his pack and unlocked it, and there was just enough light from the torch poles outside the tent for them to see the gleaming board.

"Here we are," Fallon said, pointing to their pieces on the board. "There is the black queen, right next to us. The king is already here in the camp, it seems. Look how close we are."

"Martin was right," Trynne said, pointing to the white king across the board. Another white knight was near it. "Dieyre and my father are still to the east, but we're closing the distance. Only a few squares away."

Fallon nodded and gently closed the lid and locked it. "Then let's keep going. I don't want to be here in the morning when new orders arrive."

"Agreed."

Fallon rose and then held out his hand to help her rise, a simple kindness that meant even more in this place drenched in gloom and despair. Working silently, they secured their gear and left the tent. Most of the soldiers were asleep, but there were a few clustered together, staring at the abbey burning in the distance and muttering among themselves. Soon the camp was behind them and they took an eastward road through woods. The sentries posted there merely nodded in respect as they passed, and she was grateful that Martin had provided, although unintentionally, the means for them to pass unmolested.

After the fatigue of several hours of walking in moonlight, they shed their tunics in the bushes. Wearing them deeper into enemy territory would be foolhardy. Not long after, Trynne felt something ahead on the trail, the presence of Fountain magic.

"There is a Leering ahead," she whispered.

Trynne found it just off the road, hidden amidst thick brush. The face had been carved into an existing boulder. As she approached it, she felt its magic calling to her. It captivated her in a strange way, and she felt the ripples and murmurs of the Fountain. It felt familiar and peaceful—a stark contrast to the horrors of the dungeon and the hetaera lair in Dochte.

Fallon walked around the boulder, inspecting it from all sides. "The carvings are new," he announced.

Trynne was trying to understand why the stone felt so appealing. A sudden insight struck her. It was a water Leering. As if activated by the thought, the eyes on the carving glowed bright red and water started gushing from its mouth. Fallon scrambled backward in surprise, making her smile.

"You frightened me," he said, laughing.

"I didn't do it on purpose, Fallon," she answered. After tugging off her gloves and stuffing them into her belt, she reached out and bathed her hands in the water to clean them and then cupped some to drink. After the long hike, the drink was delicious. She splashed some on her face before stepping aside to give Fallon a turn at the Leering.

"I wish we had these in our world," he said with a grin. He wiped his mouth on his sleeve.

"We do," she answered and saw his head tilt in surprise and curiosity.

"Really? Are they like the carvings in the castle of Ploemeur?"

She shook her head. "No, those are just decorations. They cannot summon power like this." She thought about the ones in the caves of Glass Beach in Brythonica. But Fallon didn't know about those, and she couldn't tell him the secrets of her mother's line. "I saw one in Gahalatine's pavilion. It probably came from this world."

Fallon shook water droplets from his hand, his expression darkening at her words. She could see his face through the light of the Leering's burning eyes.

"Ah." A feeling of awkwardness rose between them. "I've never been *there*," he added, trying to lighten the mood, no doubt.

"This was back at the battle outside Dundrennan. He said that they were from another world, so I assume it must be this one," she said, remembering that night in his tent. When they had arranged the truce between their realms. When she had agreed to become his wife. The feelings in her chest were so different now . . .

Fallon's words interrupted her thoughts. "Can I ask you something?"

She turned to face him, dreading what was coming. "I'm not sure that would be wise, Fallon. We're both exhausted."

He smirked at her gentle warning and rose, rubbing his hand along the curved top of the boulder. She felt small and miserable and envious of his height.

"I'm not going to ask you anything inappropriate, Trynne. You needn't worry."

"Will it be impertinent?" she asked, managing a small smile.

"No, nor impudent. However, it is *pertinent* to the situation. Trynne, as much as I wish it were otherwise, you are a married woman. We are alone together, so I recognize the unusual circumstances here, but I just . . . well, I'm curious about how Gahalatine won your hand. When you disappeared with him and that ugly Wizr of his, I could do nothing but wonder what would happen. Then you came back, and your agreement had been made. So . . . how did he win you?"

"Why are you so curious?" she asked him, sitting down in the brush poking up next to the Leering, away from little rivulets that had formed beneath the stone face. They didn't need the water anymore, and the Leering's eyes were cooling, the flow of water decreasing to a trickle. Somehow it had ebbed on its own, as if sensing they no longer needed it. The clacketing of nocturnal insects encroached on the quiet.

Fallon scrubbed his hand on the rock again before sitting down, choosing a spot on the opposite side of the Leering from her. "I have no question why he chose *you*, Trynne. Surely part of it was political, because the Wizrs were going to force him to marry. That is what Genny has told me, anyway. It was clearly to his advantage to choose you, in every way. But I'm curious about . . . how you *feel* about him. Are you glad you made that choice, knowing what you know now?"

"Fallon," she sighed out, leaning her head back against the boulder. Darkness settled between them as the moon continued its descent. She was grateful she couldn't see his face. "Why must we talk about this?"

"I think I already know. Please, Trynne. I may be jealous of the man, but I concede defeat. I tried my best to stop him at Dundrennan. I . . . I convinced myself that if I could turn the tide of the battle, if I could stop the threat to our kingdom, you might have me. I did my very best, but it was not nearly good enough. In fact, I would have died if you hadn't saved my life. I still have a gruesome scar on my knee, and I'm proud of it. So, given what happened, I want to be sure that you are happy and will be happy. After we rescue your father from this fell place, and you return to Brythonica and your husband, I want all to be well. His memory lapse—and your father's—is a piece of magic that I think we can break. Regardless, Gahalatine was wise for choosing you. Why did *you* choose him?"

Trynne licked her lips, bracing her arms on her knees as she nestled against the stone. "My feelings about Gahalatine are complex at the moment. I don't plan on talking to you about them for long. Not with all that's passed between us, Fallon." She rested her cheek on her arm. "I told you that my mother had a vision about my marriage. She knew I would not marry you. In that moment in his pavilion—when I realized he was willing to offer me anything to win my consent—I saw that I could save my people. That I could save Genny and Kate and Drew and everyone else that I love. That I could save *you*. I don't condone Gahalatine's ambition, but I understand how he came to be that way. I was not very kind to him that night." She laughed a little at her own choice of words. "I rebuked him."

Fallon chuckled softly. "I know what *that* feels like."

"But he took it graciously," she added with a smile.

"As I did *not*," he countered.

"True, he is at once prouder and humbler than you, Fallon. But he's not evil. He has done good. He has struggled against the Wizrs of his empire. I respect him. Admire him, even. If I didn't, I don't think I could have brought myself to marry him."

There was silence after that. She heard him breathing softly and wished she could see his face. She waited for a reply, wondering if one would come.

"That's what I thought, Trynne," he said with a sigh. "I didn't think he was a monster then. And his treatment of you when he returned from Chandigarl? He was clearly deluded by others. I'm not angry with him anymore. I may even forgive him someday." Then he snorted. "Someday. Let's rest until daybreak. I'm feeling very tired. Would you mind taking the first watch?"

She nodded and yawned. "We are so close. Maybe we'll even find my father tomorrow." As much as she wished to carry on, it would be dangerous to travel after the moon set, and she was as exhausted as Fallon seemed to be. The boulder against her back felt as inviting as a pillow.

"Thank you," he said gratefully, and began to position himself for better comfort. She sat in the stillness, listening to the quiet buzz of night insects. The wind rustling through the green. Her eyelids started to droop with fatigue, but she strained to stay awake. When her eyes fluttered shut, she promised herself it would just be for a moment . . .

♦ ♦ ♦

It felt as if her eyes had only been closed for a fraction of a moment when Fallon started yelling. She came awake with a start, her heart suddenly in her throat, her hand groping for a sword.

Fallon was standing, brushing himself off by the Leering. It was almost dawn, and the woods were gray but still bright enough for her to see the panicked look on his face. Huge spiders skittered away from him as he brushed them off.

She sat up abruptly, only then realizing the spiders were all over her too. They were in her lap, crawling up her tunic front, on her arms and legs.

The groan of fear and disgust that came from her throat was not ladylike at all as she jumped to her feet and started stomping and dancing, anything to get them off. Fallon soon rushed over to her, swatting them away from her clothes. There was nothing romantic at all in the way he fondled her. She saw little red bites on his chin and cheek and it made her nearly scream to think of spiders crawling over their faces while they slept.

In a few minutes, the huge spiders had all dispersed and the two of them leaned over, hands on their knees, breathing hard and trying not to laugh at each other.

"I want to go home," Trynne moaned, shaking her head and shuddering with terrors.

Fallon nodded, still overwrought by the episode. "I've not seen *that* before," he said, laughing nervously. "Your face, Trynne."

"What?"

"Did they bite me too?" He touched one of the spots on his chin. "It hurts! Summon the water again. Please."

She thought that was a great idea. With a thought, the Leering flared to life again, the water gushing from its mouth. Fallon stood aside for her to go first, so she knelt by the Leering, pressing her hand against the stone to steady herself, and cupped her other hand to gather water.

Before she drank her first mouthful, something strange happened. A window opened in her mind, as forcefully as if shutters had slammed open. She saw, in her mind, a man kneeling by another water Leering. Intuitively, she knew she was seeing something happening somewhere else, at that very time. The man was also touching the boulder, and he became aware of her the same instant she was aware of him.

They both looked up.

And she saw her father's face for the first time since he'd disappeared.

♦ ♦ ♦

The king's army has reached Averanche. Westmarch offered no resistance. They were too confused by the conflicting tidings to do anything other than join forces with their king. Averanche is a formidable castle, and it will not be easily taken. They can be supported by sea.

But Averanche is not the goal. I've persuaded the king to pretend to siege this fortress and draw Captain Staeli's army toward us. But I have an errand to attend to first in the grove in Brythonica. They cannot be allowed to return.

Morwenna Argentine

♦ ♦ ♦

CHAPTER TWENTY-TWO

The Fountain

Trynne would have recognized her father's face anywhere, but the many months he had been away from home had changed him. The distinctive patch of white in his hair had been joined by some gray at his temples. He was weather-beaten and sunburned and had a new scar across his brow. Seeing him brought a visceral rush of emotions—longing and sadness and exquisite joy.

He was clad in rough soldier's garb, the dirty tunic of a knight from a different realm. The sigil on his chest was not that of Comoros, and the fabric was a dark red, the color of wine, with a black fringe. A sword was buckled to his waist, a dagger too, and his boots and pants were soiled with the mire of the wilderness. A chain hood was pulled down around his neck, revealing a mottled beard that was untamed and rugged.

Her fingers tightened against the stone as if she could claw her way through the rock to reach him. The Leerings linked them together. She felt a series of Leerings like a trail that connected the land between them. He was to the east and a little south.

She was about to speak, to call out to him, but his eyes locked on hers. He abruptly removed his hand from the stone and the connection between them snapped.

The pain of the separation was physical. Trynne clutched at her chest, feeling tears sting her eyes.

"What's wrong?" Fallon asked, wiping his mouth. He stared at her face in confusion.

Her throat was so thick, she could not speak. Awash in emotion, she struggled to breathe. She'd seen her father's face. He was alive, that very moment, at another Leering. There was no look of recognition in his eyes when he saw her, but how could there be? What had he seen but a disheveled, spider-bitten stranger?

"I saw him," she gasped, panting, trembling.

"Who?" Fallon came around and dropped to one knee beside her, putting a hand on her shoulder.

"My father," she whispered, gazing into his face. She wasn't sure whether to smile or sob.

Fallon's eyes lit up with joy at the news. "Where is he?" he asked her fiercely.

She grazed her palm across the stone. "This one is connected to other Leerings. There's a chain of them. I saw them in my mind. He may be a day or two away from here, but I clearly saw him. He was in the wild, like we are. I saw him, Fallon!"

He pulled her into a hug and they savored the moment of discovery together. Her cheek pressed against his neck and she squeezed him hard, feeling gratitude swell inside her heart.

Fallon broke away first, but he kept his hand on her shoulder and squeezed it. "It's worth all the horrors of Dahomey if we can reach him. I'm not weary anymore." He rose to his feet and then held out his hand to help her up. She accepted his help, nodding energetically. The morning intrusion by the spiders was now forgotten.

As they walked through the dense forest, Trynne wondered what she would say to her father when they met again. He wouldn't remember her, although part of her was desperate to believe that he would. No, he would likely be distrustful at first, but she would find a way to earn his faith. Even if he didn't believe her, she would use the Tay al-Ard to bring them all back to the ruins of Muirwood.

They had to get back to Ploemeur. The urgency of that thought squeezed her very bones. It made her determined to keep up with Fallon's long stride.

The forest was thick and decaying. The trees gave off a foul stench and the underbrush was thick with scurrying rodents and snakes. They had quickly learned to march with sword in hand. The serpents shied away for the most part, but some hissed in challenge and barred the way.

She felt her power dripping away—the result of her instinctively using her Fountain magic to sense for dangers. But it was worth it if they could avoid deadly snakebites.

They stopped for food after finding another Leering and getting fresh water from it. There was no vision this time, but she could still sense the location of the next one. They checked the position of the Wizr board and saw the pieces were arrayed differently. The black queen had moved one square closer. Other pieces were moving in from the north side of the board, beginning to converge on the corner where Dieyre and her father were nestled.

The armies would clash within days.

◆　◆　◆

The road kept them going east, but it was not well tended and they had seen no other travelers.

Sleeping in Dahomey, if you could call the fitful slumber that, wore away at them. It had become impossible to travel at night, for the road was heavily shrouded and was nearly invisible, and they dared not risk traveling by the light of torches. One remained awake while the other slept, but their bone-deep weariness forced them to change guard every few hours as best they could manage. They skulked in the woods and slept uncomfortably.

The next morning, they awoke to find they'd been attacked by another silent enemy. Scores of ticks had crawled inside their clothes and attached to their bodies to suck their blood. When the light revealed the infestation, they again marveled at the inhospitable woods.

"Nasty little beasts," Fallon said in annoyance, squeezing one between his fingernails and plucking it out. "We'd best remove them all now before moving on. We'll be sore all over if we don't."

They finished their ablutions separately before continuing down the overgrown trail hardly wide enough for a cart. During the journey, they spoke sporadically, both trying to preserve their strength while keeping a relentless pace. They spoke of their childhood in Ploemeur, of shared memories, and of the antics they'd engaged in as children—all of it utterly foreign to their current circumstances. Fallon had always resented missing out on their parents' adventures under the despotic rule of King Severn, but he admitted that their own struggles had thoroughly altered his views on the matter.

They planned to stop and rest once they reached the next Leering, but they had not come upon it yet and the day was fading fast. They trudged on silently. Trynne found herself wondering where they were on the board. How many squares had they crossed already? She wasn't sure how vast Dahomey was. The terrain was rugged and the constant marching up and down the hills had grown tiresome.

As dusk began to drain away the sparse light, she sensed Fountain magic ahead in the distance. She hastened her steps and touched Fallon's arm.

"Ahead," she warned in a low voice.

He slowed down, turning to gaze at her worriedly. "What is it? A Leering? I only hear some annoying jackdaws."

"I sense a Leering, but also Fountain magic coming from a person," she answered, and he nodded in understanding. Both already had their swords at the ready. As they proceeded, Trynne continued to sense the presence of several Leerings. These were active ones, radiating a form of magic in a circular area. She grew more cautious, but she didn't let it slow her down.

A thickening, roiling mist hung over the trees ahead of them.

"Fog?" Fallon said curiously, his brow wrinkling. "Reminds me of Guilme."

"Only this fog isn't natural," Trynne said, growing more alarmed. She reached out with her magic, probing for danger, and felt a dark force hidden in the layers of the mist. Pouring out more magic, she found a cave hidden within a series of huge boulders. A creature—no, a hulking monster—waited inside. It had one weakness. Sunlight.

It was nearly nightfall.

"Fallon—" she started to say in warning, but before she could explain, she felt another Leering flare to life. The other Fountain-blessed person was just ahead, closer than the monster. This presence she felt was definitely human.

Fallon stopped, held up his hand. "I hear water running," he whispered.

She heard it too. A water Leering, then.

The mist grew thicker. Seeing ahead through the trees became impossible.

"There is someone just ahead of us," Trynne said. "And there is also a beast in the woods. I don't know what it is, but it is dangerous."

"I don't like this," Fallon said, shaking his head. "Could it be your father?"

Trynne nodded. "He saw me at the Leering. Maybe he came to meet me."

"But this is your father we're talking about," Fallon said, wrinkling his brow. "He doesn't know that we're friendly. This feels an awful lot like one of his traps."

"Yes, it does," she agreed. "If it is him, shouldn't we let him capture us? I have the Tay al-Ard. I can get us away quickly."

"That's true, and he doesn't know that." He looked anxious. "It's getting darker by the moment. Let's spring the trap and get ready to fly if something goes wrong."

"Agreed," Trynne said.

They walked hesitantly forward, senses alert to every sound. The mist seemed to muffle the noise, but Trynne heard the pattering sound of water flowing from the Leering ahead of them. Its two burning red eyes penetrated the mist. They slowed their approach, trying to be as soundless as possible. Fallon gazed back and forth, his mouth in a frown.

Trynne pulled the Tay al-Ard out of her belt, holding it in her left hand. The mist was so thick, it blinded them to the rest of the road, but she noticed the trees had been cut down around the Leering. There were dead trees everywhere, sawn down by man. The air was heavy with the pungent smell of rot. There were smaller Leerings arranged throughout the woods in a larger circle, and she sensed they were summoning the mist. But the water Leering was the most powerful one.

"I don't like this place," Fallon whispered. His body was as taut as a bowstring.

The Leering's eyes were livid with fire, exposing its face. This one was carved to look like a woman. A grim-faced woman with a haughty look and a stern expression. There was something huddled before the Leering. At first, Trynne thought it was a stone, so she startled when it straightened to a man's height. This was the person she'd sensed. He was wearing a wine-colored tunic, but a cowl concealed his hair. The person was Fountain-blessed. Trynne could sense the magic radiating off him.

Continuing forward, her stomach roiling with concern and hope, she started closing the distance between them. Fallon kept close to her, enough that she could reach out and touch him if they needed to use the Tay al-Ard. The cloaked figure turned and she saw her father's face beneath the hood.

She nearly gasped in relief—*Fallon* did—but something wasn't right. The man looked like her father. But the next instant she sensed the magic, sensed the disguise.

"Who are you?" Trynne challenged, reaching out with her magic.

"Who do you think I am?" came a reply in her father's voice. Trynne sensed the presence of other men, soldiers, slinking through the trees, coming around them in a wide circle. None of them had drawn a weapon, but they were closing in on them like a net.

"I know you are *not* Owen Kiskaddon," Trynne said, trying to tame the anger in her throat.

"And you answer me in the language of Kingfountain!" said the man. "Did you notice I switched? Only someone from that world would know the speech. Thank the Fountain!"

"Who are you?" Trynne demanded angrily, gritting her teeth. She stared at him, half-seen through the glare of the Leering's burning eyes.

"My name is Esquivel," he answered with a light chuckle, almost giddy. "They call me Quivel here. King Dieyre wishes to see you both. Will you come with me?"

"Do we have a choice?" Fallon asked, looking from side to side at the shadowy forms of the soldiers emerging from the gloom. He edged next to Trynne, his boot touching hers.

Esquivel held up his hand and Trynne saw the black beetle-shaped ring on his finger. The Tay al-Ard wrenched from her hand and flew into the man's outstretched palm. He caught it deftly.

"Actually," Esquivel said in a cunning tone, "no."

CHAPTER TWENTY-THREE

Quivel

Quivel chuckled to himself as he saw their immediate consternation. "You're both gifted with weapons, no doubt. You could choose to stay here in the woods. You could *try* and kill some of these soldiers—they're quite good—but if you survived, it wouldn't do you much good. A very wicked and frightening monster that hunts this blighted land would make a meal of you. Nasty business, that. I, for one, would prefer using this"—he wagged the Tay al-Ard—"to bring some of us back to the king's camp tonight and discuss things further over a succulent roast boar smothered in honey and treacle glaze. I believe that was what I saw roasting on the spit." He scratched his neck, and the illusion dissolved. Tattoos sprouted up from the skin he was scratching, entwined in patterns that reached all the way up his face.

"You're one of the Dochte Mandar," Trynne said, her mind working furiously.

"And *you* are also Fountain-blessed," he replied, gazing at her pointedly. "No use denying it. We can sense each other. Come now, put the blades down. Let's be civilized, unlike these barbarians who cannot understand a word we're saying. They only know Dahomeyjan. If you prefer a long, bloody battle, go ahead," he said, waving a hand dismissively. "I'll use this Tay al-Ard to come back later after they've subdued you."

Trynne wrestled with indecision. The soldiers were closing in like a net. Between her and Fallon, they might succeed. But it would drain Trynne's magic. She could ill afford to lose all her reserves.

Threat and mate.

"Not interested?" Quivel asked. "Very well. Have it your way." His true face had finally been revealed in full. He had a long nose and a set of bushy eyebrows, which he lifted with expectation.

Fallon let his sword fall to the ground and it hit the marsh grass with a heavy thump.

Trynne sheathed her blade in its scabbard.

Quivel smiled. "A good choice. Come, sir. Sheathe your weapon. Let's not leave it behind. Swordsmanship is highly prized where we're going and you both look capable." He motioned with encouragement for Fallon to retrieve his sword and sheathe it, which he did.

"There. Let me see. If I bring the two of you, plus me, and maybe four others, that should drain the Tay al-Ard enough for it to be thoroughly unusable until morning." He wagged his eyebrows. "I do know how these work, after all. Clever invention. And some cuffs for your wrists. That will give me more assurance." He turned to one of the soldiers and uttered the command in his language. Trynne understood what he was saying—*tie up the prisoners*—and felt a pang of gratitude for her mother, who'd encouraged her study of the words of power. Xenoglossia had been vital for both her and Fallon on this voyage.

Quivel waited as both Trynne and Fallon's wrists were bound behind them with chains and cuffs. The soldiers, all dressed in the wine-red tunics fringed with black, fell in all around them. They were hardened men, each bearing scab marks on their faces, and some afflicted with oozing sores. Fallon's jaw was clenched and his eyes blazed with fury, never veering from the Dochte Mandar.

"Wait here for my return," Quivel told the remainder of the soldiers after choosing four to accompany them. "The Leerings will protect you from the Fear Liath so long as you stay near this one. If you leave the grove, you will die. Is that plain enough? Good men. Now, let us be going."

Trynne gazed at the Tay al-Ard, her soul in turmoil. It had been stripped away from them so easily . . .

Was it her father's cunning that had trapped them? She had never beaten him in a game of Wizr. Not once.

The roar of a massive beast emanated from the misty woods, following by an ominous snuffling noise. Some of the soldiers rocked from foot to foot, looking around nervously.

"Sunset," Quivel said with a satisfied nod. "The hunt begins. Shall we?"

He held the Tay al-Ard close to him, and the soldiers gripped Fallon and Trynne's arms before reaching out to touch Quivel's arm, the one that possessed the magic. There was a swirl of motion, a dizzying spin, and then they were inside a pavilion that smelled strongly of cedar. It was spacious and decorated for comfort with stacks of chests, a table with a map and measuring tools, and several large pillows on the floor. There was a Leering in the center of the pavilion and Trynne felt Quivel's magic brush against it. The eyes started to glow red and it produced light and heat.

"Two of you stand guard outside," Quivel said. "The other two, stand over there and keep watch. If either of these two attempts any murder, you may beat them at your leisure. Understood?"

The chief soldier nodded and they assumed their positions.

"I thought we were brought here to see the king?" Fallon asked, looking around the otherwise empty pavilion.

"Not yet." He stuffed the Tay al-Ard into his belt and then motioned them toward the Leering. "Sit down there. I have questions before you see the king. Go on. Sit." He gestured with a slight frown of impatience.

Fallon glanced at Trynne and she nodded. She could free them from the chains in an instant. It would only take a single word of power. But it would be best if Quivel didn't know she'd trained as a Wizr. Outside the pavilion, she heard crackling cookfires and soldiers milling around talking and complaining about the quality of the rations. Smoke lingered in the air, making it hazy. Trynne eased down next to the Leering and Fallon joined her.

Quivel looked satisfied by their act of submissiveness. He lowered his voice and approached them in a very candid manner. "Very well, I'll get to the point. I need to get off this world. Things are going from bad to worse. I was told a man would be sent to take my place. A thief lord. Where is he? Do you know of him?"

Could it be?

Fallon turned his head and looked at Trynne. "You mean Dragan?" he asked.

Quivel's eyes brightened. "Yes! That's the one. He's supposed to be here collecting the treasures, not I."

"He was captured," Trynne said, keeping her voice steady.

"Blast it," Quivel muttered, and began to pace. "That explains why he wasn't with you. Everything is going wrong. The plan is unraveling. These people are on the verge of slaughtering each other. Three armies are marching here right now. If we don't get away soon, we'll all die here. So, perhaps we can cooperate. Dochte Abbey is burned. That was to be the signal that the final war was starting. I saw you both"—he said, wagging his finger at them—"standing near her. Queen Ereshkigal, that is. Nasty creature. I wasn't there, but I saw you through the Leering in the cell. When you vanished, I knew you had a Tay al-Ard. So, let us help one another, shall we?" His voice had a desperate edge to it. "You don't want to be trapped here any more than I do. I think Rucrius intended to abandon me. Too much time has passed since I last heard from him."

"And you won't," Trynne said, trying to understand the maze of words. "Rucrius is dead."

The news struck Quivel like a blow. His cheeks twitched with dread. "No," he gasped. He continued pacing, shaking his head in wonderment. "It's worse than I feared. We *need* to get away. Dieyre is luring the other kingdoms here for a final conflict. The strategy is elegant and simple. He'll get them all to fight each other through treachery and deceit. You see, the curse in these woods takes its toll on everyone who enters. His camp is shielded from it for now. Ereshkigal wants everyone dead, so she'll never withdraw. Not even if her men are dying in droves. There will be no one left. Is Morwenna still waiting to bring you back? Does she not have the ring still?"

So he knew about the ring. And he was allied with Morwenna and assumed the same was true of them. Trynne adjusted herself into a more comfortable position, trying to come up with a strategy.

"Do you think she would let it go willingly?" Fallon asked with a snort. "We were sent to get Kiskaddon and bring him back. Help us, and you'll be helped."

Quivel's mouth turned into an angry frown. "You intend to leave me behind. I don't think so. I will not be stranded here. There are two of you, so who was—"

Fallon leaned forward, his voice rising angrily, "If you hadn't drained the Tay al-Ard, we could all be back at Muirwood right now. I *know* the plan for leaving. You don't. I know the password. You don't. Now bring Kiskaddon here and release us. Don't be a fool, Quivel!"

The Dochte Mandar stopped pacing. He glared at Fallon. "You will *not* leave me behind. I figured out Rucrius's plan long ago. Gather up all the gold in Comoros, Dahomey, and everywhere else in this cursed place. The plague is killing everyone anyway. The dead do not need wealth. We can do it without him. We'll bring the gold back to Chandigarl through the treasure ship sent to take Brythonica. Crisis averted! There's no need for Gahalatine to defeat the people in this world, they're too busy defeating themselves!" He began muttering to himself. "So Dragan was captured and now I'm to be left behind." Finally, he stopped pacing.

"I'll frustrate Morwenna's plan," he announced. "I can get Kiskaddon *and* the gold. At least enough of it to make this disastrous mission worth our while. But I need a way out of here. I want more than promises. They'll all be dead within a fortnight. Mark my words. The disease is ravaging every city and still the rulers squabble like beggars over dried figs." He snorted.

"Then let us strike a bargain," Fallon said. "None of us want to be trapped here. I know where they are keeping Dragan. He wanted to come here."

Quivel gave Fallon a sharp look. "Who are you?"

"The truth? I'm Fallon Llewellyn. Head of the Espion. Morwenna has seized the throne."

Quivel's nostrils flared. He looked from Fallon to Trynne and then back again. "And you have the ring? You can get me out of here?" he asked.

The pavilion door rustled and one of the soldiers poked his head in. "My lord, the king is coming."

Quivel straightened. "Here?"

"Yes!"

Trynne sensed the approach of two Fountain-blessed people coming toward the tent. She squirmed beneath the chains, feeling the mounting tension in the air.

Fallon ground his teeth. "Take these chains off, man. Let me help you!"

"There's no *time*," Quivel snapped, looking more agitated. "Just tell Dieyre that you are defectors from Comoros come to join him. We captured you and brought you here. Why is he coming now? This makes no sense!"

A voice grunted from outside the tent. Trynne sensed the presence of the two Fountain-blessed just beyond the thick material. Sweat gathered at her brow and beneath her arms. Her mouth went dry with anticipation.

The tent parted and a man ducked inside. He wasn't someone Trynne recognized, but he was a handsome fellow with unruly dark hair and a close-trimmed beard. His jaunty attitude reminded her of Fallon if she were being honest. From the way he glared at the soldiers who had blocked the entry, she could tell he was very self-assured, very accustomed to being obeyed. He wore a royal tunic that was travel stained but still impressive. It was the same color as the tunics worn by his soldiers, except an oak tree was emblazoned on the front in silver thread.

Arriving just behind the king was her father. Her heart lurched seeing him, wearing the same garb she had seen in her vision at the Leering. He looked stern and serious, his eyes full of distrust for the Dochte Mandar.

"Your Majesty!" Quivel said, bowing obsequiously. "You do me honor to visit my humble tent! Surely I would have come to you!"

"How long were you planning to wait before telling me you'd arrived with the prisoners, Quivel?" the king said. "Stiev was right, as ever," he said, nodding toward Owen. "He said you'd interrogate them yourself before bringing them to me as ordered."

Quivel's eyes widened in surprise, and his mouth gaped open, quivering as if he was seeking the words that would earn the king's forgiveness.

"I've never had a more cunning or clever man serve me," the king said. "Faithful. I've never seen the like. Well, not since all the mastons departed!" he added with a chuckle. Then his eyes narrowed angrily. "Get out."

"My lord, let me—"

"Get out!" Dieyre snapped.

Quivel looked like a beaten pup as he skulked out of the tent with his two guards, the Tay al-Ard still stuffed into his belt. Trynne turned and looked at her father, saw him staring at her. His magic reached out and swelled around her, probing her for weaknesses, for information.

He could sense her power, just as she could sense his and the king's. She saw his eyes narrow slightly, but he looked at her with an utter lack of recognition. As if she were a stranger with no connection to him at all.

Her heart pounded in her chest. She feared she'd not be able to speak. Here, at last, was her father . . . and he didn't recognize her.

"And so here you are," the king said, sauntering up to them and grinning with conceit. "You were both seen at the Leering marking the trail. Stiev told me, of course. He always tells me things. My quiet warrior. A young man and a young woman lost in the woods, following my trail of Leerings." He crouched down near Trynne, looking at her profile, at her face. He had a familiarity about him, as if he normally treated everyone as though they were long-lost friends. "You could almost pass for a boy, but I have a discerning eye. You're a lass in disguise." He scrunched his nose. "Are you come to warn me that my kingdom is about to be destroyed? Or did you simply miss boarding the ships with all the other mastons?" He offered a small, resentful chuckle, but he didn't look like he wanted or expected an answer.

Trynne did not understand what he meant. But she used her magic to test him. To lay bare his soul. He was skilled with the sword, much more so than most of the champions of the Gauntlets back home. He was proud of his skill, proud of his reputation. His body was lean and hard and muscled. He had cat-quick reflexes and a penchant for fighting unfairly. But his greatest weakness was inside his mind. He had tried to win a woman's love and she had spurned him, even though she had loved him in return. The regret was a bruise on his soul that couldn't heal. In Trynne's mind, she could see the girl's face emblazoned in Dieyre's thoughts like a burning torch. He still pined for the girl. He would do anything to get her back.

"Quivel said he saw you through the Leering in Dochte," Dieyre said, straightening and folding his arms imperiously. "How is Hillel? The *imposter* queen. I know who she really is—a wretched, nothing more." He smirked as he said it. "I remember the first time I met her.

Poor waif. So tongue-tied. Though women usually are around *me*. Have these two brought to my tent, Stiev. We need to find out why Quivel was being so sneaky. I'd bash in the faces of every Dochte Mandar if I could, only I *need* them." The last bit was said resentfully.

"I will, my lord," Owen said. The king exited the tent, leaving two guards behind.

Trynne's father came and knelt before her, studying her with wary interest. He reached for her arm to help her rise. His touch brought so many feelings swimming through her.

"Father," she breathed softly, willing him to believe her, to trust her. To remember her.

CHAPTER TWENTY-FOUR

Discernment

Owen's hand froze, his eyes widening with shock at her whispered word. *Father.* Trynne felt the Fountain magic stirring with her, a spark of it moving unbidden to his hand, still holding her arm. He gasped, his eyes staring at her face. Not with recognition, but with hopefulness, with eagerness.

"Do you know me?" he asked tremulously, his voice husky and soft.

"Know you?" she said with tears catching in her throat. "You are my father. And we have come a great distance to find you. To save you from this place."

His hand still loosely grasped her elbow, and magic flowed more freely between them, binding them together. She felt it emanating from the Leering she leaned against. Somehow the magic was confirming her words, enabling her to speak the truth with convincing power.

"Who am I?" he whispered huskily, his expression rife with desperation and relief.

"Your name is Owen Kiskaddon," Fallon said with deep respect. "You were practically a father to me as well. This is your daughter, Tryneowy. But you always called her Trynne."

"Trynne," Owen said in bewilderment. As he said her name, a series of chills rushed down her spine and she trembled.

"Papa," she said, letting the tears come, letting them wet her lashes and streak down her face. She wanted to hug him, but her wrists were still bound in irons.

One of the soldiers who had been guarding the tent door slipped outside and walked away quickly.

Owen glanced over his shoulder, watching the man go, and then quickly rose, his face darkening. He let go of her arm but then turned back and looked at her.

"Why can't I remember?" he asked in desperation.

"Your memories were all stolen," she replied. "What name did the king call you? Stiev?"

He nodded slowly.

"You were raised in a place called Dundrennan," Fallon said. "Under the tutelage of the duke of the North, Stiev Horwath. My great-grandfather. Just as I was raised under yours. You are not from this world. You were brought here by treachery, by the deepest treason. We came to fetch you home."

Owen nodded as Fallon spoke, his look one of bewilderment but acceptance. He rubbed his wrist as he gazed down at them. "My only memories begin in a dark cell. I was kept drunk and masked. I used to have a ring on my hand. The callus is still there. Did I . . . did I have a wife?"

"Yes!" Trynne said, her chest throbbing. "You still do. Her name is Sinia. She's not been the same since you vanished."

"The ring you wore," Fallon said urgently, "allows its wearer to pass between the two worlds. The ring was stolen from you, but I retrieved it. With it, we can get back home."

"I must return to the king," Owen said.

"No," Trynne said, shaking her head. "I won't let you out of my sight again."

"If I don't leave now, the king will suspect me," he answered. He started walking toward the tent door and Trynne uttered the word of power to unlock the shackles. They fell away instantly, clattering to the ground. The remaining guard stationed at the door looked over at her in startled surprise. Suddenly Owen struck him on the temple with the hilt of his dagger and then caught him before he collapsed. He dragged him away from the door and lowered him to the ground.

Trynne was about to summon the word of power to open Fallon's cuffs when she saw him stand, the cuffs dangling from only one of his wrists. He grinned at her.

"An Espion trick," he said wryly as he removed the other cuff.

Owen smiled. "Take his tunic," he said, motioning to the comatose soldier, "we'll move around easier. Now we just need to find one for you," he finished, looking at Trynne. She invoked her magic ring and suddenly her tunic was transformed to the wine-red one. He jolted when he saw the transformation.

"This will work," she said. Fallon gave her a smile and then hurried over to the soldier Owen had knocked out. Moving quickly, he removed the man's belt and tugged off his tunic.

"We need to find Quivel," Fallon said as he cinched his sword belt over the tunic.

"I know where he is," Owen said. "He's watching the tent."

"I can sense him too," Trynne said. He was nearby. His presence was so subtle that she hadn't noticed it. She turned around and then pointed. "That way."

"I've never trusted Quivel," Owen said. "He's the one who came for me in the cell in the dungeon. I knocked him out and changed places with him. He found me, and he's been my shadow ever since I escaped. I'm not going back to that dungeon."

"I'll get the Tay al-Ard back," Fallon said. "If either of you go, he'll sense you coming. He won't be able to sense me. Wait for me here. Once I have it, I'll come back and slice a hole in the back of the tent."

"Fallon," Trynne said worriedly. She didn't want him to go away either. "I'll do it."

He smiled confidently at her. "I'm actually better at this kind of work," he said. "If you two stay here, it'll keep his eyes fixed on the tent. I'll be back soon."

There was a wrenching feeling in her heart. She wanted to kiss his cheek and thank him, she wanted . . . but it wouldn't be right. It wasn't even right to entertain such thoughts. Instead, she steeled herself and nodded for him to go.

He slipped out of the tent, leaving her and her father alone together for the first time in a year and a half. She hugged him fiercely, even though he could not remember her, pressing her cheek into his chest. The tears welled up again when he patted her back and returned the hug. It was the hug of a compassionate stranger, but it was still a relief to have him again.

"I've missed you so much," she whispered. "So much has happened. So many troubles."

"I can't tell you how relieved I am," he said gently. "Not knowing yourself is such a torment. Yet I felt I had a family somewhere. There was an ache inside of me that is finally starting to mend. I can't explain it, but I have been guided. Led, even, to this place. When I saw you kneeling by the Leering"—he laughed softly—"something about you spoke to me. I knew I needed to find you. To understand who you were."

She looked up at his face, saw the awakening tenderness there. He had accepted and believed her words. His memories had been stolen from him, but not his sense of discernment.

"We will get your memories back, Papa," she promised, squeezing him hard. "And if not, then I will tell you all the stories you once told me. Of Ankarette Tryneowy, the queen's poisoner, and how she saved your life. Of your childhood with Elysabeth *Victoria* Mortimer. Of how you fell in love with my mother, Sinia Montfort. Of Severn Argentine, the king you served and then deposed." Her heart twisted with anguish. "Who died defending his rival, our true king. Of Severn's daughter, Morwenna, who betrayed us all." A spike of red-hot anger jammed into her mind at the thought of the poisoner.

Owen pulled away from her, cocking his head slightly.

"What is it?" she asked, her hand going for her sword hilt.

"The king's come back," Owen said.

Moments later, the tent door ruffled and Dieyre stalked back inside, his face a mask of anger. He gazed at the guard sprawled on the ground, at Trynne standing beside her father, her hands free of bonds.

"What is the meaning of this?" he demanded, drawing his sword. "Where did the other one go? Are you helping them escape? Answer me, man!"

"This is my daughter," Owen said evenly. "I must leave your service."

"Impossible. You cannot leave me," Dieyre said, shaking his head, stepping forward in a defensive stance. "I can't win this fight without you, Stiev."

"I've given you all that I can," Owen said. "My mind has been in a fog. Now I know why."

"I *need* you!" Dieyre shouted angrily. He looked at Trynne with resentment. "Where did you come from? What land do you hail from?"

"I am not from this land. And neither is my father," Trynne answered. "We owe allegiance to another king."

"Oh? And what king is that?" he spat. "The King of Comoros? His will has been twisted into knots by a hetaera. So have the others—even my own mind was corrupted until I met *him*," he said, trembling with rage and pointing his sword at Owen. "Until he came. My mind has been cleared at last. He's the only thing that has broken my wife's grip on me. That scheming she-devil and the lost abbey she's building! She cannot control me when he is near. So no, you aren't going anywhere." There was violence in his eyes.

Trynne drew her blades.

"You think I'm afraid to kill a girl?" Dieyre said with disdain. "I once had a girl thrown into a pit of flames. I've watched the innocent burn. I have no compunction against killing my enemies. I'm the best swordsman in all the realms. Even better than your *father*." He glared at them both, his eyes cruel and dark.

Owen put his hand on Trynne's shoulder. His other hand gripped the hilt of his own sword. He shook his head no.

"Trust me, Father," she said, looking at his face. "Captain Staeli, the man you assigned to protect me, has trained me well."

She knew Dieyre had a penchant for cheating—one of many flaws that assailed him. He relied not only on his reputation to instill fear in his opponents, but also on subtlety and deception. In other words, he cheated.

She stepped away from her father and invoked the ring to alter her appearance. She assumed the guise of the Maid of Donremy, whom she had seen in her visions of the Oath Maidens of the past. Dieyre looked at her in confusion. Then she shifted again, becoming the Painted Knight, half her face colored blue.

"What trickery is this?" Dieyre snarled, brandishing his sword.

Trynne shifted her appearance to that of Morwenna Argentine. Dieyre looked on in fascinated confusion, his eyes darting from her to her father, as if expecting the ruse to lead to a feint attack. He flourished his sword, but he did not attack her.

"You've disrespected women all your life," Trynne said. "You think them beneath you." She shifted again, invoking the face of the woman she'd seen in the king's mind. The one he had loved and then lost.

Dieyre's composure broke completely. "Ciana!" he hissed, as if seeing an apparition inside the tent. His arm started shaking. She saw his mind was completely overcome. She'd struck him at a primal level, and his body reacted despite his years of training.

Despite the fact that he knew it was a trick.

Dieyre lunged at her to try to stab the ghost image of his beloved to death. She'd been counting on that, for her power was always strongest when she was on the defense. The magic came to her aid. With reflexes faster than a snake strike, she stepped aside from the lunging thrust meant to skewer her and trapped his wrist against her body with her elbow. She stepped forward, twisting as she moved, and smashed him in the cheek with her forearm.

Dieyre tried to lever his boot around her, but she hooked his instead and suddenly he was falling backward on the ground. She released the trapped wrist and let him fall hard. His eyes were frantic, but he'd managed to keep his sword. He waved it in front of him on the ground, trying to deflect attacks that weren't coming.

Trynne walked around him, and he scuttled backward.

"You will soon be the king of nothing," she told him. She kept the image of his beloved on her face and taunted him with it. The flow of the Fountain came to her, the words gushing from her mouth. "You have refused to believe the warnings. You were given a chance to forsake your pride, but you denied it. If you survive the battle that is coming, you will rule over dead men's bones. All your life you have sought something you could never obtain. And now your destruction is certain."

His teeth were bared like an animal's, his eyes flashing with mortal hatred. "Will your ilk never stop *preaching* at me! I would have submitted if I'd gotten her! If I'd gotten what I wanted! I would have given up everything, but no, the Medium wouldn't give me what I wanted."

"What you craved was unattainable. And even *it* would not have satisfied you," Trynne said. "There is nothing you can do to stop the end now. Nothing."

"Enough!" Dieyre snarled. He twisted his body, trying to lunge at her with his sword.

She stabbed her blade down and impaled his forearm with it, the blade buried deep in the earth beneath the tent. Dieyre stared at the weapon in horror, his cheeks twitching as the pain started to bloom inside him.

The agony had to be intense, but he did not cry out in pain. Instead, he opened his mouth to call for his guards.

Owen knelt and clubbed him on the temple with his dagger.

All went silent.

We have Staeli's army surrounded, and yet he refuses to yield. Heralds between camps issue back and forth to press the negotiations. He says he will not surrender without direct orders from Trynne. She is nowhere to be found, of course. The king wishes to prevent needless bloodshed. How weak he is. Brythonica is without protection. I walked the shores of the beach of sea glass just last night. There was no one to stop me. No guardians save a small group of soldiers whom I easily deceived. I sensed magic coming from the caves along the rocky shore. If I still had the ring of the grove, I could have found out what was hidden there, but now I must wait until the tide goes out to discover Sinia's secrets. There must be a reason she always strolled that beach. I'm determined to find out why.

Morwenna Argentine

CHAPTER TWENTY-FIVE

Prey

While Trynne bound up the King of Dahomey's wrist wound, her father shackled and gagged him. They hoisted up his body and concealed it under a pile of fur blankets at the side of the tent, but before the last blanket settled atop him, the sound of ripping fabric filled the space. Trynne whirled around to find a dagger shearing through the back wall.

Fallon stuck his head through the hole, his eyes bright, his grin cocky and victorious. "I have it," he said.

She wanted to hug him right then and there. Instead, she gripped her father's arm and they hurried over to the tear in the tent wall and stepped into the darkness of the night. The soldiers were all gathered around cookfires for heat and their supper, so no one paid the three of them any mind as they tromped through the large camp.

"Where is Quivel?" Trynne asked as they passed through a veil of smoke that stung her eyes. A set of soldiers was roasting a serpent to supplement their meat.

"Over there," Fallon answered with a gesture. "I knocked him out and took the Tay al-Ard and his kystrel."

"This way," Owen said, leading the way through the camp. "There are over twenty thousand soldiers camped here. It'll take some time for us to cross the army and reach the woods. Dieyre will send hunters and maybe a kishion after us."

"We just need to hold them off until daybreak," Trynne said. "We have a magical device that can take us where we're going. It just needs some more time to rest before we can use it again."

"Should we try it now to be sure?" Fallon suggested.

"It wouldn't hurt to try," Trynne said.

"Touch my arms, then," Fallon said. They did as he asked and he invoked the Tay al-Ard.

Nothing happened.

"Where are we going?" Owen asked.

"To the ruins of Muirwood Abbey," Fallon said. "There's a portal back to our world there." He lifted a hand. "Quiet."

A horn sounded behind them, and an instant hush descended on the camp. The soldiers stopped what they were doing and gazed back into the darkness as if waiting for something.

"That didn't take long," Owen muttered. "There's more to come." Three long blasts from the horn followed the first. "Three blasts. Enemies sighted. The captains will be gathering for orders and they will describe us. The whole camp will be on alert. No one will be able to enter or leave the camp until the truce sound is called."

"We need to find an abandoned tent," Trynne suggested.

"No, we won't have any trouble leaving," her father said. "Few guard the south of the camp, the area toward the mountains. I know all the patrol patterns and passwords. I established them," he added, chuckling softly.

◆ ◆ ◆

The moon was bright overhead as they continued to climb higher into the mountains, the trees growing sparser the higher they went. Trynne's legs burned from the climb, but she was determined to keep going. The sound of hounds called in the distance, gaining ground.

They stopped to rest on the mountain trail, taking in huge gulps of air.

"The air . . . is getting thinner," Fallon said, gasping. He mopped sweat from his brow. "How far behind us do you think they are?"

Owen folded his arms, leaning back against a rock, his breath whistling in his chest. "Closer than I'd like. They've been moving quickly now that they're on our trail."

Trynne spotted several points of light at the base of the mountain. "They're carrying lamps or torches," she said, gesturing to them.

"Best to keep going, then," Owen said. "The torches will be at the rear, not the front. The dogs don't need the light to hunt us."

"That means they're even closer than they look," Fallon said.

"We were never going to make it very far," Owen said with resignation. "Come on."

They continued up the trail, the night air cold against their necks. Trynne was fatigued by both lack of sleep and the trials of their difficult journey, but she was relieved that her father was with them. Even without his memory, he seemed much the same to her, always plotting ahead, pinpointing enemies' weaknesses.

Huge broken fragments of rock were jumbled around, making their progress slower and more arduous. As they moved higher into the pass, the smells changed. There was a minty scent to the air, and she noticed some long-leafed plants choking the scrub alongside the mountain trail. She bent and snapped off one of the leaves. It was soft as felt and gave off the pleasant odor.

Suddenly, Trynne sensed a pulse of Fountain magic at work on the trail below them. Owen stiffened at the same time, holding up his hand to halt them.

Lightning exploded from the cloudless sky and struck a tree to their left, turning it into a tower of flames. The noise of the thunder was deafening, and the air sizzled with heat and danger.

"That's the power of the Dochte Mandar. We need shelter," Owen said. The crackling noise of the burning tree filled the quiet that followed the clap of thunder.

"Aspis," Trynne said, conjuring the word of power to form a shield around her and those near her. There was a risk that it would draw the Dochte Mandar to them, but the danger in not acting was greater. As if they were indeed summoned by her show of power, more bolts of lightning zigzagged across the sky—enough that it was soon as bright as day.

The shield drained Trynne's store of magic, but she held it up to protect them as they climbed. More stabs of lightning continued to strike all around them, blasting trees and shattering stone, and the thunder ricocheted off the stone of the mountainside, magnifying the noise.

Trynne's heart was hammering with fear, but she was grateful for her magic. She sensed it was their only protection against the Dochte Mandar.

Suddenly, she felt her shield rip away. Quivel was amongst those chasing them, she sensed, and he had just countermanded her word of power. They were vulnerable to the lightning strikes now.

"We need shelter!" Trynne cried out.

"A cave! Over there!" Fallon shouted over the tumult, pointing. Off the trail, through the gorse, they saw a place where the stones had fallen and created a small warren. They trampled through the green, hurrying to reach the safety of the cleft of rock.

Fallon reached it first and ducked his head inside. He nodded and then waved them forward as more lightning crackled through the sky. Owen ducked his head and entered the cave. Then Trynne. Then finally Fallon. His eyes were bright with fear and excitement as he moved deeper into the shallow cave. This time his height was no advantage—he had to duck very low to follow them inside.

Fallon lowered onto his haunches and gazed back out the cave entrance. The landscape was brightened' every few moments by fresh displays of celestial power. The rocks thrummed with the pressure from the thunder. Trynne pressed her sweating palms against the stone. The cave was dark, but the sporadic lightning bursts helped them see each other. The air had a tang to it, the smell of dross from a smithy's forge.

"It won't take them long to find us now," Fallon muttered, wiping his hand across his whiskers. "I should have killed Quivel. I was tempted to. He's desperate to leave and he knows we have the Tay al-Ard. If he doesn't catch us before dawn, he never will."

A moment later, complete darkness fell.

"They're coming," Owen whispered after the stillness became prolonged.

They all quietly drew their swords in preparation.

The sound of hounds baying started up again, much closer this time.

"Do we run?" Fallon asked softly.

Trynne felt the seclusion of the cave would offer more protection. At least they would know no one was coming at them from behind. "I think we fight it out inside here," she said. "The entrance isn't very big. They won't be able to charge us in large numbers. It's as good a place as any to withstand a siege. We need time, that is all."

"If the device you have can truly get us out of here," Owen said, "then yes, this would be a good place to make a stand."

"Just like Dundrennan," Fallon said, glancing back at her with a smile of remembrance.

As he said the words, she recalled being on top of that tower with him, the stars glittering like jewels above them as he took her into his arms and kissed her. The memory of that kiss still haunted her. It made her yearn for what might have been. Was he remembering it as well?

"I can hear them," Owen said. His sense of hearing had always been exquisitely sharp. As they quieted their breathing, soon they could all hear the noise of the dogs snuffling through the brush toward the cave. Within moments, the hounds reached the entrance and started barking fiercely.

Men shouted to each other. Then the bob of torches and light came nearer, revealing the menacing hounds outside the cave. The slavering noise, the scratching of claws against the gravel—all showed the beasts' eagerness to attack.

". . . the dogs, they can't hear us. Silence them. Come on." It was Quivel's voice.

The hunters came and pulled the dogs away by their collars. The noise of tromping men filtered into the space.

"Can you hear me now?" Quivel asked. "Look, it's not sunrise yet. Cannot we bargain? There is no magic I can use to force you to come out of there. I know that. But I'm content to kill you by other means if it prevents me from being trapped here. I have some poisonous leaves. If I make a fire and blow the smoke in there, you will all sicken and die. Then I can take back what you stole from me. But I cannot leave unless I know who is waiting for you on the other side. So can we not be civilized at—*nnnnghh!*"

An arrow struck Quivel in the breast, spinning him around and dropping him. The dogs started howling again as the whistle of arrows filled the air. The hunters began to shout in panic, and the hounds went into a frenzy of terror. They jerked free of their masters and fled.

Fallon craned his neck, expression full of surprise, trying to see what was going on, and Trynne couldn't help but do the same. Arrows had rained down on the sentries outside the cave, dropping them one by one. The others began to flee in confusion, dropping their torches and scattering back toward the trail.

The commotion ended and darkness settled in once again. But there was a little glimmer in the sky, the faintest touch of dawn that brought Fallon's face into the grayish light. His gaze was still fixed on the entrance to the cave.

The noise of boots scrambling down the rocks was followed by the thud of someone landing before the cave. Gravel crunched beneath the heavy steps. They heard the noise of a man hocking and spitting.

"By Cheshu, look at them run," Martin said gruffly. He sniffed. They could see his boots and lower body. He stepped on Quivel's chest and yanked the arrow out of the dead man. Then he ducked low, his frame filling the gap. "Come on out, my little ferrets. They're on the run now. They'll trouble you no more."

Fallon smiled. He shuffled forward a few paces. "How many men did you bring, Martin?"

"Just Deven and a few others. A good hunter with a bow is worth twenty men with naught but swords. The hunter is patient. The prey is careless. I don't think they realized they were the prey until the end."

CHAPTER TWENTY-SIX

The Crooked Tree

Despite the reassuring tone in Martin's voice, Trynne was distrustful. Fallon looked ready to head out, but she caught his arm and gave him a warning look. "How did you know we'd be here?" Trynne asked the grizzled hunter. She couldn't sense anyone who was Fountain-blessed or possessed magic. Still, she did not feel entirely safe.

"Bah," Martin said with a snort. "Didn't know that, lass. But I won't mistake this for coincidence. I have seen enough in my years to convince me the Medium is real. I knew you two were heading to Dieyre's army to seek your father. There were rumors about Dieyre's new strategist. I pieced it together.

"I've had my Evnissyen up in these mountains for weeks trying to find a back way in, since the front is heavily guarded. Deven and I made haste here and arrived last night. We were on the lookout for you. We camped high up, so we saw Dieyre's hunters chasing you. I told you I would aid you if I could."

His gaze shifted to Owen. "I'm guessing you found the one you've been seeking?"

Martin was a canny hunter. She had assumed that he would try to follow their trail through the cursed woods if he decided to follow them.

But now that she thought on it, he had already suspected their destination. It made sense that he had taken the safest way there.

"I'll go out first," Fallon said to her. "I think we'll be all right."

Although she was still hesitant, she gave him a nod and gripped her sword hilt, ready to fight if need be. Ducking low, Fallon crept toward the edge of the cave and soon emerged.

"Well met, Martin," he said. "Hello, Deven."

"Well met, indeed, by Cheshu," said the hunter. "Deven, take the rest of the Evnissyen and hunt down those who escaped. Claim their uniforms and badges. They will come in handy later, I should think. I'll take yours too, lad, if you'll not be needing it."

The sky was beginning to brighten, each moment bringing more light to the interior of the cave. She glanced back at her father. He was watching the entrance, his eyes squinting in the gloom. Reaching out, she put her hand on his shoulder.

He gave her a sad smile and then nodded. "I think we are safe." They left the cave together and joined the others.

"So where are you bound?" Martin asked when he saw them. "You can't go back to the queen. When you disappeared like that, snuffed and vanished like a conjurer's trick, she was all too keen to find you. The whole army is on the look for ye. I can get you a boat if you need one. The Evnissyen are loyal to *me*."

"The question is," Fallon asked, "why are you still loyal to *her*?"

Martin's face scrunched up at the question. "You are young, lad." He bared his teeth in a grimace. "You don't understand the pull of family."

Fallon's face became intense and serious. "I think I do."

"So long as there is a spark of hope—a single ember burning in the ashes, the faintest puff of smoke—that my granddaughter can be saved, I will cling to it. The Myriad Ones have her, lad. It's plain enough to see. There was a time, years back, when she was an innocent. We cannot return to the past. No traveler can. But so long as I have memories of her then, it makes me determined to see that cursed hetaera Leering smashed into rubble."

Fallon pursed his lips and nodded. "I see that you cannot be swayed from your path."

"Aye, lad. That Leering was taken somewhere. And I mean to find it."

Trynne admired his courage, his unwillingness to accept that his granddaughter was lost forever. Maybe it was a foolish hope. But it was the kind of hope that she herself had clung to after her father's disappearance. Now her father stood by her side—evidence that some hopes were fulfilled.

"I had wondered if we could persuade you to join us," Trynne said. "This war is going to destroy all the kingdoms. Dieyre knows it, but he still won't back down. It's not too late to escape, Martin. You can come with us to Muirwood and leave this place." She hoped he would say yes. She would like to introduce him to Captain Staeli.

Martin sniffed and brushed his forearm across his nose. "Muirwood after all, is it? The sun rises and sets there it seems. I do appreciate the offer, lass. You may not be maston in name, but you have a maston's heart. And I miss that. But my duty is here. I was given the choice to abandon my granddaughter before and I wouldn't. I still won't."

"I'm glad we met, Martin Evnissyen," Trynne said.

"Aye, lass. Me too. You remind me of someone else. She had your spunk. You don't look much alike, but you still remind me of her. She led the mastons to safety, to another land across the sea. They'll return someday to reclaim the ruins we leave behind. But be careful. The sheriff of Mendenhall has refused to join the queen and skulks around the grounds looking for mastons to kill."

"Thank you. I don't know if this will help," Fallon said, gripping the hunter's shoulder. "But Dieyre said his wife was building another abbey, one that is concealed somewhere in these mountains. Perhaps that is where the Leering can be found."

Martin nodded. "Then Deven will help me find it."

A ray of sunlight pierced the trees over the horizon and stabbed Trynne's eyes. The new day had finally dawned and she felt hope spark inside her.

She touched Fallon's arm. "It's time to go."

He looked at the tiny speck of sunlight. There was a sad look on his face, as if he was sorry that Martin wouldn't be joining them. Then he removed the tunic marking him as part of Dieyre's army and so did her father. They handed them over to Martin.

"Farewell," Fallon told the man.

"I'm not very keen on good-byes," Martin said, chuffing. "But I bid you one all the same."

Fallon brought out the Tay al-Ard. A slight breeze ruffled his hair. His eyes were wells of emotion, but he grinned at her as he held out the device, nodding for her to take hold of it. She clasped it, her hand touching his. Owen placed his hand on her arm, catching on quickly.

The magic yanked them away.

♦ ♦ ♦

They emerged at the crooked oak tree whose branches were so thick and heavy they sagged to the ground.

They had also appeared amidst a small camp of sleeping soldiers wearing ragged and filthy tunics. A small cookfire at the center of camp was full of cinders, and the makeshift spit straddling it had been stripped of all but the last charred bones.

"What in the blazes!" said the sentry, who had seen them appear out of nothingness. "Get up! It's them! Up!"

At least a dozen men slept near the tree. Suddenly blankets whipped up across the camp as the rousing soldiers moved, groping in the semidarkness for their swords. Fallon was the first to act, kicking one of them in the head as he struggled to sit up. Trynne and her father unsheathed their weapons as the small camp came alive, responding to the frantic urging of the lone sentry. There were curses and oaths and Trynne found three men charging her and her father in moments, filthy battered swords at the ready. She blocked an attack with one of her swords, clubbed the man on the head with the hilt, and then whipped her blade around to stab another man as he rushed at her. Her magic rushed to defend her, but her father moved in and struck down the third man.

One of the men had throwing axes, and she watched him train his eye on her as he hurled one of his weapons. She stepped back and the axe whirled just past her, the blade sticking into the rough bark of the oak tree. The man scowled as he hefted another and threw it. She dodged that one too and it sailed past her and bounced off the trunk. The man readied his third axe, coming closer before he threw it at her.

His aim was true, but she crossed her swords in front of her and the axe deflected off her blades.

The axeman's eyes bulged at her prowess and he turned and bolted, shouting for help. "Sheriff! Sheriff! Down here! Down here!"

Fallon had brought down five or six men himself. Owen had disarmed another, and the remainder fled, shouting for reinforcements. The calls were answered by men hidden in the ruins of the abbey. Trynne's heart was pounding from the unexpected fight. She turned around in a full circle, reaching out to find danger, and discovered that the woods were teeming with soldiers, most already awakened by the chaos.

She kept her swords out and backed toward the tree. "Fallon, get us out of here," she said worriedly, sensing the presence of others converging on their location.

Fallon had sheathed his sword and tugged off his glove. "Lord Owen," he said, coming near. Trynne saw him tug at his own finger.

"This is yours by right and duty. Put it on. You must be the one to use it."

The noise of boots crunching in the woods came from all around them. "Fallon, can't you bring us back like you brought us here?" Trynne asked, confused.

Owen held out his hand and groped for the ring. He slid it onto his ring finger and then clenched his fist.

"What do I do?" he asked Fallon.

"Trynne, take his arm. Put your palm on the tree so that the ring touches the bark. The magic will bring you back to the grove in Brythonica. You'll reappear in the cave."

The way he said the words implied that he would not be going with them. A spear of panic spiked into her stomach. "Iago Fallon Llewellyn, you are coming with us!"

She watched him take several deliberate steps backward, away from them, away from the tree.

"I can't," he said, shaking his head.

"Fallon!" she said angrily. It felt as if everything inside her was as jumbled as rocks tumbling down a mountainside. "Get over here."

"I can't, Trynne!" he said, shaking his head. He unslung his pack. "I've put a note explaining things in the chest. The key is in the pack. Take it with you. Save Kingfountain from Morwenna. I cannot go back with you."

He hefted the pack by the strap and threw it to Owen, who caught it with a grunt.

Fallon kept backing away, shaking his head. "I choose to stay willingly. It must be done willingly or the magic won't work. Good-bye, Trynne. Good-bye, Lord Owen."

The haunted look on his face devastated her. He had known he would not be coming back with them. He'd kept it to himself, not telling her the full truth until the very end, when there was nothing she could do about it.

A memory from Myrddin's cave flashed through her mind. The Wizr had said something about rules separating the worlds. He'd seemed on the verge of saying more, but he'd shifted his attention to Fallon and stopped himself. *I will say nothing more on that. I see it clearly. There are rules. I did not create them. Even I must abide by them.* Myrddin's gift from the Fountain was the ability to read people's minds. He had silenced himself because he'd seen Fallon's intention to sacrifice himself for her father, to trade places with him. Fallon would remain behind so that Owen could leave. It was why Quivel was so desperate. He had been left behind and had wanted to bargain his way back to their home world.

"No," Trynne said, stifling a sob as she stared at Fallon's retreating form. He was nodding at her now, seeing that she finally understood. She recognized Dragan's role as well. It had been Morwenna's intent all along to trap him in this place. But her plan had changed after he was captured. He knew too much, so she'd wiped away his memories before he could denounce her.

Her heart swelled to the point of bursting. Fallon had done everything in his power to save her father. But in so doing, he had condemned himself to a world that would be destroyed by plague and violence.

"Go," Fallon said tenderly. "There was no other way. One of us had to stay. If you can't be mine, then it's better this way. Tell my parents. Tell my sister. I chose this willingly."

"Over there! I see them by the oak!"

The noise of people crashing through the woods shattered the moment. Fallon drew his sword and turned to face the soldiers rushing toward the tree.

Hot tears streaked down Trynne's face. She loved Fallon so much in that moment, it stole her breath away. She would never love Gahalatine like this.

Owen stared at Fallon, hesitation in his eyes. She was duty-bound to save Brythonica, so she could not stay. It would have been impossible for her to choose between them. She loved both of them deeply. Fallon had made the difficult choice for her. It felt as if her heart had been ripped in half, but she clutched her father's arm.

Trynne hung her head and began to sob as her father placed his hand on the crooked oak. A prick of light came from the tree, swelling until it was so bursting and dazzling it hurt—a radiance so penetrating that she had to hold up her hand to protect her eyes.

Then everything moved.

CHAPTER TWENTY-SEVEN

Wizr Board

The brightness of the glen was replaced by the darkness of the cave. The sounds changed from the ruckus of charging soldiers to the lapping, quiet thrum of a small waterfall moving across stone. Even the air smelled different. It carried the faint scent of eucalyptus. Brythonica.

Home.

Owen put his hand on her shoulder. Light filtered back from the entrance of the cave—just enough for them to see each other in the darkened interior, while the world outside was swathed in rich, vibrant color. She could see the stone plinth, covered with a sheet of crumbled oak leaves. The silver bowl was still chained there, brimming with the Fountain's magic. She felt so depleted, so drained, yet the grove was a place for magic to be replenished.

"Oh, Papa," she cried, clinging to him with joy and misery, her heart cleft into two separate pieces. Part of her was dead inside, afflicted by the loss of Fallon.

There was a hesitation on her father's part. She was a near stranger to him in his present state. But she couldn't help herself. It was still *him*, and he was back after such a long absence. Gratitude welled up inside her, squeezing past the tears still falling from her eyes.

Thank you, she whispered silently to the Fountain, hearing the gentle murmur of the nearby brook.

And then there was the crackle of breaking twigs outside the cave and she felt her father's hand stiffen on her shoulder.

"We're not alone," he whispered.

Trynne's relief at making it back home and her grief at losing Fallon had blinded her to the possibility that Morwenna might have left allies to thwart their return. She reached out with her magic and sensed dozens of soldiers, maybe more, hunkered within the confines of the grove. They were armed. They were waiting for them to emerge.

Trynne lacked the strength to fight so many. She was exhausted from the ordeal, from lack of sleep, and her reserves were diminished. Even someone who was Fountain-blessed had limits.

She could sense the soldiers creeping toward the mouth of the cave. When they all arrived, she and her father would be overwhelmed. These men probably had orders to kill them. If she returned with her father, it would upend Morwenna's plans.

Owen drew his sword. "We're going to need to fight our way out of here," he said softly, looking into her eyes.

Too many. There were too many.

Then the idea struck her. A defense that could help them.

"Father," she said. "You see the silver bowl? Fill it from the waterfall outside the cave and then pour its contents onto the stone plinth. I'll distract them until you do. It will even the odds. Prepare for a violent storm."

"I don't understand," he said, shaking his head.

"You will," she promised, giving him a crooked smile.

Trynne breathed in the sweet-smelling air as she drew her twin blades. In her mind, she invoked the magic of her ring and turned herself into the Painted Knight, making her face half-blue, changing her outfit to look like the armor of the Maid. Then she marched out of the cave, swords in hand.

"There, there!" someone shouted.

The twangs of crossbows sounded across the grove, and missiles flew at her from several points. She felt herself wrapped in the oath magic and time seemed to slow, allowing her to jerk and dodge the bolts, which clattered harmlessly into the rocks behind her. Trynne marched forward, swinging her swords in matching circles as she had practiced thousands of times. Onward she walked, each footstep thudding in her ears, moving past the stone table, past the silver dish, bringing herself into the middle of the soldiers who were converging on them. The men wore black and carried the badge of the white boar. Men of Glosstyr.

They readied to charge. She saw their anxious, determined looks. She was completely outnumbered.

Trynne stopped on the gently sloping ground, well ahead of the plinth. She was nearly surrounded now—at least twenty soldiers at full alert with unkempt beards and angry frowns had fallen in around her.

They rushed her at once.

Trynne reacted in a blur of motion, her strength sustained by the power of the Fountain, even as she felt it ebbing quickly. She blocked the thrusts that came at her, deflecting blades and countering with her own. She did not fight to kill these men, just to hold them off, to fix their attention on her, giving her father a chance to slip out of the cave and seize the silver bowl. Shouts and grunts filled the calmness of the grove. The men were all bigger than her, but she was quicksilver fast, dodging away from thrusts and jabs, responding with two blades at once to trap and then disarm her opponents. Still, their sheer numbers were like a swelling tide, one that would drown her given enough time.

"There's the other! It's Kiskaddon!"

"Kill him!"

These men had clearly been chosen for their resentment against her family, against her husband. These were soldiers of Glosstyr, men fiercely loyal to Severn, not the Sun and Rose, and their loyalty still bound them. Trynne could not stop those who charged toward her father with murderous intent.

She cracked skulls with the hilts of her swords, slammed her elbows into chins and noses. But there were still too many, and she felt her limits straining. Someone grabbed her by the collar, and she felt her boots slip on the brackish ground. She whirled and collided with someone who punched her in the ribs with a gauntlet-encased fist. Another blow struck the back of her head and pain erased every other sensation for a moment. She knew she was going to fall an instant before it happened—and then she slammed flat on her back with a heavy thud.

One of her swords was gone, but she kicked a man in the knee and fought from the ground as she watched the web of swords converging on her.

And then the crack of thunder sounded, so loud it nearly deafened Trynne. So loud it stunned the warriors and suspended their assault.

A few drops of water fell. Then it started to hail.

Huge chunks of ice began to plummet into the grove. They fell amidst the soldiers, who began to shout and wail in terror and panic. Some tried to flee, only to be struck down by the apple-sized stones. The storm buffeted the men of Glosstyr, knocking them down mercilessly. Some tried to cover their heads and seek shelter in the nearby woods.

Trynne felt the ice slamming into the ground all around her, but she was surprised to realize that none touched her. Then her father was at her side, shielding her body with his. He didn't realize that their variety of Fountain magic protected them from the icy deluge. He looked frightened and awed by the display—the way Trynne had felt the first time he had shown her the power of the grove. The ground was soon blanketed in white, the leaves of the oak tree stripped away. The storm seemed to last forever, but it finally ended, and sunlight glittered across the frozen grove.

Heaps of men lay scattered around. All their foes were down. Trynne lifted herself up on her sore arms. The only noise in her throbbing ears was the sound of heavy breathing—hers and her father's—and the trickling sound of the waterfall. She sensed no other life in the grove and she realized that the Fountain had slain all the men of Glosstyr.

Then the sweet trilling of birdsong filled the void, the hauntingly beautiful sound that never failed to move her after the devastation wrought by the grove's storms. She sat up and Owen sat down, stunned at the chorus that swelled in the air. He stared at the oak tree that was no longer barren but full of a variety of birds, each singing a part of the melody. As they filled the sky with music, the buds of the oak tree regrew and suddenly it was complete again.

"There's someone at the tree," Owen said, looking keenly at it.

Trynne caught just the subtle shift of movement and then remembered Fallon's warning.

"Don't look at her," she said. The grove felt wrong now, hostile. "We must not look, or we'll both forget who we are. That's what happened to you before, Papa."

The ice melted away, bathing the glen. Drips of water plopped from the ferns and bracken. The gateway back to Muirwood was open. She sensed it calling her, urging her to go back to Fallon, to be with him there. The pain in her heart was real and it hurt beyond her reckoning, but she had a duty to perform in Kingfountain. She could not fulfill her own wishes at that moment. Not when so much was at stake. Still, she was determined to bring Fallon back somehow and prayed she would not be too late. She and her father sat in the quiet damp, listening as the birdsong finished. And then the portal to Muirwood closed. She felt empty inside when it did.

"That was frightening," Owen said, chuckling softly.

Trynne gazed at his expression and smiled. "The first time you came here, it was with a poisoner named Etayne. She almost died in the hail, but you shielded her too."

Owen nodded with interest. "What's our next move?"

"I guess that depends on what we see on the Wizr board."

His brow wrinkled. "Wizr?"

"That's right, you don't know of it. I suppose they don't play Wizr in that other world. You have Fallon's pack. Open it and draw out the chest."

She watched as her father did just that. Fishing through the pack again, she found the key that would open it.

When she unlocked it and lifted the lid, the first thing she saw was the note Fallon said he had left there. Her eyes fixed on it, pricking with heat. Owen gently withdrew it, staring at the paper. But her name was on the folded sheet, written by Fallon's own hand. Owen gave it to her and she held it in her lap a moment, not wanting to read it yet, unsure whether her heart could bear it.

"This is a game?" Owen asked, staring down at the confusion of pieces.

Trynne also looked at the board. Fear bloomed in her chest.

The game was nearly over.

♦　♦　♦

There was a ley line from the grove to the palace in Ploemeur. Trynne took her father there after they sipped from the silver dish, which they'd replenished at the waterfall, the water restoring their magic. She was invigorated and more determined than ever to defeat Morwenna. If only her father had his full memory going into this fight . . . She would hull the tree in an instant. But it would take time, and she sensed from the Fountain that she had little remaining. So the tree would have to face its executioners later.

Though she was tempted to bring them straight to Kingfountain, they needed answers first. Answers that would be better found in Ploemeur. When she and her father appeared in the fountain, Owen looked bewildered by the drastic change of location. It was obvious he felt like a stranger in the palace where she had grown up. The pieces on the board had revealed much, but it was still cryptic. Drew was the black king. Morwenna the black Wizr. Both were at Kingfountain. The white king, her husband, Gahalatine, was also at Kingfountain. The white queen, Genny, was isolated in the North. She saw herself and her father by themselves in the western portion of the board—two white knights. The army of pawns was no more. What had happened to Captain Staeli? His piece was no longer on the board.

As they walked down the palace corridor in their filthy, battle-stained clothes, they were met with surprise by some of the servants, who were clearly thunderstruck to see them.

"Lady Trynne! Lord Owen!"

Within moments, the palace was in an uproar. Servants crowded into the corridor, anxious to see Trynne—and especially Owen.

Trynne asked one of her mother's faithful servants to summon Thierry. The woman shook her head and said, "But my lady, Duke Ramey is warden of Brythonica now and commands a garrison of soldiers here from his duchy. Thierry is with him at the moment. Shall we keep your presence a secret? They have orders to arrest you."

"I will not hide from him," Trynne said. She had no doubt Morwenna already knew they were back. "Where are they?"

"In the audience hall."

Trynne nodded and then guided her father there. Word of their arrival was still rushing through the palace. The relief her people felt was evident—she saw it in every smile, in every bow of reverence. They had despaired that no one from her mother's line was present to protect them.

When they reached the audience hall, the doors were held open for them. Trynne and her father strode through them, and she couldn't help but think of the many events that had played out in this very room. Her father's disastrous proposal to her mother. Her confrontation with Rucrius and his Wizrs before she summoned the flood.

Duke Ramey was in conversation with Thierry when they walked inside, and his eyes nearly leaped out of his head when he saw her father.

"L-L-Lord Owen!" he said in astonishment, jaw dropping.

Thierry gazed up toward the ceiling, mouthing unsaid words of praise. He rushed to Trynne with near panic. "My lady, my lady!" He dropped to his knees before her.

"My lord duke," Trynne said, standing before Ramey. "My father has returned."

"I see him standing before me," the duke said, shaking his head. "But my eyes have been deceived much of late. Everything has changed. It feels like winter although it is spring, especially at the palace. I have orders from the king himself to arrest you, Tryneowy. To arrest you for treason." He held up his hands and shrugged. "All that I am, all that I have, my seat at the Ring Table, I owe to this man," he said, gesturing to her father. "I'll admit that I was unprepared for this possibility. No one thought you'd return."

Trynne saw the look of helplessness on his face. He was a good man. A dutiful one. She saw the conflict raging inside of him.

"Why would you think that?" she said. "This is my home. These are my people."

"I know, but things have been topsy-turvy. The king hardly acts like his old self. His grief at losing the baby has changed him. The queen is not herself either. Everyone said that you ran off with Fallon after your army lost, that you abrogated your duties, that you were a traitor. Some Espion claimed they saw the two of you in Legault. Some in Genevar. The rumors . . ." He shook his head.

Trynne looked at him sternly. "Where are Captain Staeli and Gahalatine?"

Duke Ramey sighed. "The Assizes are being held in Kingfountain as we speak. Staeli is being tried for treason. If he's not over the falls already, he will be shortly. Gahalatine is also imprisoned at the palace. The North is under revolt, Brugia too, and the king will subdue them next, now that he's overrun Westmarch and Brythonica. I was stationed here because the king trusts me, if barely. He's changed so much, Trynne. They all have. It's like what happened before. Under Severn. But what can I do? What can I do but obey the king's order?"

Trynne closed her eyes, squeezing her hands into fists. She glanced at her father, watching as he looked around the room with utter confusion. He had no understanding of the politics here. He could not help her devise a solution to the horrible situation that Morwenna had sprung on them. *She* had to do it. She had to *think* like her father.

Thierry stood up before her, his face agitated. "Lady Trynne, I must speak with you."

Things were about to get worse. She could tell just by the look in his eyes.

"What happened, Thierry?" she asked him softly.

His brows stitched together. "My lady, before Staeli was defeated, the guards who patrol the beach say they saw someone walking alone there. The tide was out. They thought . . . they thought it was you. They called for me, and when I arrived, there were footprints in the sand. Someone *had* been walking the beach. The trail led to the caves along the shore." He started to tremble. "My lady," he whispered hoarsely, "was that you? My heart tells me it wasn't. That it couldn't be. It must have been Lady Morwenna in disguise."

♦ ♦ ♦

People are superstitious. They always fear what they do not understand. They believe in traditions handed down to them by dead ancestors. They do not question how those traditions were formed. They toss coins into water and think they are transmuted into prayers.

I've gathered pretenders impersonating some of the rulers of Occitania, Legault, and Atabyrion to Kingfountain to witness Staeli's execution in the river. The rest will learn firsthand that the Fountain was displeased with Tryneowy's treachery when Brythonica is at last smothered by the Deep Fathoms. I made sure Duke Ramey was assigned there so he'd be lost. He was always too loyal to Owen Kiskaddon. All the rulers will obey or risk their domains drowning as well.

Morwenna Argentine

♦ ♦ ♦

CHAPTER TWENTY-EIGHT

Our Lady

The Leerings in the sea caves had been destroyed. All of them. The faces carved into the stone beneath the dripping moss had been shattered. The surf hammering against the rocks outside the caves announced the return of the tide. If Trynne did not leave soon, she would be drowned. She was sick inside, haunted by the realization of what Morwenna had done.

The defenses of Brythonica were shattered. Nothing protected the border of the duchy from the sea. The promise she had made to her mother had been broken. She trembled, quavering at the thought of what was going to happen.

Kneeling in the sand, she touched her face, feeling the spray from the ocean intruding. The water lapped closer and closer to where she knelt in the darkness. She wanted to sob, to surrender to her misery, but there was still fight left in her. In her mind, she could see the beautiful face of Morwenna Argentine taunting her. This was the poisoner's revenge against Owen, against Trynne's entire family. This was what would have become of Ankarette had she allowed the need for revenge to break her loyalty to the queen whose family she secretly served.

Morwenna was wreaking havoc on the politics of Kingfountain and Chandigarl. It was not just Trynne's kingdom that was threatened with destruction. Her husband's realm was in trouble as well. She had seen the bottomless depth of hatred and revenge in Rucrius's eyes during his imprisonment in her dungeon. She had seen that same look from Dieyre and Hillel. There was no slaking such a thirst. It brought nothing but curses. The only thing that could ultimately quench its fire was utter destruction.

Trynne would not allow it to happen, not while she still drew breath. When she set aside her own feelings, she could almost pity Morwenna. She was an angry woman who had let herself be twisted to darkness. But despite that pity, Trynne could not allow her to succeed. There was a way to destroy someone who was Fountain-blessed. But before that could happen, Morwenna needed to exhaust her power.

Rising from the sand, Trynne made her way back to the sharp light of the outdoors. The next wave drenched her boots as she ducked beneath the overhang. She found her father where she had left him, crouched on the beach of sea glass. He was studying the small pebbles of polished glass, gazing at the intricate shapes and variety of color. When she emerged, he straightened, hefting some of the pebbles in his hand.

"Where did these come from?" he asked her with curiosity. This beach had always been a favorite place for him and her mother. Now all that history had been stripped away. It saddened her, but if she succeeded in stopping Morwenna, there would be time to recover his memories. She was drawn back to Kingfountain. The sense of urgency was overwhelming.

"Mother told me that they are the remains of an ancient kingdom that was buried by the Deep Fathoms," she replied. "The glass from thousands of shattered windows has been rubbed along the coast of Brythonica for centuries. Down there," she said, gesturing toward the water that was hissing and rolling back to the sea, "are the remains of ancient castles and homes. The land between Brythonica and

Westmarch—your duchy—was called Leoneyis and is no more. All that land's people were drowned. Only a few survived to bear witness to the destruction. Those who had gathered to safety at the sanctuary of Our Lady at St. Penryn."

As she said the words, her mind was pierced with a spike of anguish—a horrifying premonition of what was to come. Morwenna had destroyed the borders, so there would be no protection from the flood she planned to invoke. When it happened, all the rest of the duchies would gibber in terror, afraid that they would be next. She saw the darkness that was about to overrun the land. She could not stop the floods from taking Brythonica. So she had to stop Morwenna before she could unleash them.

"We must go, Father," she said, shaking her head to try to dispel the terrible vision.

"To Kingfountain?" he asked her solemnly.

"Yes, to the sanctuary of Our Lady. Duke Ramey said the Assizes would render judgment today. This is the day Morwenna plans to destroy us. We have to stop her."

He nodded to her. "I am ready."

Trynne swallowed and looked at him fiercely. "Her magic cannot hurt you, Papa. It cannot affect those who are standing close to you either. We must get to the king quickly. We saw the Wizr board. They are at Kingfountain now. I can only pray we are not too late."

◆　◆　◆

The ley lines from Ploemeur went in all directions. It was one of the major hubs on the map that her mother guarded. But she knew if she appeared anywhere in the castle, the Espion would be waiting for them. So Trynne chose the sanctuary of Our Lady. Thousands would gather to see a royal execution. Thousands would watch as a boat with its victim nestled within the hull was launched from the royal pier and handed over to the water for justice. With any luck, they would appear as a couple of unknowns in the crowd. She did not use magic to conceal them for fear of alerting Morwenna too soon.

Trynne and her father appeared in one of the fountains on the grounds of the sanctuary, the breath misting from their mouths. Just as she'd suspected, there were thick crowds. Most were bundled in cloaks and hoods, for the weather had turned severely cold. The entire sanctuary island was filled to the brim, but they were all facing the huge castle on the hill across the river. People were speaking in urgent tones, gossiping about the results from the Assizes.

Trynne and Owen joined the crowd and she led him through the throng, heading toward the area behind the sanctuary where she knew some docks had been constructed. It was not a commonly known place.

"He's about to go into the river," someone said. "The king's guard is carrying the canoe!"

"Shhh! Quiet!"

Trynne and Owen walked hurriedly and her heart hammered in her chest.

"Kill the king's traitor!" someone shouted. "Drown Staeli in the depths!"

Trynne saw a break in the crowd and tugged her father toward the secluded part of the grounds. The people were all gathering toward the area with the best view, even small children pressing in to try to get a look. Some were on their parents' shoulders, and she could see many of them pointing toward the royal docks.

Trynne felt the panic of the moment, the worry that they were too late to prevent it. Glancing backward, she saw several men following them, motioning to each other with Espion hand signs. They'd already been spotted.

"They will truly throw him into the river?" Owen asked in confusion.

"It's the custom here," she answered, her voice throbbing with worry. "It almost happened to your parents, but you prevented it."

"We're going to the docks, over there?"

"Yes, but we're being followed—" she said, glancing back again. The men had started to jog toward them. "Run!" she shouted, gripping her father's hand.

The two of them rushed forward, assailed by the sound of rumbling boots coming up behind them. Trynne reached the stairs to the docks and they both hurried down. Their pursuers could still be heard in the distance, but suddenly the crowd went quiet, the people collectively holding their breath.

Trynne watched in helplessness as the knights upriver across the turbulent rush marched the canoe to the river's edge, carrying it on long poles. She could only watch as the knights raised one end higher and sent the canoe into the waters of the river at an angle. A body was lashed inside and her heart clenched with pain at the sight. Captain Staeli, her mentor. Her protector. Her friend.

The canoe bobbed to the surface and was yanked toward the falls, caught in the terrible grip of the river. She and her father raced down the length of the pier as the boat rushed toward them with increasing speed. There would be a host of men and women watching from the bridge straddling the mighty waterfall, which could be heard rumbling so near. They were too late! Too late!

Trynne saw the canoe speeding up as it came down the river toward the sanctuary. It would pass by the island where the crowds had gathered to watch. Drew stood at the royal docks, watching it happen. The woman at his side, clutching his arm, looked like Genny. But it wasn't. There were others milling around.

She and Owen reached the end of the pier.

"Captain!" she shouted as loud as she could, hoping he would hear her voice. Praying he would recognize it. Grief swelled inside her. She could see his beard now, could see him fidgeting in the canoe, wrestling against the ropes.

Their pursuers drew up behind them, she could tell from the sound of their bootfalls, but she didn't care. She was going to watch until the end. It was the least she could do for him.

"Lady Trynne!"

She recognized that voice.

Whirling around, she saw that Lord Amrein was one of the men running after her. He wasn't dressed in court finery, but garbed as a beggar, no chain of office around his neck. The Espion master was looking at her with relief—and then his eyes shifted to her father standing there beside her.

"You found him!" Kevan said with hope in his eyes.

And then Trynne heard the splash from behind her as another body went into the river.

Turning around in horror, she found herself alone at the end of the dock. Her father had jumped into the rush.

That was when the miracle happened.

There was a collective gasp as the waters of the river burst apart. They seemed to spread away from Owen like a scythe cutting through stalks of wheat. Her father wasn't floundering to swim, he was at the bottom of the river, on dry ground, and the river was parting before him as he moved.

The ring!

She'd forgotten about its power. She hadn't told him about it either. The Espion who thronged her stared at the display of the Fountain's power with wide eyes and open mouths.

"Sweet Lady!" one of them muttered reverently.

Trynne's heart swelled with relief. The gap in the river widened until it stretched from the island all the way to the palace. The river roared like a frantic beast, but the waters could not pass the breach.

Trynne leaped down into the void, landing on the smooth river stone that was temporarily dry. She saw her father rushing ahead, and her breath caught in her chest when the canoe wedged into the gap, unable to move forward. The rush of the river was deafening, but Trynne grinned at the sight of her father lifting Staeli from the canoe and hoisting him over his shoulder. She reached him as he started crossing the river toward the palace. In the chasm of the river, she couldn't see ahead, could only hear the frightening noise of the crushing waters straining the barrier, but she kept her eyes focused on the dry ground beneath them. Her father's face was a grimace of pain. He looked to be in agony.

"What's wrong?" she shouted to him.

"The ring is burning me," he grunted, but his eyes were fixed ahead. Staeli craned his neck until he saw her. His relieved smile was the most welcome sight she'd seen since her return.

"That was a little too close for comfort, lass," he told her with naked relief.

She touched her father's shoulder and invoked a word of power for healing, suffusing him with her magic.

Trynne felt a jolt of power coming from the other shore. It hammered against the river, trying to dispel the ring's power. Trynne recognized the magic and she feared for a moment that the waters would come crashing down on them. That they'd all go over the waterfall together. But the ring's power superseded Morwenna's magic. It could not be unmade so easily.

With each step, they drew closer to the opposite side. Trynne felt Morwenna's presence seething through the tumultuous waters. She saw the royal docks ahead, and Drew was standing there, gaping at them in surprise. There was Genny as well, her face full of wrath and hatred. The weight of Staeli's body was obviously a burden to Owen, but he lumbered forward.

"It's him! It's Lord Owen!"

244

They were just close enough to hear the words over the noise of the swollen river. The chasm of water defending them swelled like a majestic fountain, bubbling, rising higher and higher into the air.

"Use the poles. Fetch them out!" Drew shouted, motioning for his soldiers to drop their staves down to them.

Owen set Staeli down by the blackened posts of the pier, then hunched forward, breathing hard, hands on his knees.

Trynne drew her sword and sliced through the captain's bonds, freeing him. "I *told* you I'd come back," she said in his ear.

"Aye, lass. And I couldn't be more grateful."

The poles were lowered to them and the three of them climbed up to the pier, where they faced a host of the court of Kingfountain. There was Iago and Evie, the Queen Dowager of Occitania, Elyse, and many others Trynne recognized, but not Elwis. However, Trynne's attention was drawn to Drew. She saw the conflict raging inside him. His gaze went from her to Owen and back again.

As her father straightened, the towering waters suddenly came crashing down in a heave that made everyone cry out in fear. The canoe, which had been left behind, was splintered and broken in half, and the pieces hurtled violently toward the edge of the falls.

Trynne faced her king, sword in hand. He was gripping the pommel of Firebos, but she saw that it wasn't his true sword. She could sense the illusion magic around it. The sword was gone, replaced by a deception.

Yet another thing Morwenna had stolen.

"What is the meaning of this?" Drew said, his voice quavering. "Lord Owen, is it truly you?"

"This *is* my father," Trynne said, stepping forward, her eyes locking with Morwenna's.

"It's over, Morwenna."

"That is Genevieve," Drew said with alarm. But there was hesitation in his voice—a sense of growing uncertainty.

"No, Your Highness," Trynne said, shaking her head. "It is not. *Apokaluptis*," she breathed out in a low, firm voice, invoking the word of power used to unmask a disguise, to reveal the true nature of something hidden. She felt the pulse of Fountain magic in her mind, as if a large boulder had been catapulted into a lake. The ripples shot out from her in all directions.

Morwenna Argentine was suddenly standing there, to the sight and wonderment of all. Even the sword's illusion had been stripped away. And so had the disguises of many of the nobles of Kingfountain. The pair who had looked like Iago and Evie were revealed as strangers, imposters. The masks had all crumbled, and as Drew turned around in baffled amazement, he stared at his sister with a look of sudden revulsion and terror. He saw he was surrounded by strangers, and the realization of it crashed upon him like the walls of water had just crashed into the river.

"I arrest you by the name of Morwenna Argentine," Trynne said, striding forward, putting herself between the poisoner and the king.

"If you think I'll be dragged to Helvellyn willingly," Morwenna shot back angrily, "you're a fool."

"I'm not a fool," Trynne answered. It was time for a reckoning between the two of them. Trynne steeled herself for the fight.

But Morwenna reached behind her back, and Trynne caught only a glimpse of the Tay al-Ard before the poisoner vanished.

CHAPTER TWENTY-NINE

Ruin

With a Tay al-Ard, Morwenna Argentine could go anywhere in the world. But there was one place where she could do Trynne the most harm. Brythonica. Her every instinct screamed that the poisoner had gone there to flood the entire duchy, drowning it under the Deep Fathoms.

And Trynne carried in her pack the tool that could help her defeat Morwenna.

She dropped to her knee before the king. "My lord, I am still your servant. I knew of Morwenna's deception before I left to free my father. She imprisoned Genny and poisoned your child. I took Kate to save her, and it was Fallon who knew the cure. He also stole the Wizr board from Morwenna. Please, my lord, if you'll look at the pieces, you will see that I am telling the truth."

Drew knelt before her, his eyes crinkled with worry and hope. He put his hand on her shoulder. "You've saved my life again, my Painted Knight. My champion. My mind is in agony over what I almost did. How my sister deceived me. I'm nearly too ashamed to speak. She pretended to be my wife. If we had . . . then history would have repeated . . , I would have been slain by my . . ."

He shuddered at the thoughts colliding in his mind. Squeezing his fist, he pressed it against his mouth, shaking his head in horror. "You saved me. You saved me from the worst possible fate."

Trynne's relief was superseded by the urgency of her task. "My lord, the Wizr board."

"Yes, yes—pull it out."

Trynne undid the straps while Kevan ordered the king's guard to surround the imposters. "Take them to the dungeon and hold them there for now. Fetch Lord Gahalatine from Holistern Tower and bring him here."

Trynne's head turned up sharply at the orders.

"I could not order his death, even for treason," the king said softly. "Not when so many lives were at stake. I would not have so many deaths on my shoulders. He was true to you, Trynne. He and Captain Staeli did their best to stop me."

The king turned his gaze to the grizzled captain. "You, sir, have been faithful to the last. I'll make a duke out of you, ere this is over. You have my word."

Trynne hefted the chest by the handle and pulled it out. Putting the key into the lock, she twisted it and then raised the lid.

The colors had changed once again. She saw Drew as the white king, surrounded by two knights—her and her father. Morwenna, the black Wizr, was across the board at Ploemeur. Trynne's heart sank even though the sun had begun to penetrate the cold.

"My lord, I *must* go!" Trynne implored. "She has already ruined the defenses of Brythonica. If she summons the waters, my people will drown!"

Drew stared at the board in wonderment. She could tell he didn't understand how it had been preserved from Rucrius's attack. But it was not a time for questions. He lifted his hand and set it on the piece on the board that represented her. She felt the grinding sensation, the rumble of trembling stone beneath her.

The king hesitated, his fingers poised to move the piece.

"What if I lose you?" he said, gazing at her with fearful concern. "The Wizr is the most powerful piece."

"Send me," Trynne begged him.

The king glanced up at Owen. Trynne didn't look to see her father's reaction. She stared at the king, willing him to move her piece.

And he did.

◆ ◆ ◆

The skies over Ploemeur roiled with seething black clouds. A violent sea storm was arriving, and the wind howled like unleashed demons. Trynne appeared on the beach in the midst of the tempest. The gale whipped her loose hair around her face, and she staggered a bit on the sandy ground, shielding her eyes from the gusts.

The beach had transformed.

All her life, she had walked along this beach, at high tide and low tide, and yet she'd never seen it like this. The sea had receded for nearly a mile, exposing rocks and boulders she had never seen before. There were glistening tide pools, radiant with the colors of vibrant life. But some of the boulders that had been revealed were clearly shaped by men—the bony fragments of castles that had once existed in might and triumph before being swallowed by the depths. Almost as far as she could see, there were mounds and squares and fallen arches covered with seaweed. These were the rotting bones of Leoneyis. She stared at them in awe, trying to discern the edge of the sea.

Trynne heard shouting, and turned toward the source. In the midst of the sloping wet sand, she saw two figures. Fountain magic radiated from both of them. One was Myrddin with his crooked staff. The other, Morwenna.

"Don't you see, I don't care if we all drown!" the poisoner was shouting. "Not even you can withstand the power of the sea, old man!"

Trynne gazed in horror as the biggest wave she'd ever seen came at the bay like a devouring monster, all thrashing foam and froth and weight. When Rucrius had turned the river outside Kingfountain back, it was nothing compared to this. There were cries of fear from throughout Ploemeur as the people began fleeing to higher ground.

"*Aspis!*" the Wizr Myrddin commanded, slamming his staff into the sand.

Trynne stared at the coming flood with terror. No shield could hold back the entire ocean. It had taken multiple Leerings to fence it in. Dread sickened her.

"You won't stop it!" Morwenna taunted.

Trynne shuddered as the wave engulfed the stone ribs and skeletons of Leoneyis. As soon as the waters struck the beach, Trynne shut her eyes, unable to watch the devastation. Her heart hurt for the people she had promised to protect. It was better to die with them, even though she had the power to flee. Better to share their fate than live through the guilt of surviving it.

The clang of Fountain magic buffeted the beach and knocked Trynne to her knees. She opened her eyes, confused, and watched as the wave was shoved back, smashed against an invisible wall that protected the beach. It was as if a huge glass orb had been put over the beach. The waters of the ocean, tangled with huge skeins of seaweed, loomed far over Trynne's head, high in the sky. But a dome of power protected the city, and the surf, despite its fury, could not claw over the rounded top. The torrent, losing its power, slid down and crashed back into the sea.

Morwenna's eyes blazed with fury.

"No! You will not stop my revenge!"

"I will stop it as long as I must," Myrddin answered. She felt his magic receding from such a display. His shoulders hunched and sweat dripped down his cheeks. His stores of magic were incredible, but even he had his limits.

Trynne marched down the beach to join him.

"Hello, little sister," he said coyly. "Your *pethet* friend warned that you may need some help."

Smiling in spite of herself, she nearly gave him a hug. "Thank you, Myrddin. Thank you for coming back."

"Tsk, it was the Fountain that sent me. The need was greater *here* this time. It does not abandon the faithful." He gave her a pointed look, and she felt her insides quiver with joy.

"So both of you will try to stop me?" Morwenna scoffed. "You have no idea the power I can summon. The land exists only because the sea permits it! The Deep Fathoms have always been here, but they were bound and tethered. Restrained. I will break every bond. Water is the source of life. And of death. I will drown the world. You cannot stop me!"

Myrddin's eyes squinted as he gazed at Morwenna. "I cannot defeat her," he said in a low voice to Trynne. "Our power is equal. She knows this. I can counter what she does, but only until I run out of strength."

"What must I do?" Trynne asked.

"You are an Oath Maiden. Do what your memories tell you."

Morwenna hooked her fingers and swirled her arms, a sick grin on her face. Suddenly, the huge ropes of seaweed that littered the beach inside the shield rose and flew at Trynne and Myrddin. While Trynne immediately drew her swords and began slicing the tangled seaweed as it tried to enwrap and tangle her, Myrddin twirled his staff, drawing the water out of the skeins so they dropped limply to the beach. Morwenna's face flashed with fury again. Her stores were dropping too, but Trynne sensed the Wizr was right—they were evenly matched.

One of the ropes of seaweed wrapped around Trynne's leg to yank her down, but she felt the magic die and the rope go limp. It trembled and throbbed, the magic pulsing inside its orange-brown layers. It was trying to obey Morwenna and entangle Trynne. Yet it could not.

And she understood why. Morwenna's deceptions could not affect her. Neither could her power.

The water had receded again, but it was drawing up its strength for another rush. Trynne felt snapping sensations under her skin, the breaking of ley lines. *The Hidden Vulgate*'s dark magic had an even larger scope than she'd feared. Myrddin's face twisted into a scowl.

"You'll not escape death," Morwenna said. "We will all die in this place. You broke my Tay al-Ard, and I will break your staff! None of us shall flee. We will be buried beneath a mountain of water. I summon it!"

The sea was swelling with her every word.

"Not yet, lass," Myrddin said, shaking his head. Trynne sensed his magic building up to defend them. She sensed his knees paining him, his shoulder throbbing.

Suddenly Morwenna staggered backward and the wave collapsed, losing its energy too soon. Sweat dripped from Myrddin's nose.

"I can't hold her forever, sister," he said coaxingly to Trynne. "It is *you* who must defeat her. Not I."

"I know your weakness, old man!" Morwenna scoffed. "I know why you keep to the shadows. I've read *The Hidden Vulgate*. I read how Nimuë enslaved you with a kystrel. How she tricked you into that cave and sealed it with the Fault Staff. Men have ever yielded to desire above all else. You're afraid of me, *Maderos*. You've always been afraid of how I can make you feel."

Trynne felt power behind her words, power that was unseen, yet just as dangerous and deadly as the storms Morwenna was summoning.

"I have the kystrel's taint," Morwenna purred. "Don't you wish to see it?"

Trynne felt Myrddin's shield waver. He closed his eyes, gripping his crooked staff with both hands, pressing it into the sand deeply, as if he were driving it into the heart of the earth. His face was dripping with sweat, but his cheeks were calm. His shoulders drooped.

"Leave him alone," Trynne said, standing in front of Myrddin.

"Everyone will suffer," the poisoner snarled. "You have always been so faithful. Look what it has gotten you. Look what it has done for your people. The Fountain is not alive. It is not benevolent. It is cruel and murderous and violent! It would drown a million people to spite a handful. We are right to fear it."

Trynne continued walking forward, closing the gap between her and the poisoner. "You speak lies, Morwenna. You may have grown to believe them, but they are still lies."

"Are they?" Morwenna challenged. "Why would the Fountain have let me destroy the Forbidden Court? I was the one who summoned the storm. I destroyed half the city. And the Fountain *let* me! It did not intercede. The East Kingdoms will never be grand again. Even if you could kill me, and I don't think you have the heart to do it, they will all die anyway. I kissed Gahalatine, Trynne. Pretending to be you, I kissed him. My kiss is deadly."

The words stabbed into Trynne, especially since she sensed they were true.

"There is no cure for its poison," Morwenna continued. "And when he dies, the East Kingdoms die with him. The Fountain let me do this! It obeys whoever *forces* it to obey. It is a matter of will. And *my* will is stronger than yours. Than both of yours combined!"

Trynne saw the sea beginning to collect again, preparing for another onslaught. Myrddin's shield was buckling. She reached out with her magic as she approached the poisoner. Morwenna's weakness was the same as any Wizr's. She was strong and hardened by training. She was more than a match for Trynne. But her weakness was her neck. If she could not breathe, her powers would fail her. Could Trynne cut off her head as she had done to Rucrius? She wanted to kill her out of vengeance. But she had sworn an oath never to do that. She listened for permission from the Fountain.

All was silent in her mind.

She was supposed to capture Morwenna, then. Bring her to justice at Kingfountain.

Trynne dropped her twin swords. The two blades embedded in the sand. She kept walking down the slope of packed sand, weaponless. The swords would only kill Morwenna. There had to be another way.

Morwenna's lip curled into a sneer. She drew one of her daggers. Wet poison glistened on the blade.

CHAPTER THIRTY

Drowning

Morwenna's eyes flashed and a pulse of magic seared at Trynne. It had no effect. Then sand exploded from the shore, sending up a blinding haze of stinging pebbles and grit that whirled around in a vortex. Trynne walked through it, shielding her eyes. She could no longer see Morwenna, but she could still sense her. The poisoner was retreating deeper into the ruins of Leoneyis.

Trynne trudged forward, sensing the barnacle-encrusted pillars that rose around her, the bones of the ancient kingdom. The wind died down, giving her relief from the pelting sand. She couldn't see Morwenna anymore, but there was no mistaking where she was concealing herself—she'd hidden behind some of the broken fragments of rock. Trynne saw the tide still stretching out, building up for another colossal charge. She had to hurry, had to defeat Morwenna quickly enough to stop the surge. Glancing back, she saw Myrddin on his knees, still gripping the gnarled staff in his hands, head bent low. But she also saw others flocking to the beach, the citizens of Ploemeur coming out to see what was going on. She wanted to scream at them to flee, to get to higher ground. They were arriving in droves.

"I've waited for this," Morwenna taunted, her voice ghosting behind the rocks. "For the chance to face the Painted Knight myself." Despite all the seaweed and encrustations, Trynne could see the carved face on the rock—as ancient and decayed as the ruins itself.

"I do not seek revenge against you, Morwenna," Trynne said. "I arrest you by command of the king. Your brother, whom you betrayed."

"My brother," the poisoner laughed. "The son of a coward. The heir of a withered dynasty. He doesn't deserve to wear the tunic of the Sun and Rose. He didn't *earn* it, as my father did. You should know all about betrayal. Your father betrayed mine."

"My father served the Fountain. And *your* father served the true king. He gave his life to defend Kingfountain." Morwenna continued to retreat deeper into the hulking stones. Beautifully colored starfish clung to many of the ruined buildings, and vagrant strands of kelp draped across the stones. It was getting colder, darker, as she followed Morwenna deeper into the ruins.

"Your father tricked mine through the help of a poisoner. Isn't it fitting that you've been duped by one as well? Ankarette was afraid of my father, you know. She was afraid to face him."

"I'm not afraid of you," Trynne said.

"We're both going to die in this place. I will not come with you to stand before my brother. To be dragged to an icy mountain. Chandigarl will perish by flood. And so will Brythonica. No one will remember your name or who you were named after. Is it any wonder that those who love you forget you? You've always been forgettable. Do you finally see how insignificant you are? It's a pity your mother isn't here to see your next failure."

Morwenna was trying to goad her, to make her give in to her anger. Her desire for revenge. Trynne kept her emotions bottled up, sensing for weakness, waiting to be attacked so that she could use her powers to their best advantage.

"It's a pity Fallon isn't here to witness *your* failure," Trynne said with a hard edge. "How it must gall you that he chose me, disfigured and short, over you. It tortured you so much that you had to steal his clothes just so you could pretend he was yours."

Morwenna stepped out from around a boulder, emerging behind Trynne. She whirled to face the poisoner, who was gripping her dagger so hard her knuckles were bone white. The curl of her lip was almost that of an animal about to attack.

"He only pitied you," Morwenna said darkly.

"He loved me," Trynne shot back, her heart racing in her chest. "He sacrificed himself so that my father could return to Kingfountain. He outsmarted you. He saw through all your tricks."

"And you've condemned him to die in that forsaken land with all its forsaken thrones," Morwenna spat. "That alone would give me reason enough to hate you. At least we die together. Like sisters. *Invocamorayim!*"

Trynne had never heard that word of power before. But she sensed its potency. It felt as if Morwenna had unleashed the entire ocean instead of just a few waves. The binding was loosened and an avalanche of water was let go. It was a command to flood the earth, to break loose all boundaries.

Dagger in hand, Morwenna rushed Trynne, slashing down with the poisoned blade. Trynne caught the poisoner's forearm with her own, punching her other fist into Morwenna's sternum. She couldn't think, only act, as Morwenna's boot came spinning up at her brow, forcing her to duck. They traded blows, each one connecting, each one causing the other pain.

A searing rip of pain tore Trynne's arm. She saw her own blood on Morwenna's dagger, saw the delight of victory on the poisoner's face. Morwenna's boot connected with Trynne's stomach, knocking her down, but she rolled backward and landed on her feet again. Pain bloomed down her arm, as if a torch had been pressed to the wound. Her bone felt as if it were on fire.

Morwenna kicked at her again, but Trynne dodged the blow and the boot hit a stone instead. Wincing, Morwenna grabbed Trynne's arm with her hand. The dagger followed, coming right for her throat.

She caught the blow, gripping Morwenna's wrist, and then flipped her down on the sand. She followed through, hoping to slam her nose, but the poisoner spun in the wet sand and kicked Trynne back against the rocks. The waves were rushing toward them now, moving like white storm clouds.

Trynne had to break the spell, had to smother Morwenna's power. With her arm throbbing from the poison's fire, she invoked her power of speed and rushed up to Morwenna. It felt as if time had slowed down to a crawl. She saw the glitter of sunlight off the white crests of water. Saw the waves engulfing the rocks slowly, crashing into them at a turtle's pace. Trynne kneed Morwenna in the stomach, bending her double, and then wrapped her good arm around her neck in a vice and clasped her hand around her wrist to secure the lock. The chokehold would rob Morwenna of air in seconds.

She felt a pinprick of pain on her forearm and sensed the ring on Morwenna's hand, its secret needle exposed. The poison was fast acting and Trynne's arm went numb. Still, she gripped Morwenna's neck, arching her backward. The dagger stabbed Trynne's leg once, twice. She endured it, feeling the ribbons of blood running down her leg. Then her leg was on fire with pain as well.

Her grip on Morwenna's neck tightened. She'd cut off her air completely. Morwenna thrashed, unable to breathe, her consciousness fluttering. A hand, the nails gritty with sand, clawed at Trynne's face. She felt another stab of the needle ring on her slack cheek.

Then the waters hit them. Trynne and Morwenna crashed against the rocks, both upended by the force of the raging surf. It ripped the poisoner out of Trynne's arms and sent her tumbling end over end.

Her mouth was full of the horrid taste of saltwater and she choked. There was no up, no down. Her head struck against stone and all went black.

Her last thought as she struggled to breathe was the realization she was drowning.

♦ ♦ ♦

The first noise Trynne discerned was the sound of a seagull. Her clothes were drenched and she felt the sucking of the sand as a gentle wave lapped across her, lifting her slightly and then settling her back down. The water was so cool against the fire burning on her leg. She couldn't move, although she tried. Her entire body was paralyzed. The webbed feet of the seagull pattered up to her and she thought drowsily that it might start pecking her hair.

"I found her!"

The voice was garbled through the seawater still in her ears. She heard the slapping noise of boots against the wet sand and then suddenly two sets of arms were pulling her away from the clutch of the sea. Her head drooped low, her hair thick with sand. She felt the particles everywhere, but she couldn't budge. The poison was doing what the water could not. Killing her. She felt every heartbeat, for each one was shuddering in her chest as her heart gave out. Was she even breathing? *Could* she breathe?

"It's Lady Trynne! We found her!"

She wanted to speak, but could not so much as grunt. She'd never felt so exhausted, so drained. Her Fountain magic was empty, completely empty.

"Bring her here. Come now, over here." It was Myrddin's voice.

"She's not breathing," someone said.

"Look at all the blood. Is she even alive?"

"Of course she's alive," Myrddin crooned. "Have you ever heard of a Fountain-blessed drowning, eh? Don't be a *pethet*, of course she's alive. Bring her here."

Her heart was beating painfully. The pain in her arm and her leg was so intense she wanted to cry out.

"There, there, little sister. All will be well. All is well. Lay her down."

She saw the sun in the sky. She tried to blink but could not. The worried faces of several of her people passed before her gaze.

"She's dead," one of them whimpered.

"She's not dead," Myrddin said. "She's only asleep." Then he bent over her and she saw his face, saw the gentleness in his look, the admiration. He gazed down at her tenderly. The sun was just beyond his thick dark hair.

Her heart stopped. She felt herself moving toward the light beyond Myrddin, but a single word stopped her flight.

"Nesh-ama."

All the pain, all the weariness vanished. She felt tingling all over her body. The burning fire from her wounds vanished, replaced by tender skin. She took in a breath of air and it tasted delicious. The smells of eucalyptus, of seafoam, of oysters filled her senses. Trynne stared up at Myrddin, saw him leaning back from her with a smile on his face.

"There, lass," he whispered. "You'll be mending now."

She saw him stuff some shriveled green moss into a pouch at his waist.

The voices whispered with reverence around her. "She's alive!" "She's alive!" "Tell Thierry. Quickly!"

Somehow they had been saved. Her people had not been drowned after all.

Myrddin grasped his crooked staff and winced as he tried to rise. He was clearly weak, the battle must have drained him considerably, but he still managed to make it to his feet. Gripping his staff, he reached down and caught her hand and helped pull her to her feet.

She was on the beach of sea glass. It had been restored to its previous state—the bones of Leoneyis hidden again beneath the waters—and the very familiarity made her gasp with relief.

"I thought . . . I thought the flood," she managed. It still felt new and difficult to breathe again.

Myrddin cocked his head and looked at her curiously. "You thought what, little sister?" She could almost feel him reading her mind, plucking out her thoughts like one would harvest ripe berries. "That the Fountain would abandon the people who were always faithful to it? Look around you, lass. The beach is crowded. Yet the people follow the covenant, only removing one chest a year. They honor the Fountain not just with their hands, but with their hearts." He tapped his chest with a cluster of fingers. "And so the Fountain honors them. It honors *you*."

"But the Leerings," Trynne said, confused. "They were all destroyed."

He gave her a knowing smile. "And who do you think, lass, who do you think put those Leerings there in the first place? Who put them there before he was trapped in a stone cave and banished to another world?" He wagged his bushy eyebrows at her. "This beach is sacred because it is a reminder of what happens when a people forsakes the Fountain. It will now be a reminder that the Fountain can be a great protector as well. Look," he said, chuffing, shaking his head. "So meek. I don't see that in every world. They want to see you, little sister. They know that *you* saved them."

"But I didn't," Trynne said, shaking her head. She was so weary, but grateful. Tears pricked her eyes. "It was you."

"No, lass," he said. "Your need summoned me here. And now I must return to see things finished. To write the rest of the story. I can't leave that *pethet* in my cave for too long, you know. He's a bit too curious, that one."

Trynne's heart lurched. "Was there no way . . . no way to bring him with you? Cannot my father go fetch him? I . . . I thought the rule was that only two could cross at a time?"

Myrddin shook his head, his eyes full of sadness. "It doesn't work that way, little sister. I didn't create the covenants that separate the worlds. Even I must abide by them. Someone must willingly trade places. And so I must go back and fulfill what the Fountain sent me to do." He bent down and kissed the top of her head.

"Myrddin?" she said, her voice breaking.

He arched his eyebrows at her.

"Would you tell him . . . would you tell Fallon that I love him? That I wish . . . with all my heart, I wish things could have been different between us. He's truly the best of men." Tears thickened on her lashes. She would start weeping uncontrollably if she said any more.

Myrddin pursed his lips. He touched her shoulder comfortingly. "I will. Farewell, Oath Maiden. Until we meet again on another shore. May the Fountain always bless you."

She sniffled and wrapped her arms around him and buried her face against his chest. She felt his hand stroke her sandy hair. Then she pulled away and smiled at him with her crooked smile.

"Good-bye, little sister," he said tenderly.

When she turned, she saw a larger crowd had gathered around them. The people of Ploemeur had all joined them on the beach. She started to walk through them, and they parted to make a path for her. The looks of awe and reverence on their faces humbled her. To them, she was a manifestation of the Fountain. The one who had saved their kingdom from drowning in the sea.

She saw Thierry marching toward her from the palace, his face full of wonder. When he reached her, he gripped her shoulders and then kissed her on both cheeks.

"My lady," he said, whispering the words like a benediction. He pitched his voice lower. "We found her. Severn's daughter. She too washed up on the beach. She's alive, if barely."

Of course she would have survived too. She was Fountain-blessed.

Trynne sighed. "I must take her back to Kingfountain."

Thierry nodded sagely. "Yes. But she is not as hale as you. She's nearly dead. And from the looks of it, she was attacked in the waters. Her hand is missing. And we found this."

He held up a single serrated tooth the size of a hunting dagger.

♦ ♦ ♦

Dearest Trynne,

I must write this note now in case there is not time to explain before we are separated. You know how I've hated the secrets between us, from the time you learned about your father's fate and wouldn't share it with me to my intrigues with the Espion and the search for your father that I concealed from you.

If you knew that one of us would need to remain behind, you would have sacrificed yourself. I know you too well, Trynne Kiskaddon. So here is the last secret that I learned from Morwenna when I poisoned her. The guardian of the grove who bears the ring can pass between worlds. They can bring one other person with them. But they cannot take someone away without exchanging with someone who is willing. There must be a balance exacted, or the magic will fail. Morwenna learned this from The Hidden Vulgate *she found in Pisan, which contained a story about the grove, the silver bowl. It talked about a man named Owain who became the master of the ring and crossed worlds. It was a secret Owain only shared with King Andrew. The king was taken to that other world to be healed after his mortal injury by his bastard son. A son sired because of his sister's deceit.*

The Dochte Mandar have been looking for King Andrew's posterity in the other world. Apparently, only a certain family can use the Medium—or the Fountain magic as we call it. That family descended from our world originally. I hope to learn more about it while I stay. If I can find the remnants of that family, then I will swear my loyalty to them.

Trynne, this is for the best. It would torture me to live in a world where you are married to another man. I would rather be here all alone. I cannot walk away from these feelings for you. I've kept Morwenna's kystrel to keep her from using it against you. I don't think I could have stood by and watched you destroy her, even though you must. It would have been too painful, because she was, for a time, a dear friend. Know that my heart will always belong to you.

To stay here, this had to be done willingly. No one forced me, Trynne. But I need to step aside so that Gahalatine can have you and so that we cannot be tempted to do something that would bring shame on both of us. I will live my life in this world with the burning hope that we may reunite again when we both reach the Deep Fathoms.

With all my love,
Fallon

♦ ♦ ♦

CHAPTER THIRTY-ONE

Nightmares

In her dream, Trynne was slogging through the fetid swamp surrounding Muirwood Abbey, being hunted and chased by baying hounds. She was trying to find Fallon. There were occasional glimpses of him up ahead, but every time she tried to call out to him, to plead with him to stop, she was too breathless to speak. Her eyes blinked awake and the dream began to dissolve like dew under rays of sunlight.

Trynne had spent much of the two days following the confrontation with Morwenna sleeping and regaining her strength. The rest was fitful, and she'd often awoken with her pulse racing, fearing someone wanted to hurt her.

Each day she checked with the healers on Morwenna's progress. The poisoner had not regained consciousness for more than brief moments, just enough to sip some broth. She had lost a lot of blood, and the injuries all over her body were frightening. There was no spark of Fountain magic in her. Trynne made sure she was guarded night and day.

As Trynne stared at herself in the mirror, looking at her simple soft gown, she saw that her own scars had indeed healed. At least the ones on the outside. Her hair was clean and brushed, her skin scrubbed relentlessly to free it from the caked-in dirt from her perilous journey. She had bruises on her arms and puckered skin that had been stitched and restored. As she gazed at herself, she felt older than her years, wearied by the ordeals she had faced.

She blinked, feeling suddenly on the verge of tears. Her husband, Gahalatine, had been kissed by Morwenna. He was infected by the disease that she had sensed while in the world of Muirwood. There was a no cure for it. What fate did it spell for Gahalatine's people, for the East Kingdoms? Was Morwenna right? Would the game end with Gahalatine's death? Would his vast domains incur the floods of the Deep Fathoms? She dreaded it was so. Surely Sunilik was still on his way back to those lands. The journey took several months at sea.

A soft knock sounded at the door, and Trynne turned in her seat, feeling some of her stitches pull with the movement. She winced before calling out, "Yes?"

The door was opened by Thierry. "Good morning, my lady. I knocked softly because I wasn't sure if you were still abed. You look much improved."

Trynne rose from her seat and walked to him. "Has Morwenna awakened?"

He shook his head no. "She is still fighting for her life. She murmurs in her sleep. No, I came with news. King Drew's herald just arrived. The king is at his heels with your father and Captain Staeli. They've crossed into Brythonica with a small retinue of knights and are coming to Ploemeur. They should be at the palace by midday."

Trynne's brow furrowed. "He's come here? I was going to go to Kingfountain to—"

Thierry held up his hand. "I took the liberty, my lady, of dispatching a trusted servant to the palace to apprise the king of your success in capturing his sister. And of the injuries you sustained. But my messenger found them already en route. He returned with the herald after delivering the message. The king is eager to declare to the world that you are no traitor to Kingfountain, but its greatest hero. Your husband was too ill to ride."

She blinked with surprise—so full of emotion she was not sure how to interpret her feelings. "And my father is with them?"

"He is indeed. They stopped at Tatton Hall yesterday. Apparently there was a great deal of commotion upon his arrival." Thierry grinned at her.

Trynne nodded, feeling how strange the world had become. "If they've entered the borders of Brythonica through Westmarch, they will come by way of the grove, will they not?"

"Aye," Thierry said. "I thought you might care to meet them there?"

Trynne nodded. "I would. Please keep a constant vigil on Morwenna. I don't think she is a danger to anyone in her state, but I dare not take that for granted."

"Of course, my lady." He paused, hesitating.

"What is it, Thierry?"

"Will you . . . will you be staying among us for a while? Or do you plan to return to Averanche? The people long for you to stay. To remain and accept your rightful place here. There have been flowers sent to the castle, baskets of berries and jams. Small tokens of respect and honor. They continue to come daily, hoping for a glimpse of you. I know you prefer your privacy. But the people still need you."

She knew that it was truly the Fountain's power that had saved them, but his words humbled her. Still, she longed to walk the battlement walls of Averanche, to start training again with the Oath Maidens. With Captain Staeli.

"When I go, I won't be gone for long, Thierry," she promised, touching his arm. "I'll return soon."

"Of course, my lady," he said, bowing respectfully.

◆　◆　◆

Trynne was grateful she had taken a cloak with her to the grove, for it was cool in the shade. Dark, violent memories from her last visit to the grove flashed through her mind and made her tremble. The dead had all been cleared away and buried in the woods. New leaves had fallen across the stone plinth, and the silver dish looked ancient as it stood before the broken stones of the cave. She gave the huge oak tree a wary look. It wasn't as enormous as the one they had discovered beyond the abbey's ruined walls, but could it really be a coincidence that both were oaks?

Fallon's suggestion surfaced once again in her mind. Would it restore her father and Gahalatine? She gave it a wary look, careful not to gaze at it for too long. She didn't want her own memories purged. The tree felt docile, harmless. But so did the silver bowl until the water was poured from it.

She heard voices in the distance and the tramping of boots through brush. She sensed the presence of a Fountain-blessed and suspected it was her father. But after all the difficulties she'd faced in her young life, she was no longer willing to take anything by chance. She walked away from the grove and soon met the king, her father, and Staeli along the path. The other retainers held back, keeping their distance.

"Lady Trynne," the king said, staring at her in awe.

"Your Majesty," she replied with a bow. Then Trynne smiled and gently embraced her father. He hugged her back, but there was still a certain aloofness in his eyes, the look of a stranger. She had gotten part of him back. She wanted the rest.

"Captain," she said, smiling fondly.

"Hello, lass," he said with a small bow.

"I was fearful we'd find you laid up on a sickbed," Drew said. "But we find you roaming the woods, much recovered. Your family has always healed quickly. It's good to see you so hale," he said, reaching out and taking her hand. He kissed it in a token of utmost respect.

"Have you sent for Genny?" she asked.

Drew nodded. "I told her that I would come to Dundrennan myself. To await me there. I understand that she is safe, that she has our child. Kate's health is still not fully restored from the poison administered to her, but she is recovering. I thought . . . she was already dead." His countenance fell. "I'm troubled at how the grief affected me. How it blinded me to my sister's illusions. Your father has explained his journey to me. The realms he visited and the trust he earned serving the King of Dahomey." A smile quirked on his mouth. "It does not surprise me in the least. But can nothing be done for his memories, Trynne? He has lost all his past. I still sense the same personality in him, but it truly is a grievous curse for him to lose his memories."

Trynne stared at her father, seeing the anguish in his eyes. He wanted to remember. She wanted it too.

"Fallon was the one who unraveled all of Morwenna's secrets," Trynne said.

"I never thought to admit this, but I do miss him," Drew said seriously. "I've not only lost my brother-in-law. He has changed much over the last years. And he gave up his own future, willingly, to trade places with your father." He shook his head in wonderment.

"Fallon believed that the oak tree yonder is important. I have hoped that Morwenna would revive soon. I have so many questions for her."

Those questions had been running through Trynne's mind again and again over the days of her convalescence. Where had Morwenna hidden the blade Firebos? Where was her father's scabbard?

Drew pursed his lips. "She may be too vengeful to help us. She's guilty of treason, and I intend to see that she suffers a traitor's fate. I had compassion for her before, but I see that she has repaid it with even more treachery. Lord Amrein has been in disguise all this time. He feigned his death after he was poisoned, not knowing whom he could trust. He was hiding in the sanctuary of Our Lady."

"Poor man," Trynne said sadly. "I agree that Morwenna has no incentive to be useful. So I recommend that we cut the tree down, as Fallon suggested."

"Are you sure, Trynne?" Drew asked. He raised his eyebrow at her. "Might it have unintended consequences?"

"It might," Trynne said. "But I cannot think of another way. I wish Liona's husband were here with his axe."

Drew smiled. "Shall I send for him?"

Trynne laughed softly. "I'd rather not wait. Your knights can do the work if you call for them."

Trynne noticed a butterfly with pale blue wings flutter up and land on her father's shoulder. It was a *Sinia* butterfly, the breed her mother was named after. As her eyes fixed on it, she felt an overwhelming feeling in her heart, a deep foreboding about cutting down the tree. It felt like a cloud passing over the sun. It felt *wrong*. The butterfly suddenly leaped into the air. Trynne tried to follow it with her eyes, but its path was too erratic. Then she realized that people were shouting from a distance.

Drew reached for his sword, his face furrowing with concern. Staeli turned and frowned, walking toward the noise—as he ever walked toward danger. There was a man rushing forward, trampling through the trees in his haste. He was accosted by the king's knights, but he struggled against them, trying to reach Trynne.

"Who is it?" Owen asked with concern.

Trynne and the others approached and found a dark-haired man gasping for breath, wearing the tunic of her household. It was one of Thierry's underlings, a clever young man named Lapiyerre.

"Unhand me!" he said, trying to shake loose of the sturdy knights. "My lady! I am sent from your steward, Thierry. My name is . . ."

"Yes, I know who you are," Trynne said, coming closer. His face was agitated and nearly bursting with excitement. "What is the news?"

He looked so relieved, but his eyes bulged when he realized that she was with the king and her father. He swallowed awkwardly. "My lady, her ship. The ship. Blast it all, your *mother's* ship! It's arriving in the harbor as we speak. Lady Sinia's ship has returned!"

Trynne stared at Lapiyerre in surprise and happiness, which slowly transmuted into sickening horror. Her mother had returned. Trynne would have to tell her about Gannon's murder, about Owen's lack of memories. She felt herself swaying and wondered if she would faint. A hand lowered onto her shoulder to steady her. It was her father.

He looked at her keenly, his eyes full of concern. "I learned about Gannon while we were at Tatton Hall," he said softly. "About my parents. We must break the news to your mother before anyone else does. Wouldn't you agree?" He gave her a reassuring look.

Trynne bobbed her head, trying to maintain her composure. She'd thought she would have more time to prepare herself for this moment, but at least she wouldn't have to bear the burden alone.

She put her hand on her father's forearm and nodded. Then she reached out her other hand and offered it to the king. "We should go at once. I will take us there."

◆　◆　◆

Trynne's stomach was twisting into knots of worry. She wanted her mother to see Owen by her side as the ship landed. The king and Thierry were there, and so was Captain Staeli, ever watchful. A crowd had gathered, and the watch had been summoned to push the onlookers back, to make room so that the family could gather privately first. The sun was bright overhead, but there were plenty of cool sea breezes to keep the heat from burning them. It was a terrible moment to talk of death. To describe the near ruin of Kingfountain.

Please let her understand, Trynne prayed silently, squeezing her hands behind her back. She was trembling with anticipation. The boat arrived with the noon tide, and she spied Captain Pyne at the main deck. The ship looked worn and weather-beaten. It had been at sea for so long. Trynne couldn't help but remember a different day, long since past, when this same boat had prepared to disembark. Her mother heading off on an unknown adventure, driven to heed whispers from the Fountain.

Commands were shouted and the crew responded sharply and with great order. Ropes were thrown overboard to secure the vessel. Each moment was an agony to Trynne as she prepared to explain the absence of her little brother, the boy she had been charged to protect. Guilt wormed inside of her.

She felt her father's arm lower around her shoulders in a comforting gesture. "She will understand, Trynne," he whispered. "Won't she?"

Trynne was so worried about her own feelings, she'd failed to recognize his. This was a man who had lost all recollection of his wife and his children. Gannon's loss hadn't stabbed him as deeply because her brother didn't exist in his memory. He didn't even know his wife's face, what she looked like.

The dockworkers lifted a ramp, and the soldiers aboard affixed it to the edge of the ship. Trynne caught a flash of golden hair—her mother, approaching the gangplank. Just seeing her made Trynne's whole being thrum with relief, but the feeling was quickly muted by the burden Trynne carried.

Sinia spoke in undecipherable tones to Captain Pyne for a moment and then headed toward the ramp.

Trynne saw someone with her mother. She blinked, not able to understand. There was a child holding her hand. A boy with tawny hair and a wide smile. Trynne's vision was blurred by tears and she wiped them away fast, afraid it was an illusion. But she could not be deceived by illusions. She saw the lad clearly.

It was Gannon.

CHAPTER THIRTY-TWO

The Dryad Tree

Trynne sobbed as she hugged her brother, kneeling on the sharp wooden planks of the dock, feeling his hands patting her shoulders comfortingly. Her heart felt so swollen she thought it would burst, and her breath came in soft hiccups. She gazed at her parents, seeing them together, Sinia holding Owen tightly, cheek pressed against his chest, her tears flowing freely. There was no way to describe how Trynne felt. They were a family again.

Trynne closed her eyes, savoring the relief, the confusion—she couldn't understand how this was possible outside of a dream. She feared she'd awaken and it would be gone. But she felt Gannon, smelled the scent of the sea on his skin. He was *alive*. She kissed his cheeks until he wrinkled his nose and started to shove her away.

Looking back from her brother, she saw something dangling from her mother's girdle. She sensed it was hidden and concealed by magic, but her eyes could see it—the illusion would not work on her. It was a key, a strange, ancient-looking key that was made of rusting iron and hung from a braided rope tied around her mother's waist. She felt the strange power it radiated. What was it?

Her mother caught her gaze. Then her fingers wrapped around Trynne's shoulder and gave it a squeeze. "I will explain everything to you, Tryneowy. All that I can. Later. First, we must bring back your father's memories."

King Drew approached, staring at Sinia in awe. "You can do this?" he asked, his eyes brightening with hope.

"Yes, my lord. I know now how they were taken—and how they can be returned." She inclined her head to him. "I also know where Firebos is being concealed. And my husband's scabbard." She patted Owen's chest. "It too shall be restored. All things will be made right again." Her countenance fell a bit as she shifted her gaze back to Trynne. "All that *can* be."

◆　◆　◆

Once again, they were back at the grove, but this time with Trynne's mother and brother. The noise from the cheering crowds was gone, replaced by the sweet chirping of the woodland birds and the steady pattering of the waterfall. Gannon ambled around the oak tree's roots, and Trynne felt a nervous gust of fear. She folded her arms, shuddering, still amazed to see her brother hale once again.

"I have so many questions . . ." Trynne said, turning to her mother. Sinia was walking hand in hand with Owen toward the plinth.

King Drew clasped his hands behind his back, standing near Trynne and brooding over the strange scene. "As do I," he said. "Why do I have a feeling you have already seen this moment in a vision?"

Sinia smiled at the comment and nodded to him. "When I departed Kingfountain, I said that I was being summoned back home. Back to the Deep Fathoms."

"I recall that moment quite well," said Drew forlornly. "Everything started to fall apart afterward."

Sinia turned and gazed up at the crooked tree branches of the mighty oak. "I know, my lord, but there were things we needed to know. Things that I could not learn in Ploemeur." She released Owen's hand and turned to face them. "My birth was a secret, even to me. I was found on the beach by my parents. A water sprite. A gift from the Fountain to save Brythonica from drowning. What I say here, inside this hallowed grove, must remain a secret." She looked calm and peaceful, serene, transformed from when Trynne had seen her last. "We sailed westward and had many adventures. Far away, across the farthest sea, is an island. A trail of stone boulders, cut with stone faces, led me there. Next to the island there's an underwater chasm deeper than the deepest gorge. It sinks into the very heart of the sea, and all the currents of the ocean are drawn into it. It is a gateway to the Deep Fathoms."

She paused, gazing down at the stone plinth. "We sailed into its depths. Inside the Deep Fathoms, I met my true parents." She looked up then, her expression one of tenderness and devotion. "My father rules the Deep Fathoms. In his previous life, on another world, his body was horribly scarred and he had lost his memories. My mother is a Dryad. This," she said, gesturing to the oak, "is a Dryad tree. They are spirit creatures, like water sprites, but of the earth instead of the sea." She turned and faced the tree, bowing her head respectfully. "The Dryad in this tree is my *sister*," she said, her words full of loving feeling. "I never knew why I felt so at home here. Why this place was sacred to me as a child. I could always feel its whispers beckoning to me." She turned her head to face them. "A Dryad's power is over memories. She can snatch them away with the blink of her eyes. Her kiss restores them. My sister is bound to serve the master of the ring, so she has been in bondage to Morwenna. Now that the ring has been restored to its proper owner, she will restore Owen's memories and those of the others whose memories she has taken. The lore of the Dryads is an ancient secret. These trees are truly the portals between worlds. The roots have powerful magic. The portals must be guarded. And kept secret."

Sinia turned back to the tree. "Morwenna learned about her in a secret book of magic called *The Hidden Vulgate*. It is a book of great power and greater evil. It was created, originally, by my father's brother, a terrible ruler who once enslaved all the kingdoms of his world and destroyed them. His essence is bound inside that book. It cannot be unmade. But it was hidden by Morwenna and it will remain hidden. Her connection to the book has been broken, but her hatred cannot be cured.

"A Dryad will not appear to mortals unless forced to," she said after a brief pause. "She will come if commanded by the one bearing the ring. The rest of you must shield your eyes. Kneel on the plinth, if you please."

"Can I see the Dryad?" Gannon said eagerly after approaching her. "I saw them in Mirrowen."

Sinia smiled at him and tapped his nose. "We are in the mortal world now, Jorganon. You must resist the temptation to look."

He frowned at the request and then joined Trynne and Drew as they knelt on the stone plinth. Trynne obediently shut her eyes and put her hand on Gannon's shoulder to help him be still.

There were no words said. The wind rustled the branches and wafted the scent of eucalyptus throughout the grove. It was interesting how the lack of sight made Trynne's other senses heighten. The drone of a bumblebee could be heard in the woods. And then she heard it, the little crack of a stem. Then the delicate crunch of fallen leaves trod by bare feet. She felt the Dryad's Fountain magic, sensed that another person had joined them in the grove. The compulsion to look was fierce. It clawed at the back of her mind, demanding that she witness the being who had stolen her father's memories. She squeezed her eyes shut, breathing deeply. She could feel Drew shudder beside her.

Amidst the cacophony of voices inside her head, she still heard the trickle of the waterfall, the warble of birds. And then she heard the tiniest sound—the press of a kiss. If she hadn't been kneeling so close, she wouldn't have heard it.

Followed by the sound of her father gasping.

"You may look now," Sinia said reverently, her voice thick with tears of joy.

Trynne opened her eyes, staring up at her father. He stared back in recognition, his eyes sparkling with tears, his face awash with a thousand conflicting emotions. He sank to his knees, clutching Sinia's waist, and buried his cheek against her abdomen while she stroked his hair, breathing fast and hard as if he'd jogged up the side of a hill. The look of a stranger was gone. Owen was finally himself.

Trynne crawled to him and hugged him, clutching him fiercely, with all the love in her heart.

"Trynne," he gasped. "There you are! My *Trynne*!" He trembled like a leaf, as if all his strength was gone. "I'm . . . I'm breathless," he said. "It's all back. All of it. I remember . . . everything. Everything I've ever said. Jumping into the cistern. Ankarette's smile." His voice choked with emotion. "I never realized how sick she was. She was dying before she met me." His trembling intensified. "I can remember every missive I've read. Every conversation. My mind is going to crack into pieces."

Sinia dropped down to her knees, holding him protectively, drawing Trynne and Gannon close as well. "The magic of a Dryad's kiss is potent. You'll remember everything in greater detail. Every book you've ever read, my love. Or will read. You will be an even stronger servant to your king. I experienced the same when my mother kissed me. It takes some getting used to."

Trynne looked hungrily at her mother. "Do you know what has happened to us, Mother? Did you see it from the Deep Fathoms?"

Sinia nodded. "I'm so proud of you. So proud of what you've done. This is what you were meant for, Trynne. I understand that now. I was blinded to it by my concern for the safety of my people."

Trynne warmed at the sentiment. She'd long carried the guilt of not continuing her Wizr training. "So Gahalatine can get his memories back?"

"Yes. And Dragan too. But it cannot cure Gahalatine. He will die from Morwenna's kiss."

Trynne's heart sank. She'd hoped his fate would be different. "And his people? Are they doomed to perish?"

"I have seen visions of the future, Trynne. I cannot speak of all that I know, but Gahalatine has a special gift from the Fountain. His words are convincing. He must use his gift to persuade his people to enter the treasure ships that he had them build. Those who hearken to his word will live. Those who don't believe in the judgment of the Fountain will perish. He must be returned to Chandigarl at once. His sickness will kill him swiftly. But he still has the chance to save his people."

Trynne's throat closed with tears and she felt sadness but also gratitude. Some would listen. Some would heed the warning. "Mother. What of Fallon? Have you seen a vision of Fallon?"

Her mother's look became somber. "I have, Daughter. I cannot bring him back. Neither Myrddin nor I can change the covenant that binds the portal. The offer must be made by one who is willing. And I have seen our futures here in this world."

◆　◆　◆

Gahalatine had been confined in illness to a part of the palace that was little used and visited. It wasn't the traitor's tower of Holistern, but it felt like a dungeon nonetheless. A guard was stationed there to keep others *out*, not Gahalatine in. Trynne gestured for the man to open the door. She heard her husband's hacking cough before she entered.

She found her husband, sick on his bed, drenched with sweat, and racked by chills. He had gray shadows beneath his eyes, and the signs of his mighty strength were already beginning to wane. As she entered, he scooted back on the bed to try to sit up, stifling a cough on his fist. His hair was slick with sweat.

"You did return," he said gratefully, his voice hoarse. "Others t-told me"—his words were interrupted by a cough—"Lord Fallon remained behind."

She approached his bedside and reached out and touched his leg in sympathy. "It grieves me to see you like this," she said sadly. "I kept my promise."

He blinked and nodded, looking uncomfortable and achy. "I knew it wasn't you," he said, shaking his head. "The strangest feeling wrapped around me when she entered the tower. It was . . . wrong—so different from how I felt with you in Ploemeur. How I feel with you now. I knew that Morwenna could disguise herself. She does so convincingly. But I still knew. She tried to kiss me and I turned away. It felt . . . wrong. Vindictive. She kissed my cheek instead. And now I am cursed to die." He looked at her sadly, but proudly. "I kept my promise too."

Her heart tugged with anguish. She grasped his hand in hers and slowly began to feed him with her magic, helping him recover some of his strength. She watched the color come back to his cheeks. The tremors began to fade.

It would not cure him. But it would sustain him a while longer.

◆ ◆ ◆

The king's council had gathered in the audience hall of Kingfountain palace at the massive Ring Table. This was the first time since Morwenna's assault on the princess that the king's loyal subjects had come together without disguise or illusion. Trynne and Sinia had used the ley lines to summon together those rulers whose presence had previously been faked by Morwenna's magic.

Trynne stood alongside Gahalatine, holding his hand to continue lending him strength, watching with tender feeling as Lady Evie and

Iago hugged her father. He was thronged with well-wishers, but she could tell by the look in his eye that he'd prefer to be closeted in the Star Chamber with Lord Amrein discussing politics or on the beach with Sinia than to be the focus of so much attention. Genny was there, gripping her husband's arm possessively, and so was Kate, being held and kissed repeatedly by her grandmother, Lady Kathryn.

Only Fallon was missing. Turbulent feelings bubbled up inside Trynne, like one of Liona's stews in a cauldron, and she dabbed at her eyes. The sight of his empty chair at the Ring Table filled her with pain. She could imagine his boundless energy, watching for a prank or a quick jest.

Gahalatine released her hand and put his arm around her shoulders. His memories had now been restored by the Dryad's kiss and his entire demeanor toward her had changed. He was chagrined, humbled, and miserable. He already had a clawing cough, but he was determined to do everything in his power to save his people from destruction. They would leave via the Tay al-Ard immediately following the meeting.

"It will take the king a while still to calm the room," he told her gently. "Can I confess something to you?"

She turned and looked at him. Before he'd lost his memories, he had acted like a stranger to her. His sense of right and wrong had been warped by Morwenna and the Wizrs of his realm. He saw now that he'd been deceived, that she was true and faithful. That she had not tricked him into defeat at Dundrennan. It gave her peace of mind that he believed her once again. There were horrors to come, but they would work together to help the people of the East Kingdoms.

"What is it?"

"While you were gone to the other world," he said, "I learned that you and Fallon Llewellyn were . . . I'm trying to put this delicately, that you both shared feelings for each other. That he had loved you for some time and proposed marriage. But you rejected him. Captain

Staeli confirmed this. I asked how worried I should be that the two of you were alone together."

She swallowed and glanced over at Captain Staeli, who was looking strangely at one of the chairs. He was rubbing his hand along its carved top. The king was making him a duke for his bravery and steadfastness, and this was the seat that would be his. Duke Staeli. It made her want to laugh with joy and pride.

"What did he tell you?" Trynne asked, glancing back at her husband.

His eyes narrowed and he smiled. "He said I'd be a fool if I didn't trust your loyalty. He said you'd do your duty no matter what." He turned and took her hands in his. "Before you left, I couldn't remember who you truly were. Now that I remember it all, there's something I need to say. If I had known how deeply you cared for him, I wouldn't have asked you to be my wife. I can see, probably more clearly than ever before, that the Fountain was preparing me for a greater service than I had imagined. Your willingness to sacrifice your peace and happiness for your kingdom has inspired me to do the same. I will die soon, Tryneowy. Nothing can alter that. But I will die a changed man, and it is because of you.

"I let my ambition and pride get ahead of my honor, but no longer. When this meeting is over, I intend to speak to your parents and insist they declare our marriage invalid. It is in keeping with the traditions of my people, for you are still not of age. It is honorable. And I will feel better if you are set free ere I die." He patted her hand affectionately.

A lump filled her throat. "It's my intention to help you save your people. To go the length and breadth of your empire with you to issue the warning. To tend to you while you are sick and uncomfortable. Don't cast me aside so quickly, Husband."

Gahalatine's eyes closed and he sighed. "Your words comfort me."

"I'll not forsake you," she whispered.

He had tears in his eyes when he opened them. He pressed a kiss on her hand. "Thank you." Then he turned his head away and barked out an anguished cough.

The commotion in the room began to still as King Drew called for those assembled to take their places at the Ring Table. Trynne's heart brimmed with emotion as she walked, hand on Gahalatine's arm, toward their seats.

As they approached, she was a little confused to find her father standing behind the chair on Drew's right side. It had always been his seat—the Siege Perilous. She saw him pat the edge of it and nod for her to take it. Her eyes widened with surprise.

"Yes, Trynne," Drew said, gesturing to the chair. "You are still my champion and deserve the seat of honor."

CHAPTER THIRTY-THREE

Faithful

Trynne had spent so many weeks in Chandigarl that she had forgotten that sunset in the East Kingdoms meant sunrise back at Kingfountain. She was exhausted from the ordeal that was now over. Her husband was dead, and the people—those who had hearkened to him, and there were many—were hunkering in treasure ships that had escaped into the open seas. Drew had offered refuge in his realm to those who were willing to come.

The repaired ley lines had brought her back to the palace fountain in Kingfountain, where she had anticipated finding Drew and Genny. Then she would return to Ploemeur to inform her parents of the events. She was greeted by the king's guardsmen, one of whom gave her a strange look.

"Good morning, Lady Trynne," he greeted, bowing respectfully. There was something in his eye, the quiver of a smile on his mouth.

"Is everything well?" she asked him. She was bone weary from the long day, the emotional farewell. It was so odd to see the bright sunlight shining through the hall curtains beyond, to hear the hurried steps of servants preparing for the new day.

"Indeed, my lady." He bowed again and the two guardsmen regarded her silently as she passed.

She was exhausted and probably reading too much into it. As she walked down the corridor, she kneaded the muscles at her shoulder. The smells of the palace were so different from what she'd grown accustomed to in the months since she had departed. She had returned occasionally to provide reports and seek counsel, but she'd pushed herself to her limits trying to help Gahalatine save his people, all the while tending to him as his health was ravaged by the debilitating sickness that would eventually end his life. She had used her magic to stave off the symptoms for as long as she could. But the fatal kiss was indeed that in the end.

She looked forward to returning to Averanche. It had been a long time since she had stayed in the quiet castle. What she needed, after a long rest, was a chance to spar with Captain Staeli.

But no—she caught herself, feeling a wince of pain.

He was a captain no longer. Had the ceremony already happened investing him with his dukedom? He would continue training the Oath Maidens, of course, but probably in his own domain. She was happy for him. He deserved the reward and recognition. But she would miss him deeply.

Her mind fluttered with a variety of thoughts as she approached the queen's chambers. Her first visits were always to Genny. She longed to see her friend, missed their long talks and the confidences they shared. At least she would catch up on the latest news before she went to see her parents. Her mother, she knew, had been working on carving new Leerings at the beach to replace the boundaries destroyed by Morwenna. The effort would require some time, but they would be able to stand for another thousand years when they were done.

One of the queen's handmaids opened the door before she arrived. The girl turned back and announced her arrival. Trynne thanked the girl as she crossed the threshold.

There were Genny and Mariette, speaking in low tones. Mariette looked stricken, her eyes rimmed with red.

"Is all well?" Trynne asked with concern.

Mariette blinked quickly, brushing away the fresh tears. She nodded, her voice too thick to speak. Genny patted Mariette's shoulder, giving her a comforting hug. Genny was always the source of relief. She had such a compassionate heart. The events of the past had affected the queen deeply, yet she was still attuned to the needs of others.

"It will be well," Genny said, patting Mariette again. "All will be well."

"I know. I just . . . I know." She straightened and came to Trynne, brushing a kiss to her cheek. The tall warrior maiden had to stoop low to do so, but she was loyal and fiercely true. Trynne watched her go and then arched her eyebrows at the queen after she'd left.

"Troubles with Lord Amrein?" Trynne asked.

Genny smiled at the comment. "Not this time. Although I do think she's growing weary of waiting for him to ask to marry her. But that's not what's troubling her. It's so good to see you again, Trynne." The queen embraced her, and there was such warmth and friendship there. The queen had a sweet fragrance in her hair. The dusky smell of star jasmine.

"I'd forgotten it was morning here," Trynne said, pulling away. "I'm exhausted."

Genny squeezed her hands. "You do look tired. But you won't hasten away? I'd like you to stay a little while."

"Very well," Trynne said. "What news?"

"Tell me your news first."

Trynne nodded and started to pace, but Genny hooked her arm. "Let's walk as we talk. It'll help refresh you."

Trynne accepted the invitation, even though she had been active all day. A servant came to say that breakfast was about to be served in the audience hall, but Genny waved the girl away after inquiring if Trynne was hungry.

She was not. She wasn't sure she ever would be again.

"It is finished, Genny. We saved as many people as we could. The ships were launched from their various harbors. According to my mother's vision, we evacuated the most impacted realms first. In the end, Gahalatine was too weak to travel. He stayed at the zenana after his palace burned down. The Dochte Mandar and the Wizrs had fled, along with any hetaera. Sunilik helped drive their influence out. He's going back to the oasis, where he will rule once again. It will not flood in the desert, thankfully."

"That is good news," Genny said, steering her along the corridors. The sunlight shone on the queen's hair. "Reya will be happy, and she and her husband will enjoy visiting there."

"So Reya and Elwis were married at last?" Trynne asked.

Genny smiled pleasantly. "Indeed. So much has happened."

"I want to hear about all of it," Trynne insisted.

"Your news first. Tell me more about Gahalatine. His death must have been very difficult for you."

Trynne nodded, feeling the sorrow well inside her. "It was difficult watching someone so hale fail so quickly. He shrank before my eyes. But he was determined. He spoke vigorously about the corruption within Chandigarl, the focus on wealth and riches above all. He defeated the rumors about us and told the truth about what had happened. Most believed him. Many did not—they refused to accept that the flood was coming. They made any number of excuses for why it would not. But it all came down to the fact that they didn't believe it would happen. He sorrowed because of it, especially since there were so many trappings of belief—the fountains, the prayers, the symbols—throughout the realm. Yet many saw them merely as decorations. They wore their beliefs on the outside, not the inside."

Genny gave her a sage look. "I fear some of our own people would have done the same." She sighed. "Even after the miracles that were shown months ago, I've already heard whispers that some of the people are doubting what they saw."

Trynne patted Genny's arm. "Gahalatine had great faith in the Fountain."

Genny gave her a sidelong smile. "You helped strengthen it for him, Trynne. Being there in his sickness took great courage. I'm grateful that your mother's vision showed you'd return to us unharmed. Many of the people who refused to leave probably were unwilling to forsake their treasures. All we have will be reclaimed by the Deep Fathoms eventually. Why cling to what is not truly ours?"

"Well said," Trynne offered. "I'm at peace with Gahalatine's death. I'm still not at peace with what Fallon sacrificed. You're his sister, so I suppose we get to commiserate with each other. How are your parents handling it? Do they mourn?"

Genny looked away, as if the words were too painful. They walked in silence alongside each other for a while before the queen responded. "Both of them, as you can imagine, are hurting still. Yet we're also proud of him. There was a time, not long ago, when we all feared the worst would come of him. Didn't we?" She tugged on Trynne's arm. "He was utterly unpredictable, but he changed. Part of it was because of your father's influence on his life. But the larger part, I think, was because of you."

Genny gave her a poignant look that made Trynne want to hide in a closet and cry. But she was determined to be strong. Her mother had promised that everything that could be made right would be. She would trust in that.

"Are you ready for the news, then?" Genny asked somberly. When Trynne nodded, the queen continued. "Morwenna's trial was completed last week and the Assizes rendered judgment. Nothing was rushed, and copious records were made. Polidoro performed the task of recording the proceedings with great diligence. We will be judged in the future by how we treated Morwenna Argentine."

"Treated—you mean she's dead?" Trynne asked, her soul feeling a pang of unexpected sorrow.

Genny nodded. "Looking at the record of the Maid, it is clear in retrospect that she was Fountain-blessed and only sought to do the Fountain's will. She was judged harshly and condemned because of politics. We did not want to replicate the mistake, so we refused to rush to judgment. Your evidence played a strong role in the decision, but not yours alone. She was feared at the poisoner school in Pisan. As the pieces came together, the conclusion was inescapable. She had committed treason in every possible way. And so she was condemned."

Trynne breathed through her nose, trying to suppress a shudder. "Was she chained to the rock like the Maid? In Helvellyn?"

Genny shook her head no. "Sinia had a vision of her execution. In the records, the way to kill a Wizr is to bury them with stones. It was how they tried to kill Myrddin, if you remember the legend." She laughed softly. "She was taken to a cave without food or drink and a stone was dragged forth to cover it. She railed against the king the entire time, during the trial and after. She didn't go to her death quietly. Well, at least until the stone covered the door. Your father stood vigil with guards for ten days. When they removed the stone, she was dead."

Trynne's voice quavered. "I'm grateful that I didn't have to be there."

Genny stopped and touched her shoulder. "Drew insisted you should not be," she said gently. "He felt—we all felt—you'd been through enough. She is gone forever. Dragan's end—well, that is a somewhat different story."

"Truly? Were his memories restored?"

Genny nodded solemnly. "Apparently the anguish of them drove him mad. Perhaps the clarity of the Dryad's kiss finally made him realize that *he* was responsible for his daughter's death, not your father. He hanged himself two days later."

"Let's keep walking," Trynne suggested. "This talk is too gloomy on such a morning."

"It is indeed," Genny said. "It needed to be said, though. Not all of Gahalatine's Wizrs were captured, were they? Any or all of them could prove troublesome later. Drew is watching the Wizr board closely. What happens now that the game has ended? None of us knows. Thankfully, we do have our own Wizr—and that is a comforting thought."

Trynne smiled, missing her mother very much. She thought of her father having to participate in Morwenna's execution. He'd never be rid of that memory. The Dryad's kiss guaranteed it.

"There is one more piece of news. A small matter," Genny added. They'd walked around the castle in one giant circle. It amazed Trynne that they'd ended up at the part that led to the garden with the magnolia trees. Genny was tugging her toward the door, but Trynne resisted, pulling back.

"I'd rather not go that way," she said, shaking her head. The memories of that place were more painful than ever now that she was separated from Fallon.

"Come with me," Genny said, her eyes shining. It was then that Trynne began to sense the presence of another Fountain-blessed coming from the garden. She felt the lapping of the Fountain's magic, realized it had been growing steadier as they'd neared the gardens. She sensed someone's presence.

Trynne looked at Genny in confusion. "Is Father here? Mother?"

"They arrived last night," Genny said with a quivering smile. "They knew you'd arrive this morning."

Of course they would. She was about to charge through the door to see them, but Genny caught her arm. "As I said, there is one more bit of news." She paused, licking her lips. "It's regarding your friend, Captain Staeli." Genny had tears in her eyes. She swallowed, trying to keep her composure. "It's why Mariette was crying earlier."

"Is something wrong? Did something happen to him?" Trynne asked in anguish.

"Yes, in a sense. He . . . he rejected the king's offer to become a duke. He said"—here she stumbled, the tears spilling from her lashes—"that *your* happiness was worth more to him than his own. He's left Kingfountain forever. Willingly." Genny smiled sadly, her fingers squeezing Trynne's arms. The realization finally dawned on Trynne, striking her with the force of a hundred waterfalls.

Fallon.

Fallon was *here*.

"We spent most of the night talking," Genny said, sniffling, dabbing away her tears. "He's changed so much. I'm so very proud of him. Go, Trynne. He slipped out of my rooms through the Espion tunnels and said he would meet you here."

Trynne felt her heart bursting. She pressed a hurried kiss on Genny's check and rushed through the door and into the immaculate gardens. *Where . . . where?* She sensed the person who was Fountain-blessed, half-hidden by the trees. The soft grass absorbed her harried march. Her tears were blinding her, her throat swollen to the point she almost couldn't breathe. Where were her parents? She saw someone standing against one of the magnolia trees, half-hidden.

"Fallon?" she called, half croaking with emotions.

Boots disappeared. And then a seed pod sailed from the tree and landed right in front of her. It was well past summer and the season for seed pods. A few crisp white magnolias could still be found amidst the waxy green leaves, and the smell of them filled the garden. She bent down and picked it up, realizing that it was the one Fallon had stolen from the garden in Dochte Abbey.

While she crouched down to retrieve it, she saw him sauntering away from the tree. He'd changed. He looked a little older, a little wiser. There was his knowing smile, the delight that he had kept her in suspense. And it struck her forcibly that the magic of the Fountain was radiating from *him*.

Cradling the seed pod in her hand, she rushed up to him and they collided with a fierce hug, and he hoisted her off the ground and spun her around. She squeezed him, trying to break him in half with violent affection as he twirled her across the lawn, chuckling softly. Everything was spinning in her mind, but it felt so good to be in this moment, so reassuring. The news was still raw, still fresh, and tears streaked down her cheeks.

The spinning slowed and then Fallon set her back down. He continued to hold her, more gently but still possessively. Their bodies swayed a little and then she felt his lips press against her hair. He was so tall it was insufferable.

The reality of him being there, him being with *her* inside *their* garden was almost too much to believe. She found herself pulling back and then she thumped him on the chest with a clenched fist three times, saying, "You . . . you . . . you . . . I'm not even sure what to *call* you right now."

"So you missed me?" he asked with a heart-melting smile. "Not as much as I missed you. Trynne . . . I don't even know where to start. What I've learned studying with Myrddin. What I've learned staying at the ruins of the abbey." He shook his head. "We have plenty of time to speak of that later. Seeing you . . ." He shook his head in wonderment, gripping her shoulders with both hands and pushing her back a little. "I just want to drink you in. To savor this moment. How I feel right now." He sighed deeply. "I'm usually not one to struggle with words."

"Then don't start now," she said, seizing him by the tunic front to pull him even closer. "Captain Staeli . . . he traded places with you?"

Fallon nodded. "I didn't hope for it. I had no expectations. I only found out when your father came for me . . . yesterday? I can hardly fathom it. I was living at the ruins, in the little kitchen."

"But what about the soldiers? What about the sheriff's men? You have to tell me everything!"

"What's so important about all that?" Fallon scoffed.

She wanted to hit him. "When we left you, I thought you'd been captured!"

"Please, Trynne! You give me no credit at all. The sheriff of Mendenhall is a blazing idiot. I slipped behind the oak tree and pretended to be one of the injured ones. Then I stole away in the confusion and hid in that huge mound of stones." He snapped his fingers. "It was easy. I hid in the cave outside Myrddin's lair until he returned from helping you. I could spend weeks telling you all this, but it's not what I've been waiting for. I've been waiting for *you*. Waiting very patiently, I might add." He looked down at her face and then tipped her chin. "And even your *mother* has said yes this time. Please don't tell me no again."

"I don't understand," Trynne said, shaking her head. It felt like the world was still spinning.

His thumb caressed the side of her mouth. "Her visions don't always show the full future at once. She did *see* you marry Gahalatine. But she has also seen *this*." He leaned down and kissed her where he'd touched her mouth. The brush of his lips awakened a ravenous hunger inside of her.

He pulled back, his expression softening as he looked at her. "Staeli, whom I will esteem forever, saw little worth in a dukedom for an old bachelor like himself. When he heard the story of what *I'd* done, it gnawed at him like a hound on a bone. He felt it wasn't right that you'd be left without a husband after all you've done. And that I was stranded in another world because of what I'd done. So . . . he went to Lord Owen and asked if he could trade places with me." He reached up and smoothed some hair from her forehead. His touch made her skin tingle.

"Naturally, Lord Owen consulted with Lady Sinia, who can, as you already know, see the future. She had already seen it and had not said anything because it needed to be done willingly. It didn't happen right away. She wasn't sure how long it would take. She saw it happen after Gahalatine's death, and they have been preparing to fetch me ever since."

Trynne felt unworthy of so much devotion. In her mind, she saw Captain Staeli's gruff manner. He wouldn't want recognition or thanks. Seeing her happy would please him very much.

"I could cry," she said, hiccupping. "What's to become of him?"

"I already have shed plenty of tears," he boasted. "But your mother's vision appeased me."

Trynne looked at him in confusion.

"Apparently, the posterity of our good captain will continue to be of service in the future. Yes, our dear bachelor will find love. Surprising, I know! Your mother had a vision that the mastons would return someday. They will lead the fight against the hetaera. She saw in a vision that a hunter and his hound would protect a banished princess. I don't recall if it was his grandson or great-grandson, but Staeli is supposed to stay in that world. He's done the Fountain's will."

Trynne tucked the seed pod into her girdle and then squeezed Fallon's hands. Bringing them to her lips, she kissed them. "I'm so thankful. And you . . . *you*, Fallon, of all people, have become Fountain-blessed at last? Truly?"

He nodded in a very humble way. "It happened at the grounds of that abbey after I let you go. Myrddin has an extensive library and I read a great deal while I was away. I learned about apple orchards and abandoned kitchens. And I learned I can summon fire from stone. That I can sense danger before it comes. But the greatest gift of the Fountain, the gift that I've always wanted, was discernment." He smiled and placed his hand on her cheek. "I can hear people's thoughts, Trynne. It's the same gift Myrddin has. I'm still raw with it. And I have to be cautious not to misuse it. But I've always tried to understand people's true motives. It's what always attracted me to the Espion. I know when someone is lying, when they are being sincere. I've much still to learn, but Myrddin gave me a book of sorts to bring with me. To help me continue to grow this gift."

Her heart thundered in her chest as he spoke. The joy of this moment was almost too much to bear. "I love you, Fallon Llewellyn. I've loved you for a very long time."

"I know," he said with a sly look. "You don't know how much I've wanted to hear you say it. You'll bring Averanche as your marriage portion," he said with a shrug. "And I fancy that little castle and its view of the bay. But I hope you won't mind staying in Dundrennan more often? I am still a duke, after all. At least, I think I still am. Genny didn't say anything about my title being revoked, did she?"

Trynne shook her head and gripped his collar with both fists. "I've told you that I love you. Now you'd better return the confession yourself."

"As my lady commands," he answered. And he showed her in a kiss, this one even more passionate, more full of promise, than the one they'd shared in the tower of Dundrennan when the night sky was exploding with stars.

EPILOGUE

Leoneyis

The scene felt hauntingly and poignantly familiar. Years ago, Trynne had stood as an onlooker as Genevieve prepared for her wedding nuptials. Some of the same women were present, and it was the same chamber, but this time they were preparing for *Trynne*'s wedding. As Trynne looked at her reflection in the mirror, she smiled at her friends. Her *family*. Genny and Lady Evie stood to either side of her, and her mother stood behind her, her hands on her shoulders.

"You look beautiful, Tryneowy," her mother said, and leaned down, kissing her cheek.

"Thank you," she said, not feeling fully deserving of the praise, but she reached for her mother's hand and gave it a gentle squeeze. Their relationship had relaxed substantially following her mother's return from the Deep Fathoms. There was no longer the pressure of Trynne's concealed destiny, the mismatched hopes.

Genny had helped Trynne select a dress in the style Fallon preferred, but one that suited her own tastes by being less ornate than others might want. The red velvet gown had a gold trim all around the neck and bodice, sewn with Genevese pearls, and a high girdle set with beads of sea glass that normally would have cost a fortune had the bride not been the daughter of the Duchess of Brythonica. The multilayered sleeves were rolled back, exposing matching cuffs that copied the interior pattern of the dress—which was a beautiful series of tangled vines and butterflies. Sinia had brushed Trynne's hair to a luxurious shine, and there was a slight curl to it as it lay across her chest.

Trynne was trying to breathe and finding it difficult because her heart was beating so fast. In the mirror, she saw Reya speaking to Mariette and wished that she could have a moment alone with her mother before being hurried away to the ceremony. After the wedding, Trynne would take her husband by the ley lines to Dundrennan, where they'd have a feast to celebrate the evening. But that was not all. Trynne also planned to take Fallon to Marq for a gondola ride, and together they'd visit the other places she'd longed to see. She caught her reflection smiling at the thought.

"It's almost time," Sinia said, patting her shoulder.

"You are going back to Brythonica tomorrow?" Trynne asked, turning her head and gazing up at her mother.

She nodded. "I've had another vision. The ships will be arriving soon. It's been three months since the flood."

Trynne nodded. The treasure ships were coming for refuge and safety.

"What was your vision?" Trynne asked her. Sometimes her mother told her about them. Sometimes she did not. One thing she'd learned about life was that there'd always be mysteries. She noticed the strange iron key dangling from her mother's girdle, still sheathed in magic. No one could see it except for Trynne's father and herself. Her mother had said she would tell her later where she'd gotten it and what it meant, but the time had not yet come. The last month had been a whirlwind.

"I've seen the solution to the problem of the ships," Sinia answered, stroking a finger through Trynne's hair.

"What is it?"

Her mother smiled. "You'll hear about it soon enough. All the world will hear of it when it happens."

"Can you tell me?" Trynne asked eagerly, but she didn't push further.

There was a gasp of surprise and a flurry of outrage as Fallon appeared through a secret Espion door and entered the room in his wedding finery.

"Iago Fallon!" Lady Evie thundered. "You aren't supposed to see her yet!"

"Since I already *did* see her, does that mean the silly tradition no longer matters? This is a quiet wedding, not a state affair. There should be some leeway for rules to be broken here and there. Out, out—all of you. This is taking far too long. Give us a quiet moment ere the bedlam begins. Go on, Mother, you know I love you, and you and Genny outrank me, but do obey your son on his wedding day. As a personal favor? All of you, go! I'd have a word with my bride-to-be and her mother."

There were protests and more commotion, but Fallon had his way in the end, and soon the ladies were escorted away, all save Trynne and Sinia. The room was quiet and peaceful after the door closed behind the last lady. Trynne thought Fallon looked rather handsome in his wedding clothes, which were not ostentatious, but more in line with the solemn traditions of the North.

Fallon stood there, arms folded, gazing at Trynne with a look of admiration and appreciation. "Well now, my love. That gown suits you exquisitely. Exactly. Unequivocally. My sister has great taste."

"It's against tradition to see me before the ceremony," she pointed out.

He laughed. "When have I ever been a servant to tradition?" Then his smug look softened. "Actually, I figured you would want some time alone with your mother, and all the other hens were still fussing over you." He shrugged. "My first wedding present to you. Lady Sinia." He bowed to her respectfully. "You have always been a second mother to me, ever since I was a boy growing up in Ploemeur. I hope it will not offend if I begin to address you by that title. You have another son, but I do hope to be considered one of yours."

Sinia strode up to Fallon and embraced him, pulling down on his neck and kissing his forehead. "You've always been family to me," she said, patting his cheek. "As I knew you would be long ago. When I prepared on *my* wedding day."

Fallon was abashed by her compliment and turned to escape out the secret door again.

Trynne called him back. "Fallon?"

He stood there, head cocked slightly, listening to her with quiet respect. He didn't ask her what she wanted. He already knew.

"Thank you," she said, feeling that the happiness in her heart at that moment was just a taste of what she could expect in the years to come.

He smiled at her. "Don't keep me waiting long," he said with an impish smile. "We've been waiting long enough."

AUTHOR'S NOTE

One of the things that I've always admired about Jane Austen's writing is her ability to flesh out believable characters, flaws and all, and especially caddish villains such as Wickham and Willoughby from *Pride and Prejudice* and *Sense and Sensibility*. When I created Fallon's character, I wanted to cast him in their mold, yet give him an ending that showed a person can change. Both Trynne and Fallon go on incredible character journeys during this series. I was rooting for him the whole time.

I also had an enormous amount of fun with this series blending in themes and crossing over into my other worlds. Astute readers will recognize the nods from both of the Muirwood series (Lia's kitchen, Dochte Abbey, kystrels, etc.) to Whispers from Mirrowen (the Tay al-Ard, the Dryad trees, the Bhikhu) and even to my Landmoor series (Rucrius with his reflecting eyes was a Shae if you noticed that, and the Everoot that helped heal Trynne at the end). Blending different aspects of my worlds together in this series made it so fun and delighted my editor when I pitched the idea to him. I hope you've been delighted as well.

The reaction to the Kingfountain series has been such an honor and very humbling. Thank you for being part of my journey as a writer. I have so many stories still left to tell. Every time I get a book idea, I send myself an e-mail with the details to store it in a folder to look at later.

By the time you get this Author's Note, I'll have already decided what I'm doing next and will likely have written it and been done. But at this moment, the future is a blank page.

It's like that for all of us. What we do tomorrow starts with a thought. Truly the best way to predict your future *is* to create it. Wise words from Alan Kay at Xerox PARC.

Until we meet again.

P.S. If you are still hungering for more in the world of Kingfountain, I have written another stand-alone novel, which tells the origin story of Trynne's namesake, Ankarette Tryneowy. Watch my website for the announcement of *The Poisoner's Enemy* in early 2018!

ACKNOWLEDGMENTS

It takes a special kind of person to endure suffering cheerfully. As always, my sister Emily endures the pangs of suffering week by week to read my books as I write them. My daughter Isabelle joined in this time and has been a source of encouragement and support and a tireless advocate for Fallon. I also let one of my good friends and early readers, Robin, give it a try after she asked to read weekly, but eventually the strain proved too much and she begged me to stop sending her chapters until it was done.

I'd also like to thank my awesome editorial team for their continual support and suggestions. Jason Kirk: editor, shark lover, and partner par excellence, Angela "Eagle Eyes" Polidoro, and Wanda Zimba. Their capacious memories often save me from myself. Thanks also to my wonderful early readers who see these books before you all do and are still my friends after cliffhanger endings: Robin, Shannon, Karen, Travis, and Sunil.

AN EXCERPT FROM

JEFF WHEELER'S

THE WRETCHED OF MUIRWOOD

There is a difference between a wretched and an orphan. An orphan is literally a child whose parents are dead. It is a pitiable state, to be sure, but the child still knows, by means of relations or guardians, who their parents were and what Gifts they have inherited. The necessary rites can or already have been performed for them, binding them through the Medium to their ancestral forebears and the consequences appertaining to them.

A wretched is like an orphan. They have no family, no relations, no one willing to own them or care for them. Their parents may be alive or dead. They are often born in secret, with no one aware of their coming into this second life, except for the unlucky souls who find them abandoned on Abbey steps in the dark of night. After laboring and searching the most ancient references, I have thus concluded that the original meaning of the word is this—a wretched is someone deserving pity. And by this definition, I say that those children found in this state are appropriately named.

—Cuthbert Renowden of Billerbeck Abbey

CHAPTER ONE

Cemetery Rings

Lia lived in the Aldermaston's kitchen at Muirwood Abbey. More than anything else in the world, she craved learning how to read. But she had no family to afford such a privilege, no one willing to teach her the secrets, and no hope of it ever happening because she was a wretched.

Nine years before, someone had abandoned her at the Abbey gate and that should have put an end to her ambitions. Only it did not. One cannot live in a sweet-scented kitchen without hungering after pumpkin loaves, spicy apple soup, and tarts with glaze. And one could not live at Muirwood Abbey without longing to learn the wisest of crafts—reading and engraving.

Thunder boomed above Muirwood Abbey, and water drenched the already muddy grounds. Lia's companion, Sowe, slept next to her in the loft, but the thunder and the sharp stabs of lightning did not wake her, nor did the voices murmuring from the kitchen below as the Aldermaston spoke to Pasqua. It was difficult waking Sowe under any circumstances, for she dearly loved her sleep.

Running drips dampened their blankets and plopped in pots on the kitchen tiles below. Rain had its own way of bringing out smells—in wet clothes, wet cheeses, and wet sackcloth. Even the wooden planks and the eaves had a damp, musty smell.

The Aldermaston's gray cassock and over-robe were soaked and dripping, his thick, dark eyebrows knotted with worry and impatience. Lia watched him secretly from the shadows of the loft.

"Let me pour you some cider," Pasqua said to him as she fidgeted among the pots, sieves, and ladles. "A fresh batch was pressed and boiled less than a fortnight ago. It will refresh you. Now where did that chatteling put the mugs? Here we are. Well now, it seems someone has drunk from it again. I mark these things, you know. It was probably Lia. She is always snitching."

"Your gift of observation is keen," said the Aldermaston, who seemed hurried to speak. "I am not at all thirsty. If you . . ."

"It is no trouble at all. In truth, it is good for your humors. Now why did they stack those eggs that way? I ought to crack one over the both of their heads, I should. But that would be wasteful."

"Please, Pasqua, some bread. If you could rouse the girls and start the bread now. Stoke the fires. You may be baking all night."

"Are we expecting guests, Aldermaston? In this storm? I doubt if a skilled horseman could ford the moors now, even with the bridges. I have seen many storms blow in like this. Hang and cure me if any guests should brave the storm tonight."

"Not guests, Pasqua. The rivers may flood. I will rouse the other help, maybe even the learners. If it floods . . ."

"You think it might flood?"

"I believe that is what I just said."

"It rained four days and four nights nigh on twelve years ago. The Abbey did not flood then."

"I believe it may tonight, Pasqua. We are on higher ground. They will look to us for help."

Lia poked Sowe to rouse her, but she mumbled something and turned the other way, swatting at her own ear. She was still completely asleep.

The Aldermaston's voice was rough, as if he was always trying to keep himself from coughing, and it throbbed with impatience. "If it floods, there will be danger for the village. Not only our crops chance being ruined. Bread. Make five hundred loaves. We should be prepared . . ."

"Five hundred loaves?"

"That is what I instructed. I am grateful you heard me correctly."

"From our stores? But . . . what a dreadful waste if it does not flood."

"In this matter, I am not seeking advice. I am impressed that we should prepare for flooding this evening. It is heavy on me now. As heavy as the cauldron in the nook. I keep waiting for it. For the footsteps. For the alarm. Something will happen this night. I dread news of it."

"Have some cider then," Pasqua said, her voice trembling with worry. "It will calm your nerves. Do you really think it will flood tonight?"

Straightening his crooked back, the Aldermaston roared, "Do you not understand me? Loaves! Five hundred at least. Must I rouse your help myself? Must I knead the dough with my own hands? Bake, Pasqua! I did not come here to trifle with you or convince you."

Lia thought his voice more frightening than the thunder—the feeling of it, the heat of his anger. It made her sink deep inside herself. Her heart pained for Pasqua. She knew how it felt to be yelled at like that.

Sowe sat up immediately, clutching her blanket to her mouth.

Her eyes were wild with fear.

Another blast of thunder sounded, its force shaking the walls.

In the calm of silence that followed, Pasqua replied, "There is no use yelling, Aldermaston, I can hear you very well. You may think me deaf, by the tone of your voice. Loaves you shall have then. Grouchy old niffler, coming into *my* kitchen to yell at me. A fine way to treat your cook."

At that moment, the kitchen opened with a gusty wind and a man slogged in, spraying mud from his boots with every step. His hair was dripping, his beard dripping, his nose dripping. Grime covered him from head to foot. He clenched something in his hand against his chest.

"And who do you think you are to come in like that, Jon Hunter!" Pasqua said, rounding on him. "Kicking mud like that! Tell me that a wretched is found half-drowned at the Abbey gate, or I will beat you with my broom for barging into my kitchen. Filthy as a cur, look at you."

Jon Hunter looked like a wild thing, a mess of soaked, sodden cloak, tangled hair with twigs and bits of leaves, and a gladius blade belted to his waist. "Aldermaston," he said in a breathless voice. He mopped his beard and pitched his voice lower. "The graveyard. It flooded. Landslide."

There was quiet, then more blinding lightning followed by billows of thunder. The Aldermaston said nothing. He only waited. Jon Hunter seemed to be struggling to find his voice again.

Lia peeked farther from the ladder steps, her long curly hair tickling the sides of her face. Sowe tried to pull her back, to get her out of the light, but Lia pushed her away.

Jon Hunter pressed his forehead against his arm, staring down at the floor. "The lower slope gave way, spilling part of the cemetery downhill. Grave markers are strewn about and many . . ." He stopped, choking on the words. "Many ossuaries were burst. They were . . . my lord . . . they were . . . they were all empty, save for muddy linens . . . and . . . and . . . wedding bands made of gold."

Jon put his hand on the cutting table. His other still clenched something. "As I searched the ruins and collected the bands, the part of the hill I was on collapsed. I thought . . . I thought I was going to die. I fell. I cannot say how far, not in all the dark, but I fell on stone. A shelf of rock, I thought. It knocked the wind out of me. But when the lightning flashed again, I realized it was . . . in the air. Do you understand me? Hanging in the air. A giant block of chiseled stone. But there was nothing below it. Nothing holding it up. I was trapped and shouted for help. But then the lightning flashed anew, and I saw the hillside above and the roots of a withered oak exposed. There is nothing but a tangle of oaks in that part of the grounds. So I leapt and climbed and came."

The Aldermaston said nothing, chewing on the moment as if it were some bitter-tasting thing. His eyes closed. His shoulders drooped. "Who else is about tonight? Who may have seen it?"

"Only I," Jon Hunter said, holding out his hand, his mud-caked hand. There were several smeared rings in his filthy palm. "Aldermaston, why were there no bones in the ossuaries? Why leave the rings? I do not understand what I beheld tonight."

The Aldermaston took the rings, looking at them in the flickering lamplight. Then his fingers tightened around the gold bands and fury kindled his cheeks.

"There is much labor to fulfill before dawn. The cemetery grounds are forbidden now. Be certain that no one trespasses. Take two mules and a cart and gather the grave markers and ossuaries and move them to where I shall tell you. I will help. I do not want learners to discover what you did. The entire Abbey is forbidden from that ground. Have I spoken clearly? Can there be any doubt as to my orders?"

"None, Aldermaston. The storm is raging still. I will work alone. Do not risk your health to the elements. Tell me what must be done and I will do it."

"The rains have plagued us quite enough. They will cease. *Now.*" He held up his hand, as if to calm a thrashing stallion in front of him.

311

Either by the words or the gesture or both, the rain ceased, and only the water sluicing through the gutters and the plop and drip from a thousand shingles and countless shuddering oak branches could be heard. A tingle in the air sizzled, and Lia's heart went hot with a blushing giddiness. All her life she had heard whispers of the power of the Medium. That it was strong enough to master storms, to tame fire or sea, or restore that which was lost. Even to bring the dead back alive again.

Now she knew it was real. Empty ossuaries could mean only one thing. The dead bones had been restored to the flesh of their masters, the bodies reborn and new. When the revived ones had left Muirwood was a mystery. Lia was eager to explore the forbidden grounds—to see the floating stone, to search for rings in the mud herself.

And at precisely that moment, the moment when she realized the Medium was real, with her heart full of thoughts too dazzling to bottle up, she saw the Aldermaston turn, gaze up the ladder, and meet her eyes.

For the brief blink of a moment, she knew what he was thinking. How a young girl just past her ninth nameday could understand a world-wise and world-weary Aldermaston did not matter. This was the moment he had been dreading that evening. Not the washed-out grave markers, the empty stone ossuaries, or the rings and linens left behind. It was knowing that she, a wretched of Muirwood, knew what had happened. That it was a moment that would change her forever.

His recognition of her intrusion was shared then by Pasqua and Jon Hunter.

"I ought to blister your backside, you rude little child!" Pasqua said, striding over to the loft ladder as Lia scrambled down it. "Listening in like that. Like you were nothing but a teeny mouse, all anxious for bits of cheese. A rat is more like it. Snooping and sneaking." Pasqua grabbed her scrawny arm.

"I won't tell anyone," Lia said, gazing at the Aldermaston fiercely, ignoring Pasqua and Jon Hunter. She tried to tug her arm away, but the grip was iron. "Not if you let me be taught to read. I want to be a learner."

Pasqua slapped her for that, a stinging blow. "You evil little thing! Are you threatening the Aldermaston? He could turn you out to the village. Hunger, my little crow, real hunger. You have never known that feeling. Ungrateful, selfish . . ."

"Let her go, Pasqua, you are not helping," the Aldermaston said, his eyes shining with inner fury. His gaze burned into Lia's eyes. "While I am Aldermaston over Muirwood, you will not be taught to read. You greatly misunderstand your position here." His eyes narrowed. "Five hundred loaves. Tonight. The food will help offer distraction." He turned to leave, but stopped and gave her one last look. It was a sharp, threatening look. "They would not believe such a story even if you told them." He left the kitchen, the vanished storm no longer blowing his stock of pale white hair. Jon Hunter plucked a twig out of his hair and gave Lia another look—one that promised a thrashing if she ever said a word to anyone—then followed the Aldermaston out. Lia did not care about a thrashing. She knew what those felt like too.

Pasqua kept her and Sowe up all night, and by dawn their shoulders and fingers throbbed from the endless kneading, patting, and shaping of loaves. But Lia was not too exhausted, the next morning, to resist stealing one of the gold cemetery rings from a box in the Aldermaston's chambers. After tying it to a stout length of string, she wore it around her neck and hid it beneath her clothes.

She never took it off.

CHAPTER TWO

Knight-Maston

Four years passed. The Aldermaston was true to his word, and Lia was true to hers. She never told anyone about the floating stone, or the alcove she and Sowe had discovered in the hillside, or the cemetery rings. The storm raging outside reminded her of the previous one from years ago. Instead of sleeping in the loft with Sowe, she tried to get comfortable on the floor near the oven where it was warmer.

Thunder rocked the Abbey grounds, and even the thick stone wall thrummed with it. The rain dripped from several loose shingles on the roof, and the plunk-plunking on the mats kept her awake. She was not certain what would be worse, grabbing a few pots to catch the water and listening to the deep blooping sound or cramming her blanket harder against her ears to muffle it.

In the darkness, something heavy lurched against the double doors, and for a moment Lia remembered Jon Hunter bursting in, bearing the news of the landslide. She sat up fast enough to graze her head against the planks of the trestle table nearby. The sound was loud, like when Getmin or Ribbs shoved a barrel full of beans into place. She heard a few low whispers and curses just outside the door, which meant it was likely a pair of learners. Sometimes they snuck out of their rooms at night to wander the grounds, but few were courageous enough to brave the Aldermaston's personal kitchen. On quiet, bare feet, she padded over and grabbed a skillet from the hook pegs, a wide, flat one made of iron. A heavy wallop on the head was usually all it took to stop a learner.

"Here we are," a man's voice whispered. "Easy there, lad. Let me look at you. Bleeding still. Let me see if the kitchen is open."

The handle rattled and shook.

"Locked. Won't be able to cross the river again if I stay here much longer . . . let me see if I can open it." A dagger came through the crack and struggled against the crossbar, making Lia skip back with shock. Learners did not carry daggers!

"There we go . . . oh piddle, the crossbar is too heavy. Sorry, lad. Looks like you will be bleeding to death here. How the Abbey help will love a corpse on the porch instead of a wretched. But what is there to do? Well, I suppose I could knock."

Lia clenched her hands around the skillet handle, wondering if she should open the doors. A firm pounding startled her. "For the love of life, is anyone there? I have a wounded man with me. Is anyone there?"

She bit her lip, wondering if she should sneak out the rear doors and waken Pasqua. The old woman snored so loudly, it would take more than distant pounding to wake her from her dreams, though sometimes she snored herself awake. Something thumped outside, and she thought she heard the chinking sound of spurs. What kind of man wore spurs? Few soldiers could afford horses. But knight-mastons could. At least she thought they could, knight-mastons and the nobles.

Thoughts of the Aldermaston did not make the choice any easier. She knew she could just as easily be scolded for deciding either way. *What were you thinking, Lia, letting two rough men into the kitchen in the dead of night? What were you thinking, Lia, letting a man bleed to death on the porch of Muirwood?*

Looking at it that way, she supposed there was really only one choice to make. How could she let a man die, especially if he was a maston? Would not the king be greatly angered if one of his knights died? Especially considering the king was renowned for his cruelty. Yet why would two of the king's men be wandering about Muirwood anyway? The gates were always locked during the night, so they must have approached the grounds from the rear instead of the village. Why? Would they treat someone kindly who helped? Perhaps a few coins? Or even greater generosity?

That decided her.

Lia set the pan on a table, lifted the crossbar, and pulled open the door—and fell over when a man stumbled inside.

"Sweet mother of Idumea!" the man gasped, flailing and sidestepping to keep from squashing her. He was dripping wet, smelled like the hog pens, and his face looked more scratchy than a porcupine. A body collapsed with a thump just outside, and she saw glistening red streaking down his face.

"You scared me, lass! Fans or fires, that is horrible to do to someone." He regained his balance, all quickness and grace, and grabbed her hand and arm to help her stand. After wiping his mouth, which caused a rasping sound, he turned and hoisted the other fellow under the arms and dragged him the rest of the way inside. As he pulled, she saw the sword belted at his waist. It was a fine sword, the pommel glinting in the dim light of the oven fires. It bore the insignia on the pommel—an eight-pointed star, formed of two offset squares.

"You are a knight-maston!" Lia whispered.

His head jerked and he looked her in the face. "How did you know?"

"The sword, it is . . . well you see, I have heard that they . . ."

"A clever lass. Quick as a wisp. Help me drag him over to that mat. Grab his legs."

She did, and helped move the wounded man in out of the rain. They set him down on the rush matting. The wounded man was younger than she first thought, pale and clean-shaven, with dripping, dark hair.

She crouched down and studied him. "I can help," she said. "Bring me that lamp. The one over there." She was anxious to flaunt her apothecary skills, earned when a rush of fevers struck the Abbey two winters ago. He obeyed and produced it.

The injured one was no older than seventeen or eighteen—a man for certain, but one young enough to still have the blemishes of youth on his face. His hair was cropped short around his neck. His build somewhat resembled that of Getmin, the blacksmith's help who loved to torment her.

"Is this your squire?" she asked. "We should have carried him closer to the fire. He is bone cold. I can start the fire quickly."

"Squire? Well, he is . . . he is a good lad. Not my squire, though. His father was a good man. How old are you lass? Sixteen?"

"I am thirteen. At least I think so. I am a wretched."

"I would not have believed you thirteen. You look tall enough to have danced beneath a maypole already."

"I am hoping to this year, if the Aldermaston lets me. I am near enough to fourteen and think he should." The blood flowed from a cut on the young man's eyebrow. She stanched it firmly with a cloth. It might take a while to make it stop as the cut was deep. She glanced up at the loft, half expecting to see Sowe cowering there, but there was no one. Part of her was glad that Sowe was asleep.

"I always try to make it to Muirwood for Whitsunday. A most profitable day it is."

"You mean the tourneys or the trading?"

"Yes, yes, the tourneys. Nothing like bumping a man onto his hindquarters. And I most gravely apologize for knocking you onto yours just now. My, look at that wound. That is a nasty cut." He looked into Lia's eyes, and she felt a sudden jolt of warmth. "Rode his piddling mare right into an oak branch. Too many trees here, lass. Too dark and the storm made it worse! Praise the Medium, we are both still alive. Let me grab another cloth, and we can wring out that one. Wait here."

Lia knelt by the limp body, her stomach buzzing, and pressed the wound harder. She looked over her shoulder and watched the knight slice a shank from the spitted hog and stuff it into a leather bag at his waist. It was followed by three buttered rolls and a whole cherry tart.

"Those are for the Aldermaston's dinner tomorrow!" she whispered in a panic, knowing exactly who Pasqua would blame. "The hog is not even done cooking yet!"

"There we are, a cloth!" He snatched one of the fine linen napkins and hurried over, licking his fingers. He held out the napkin to exchange with hers.

"That is one of the Aldermaston's napkins!"

"Is a lad's life held so cheaply here? We must stop the bleeding. Here, put your hand on this and hold it tight. The linen will sop the blood better." He grabbed her wrist and pressed her hand against the bleeding.

"That is *not* the way to do it," she said. "Here, let me fetch some things. I can cure him." Lia ran to the benches and grabbed some clean dishrags, a kettle of warm water from the fire-peg, and a sprig of blue woad. She watched as the knight grabbed two more tarts, veins of grapes, and a small tub of treacle and stuffed them into his leather knapsack.

"What are you doing?"

"Hmmm? Victuals, lass. I will leave a little pouch with coins on the mantel." He pointed to the fire.

"Pasqua will be furious," Lia muttered under her breath, arranging the healing provisions near the young man's head. She steeped the cloth with some hot water and wiped blood from his face. He did not flinch or start, but his eyes darted beneath his eyelids. His body started to tremble. She grabbed his hand.

"He is too cold. Where is his cloak?" She poured more hot water and wrung out the cloth, bathing his face a second time before wadding it up and pressing it against the cut on his eyebrow. If Sowe were awake, she could have helped pestle the woad. But Lia was left to do it all herself.

The knight's shadow smothered her from behind. She turned her head and looked up at him.

He nodded. "Woad? Ah, you studied under a healer as well as a cook? It is a useful plant. You are a good lass. Make him well. I will be back for him in three days. Keep him hidden, if you can."

Panic. Pure and sudden panic.

"What? You are not going to . . . not leaving him . . ."

"I must throw the sheriff of Mendenhall's men off our trail, lass. It is dangerous for mastons in this part of the country. Especially this Hundred." He walked quickly to the door and the rain puddling on the entryway. "Keep him safe. If Almaguer comes, do your best to hide him. His life is in your hands. I am trusting you in this."

"No! He cannot stay here. I am only a helper. I cannot . . ."

"You do what you can, lass. You do your best. I am trusting you." And he ducked his head into the rain, clenched the hilt of his maston sword, and disappeared into the storm.

Jeff Wheeler's Muirwood Trilogies—Legends of Muirwood and Covenant of Muirwood—are available from 47North.

ABOUT THE AUTHOR

Wall Street Journal bestselling author Jeff Wheeler took an early retirement from his career at Intel in 2014 to write full-time. He is, most importantly, a husband, a father, and a devout member of his church. He is often seen roaming hills with oak trees and granite boulders in California or in any number of the state's majestic redwood groves. He is also the founder of *Deep Magic: The E-zine of Clean Fantasy and Science Fiction*. Find out more about Deep Magic online at www.deepmagic.co, and visit Jeff at www.jeff-wheeler.com.